MASON CROSS

is the author of *The Killing Season*, *The Samaritan* and *Winterlong*.

The Killing Season was longlisted for the 2015 Theakston's Old Peculier Crime Novel of the Year award, and *The Samaritan* was selected for the Richard and Judy Book Club for Spring 2016.

His short crime stories have been published in magazines including *Ellery Queen* and *First Edition*. His story "A Living" was shortlisted for the Quick Reads Get Britain Reading award.

You can find out more by visiting his website at www.carterblake.net. He lives in England.

WINTERLONG

MASON CROSS

TORONTO • NEW YORK • LONDON
AMSTERDAM • PARIS • SYDNEY • HAMBURG
STOCKHOLM • ATHENS • TOKYO • MILAN
MADRID • WARSAW • BUDAPEST • AUCKLAND

For Robert Bell and Andrew Morrison
Good fathers, even better grandfathers

Recycling programs
for this product may
not exist in your area.

ISBN-13: 978-1-335-66140-1

Winterlong

Copyright © 2017 by Mason Cross

A Worldwide Library Suspense/July 2018

First published by Pegasus Books Ltd.

www.Harlequin.com

Printed in U.S.A.

WINTERLONG

PROLOGUE

Tyuman, Siberia

THE AMERICAN WALKED into Anatoli's at five minutes
after one in the morning. He paused at the door to cast
his eyes around the interior before selecting his usual
seat at the far end of the bar.

He knew the heat from the open fire would be welcome once it worked its way past the numbness in his
face. There were no other late-night customers tonight,
which suited him fine. The bartender caught his eye and
nodded, letting him know he would be over in a minute with his usual. That gave him time to take the top
layers off and make himself comfortable.

He removed the bulky gloves first and then his head-
gear: a big wool-lined trapper hat with flaps that came
down over the ears. He placed the gloves and hat on the
bench beside him and then unbuttoned his heavy quilted
coat. He heaved the weighty garment off his shoulders
and dropped it on the bench. Finally, he removed his
sweater and allowed the warmth of the fire to begin
working its way into his extremities.

It wasn't the cold that got to you, he often thought.
Not directly. The cold was manageable, as long as you
prepared for it. It was that constant preparation that
ground you down: the coping, the managing, the careful building up and removing of layers just to be able to

survive and function in this environment at this time of year. The constant mindfulness required merely to exist.

He had caught a documentary on one of the local channels a couple of nights ago about the Space Race. Naturally, it was told from the Soviet point of view, favoring Gagarin and Tereshkova over Glenn and Armstrong, but some things were universal. He thought he knew a little of what it was like to be a cosmonaut: preparing oneself to be somewhere human beings weren't meant to be. From the perspective of a late night in early December, it was hard to escape the conclusion that Tyumen should be added to that list.

The bartender was finally getting around to drawing his beer from the tap when the door creaked open and a gust of freezing wind blew in. He looked over to see two people enter. As far as it was possible to tell from their winter clothing, they were both men, reasonably tall. They wore hats and coats as bulky as his own. Beyond that it was impossible to know anything about them— age, weight, even race—until they revealed themselves.

The bartender swaggered over to him, ignoring the newcomers. He was a brawny Armenian wearing a quilted checkered shirt that showed tattoos on his neck and creeping out onto the backs of his hands. He looked like a side of beef with a goatee. The bartender placed the beer beside him and the American nodded.

"Spasibo," he said in acknowledgment.

He kept his eyes surreptitiously on the two newcomers. There was nothing outwardly suspicious about them. Probably just local men, finishing a shift at one of the nearby factories. They hadn't so much as glanced in his direction. But it paid to keep his eyes open anyway. That was why he always took this seat, with its unobstructed view of the door. Mindfulness. Living according to one's circumstances.

He took a sip of the beer and grimaced, remembering for the hundredth time how much he missed home. Or anywhere that wasn't here, for that matter. Tyumen hadn't been so bad when he had arrived in the summer, when it was relatively warm. The job paid well and the contract was open-ended. It wasn't a difficult assignment: some close protection, some investigation, the occasional requirement for the mild rough stuff. The kind of job he could do in his sleep.

The two men had almost completed the arduous process of shedding their outdoor wear, and he could see that they were both Caucasian, young, and in shape. His internal warning system upgraded them a couple of notches. There was no point keeping one's eyes open, always selecting a seat with a view of the door, if you didn't evaluate every potential threat. He had a scale that went up to ten, and he mentally assessed everyone he came into contact with on that scale. These two were nothing to cause undue concern, not so far. They had moved up to a three on the scale now. Almost certainly they were nothing more than what they appeared to be. He logged several instances of a three or four on the scale every month.

He took another drink and looked up at the television screen hanging on the wall. It was tuned to *Russia Today*. All the news that's fit to broadcast. All the news Putin wanted to broadcast, anyway. They were covering a train crash out in Moscow, but he wasn't really paying attention. He was concentrating on watching the two men out of the corner of his eye. If they had noticed him, they gave no indication. One was watching the

TV, the other trying to signal the bartender, who was making a point of keeping them waiting while drying a glass. The American had been here a number of times now, and he noticed the bartender was never so diligent at glass polishing as when there was a customer waiting.

But then one of the men produced something from his pocket. It was a large silver hip flask. The man moved his hat on the table to conceal his action from the bartender and then placed the hip flask behind it at a very deliberate angle. An angle that would allow him to watch his position in the reflection without ever staring directly at him. An old trick. Or was it just a coincidence?

Five on the scale.

He turned away from the television. He fumbled inside his pocket and withdrew his phone. It was a basic old Nokia. Buttons instead of touch screen, no Internet, no built-in GPS. He examined the screen and glanced up at the door, as though awaiting a tardy drinking partner. He allowed his eyes to linger briefly on the two men, neither of whom were looking in his direction. They were dressed like every other male between twenty and sixty he'd seen come into this bar: jeans, work shirt, heavy boots. No…not quite the same. He risked another glance at the boots. Both of them wore similar footwear, but it was nothing like what the local workers wore. These boots were expensive.

The American didn't bother adding another notch to the scale. He simply placed a five-hundred-ruble banknote on the table next to his unfinished beer and got up, pulling his coat on. He left the sweater on the bench and grabbed his gloves and hat, striding toward the door. He heard a voice from behind him as his hand grasped the handle.

"Tovarish."

It was one of the two men. He ignored it.

"Wrap up warm," the same speaker called in Russian. "It's cold out there."

He ignored the call, noting as he did that the speaker's accent was almost perfect. Almost.

The subarctic chill hit him like a tangible thing the moment he stepped into the night, ravaging the exposed skin on his hands and face.

The Jeep was parked twenty yards away, on the opposite side of the street. He hustled diagonally across to it and reached into the pocket of his coat for the keys, barely able to hold on to them in the cold. He managed to activate the remote lock and risked a glance back at the bar as his hand found the door handle.

The two men were at the doorway. They had taken the time to dress up again properly, so they hadn't been in a hurry, but there was no mistaking it now. They were interested in him.

He opened the door of the Jeep and got in. He sighed with relief when the engine thrummed to life as he turned the key in the ignition. With the temperature dropping below minus twenty, it was touch and go whether the vehicle would start. It had already let him down a couple of times. Thankfully, tonight wasn't one of those times.

He turned on the wipers, grateful that the layer of frost on the windshield hadn't had time to harden. He pulled out onto the road and drove away as fast as he dared in the snow, stealing glances in the rearview mirror as the bar and the two men receded from view.

He kept on the main road for about a mile and then took a right onto a side street. The apartment wasn't far, but he didn't want to go there until he could be sure he hadn't been followed. He couldn't risk leading them to Nika.

And who exactly were *they*? If he was very lucky, they were merely gangsters. Foot soldiers for a rival of his current employer, looking to eliminate one part of his defensive capability. If he was unlucky…

He glanced back in the mirror and saw headlights gaining on him. They had a distinctive angular shape, like flattened triangles.

The problem with losing a tail in this town was the way Tyumen was divided by its two rivers and the Trans-Siberian Railway, creating isolated zones and severely limiting the options for movement by road. He spun the wheel and took an immediate left, followed by a sharp right down an alleyway so narrow that it barely accommodated the wing mirrors. He pulled back out onto the next street and crossed the bridge over the Tura, bringing him onto the main E22 route that led west and would take him clear of the city. His eyes flashed back and forth from the road to the mirror as he accelerated.

A car emerged from the alley behind him. Same triangular headlights, like the unblinking eyes of a dragon.

Shit.

This wasn't local gangsters; it was them.

A realization hit him in the pit of his stomach. They could easily have slapped a tracker on his Jeep while he was in the bar. That would explain why they'd been so unhurried. Hell, they could have been tailing him all day, or longer.

It had been five years. Why now?

There was no way he could head back to the apartment. Not now, not in this vehicle. And yet he had to. Because in the apartment, behind a false wall, was the only thing in the world that could protect him from what was coming.

Or perhaps that wasn't true. If they were coming for him now, after all this time, perhaps nothing could save him.

The buildings on the other side became lower and more spread out as he approached the city limits. He couldn't lead them back to Nika. He hoped they didn't know about her already. His only chance was to try to lose them in the frozen wilderness outside the city and then somehow double back and disappear. But disappear where? Tyumen already felt like the ends of the earth—if they could find him *here*…

Anyway, he thought, returning to the immediate danger, it wouldn't be enough just to lose them.

He reached his free hand out and opened the glove box, withdrawing a Smith & Wesson Governor compact revolver, wrapped in two layers of cloth. It was loaded with six .45-caliber ACP rounds. He shook the gun free from the cloth and placed it on the passenger seat.

He nudged the pedal down a little more as he passed the gas station that was the last outpost of the western edge of Tyumen. The E22 highway opened up. Frozen, snow-blanketed fields surrounded him on either side. The city already seemed a long way behind him. There were small dwellings and the abandoned sites of the former Soviet collective farms dotted here and there, including one that he knew of that was just off the road about four miles outside town. On some level, he supposed he'd borne the place in mind for a situation just like this one. It was the cold, he thought. There was never a time when you weren't planning around it, even subconsciously.

The other car's headlights followed about half a mile behind him on the straight road, not quite matching his speed. They didn't have to. They had all the time in the world.

There was a dip in the road ahead. He cast a brief glance down at the matt black frame of the revolver on the passenger seat and risked speeding up a little more ahead of the dip.

The lights in the mirror winked out as he hit the down-slope, and he saw the turnoff for the farm fifty yards ahead on the right. He wasn't planning on losing them. Even if they weren't tracking the Jeep, it would be obvious he had turned off the road, and where. But he didn't have to lose them. He just had to buy himself a little time.

He slowed for the turn, feeling the heavy tires slide a little as he swung out into the road. They held. There was a clutch of barns and darkened farm buildings ahead. He knew this from memory rather than sight. The dark structures registered as a minor irregularity, slightly disturbing the alignment of the sky against the horizon. He pulled to a stop beside one of the buildings and got out, leaving the engine running and the lights on. He slammed the door and sprinted around the back of the barn. Immediately, he remembered he had left his hat and gloves in the Jeep. It didn't matter. The gloves were too bulky to fit through the trigger guard or to fire accurately, and besides, he wouldn't get the chance to freeze to death. Either he would be back in the Jeep with the heater on full soon, or he would be beyond worrying about the cold. He heard the shift of gears as the other vehicle took the turn off the main road in a leisurely fashion and began the approach.

He edged around the far side of the barn so he could lay eyes on the approach road, keeping low. He wondered if these buildings were as deserted as they looked, and decided they probably were, given that there had been no sign of life when he drove up. The side of the barn was exposed to the full force of the wind, and the temperature, which he had thought couldn't get any colder, dropped still further. Had to be twenty-five below. His hands and face were already completely numb. He would have to trust the joints in his fingers to do what his brain told them, even though he couldn't feel them move. At least he had the coat.

Finally, the pursuers appeared, pulling to a smooth stop a short distance behind the Jeep. They were driving a silver Mitsubishi Outlander. A little too new and shiny to fit in, just like the boots. He hoped they would think he was still in the vehicle, but he knew they'd be careful. The two men from the bar got out of the Mitsubishi, guns drawn. In the glare of the headlights, he saw they were wearing lightweight winter tactical gloves. He only wished he'd been as prepared.

They stayed close to their vehicle for a second, playing it by the book, checking the area. For these brief few moments, he had them at a disadvantage. They knew he was around somewhere, of course, but they didn't know if he was in the Jeep or concealed in or around one of the farm buildings. He had picked this spot because there were several potential hiding places. Three or four places he could be, but only two of them to check those places.

The pair looked identical in their winter gear. The one who had gotten out of the driver's side nodded at his partner, an unspoken signal. He began to approach the Jeep, gun extended, while the other one covered the surrounding buildings in smooth alternating motions. Mixing it up, not spending more than a couple of seconds in any direction.

Time to take the chance.

He stepped out of cover just as the second man was turning away. He raised the revolver and fired, intending to put him down with a head shot. The gun kicked back. In the cold he barely felt it. The man went down, but it didn't look like he'd hit the head, maybe just clipped the man's shoulder.

No time to confirm, he swung around just as the other one was spinning around from his approach to the Jeep, ducking down to one knee as he did so. He was ready for this, had the muzzle aimed low as he pulled the trigger twice more. A good hit this time, two .45-caliber slugs in the center mass. The guy went down.

He started to turn back to the first one he'd dropped, but he was too late.

He registered the muzzle flash from the direction of the sprawled figure before he felt the bullet. No pain, just a sharp impact in his lower right side. He followed through on the action, squeezing the trigger again and again, putting his last three bullets in the guy on the ground.

He dropped the revolver and unbuttoned the midsection of his coat, his fingers too numb to do the job properly. He reached a hand inside and felt the tear in his clothing and the wound itself. He didn't need to see it to know it was bad. The volume of blood coursing over his fingers told him that. He put pressure on the hole with his left hand and started to move back toward the Jeep, wondering if he could survive the drive to the hospital.

And then his problems really began.

From a distance away, he heard the familiar noise of another engine slowing to take the turn. He looked back toward the highway and saw the lights of two more vehicles turning onto the access road. Distinctive triangular headlights.

He pressed down on the wound and began to run as fast as he could into the open fields. He wasn't thinking anymore. He just knew that he could not wait and fight, unarmed and wounded. He might just have time to get away, to circle back around to the main road while they were searching for him. Perhaps he would get lucky and a car would stop for him before he froze to death.

The snow was powdery beneath his feet and impeded his already stumbling steps. He wondered if he was leaving a trail of blood, but he was too weak to check. If he paused to look behind him, he might never be able to start moving again. His breathing became more labored, the freezing air savaging his lungs as he forced more of it into them. The pulse thudded in his head. He knew his heart was beating faster, which was bad news for blood loss. But if he could just keep going, perhaps he could make it.

Then he heard the dogs.

Frenzied barking, the rapid patter of paws on snow. He turned around as the two black Dobermans closed in on him fast. The biggest one leaped first, bringing him down easily. Jaws closed around his left wrist, joined a second later by another set around his ankle. Again, he felt no real pain, just pressure.

He lost track of time then, lying on the snow, staring up at the black sky, listening to the guttural snarls of the dogs. It could have been a few seconds or ten minutes later that he heard the voice. The words were in English this time.

"You had a good run. But it's over now."

The source of the voice appeared above him. Like his predecessors, he wore a coat and thin tactical gloves. He also wore glasses. It wasn't a face he recognized, but that meant nothing. He knew exactly who the man was and why he was here.

He heard a whistle and a clicking noise as the dogs' handler spoke to them and they released their grip. He didn't make any move. He had used up the last of his reserves.

"Get it over with," he said.

The briefest smile crossed the lips of the man with the glasses and then disappeared.

"Soon. You know what we want first."

"Go to hell."

The man in the glasses held his gaze for a moment, then shrugged and nodded to one of the other men. From the sounds of it, there were at least three of them. Another, taller man appeared in his field of vision, holding a cell phone. He crouched down and turned the screen so he could see it. At first he couldn't discern what was on the screen, and then he realized that it showed a video image. In close on blond hair. The camera moved out a little and a hand moved the hair to reveal a face.

His next breath caught in his throat. Nika.

Her eyes were closed, tears glistening on her cheeks. The camera reframed again to show the barrel of a gun pressed against her temple.

The man with the glasses crouched down beside him, glanced at the screen, and looked back at him expectantly.

He yelled obscenities at them, tried to lift himself up off the ground, but the bigger one easily suppressed him by pressing the sole of his boot down on his chest as he tried to get up. He yelled some more. And then he told them. He told them everything. Not because he thought it would save him, but because it might just save Nika.

The man with the glasses listened and nodded.

"Thank you."

"Now let her go. She doesn't know anything—"

The man with the glasses reached out a gloved hand, and the other one passed him the cell phone.

"Ortega?"

The tinny voice of the man holding the gun on Nika came through the cell phone's speakers.

"Copy."

"You can kill her now."

He screamed as he heard two quick gunshots over the phone. He struggled against the boot on his chest until he saw the barrel of the gun yawning in front of his eyes.

And then there was an explosion of light, and then nothing.

ONE MONTH LATER

WEDNESDAY, JANUARY 6TH

ONE

Sunnyvale, California

MY EYES SNAPPED open and for a moment I thought I was still running.

I blinked a couple of times and took in my surroundings: hotel bed, blinds open, light from a clear blue sky flooding the room. It took me a second to realize that the illusion of running was caused by the fact I was still breathing hard from the dream.

I sat up in bed. The hotel room was temperature-controlled to within an inch of its life, but I felt a chill as the covers slipped off and exposed my sweat-drenched upper body to the air. I took a few long breaths through my nose and willed my heart rate to drop to a more medically approved level.

Breathing and pulse rate dealt with, I gave myself a diagnostic knock on the head. Wow. There hadn't been a dream like that for a while. Not since the immediate aftermath of Los Angeles. I wondered if proximity was a factor. This was the closest I had been to LA since then, and although I'd been too busy to think much about the whole thing recently, it seemed like my subconscious had been doing it on my behalf.

My job is to find people who don't want to be found. Ordinarily, a third party engages my services, but I had made an exception for that case. A serial killer the

media had christened "the Samaritan" had been ab-
ducting and killing lone female drivers in LA. Some of
the details of the investigation that had been leaked to
the media reminded me of Dean Crozier, a man I had
worked alongside years before. We had been members
of a very effective, very secret military intelligence organization that found a great deal of work for our respective talents. I had a strong interest in keeping out
of the orbit of our mutual former employers, so it had
not been an easy decision to offer my services to the
LAPD. But in the end it had been the only decision. My
fears had proved grounded on both counts: Dean Crozier was the Samaritan, and I wasn't the only one who
had made the connection.

I remembered the man in glasses. The cold look in
his eyes as he held the gun steady. An unfamiliar face,
but he knew who I was.

Maybe things have changed, he had said.

I had gotten myself out of that situation though, and
things had been quiet ever since. Except that on some
level I was still waiting for the other shoe to drop.

A soft cuckoo noise chirped in tandem with the vi-
bration of my cell phone, getting gradually louder. My
morning alarm. I rolled over and hit mute.

I showered, shaved, and dressed for my appointment.
A charcoal two-button Brooks Brothers suit and a light
blue broadcloth shirt. I packed my laptop and left the
room as I'd found it. I took the stairs to the ground
floor, grabbed a bagel from the breakfast buffet, and
checked out.

Outside on the street, the sky seemed even bluer.
A cold day by California standards, but I wasn't the
type to complain about the thermometer reading fifty

degrees in January. The fresh air soothed the nagging headache the dream had left me with, and I hoped that the images still flashing before my eyes would fade along with it. There was a line of three taxis parked outside the hotel, and I got to the one at the front. I told the driver I wanted to go to Moonola House. Before I could give him the address, he just nodded and pulled out onto the road. I guessed Silicon Valley cabdrivers were accustomed to making most of their trips from hotels to one tech company or another.

I snapped open my laptop and took another look at some of the documents I had downloaded on the company I was about to visit. It sounded like a straightforward job, but they all do at first. I had time to read a couple of articles about Moonola in tech journals and one from the *New York Times* before we reached the neighborhood that was my destination.

The area looked something like an expensively designed college campus from twenty years in the future. Lots of well-maintained stretches of lawn and leafy trees. The buildings were all wide two- or three-story structures with smoked glass and steel exteriors, many of them with tasteful sculptures or water features outside. Almost none of them presented anything so gauche as a lot number or a sign identifying the name of their company. Instead, I saw lots of logos, artfully composed monograms, and the like. The driver pointed out some familiar names like Yahoo! and Google as we passed their outposts. I was grateful he knew where he was going, because I would have had difficulty navigating the maze of hieroglyphics. My job requires that I'm good at finding things, but I have my limits.

Case in point: The company I was looking for was

called Moonola. The building was another sprawling glass and steel block, distinguished from the others only by a cartoon image of a smiling cow. I wasted a few seconds trying to work out the correlation between the logo and the name before realizing that I was probably giving it more thought than the marketing team had.

"This is the place?" I asked as the driver pulled to a stop at the bottom of a path of black slate paving slabs that led to the entrance of the building.

"Mmm-hmm," he answered in the affirmative, checking the mileage and telling me the fare.

"You don't look like you belong here," he offered as I handed over the cash.

"Too old?" I asked, figuring the average age of a software guru was probably about twenty-two.

"Too dressed up."

I glanced down at my suit. Even with my natural inclination to go tieless, he was probably right.

I walked the length of the path, noting the security cameras watching me the whole way. The entrance was a double glass door, with the cow motif reproduced in frosting on the panels. It was a welcoming image to put on the front door, although the effect was undermined a little by the cameras and the sign warning that all visitors must be checked in, everyone had to swipe their pass, and NO TAILGATING. There was an intercom. I pushed the buzzer and a female voice answered immediately.

"Moonola, how may I help you?"

I gave her my name and told her I had a meeting with John Stafford, and she buzzed me in. I entered a small lobby with a flight of stairs leading to the second floor. The stairs were carpeted, and the place had a vague smell of newness. Like the recent memory of cut wood and fresh paint. At the top of the stairs was another locked door, although this one had a window into reception that let the receptionist see me. She waved at me and I heard a click as she unlocked the door remotely. Reception was another small, low-ceilinged room with no windows. The receptionist was a blonde in her mid-twenties wearing a black blouse. She sat behind a high desk.

She smiled welcomingly, but before she could speak I heard an abrupt voice from my right.

"Carter Blake?"

I turned to see another door leading to the interior of the building. A short man in jeans and a Led Zep T-shirt. He had a lanyard around his neck holding a white card, which I assumed was a security pass, but it was facing the wrong way. He had dark hair, glasses, one of those little tuft beards under his bottom lip.

"That's me," I said. "You're with Mr. Stafford?"

John Stafford was the name I'd been given. It hadn't rung any bells with me when I'd heard it the previous evening, but a little Googling had revealed he was something of a hot young gun in software. Not a Mark Zuckerberg or anything like that, at least not yet, but the kind of guy who would probably be commanding the front cover of *Wired* within the next year, and *Forbes* the year after that.

The guy with the tuft beard sighed, as though accustomed to but still mildly resentful at being defined by his association with Stafford. "I'm Greg. John's downstairs. Come on."

He had already turned to go back through the door

when the receptionist piped in. "He needs a visitor's pass."

"You haven't given him a pass yet?"

"I was just—"

"Give him a pass, Hayley."

I exchanged a brief, knowing look with Hayley as she showed me where on the form to sign, and then she gave me a red credit card-sized pass in a holder and lanyard. I took it and thanked her. "Security first," I said.

Greg snorted. "Yeah. Lot of good it did us."

I followed him through the door, and we headed along a corridor, through another security door, and down a flight of stairs. The decorators had obviously been commissioned only to cover the public-facing areas. As we got deeper into the building, it reverted to function rather than form: no carpets, cinder-block walls, strip lighting. It felt more like a bunker down here. I supposed it was, in a way.

We passed a series of door, and I could hear a faint rumble, like the engines on a cruise ship. Greg saw me looking and nodded at one of the doors.

"It's not all ours. We host for a couple dozen companies."

"Do they get a room each?"

"The big ones do."

We passed through another security door, which was the fifth time we'd had to swipe a pass, by my count, and entered a space not much larger than a phone booth. Greg waited for the door we'd used to swing shut until it clicked.

"You can't open the next door until the first one locks. This is the highest security area. Moonola servers only in the next room."

"Do you have any idea where he might have gone?" I asked, to fill the time.

He looked unimpressed. "Isn't that what you're here for?"

I didn't answer that. A green light clicked on in the last panel, and Greg swiped his pass.

We walked out into the Moonola server room. It was difficult to judge the dimensions of the space because everywhere you looked there were arrays of locked cages the height of jumbo-sized refrigerators. Inside each cage were the servers. The noise was much louder in here, so much so that I didn't catch Greg's next words. I went out on a limb and guessed it was something dismissive and nonessential. The temperature was noticeably hotter in here, despite the big air-conditioning vents in the ceiling that were blowing away, contributing to the din. I removed my jacket and folded it over my arm as I followed Greg.

We turned a few corners and made our way deep into the heart of the maze. I couldn't help but think it seemed a little anachronistic; all of these tin boxes whirring away in secrecy behind the sleek shiny devices we all take for granted these days. A moment later we arrived at what I assumed was our destination.

A man with his back to us, dressed in khaki skateboard shorts and a tennis shirt, was standing in front of an open server cabinet. He was tapping away at the keyboard of a kind of oversized laptop that seemed to have slid out of the section of the server tower just above waist level. Greg called out, but his voice was lost in the din. He reached out and tapped the man on the shoulder, but he ignored it, finishing tapping out whatever he was doing on the keyboard. Ten seconds later he hit the return key, snapped the lid of the laptop down, and slid it back into place. He swung the grilled door back into place in front of the tower and locked it before slipping the key back into his pocket. Only then did he turn around to acknowledge us.

I recognized him from the pictures I had seen on the website and on many of the articles I'd read on the company. Except that in every one of those pictures, he'd been wearing a wide grin that was just on the acceptable side of cocky. He wasn't grinning now. The confident light blue eyes were the next thing you noticed in pictures after the grin, but they were the first thing that stood out today. Only today they looked different—wounded, but purposeful. His thick, dark eyebrows were bunched close together above those eyes. His shaved head gleamed under the fluorescent lights as he walked toward me, his hand outstretched. I shook it.

"John Stafford."

"Carter Blake," I replied. "What do you need from me?"

He answered without hesitation.

"I need that son of a bitch's balls. On my desk."

TWO

Sunnyvale, California

I'VE HAD CLIENTS who would have been speaking entirely literally when they made a request like that, but I was reasonably sure that John Stafford was employing hyperbole.

"I'm afraid that's not part of the service."

Stafford didn't smile. "Let's talk upstairs."

Five minutes later, we had ascended to the second floor again. Out of the noise and the heat and the strip lighting. Back to smoked glass and expensive design and the smell of newness. The view from Stafford's office window looked out on the leaves on the trees at the front of the building. On the journey back up from the server room, we'd managed to off-load Greg, so it was just the two of us discussing the terms of the assignment.

Stafford was sitting behind the aforementioned desk: a piece of plate glass balanced on steel legs, supporting three screens arranged around a flat wireless keyboard. Far too tasteful a setup for what he had requested a few minutes before. He was a little older than I had estimated from the photographs: in his early thirties, perhaps. Not *old* old, but not exactly a spring chicken for this line of work. He looked away from me, glanced at one of his screens, then out of the window, and sighed.

He considered his response to my initial question. I could see that this was a frustration for him, having to tell somebody else what he wanted done. Technical people can be like that—they're used to solving their own problems, dazzling laymen with their mastery of the occult arts of coding or hacking or whatever.

"His name is Scott Bryant," he said after a minute. "One of my senior developers. He's worked here for the past eighteen months. Yesterday evening he walked into our secure data storage center—which you've just visited—and downloaded some very confidential, very valuable proprietary software belonging to me onto a flash drive. He hasn't been seen since."

"And you want him located so you can get your flash drive back."

"So I can get my company's future back, Blake."

"You've tried the police?" A question I generally ask. Often it's rhetorical, but not in this case.

"Of course. They sent a car around to his apartment, but of course he had cleared out. He's technically wanted, and they'll do their best to pick him up. You know what that means?"

"The same thing it means when they tell a burglarized homeowner they're looking into it?"

"Exactly. They don't get it. They don't care, because they're not paid to care."

"Which is why you're paying me to care, I take it."

"I hope so. I wanted the best, and your name came up."

"Okay. You're paying me to care, so why don't you start by telling me about this software? Starting with how time sensitive this is. Is Bryant planning to upload it to the Internet? Because if so—"

Stafford shook his head impatiently. "No. This isn't some Ed Snowden thing. This is about money. If he makes this public, it's worthless to him."

I nodded. "So he'll need to find a buyer, or meet up with them if he's found one already."

"Right."

"So what is it? What exactly has he stolen?"

He hesitated, as if it took an effort of will to discuss it with an outsider. "It's called MeTime. It's going to revolutionize social networking. Think about your Facebook page. If—"

"I haven't gotten around to Facebook yet."

He stopped and looked at me as though I'd walked off a UFO.

"But you know what it is, right?"

"Sure, an electronic tagging system that lets you upload pictures of food."

For the first time, he cracked a smile. "This will blow Facebook out of the water. It'll make Facebook look like a paper journal."

"So it's potentially lucrative."

"You could say that."

He began to give me an explanation of how unique and special his software was. He started out reasonably intelligibly, before descending into techno-babble. My attention wandered. From the lower levels, I could hear and feel the rumble of the thousands of servers. It reminded me of the thought I'd had earlier on. I pointed in the opposite direction, up to the ceiling. "I thought everything was in the cloud these days."

Stafford shook his head again. "If we'd stored this on a private cloud, there wouldn't have had to be an inside job, Blake. Some hacker in China would have had it six months ago. Physical is still best for security."

"But no system is without vulnerabilities."

"Correct."

I sat back in the chair. "I'll need his full employee record, past employment, plus anything else you've got on him."

"You got it."

"How well did you know him?"

He shrugged. "As well as any of my team. Kept himself to himself. I don't mean to say he was antisocial. I mean, he would come out for beers sometimes."

Stafford stopped and thought some more. I could tell he'd be able to reel off chapter and verse if I'd asked him how good a developer Bryant was, or what his three biggest screw-ups had been over the last year and a half. But forced to consider him as a man rather than an employee was a stretch.

"Single, I think. Or…wait a minute. He mentioned a wife once." He stopped and made a visible effort to recall the details. "Ex-wife maybe?"

"Does she live nearby?"

Stafford held up his hands in defeat. I made a mental note to follow up on that one.

"Okay, let's think about the software. Who are his potential customers? I'm guessing your rivals?"

Stafford visibly relaxed, on more comfortable ground again. "I can get you a list. We can narrow that down pretty easily. Proving anything is another matter."

"Great. Get me that and his company record as quickly as you can and I'll get to work."

"So we have a deal?"

"One last question: What do you want me to bring back? The software or Scott Bryant?"

He paused, considering the question.

"I need both, Blake. He has to go down for this." He waved his hand around to symbolically encompass the building. "I have more than thirty people whose jobs depend on this, and Bryant just sold us all out."

I sat back and considered it. "Understood. It's important to establish the ground rules up front. Now here's mine. I get half the money up front, half on delivery."

"Not a problem."

"The next one is the most important: I work on my own. As soon as you commission me to find Scott Bryant, that's it. I'll come back if I need anything from you, but otherwise you leave me alone."

"I'll need regular updates."

He slid a tastefully designed business card across the glass desk. I took it and put it in my pocket.

"Fair enough, but I'll call you. Last rule: I do things my way. That means you trust me to take any reasonable steps necessary in order to complete the job."

"I'm happy with…those decisions being taken on a need-to-know basis," Stafford said after a moment.

I smiled. "Don't worry. I don't think we'll need to bend too many rules on this one. But you never know, and that's why this rule is important. I won't burden you with the details, and you don't ask how I got the results."

Stafford nodded assent. "That's it?"

"That's it."

"Then let's get started."

THREE

New York City

EMMA FARADAY NODDED briefly in acknowledgment as the doorman stood to attention at her approach. She stepped through the open doorway and looked left and then right. Hank, her driver, was parked at the curb, twenty yards from the front door. He was short, bald, and in his sixties. He had seen her first and was already opening the rear door of the black limo.

She settled back on the leather seats and fastened her seat belt as Hank pulled out into traffic. Normally garrulous, Hank seemed to sense that this was not one of those days when his employer wanted to be chatted to. She reached into her bag and retrieved her Surface Pro. Detaching the keyboard, she placed the tablet component on her lap and switched it on. A second later, she had the file on her screen again. She had revisited this particular file on and off countless times over the past nine months and with increasing frequency over the past eleven days.

The file provided a partial history of a specific individual. The records were minutely, even obsessively detailed up until November of 2010. After that, they were culled from numerous, more casual sources. News reports. Questions asked of potential witnesses. Snatched screenshots from blurry security footage.

Faraday tapped on the screen a couple of times and navigated to the photo library. The photographs were arranged in strict date order and provided a pictorial narrative of the subtle way the subject had changed himself for the camera over the years. Expression, posture, hair length, facial hair, glasses present or absent. Everything fluctuated from image to image, except for the distinctive green eyes, which were the same in the first photograph and the last.

A soft *ping* alerted her to a new e-mail message. She tapped the screen again twice, and the image of the subject was replaced by her secure inbox. Except for the most recent arrival, the inbox was entirely clear, the way she liked it.

The e-mail was from Murphy, confirming that everything was on track for this evening's operation. The preliminary subject's location had been confirmed and verified. She only wished they could be as certain about the whereabouts of the other subject, the one in her file.

She acknowledged the e-mail with a simple "Okay," archived it, and closed the inbox window.

The subject's photograph appeared back on the screen. The most recent DMV picture, under the new name. As Hank braked for a red light, the sound of a sudden impact drew her eyes away from the screen and to the street outside. A tow truck in the next lane had rear-ended a blue Ford. She watched as the driver got out, berated the tow truck driver, and then shook his head as a symphony of horns chased him back into the driver's seat to move off, reluctantly chalking it up to experience.

She looked back to the screen, thinking about what would happen once the ball was rolling. They had a mul-

tilayered series of plans leading off from the outcome
of tonight's operation, like a formula. If A happens,
then they implement X. If B, then Y and Z. Separate
courses of action with their own branches and sequels.
In theory, they had covered all bases. But in her experience, the human element always trumped theory. And
that could cut both ways.

Murphy was beginning to disconcert her a little on
this operation. He seemed to be taking an unusual interest, to care a little too much about it. She supposed that
could be explained by the fact that he had worked with
the man in the file. There was an unavoidable personal
dimension there. She was uncomfortable with that. But
on the other hand, it made Murphy particularly valuable on this operation.

In some ways, Murphy had made things less difficult for her than they could have been, when she had
been brought in to direct the organization a year ago.
The change of personnel had been made in unfortunate circumstances—the previous director had killed
himself after being diagnosed with terminal cancer. It
had been decided that an entirely fresh way of doing
things was required.

The upper reaches of the DOD had begun to question the veil of secrecy drawn over so many operations
of the organization, even though they seemed happy
enough with the results. The organization was a *black
box*. An entity defined by inputs and outputs, with no
one able to see its internal workings. Instructions in
one side, results out the other. The detail of what went
on in the middle was lacking, and that was beginning
to make people nervous.

So Faraday had been quietly imported from the CIA.

Her track record with the agency, including an impressively disaster-free stint as station chief in Baghdad, gave her the skills, the background, and the credentials to take over as director. She understood, too, that the fact she had no dependents and kept any romantic relationships brief and entirely isolated from the job had worked in her favor.

That did not mean it had been an easy transition. The organization was the most closed of closed shops up until that point, run as near to a personal fiefdom as the US military allowed by just one man since the early 1990s. But that was where Murphy had come in handy. He had proved an able right-hand man, quelling potential dissent among the men and occasionally translating her more controversial commands into more digestible language. Freed to focus on the big picture, she had started out with one aim: to keep what worked, and to ruthlessly jettison what did not. A year on, she was pleased with the progress. Tonight's operation would begin the work of cutting one of the last remaining ties to the past.

So why did she feel so uneasy about it?

Hank started signaling and looked for a place to stop as they approached the building on West Fortieth. It was an unassuming thirty-eight-story glass and steel structure, built within the last fifteen years. It didn't stand out, certainly didn't look as though it might contain the headquarters of a secret military intelligence organization, but then that was entirely the point.

The organization had started out in a windowless sub-basement in the Pentagon more than two decades before, moving to an office park in Virginia in the late nineties to blend in more fully. After 9/11, the organization had looked ahead of its time. It had been designed as an agile, kinetic response to emerging threats; focusing on bringing together the top tier of military and intelligence operators in a small, compartmentalized unit. These attributes put the organization in a perfect position to adapt to the new world. In 2003, it had moved once again, to its present location. The shifts in physical distance from the seat of power seemed like an apt metaphor.

As Hank pulled to a smooth stop at the curb, she looked down at the file one more time. The green eyes stared back at her from the DMV photograph, as though aware of her gaze.

The subject had the ideal skill set for the work they did. An expert tracker, good with people in every way that mattered, above average on the firing range, adept in unarmed combat. A strategic thinker, too, able to respond creatively to changing conditions on the ground. Both a thinker and a warrior. Carter Black would be a perfect asset, if she were recruiting.

But more likely, within thirty-six hours, he would be dead.

FOUR

New York City

THE TWENTY-FOURTH-FLOOR conference room of the building on Fortieth Street was overheated, and the absence of windows meant that after a while you could almost forget you were in the heart of the city. If you spent long enough in here, it was possible to forget what *country* you were in. It had the feel of a bunker, nothing to distinguish it from similar rooms across the globe. Cornell Stark couldn't help but wonder if that was deliberate, given the subject matter of today's briefing.

Stark glanced around him. Twelve men in the room altogether, and he wondered how many of them knew why they were here. The only reason *he* knew was because he had been on the Crozier operation and Murphy had given him a heads-up that this was coming. The men were seated in two rows of six, facing the screen at the front of the room. At first glance they didn't look like what they were. For a start, grooming choices varied as much as they would have in a gathering of college students: buzz cuts to longer hairstyles, clean-shaven to bearded. The men were mostly dressed in cargo pants and T-shirts: the colors black or dark blue or olive green. None of them was wearing an official uniform of any kind. But a random civilian who happened to open the conference room door and look in would not mistake this group for anything but a team.

Not that anyone would be in a position to just walk in here by accident.

Stark himself wore boots, black combats, and a black tennis shirt, and he was one of the clean-shaven, short-haired contingent. He had been regular army up until a year ago, and he was still getting used to this. Not just the disregard for strict uniform and grooming standards, but the patterns of deployment. The long periods of downtime followed by a sudden call, after which he'd be expected to report within the hour and in peak fitness. Ranks were almost never referred to. The only person who was ever called anything other than their last name was Faraday. The director.

Stark checked his watch. Four minutes to noon. Which meant the briefing would begin in precisely four minutes. Murphy was a precise guy. And even had he not been, Faraday was going to be in on this one, and Faraday made Murphy look carefree and relaxed.

The other men were talking among themselves, waiting to find out why they were here. Some were shooting the shit about what they'd been doing on downtime. Some were speculating carefully about where they were possibly about to be deployed. Stark thought about the common denominators of the eleven men plus himself and decided Murphy had made these particular selections because, for want of a better descriptor, these were the most normal guys in the team. None of them would particularly stick out in a crowd, like the six-foot-eight Davis would have. They were all reasonably at ease talking to people, blending in.

Blending in would be important.

The only one who didn't quite fit that bill was Usher. Like Stark, he was sitting in silence, observing the others. He was at the far end of the front row—diagonally as far away from Stark as he could be. He wore glasses and was dressed neatly, but in subtle contrast to the others. He wore black jeans, soft shoes, and a white oxford shirt. That hypothetical civilian, in his or her brief glance into the room, might have had time to note that of all the men, Usher seemed to sit at one remove. As Stark's gaze lingered on Usher's profile, he sensed he was being watched and his head snapped around. Their eyes met. Stark smiled and raised his eyebrows, as if to say, "Do you know why we're here?"

Usher's expression didn't change. After a moment he looked away again, staring at the blank screen on the wall. Usher knew, he decided. Usher had been in LA, too.

There were men in the unit with whom Stark got on very well. There were others who proved more difficult to like. Usher was in neither of those two brackets. He was an enigma. He never spoke about anything not directly related to the job. Even then, he was economical with words, communicating exactly what he needed to as efficiently as possible. Stark had tried to engage with him a couple of times and concluded that, as smart a guy as Usher was, his brain was evidently missing the software that allows a person to interact normally with other people.

The conference room door opened and the conversation trailed off as Faraday entered, followed by Murphy. Jack Murphy was tall and broad-shouldered. Although he was wearing a dark suit, white shirt, and tie, there was no mistaking his military bearing. He was in his midforties, and although his days in the field were now behind him, Stark was in no doubt that he could still handle himself in a rough situation. The serious, focused version of Murphy had shown up today. He was the type of guy who could buy a round of drinks and fit in with the crowd at the bar, but he was capable of switching that off and projecting the persona of a cold professional when necessary. Stark wasn't sure which was closer to the real him. He reminded Stark of a politician, which explained why he'd been able to move so seamlessly into the role of deputy director. Not, of course, that anyone referred to him as such.

Emma Faraday, on the contrary, had only one side that Stark was aware of. The director was all business, all the time. She actively disliked any hint of levity. She discouraged any attempt at small talk. Stark had seen her respond to an innocent comment about the weather with a withering put-down. As far as Faraday was concerned, if it wasn't related to the job at hand, it was a waste of breath.

She was shorter than Murphy, around five six. Light brown hair pulled back in a severe ponytail, a midnight-blue shirt under a black pantsuit. She was a little younger than Murphy, too, but still older than the rest of them. Her high cheekbones and piercing blue eyes would have demanded attention even if she hadn't been the only woman in a roomful of men. Her permanent frown spoiled the effect somewhat. Thinking about it, Stark genuinely couldn't recall ever seeing Faraday smile in the year she had been in position as director.

The conversation immediately died away, and the men straightened in their seats, awaiting illumination as to why they were there.

Stark saw Murphy glance discreetly at Faraday before starting to speak. She responded with an almost imperceptible nod.

"Gentlemen," Murphy began. "I'll cut to the chase. You're about to be deployed on a mission to acquire a target. The target in question is smart, he's deadly, and he knows our methods. This is not business as usual."

"Sounds like business as usual to me," Dixon cut in, to mild laughter from some of the others. Faraday fixed the brawny Texan with an arctic stare, but said nothing.

Murphy left a pause before continuing. "First point of difference: As you may have gathered, given that you're not sitting on a C-130 right now, we're working stateside on this one."

The men were too jaded to show much in the way of surprise, but Stark noticed a couple of raised eyebrows from his vantage point. Jennings and Abrams exchanged a glance. They were sitting together, as usual. Their similar builds, hair, and features had led to Faraday mixing them up a couple of times early on, leading in turn to the nickname that both men hated: the twins.

"This is real world?" Abrams asked. If they had genuinely been twins, Abrams would have been the evil one. Stark had had to rein in his predilection for mayhem on more than one occasion.

"Real as it gets," Murphy confirmed. "Second point of difference. I told you our target knows his methods. There's a very good reason for that. He used to be one of us."

Faraday stepped forward as the screen lit up behind her, showing a low-res photograph. It showed a man in his mid- to late-thirties, dressed in a suit and wearing dark glasses. He was entering the lobby of a building, the picture taken from a security camera. A better-quality photograph appeared on the right-hand side of the screen, superimposed over the surveillance pic. This one was head and shoulders: an identity photograph from a driver's license or passport. It showed what Stark assumed was the same man: dark hair, green eyes, a carefully neutral expression, as though he didn't want the picture to reflect any kind of likeness.

Faraday said nothing for a moment, scanned the seated men with her stare. She looked as though she was daring someone to speak before she began. Nobody took her up on it.

"A couple of you in this room know who this is. For the rest of you, he's from before your time. We knew him under a different name, but he is currently calling himself Carter Blake."

FIVE

New York City

STARK WATCHED FARADAY as she paused to study the faces of the men in front of her. They were all listening intently, eyes focused either on her or on the screen. Stark saw Murphy and Ortega exchange the briefest of glances. So Ortega knew about this, too. It made sense. He was one of the longest-serving men in the room. Perhaps he, too, had worked alongside Blake. Ortega was about five seven, of stocky build, and with a white scar down the right side of his face. Stark had yet to work with Ortega, but his initial impressions left him wary. He was always quick with a joke, but Stark sensed a faint air of desperation beneath the quips. One of those men who seemed to obsess about making sure nobody put one over on them.

After a minute Faraday continued. "Blake was with us from 2003 to 2010, involved in actions in the Middle East, Central America, the Horn of Africa, and some more places we don't talk about. He was your classic triple threat—he came in on signals intelligence, but quickly proved even more adept on hum-int, and he could more than handle himself in combat. He preferred small teams." Faraday paused, corrected herself. "Actually, that's something of an understatement. His optimum size of team was one. It seems that's still the case."

She turned back to the screen and clicked the pointer

to activate the next series of images, flashing up one by one on the screen. Headshots of people Stark did not recognize. News headlines referring to missing people. And then headlines from the LAPD's Samaritan investigation.

"Since leaving under…difficult circumstances, it appears he's set himself up as a private contractor. Doing similar work to what he was doing with us and offering his services on the open market."

The blond-haired man in the front row cleared his throat. He was more powerfully built than any of the others, his black T-shirt straining over his wide arms. Stark had not worked with him before and couldn't remember his name. Something Polish, Kaminsky perhaps?

"Similar work, ma'am?"

Faraday nodded at the blond. She didn't mind being interrupted for a question, as long as it was a serious one. "That's right, Kowalski. He's a locator. He makes himself available to those who need somebody found, people who have exhausted the traditional channels or are prevented from using them. He's exclusive, tends to be expensive, and he works through personal recommendations. He's been reasonably smart. That's one of the reasons he's managed to stay off our radar for the past few years."

"Until now," Murphy said.

Faraday nodded and clicked on to the next slide. There was no one in the room who didn't recognize this one. The tall, slim man pictured on the screen had caused this secret unit a lot of trouble the previous year.

"I assume I don't need to give you Dean Crozier's résumé," Faraday said, her gaze dropping to Usher in the front row. She looked from him to Stark, who made sure to meet her gaze with an expression that said she sure as hell didn't.

Crozier had also been a member of the unit. Whereas the man now called Carter Blake had specialized in locating people, Crozier had specialized in ending them. He had been a little too zealous in the pursuit of that task, so much so that Faraday's predecessor had reserved him for deployment in parts of the world where his brutality would go unnoticed. But still, stories had circulated about him among the other men. That he hadn't confined his killings to designated targets. That he had taken enhanced interrogation to a level that made the Russian FSB look like bleeding-heart vegan hippies. There was even a story that he'd killed his own parents as a kid and had gotten away with it due to lack of evidence.

Suffice to say, nobody was overly saddened when Dean Crozier departed the unit for parts unknown. There was an unspoken suspicion that he had been dealt with permanently, on the orders of Faraday's predecessor. Unfortunately for a lot of innocent people, that hadn't been the case.

"As most of you know," Faraday continued, "last year the LAPD and the FBI uncovered evidence of a serial killer who had been operating nationwide for a time span that happened to coincide exactly with the time since Crozier left us. There were things about the killer's MO that raised some flags: the military experience, the use of tracking devices and booby traps, and most of all, the use of this weapon in the murders."

The screen changed to show a long, curved dagger.

"Crozier's signature," Faraday added. "We couldn't stand still on this. He was out of control, and that was unacceptable."

Not for the first time, Stark wondered what was most unacceptable: the dozens of murders Crozier had committed across the country, or the fact that it was clear they could not rely on him to keep his mouth shut about his past when he was inevitably caught. Given the parameters of their mission, he had a pretty good idea.

"We sent three men to Los Angeles," she said, briefly glancing at Stark and the other two she was talking about: Abrams and Usher. "They completed the job."

Reflexively, Stark looked back to Usher. This time he didn't move, his eyes staring dead ahead at Faraday. The truth was, only Usher knew exactly what had happened out at the abandoned film set in the mountains where Crozier had been found dead, along with his half sister and apparent partner in murder.

"During the Crozier operation, we hit a complication," Faraday continued. "The morning before we finally caught up with him, the LAPD managed to come up with a suspect all on their own. Needless to say, they got it completely wrong."

Carter Blake's image flashed up on-screen. It was the driver's license picture again, only this time it was part of a screen grab from an LA news channel. Blake's picture was on one side; a blond newsreader on the other, mouth open, brow furrowed. The ticker along the bottom read, LAPD IDENTIFIES SUSPECT IN SAMARITAN SLAYINGS.

"The officers concerned at the LAPD have been singularly uncommunicative on this, but we managed to piece things together. It seems were weren't the only ones who worked out it had to be Crozier. Blake did, too, and he volunteered his services to catch him."

"But it was a dumb move," Murphy said, stepping

forward again. "He had the inside track, but he had to know there was a possibility this could happen. He stayed under the radar for four years and then this."

Stark raised a hand, his eyes meeting Faraday's.

"So why are we going after Blake?"

"For the same reasons Crozier had to be put down. One, he knows too much. Two, he's a danger to society."

"All due respect," Stark said after a moment's thought, "from what you've told me, that doesn't sound like the case. He was helping the cops. He's not a killer like Crozier."

Murphy smiled knowingly and glanced at Faraday, as though to say, *Do you want to tell him, or shall I?*

Faraday didn't return the glance. She just clicked to the next slide. It showed a good-looking couple. The man was in good shape, in his midforties. He had brown hair, was wearing a dark suit and a smile as wide as the Mississippi. He had his arm around a woman: a brunette with big, expressive brown eyes and a smile that was even more dazzling than her companion's. They were pictured in front of a sea of smiling faces. In the background, you could make out red, white, and blue balloons suspended in the air.

"Do you recognize this man, Stark?" The tone in Faraday's voice was subtly mocking, and well it might be. Because there would be few people in the country who wouldn't recognize the man and woman in the picture. Their faces had been on the front page of every newspaper in the Western world five years ago.

"Of course I do. Are you saying Blake knows something about the assassination of Senator Carlson?"

Faraday took her time answering.

"I'm saying he pulled the trigger."

FIVE YEARS AGO

New York City

"Excuse me. Are you looking for somebody?"

I turned my head at the sound of the light female voice and saw its owner approaching me across the tiled floor to the lobby with speed and purpose. The first thought that popped into my head was, *Here comes trouble.* Although the question and the tone in which she'd asked it were polite, her expression said differently. It seemed to say she had a hundred and one things on her to-do list and she didn't have time to be dealing with some nobody who had wandered into the wrong Midtown office building.

She had light blond hair and was probably about five-five—though it was hard to be certain since she was wearing heels. She had blue eyes and wore subtle pink lip gloss. She had on a smart charcoal pencil skirt and a matching jacket over a cream blouse. There was a laminated identification pass clipped to the lapel of the jacket. She was carrying an iPad that I guessed had a list of those hundred and one tasks arranged in strict order of priority. She stopped two steps in front of me and looked up at me expectantly.

"Yes, I am." I smiled. "My name's—"

"Who?"

"Excuse me?"

"Who are you here to see?"

I glanced down at the pass on her lapel. In contrast to the way she was looking at me right now, the picture showed her smiling warmly. There was a barcode and a string of letters and numbers, and a name and a position: Carol Langford, Director of Operations.

"You work for John Carlson?"

Carol Langford sighed, as though resigning herself to wasting a couple more minutes on me than she'd budgeted for. "I work for *Senator* Carlson, yes. Do you know what that means?"

"It means you have a lot to do today?"

"Correct. Today and every other day. Now, if you'll be so kind as to state your business. I can either pass you along to the correct person or help you find your way out."

"I have a meeting with him."

"With whom?"

"Senator Carlson."

She blinked. "No, you don't."

"How do you know that? I haven't even told you who I am yet."

"I don't need to know who you are."

"You don't?"

She shook her head. "Because I do know that you're not the executive director of the Lake George Association, with whom Senator Carlson is meeting in twenty minutes, and you're definitely not Elizabeth Carlson, who's meeting the senator for lunch directly after that."

"How can you be certain of that?" I said, unable to resist the urge to provoke her a little more.

It failed. Rather than get more irritated, she loosened

up, giving me a sarcastic smile. "Because Mrs. Carlson is *never* early for any appointment."

I nodded. "Inside knowledge."

"No substitute for it."

Before we could circle back to the question of who I was and why I thought I had a meeting with her boss, we were interrupted by her cell phone ringing. Carol raised her eyebrows to excuse herself from the conversation and retrieved the phone, glancing at the display before she picked up.

"Senator? I'm good, thank you. I was—"

She paused, and her blue eyes flicked back in my direction. "Yes, there is a man in reception, but he…" Her gaze took on a more focused edge, and I could tell she was checking description. It felt a little uncomfortable, like being scanned.

"Yes, that's him. Okay. Now? Okay."

She hung up and composed a polite smile that perfectly matched the one on her badge. "My mistake. It appears you do have a meeting with the senator."

"Not a problem." I smiled. "I guess somebody screwed up on the scheduling."

The smile vanished at about the precise moment the realization hit me that the person responsible for the scheduling was standing right in front of me.

"Unlikely," she said coldly.

The reception desk was set between two rows of electronic turnstiles that guarded access to the rest of the building. Carol Langford asked for a visitor pass for me and we passed through the turnstiles and into one of the three waiting elevators. She hit the button for the twenty-sixth floor and the doors closed silently.

"How long have you worked for the senator?" I asked to break the ice as the elevator began its ascent.

"Almost three years, now."

"Must keep you busy."

She looked at me for the first time since the lobby and nodded slowly. Neutral expression, but I could tell from her eyes that she was amused at my efforts to work myself back into her good graces through small talk.

The floors on the display clicked past: nine, ten, eleven. A weird thought occurred to me. The ascending floors were like a clock ticking down to the last time I would ever be alone with this woman, in all likelihood. And for some reason I didn't quite understand, I didn't want that time to be over just yet.

"You know," I said, as though having given it careful thought, "if you give me your number, I could call ahead next time. Make sure there are no surprises."

She looked up at me and blinked, then shook her head in amusement. "Really?"

"Not smooth enough, huh?"

"I've heard smoother."

"Cut me some slack. I'm rusty. I've been out of the country for a while."

"You have, huh?"

The floors clicked up. Twenty-two, twenty-three. I felt the elevator begin to slow.

I shrugged. "I'm sorry, I didn't mean to offend you."

"Who's offended?" she said, which I figured could mean anything.

The digits hit twenty-six. The elevator chimed softly and the doors slid open on a stretch of hallway, opposite floor-to-ceiling windows facing east. The sun shone out of a clear blue sky over the East River, flooding the carpeted floor with light.

Carol turned left and marched down the hallway without waiting for me. I followed. Without looking back, she spoke, all business once again.

"Care to tell me what you're meeting the senator about?"

"I would if I could," I said.

"Classified?"

"Even to me," I said.

It was the truth. I wasn't sure how or why the senator had found me, but I was intrigued enough to want to find out. We passed several offices before we got to one at the end of the hall with a name plate that read SENATOR JOHN CARLSON.

She paused at the door and turned back to face me. "I'll tell you what," she said. "There's a restaurant in Little Italy I like. It's called Terradici's. Think you can find it?"

I smiled, caught off guard. "Sure. I'm good at finding things."

She nodded. "Eight o'clock, then. But only if you're confident of my ability to not screw up the scheduling."

Before I could open my mouth to respond, she turned away from me, knocked on the door, and opened it. She showed me into a big office with more floor-to-ceiling windows and a view to the south this time. Books lined the two side walls, and the carpet felt deeper and plusher underfoot than the one in the corridor. There was a big desk in front of the window and a big man behind it, already getting up to greet us.

John Carlson was young and in good shape, especially for an elected official. He wore a striped shirt.

His jacket was off, draped over the back of the chair. I was unaccustomed to meeting public figures in person, and there was an odd feeling of disconnect. He looked like he had stepped out of the television screen, or off the cover of *Newsweek*—the same build, features, the same brown hair, brown eyes, tanned complexion I'd seen so often at one remove. It took me a second to figure out what was missing: the five-hundred-megawatt smile. In its place was a look of grim focus, like he'd been preparing for this moment over and over in his head all morning. I think I knew at that moment why I'd been called in.

I held my hand out and he took it, gripping firmly and doubling up with his left hand as his eyes held mine. A real politician's shake. We said each other's names, even though we both knew them already.

"Thank you, Carol," he said, without taking his eyes off me. I glanced at her and saw her quickly recompose her features from a frown. I got the impression she wasn't used to being dismissed quite so abruptly.

She nodded. "Let me know if you need anything."

The door closed behind her, and Carlson stepped back a couple of paces, perching on the edge of his desk. He indicated the twin upholstered chairs facing the desk. I pulled one of them toward me and sat. He looked down at me, his eyes still sizing me up. I wondered if this was some kind of business manual technique to reinforce power relationships in a meeting or something.

"Thank you for coming in. I appreciate it."

"Not a problem," I said. "Have to say I'm curious."

"You want to know why I wanted to speak with you."

I took my eyes off him and looked out at the city for a few seconds before answering.

"That's just the tip of the iceberg," I said. "I'm curious about who told you I was someone you needed to speak to. I'm even more curious to find out how you found me—my apartment in the city isn't held under my name, and I'm out of the country for work a lot. That's all very curious. But the thing I'm most curious about is why you don't want anyone to know you're meeting with me, to the extent that one of your closest aides didn't know about it until the last minute."

He watched me, unblinking, while I said all this. After I'd finished, he nodded slowly.

"Fair enough. I think I can answer your questions with one word."

I kept my face impassive. "Is it a magic word?"

For the first time, I saw a hint of the famous Carlson smile. "You could say that. I hear you and your cohorts like to think of yourselves as magicians, of a kind."

All doubt evaporated. And I knew what the word was. I also knew I had to extricate myself from this room as quickly and as cleanly as possible. I cleared my throat and smiled at him.

"My cohorts?" I repeated, hoping my tone conveyed the right balance of confusion and amusement.

Carlson nodded again, but his smile was gone. He stood up, and I noticed that there were two plain manila file folders on his desk: one thick, one thin. He reached down and picked the thin file up. There was no label on the cover. He opened it and leafed through a couple sheets of paper.

"Says here you've been working for Uncle Sam for the last six years. Overseas Personnel Planning. Nice salary. Lots of foreign travel. Pretty cushy position, by the looks of it."

"It's harder than it looks."

"Oh, I don't doubt that. I don't doubt that at all. Because this is all bullshit."

He closed the folder and slapped it on the desk, staring back down at me.

"Why don't you tell me about what you really do," he said. "Why don't you tell me about Winterlong?"

SIX

Sunnyvale, California

AFTER LEAVING THE Moonola building, I took another cab back into the center of Sunnyvale and found a quiet coffee shop. I ordered a large cup of black coffee and read through Scott Bryant's employee file. There wasn't a great deal to read.

It contained the things you'd expect from any company: Bryant's résumé, submitted on his application for the job; his sickness and vacation record; details of his salary and benefits. As you'd expect from a company that employed highly skilled technicians, it also contained the successful results of his selection and evaluation tests. And as you'd expect from a company that developed a highly marketable and attractive product that could be stored on a flash drive, there was also a background report. As Greg from Moonola would no doubt have pointed out: *A lot of good that did.*

It looked as though the agency that had been commissioned to look into Bryant's background had done a reasonably thorough job. His employment history and educational qualifications were bona fide, matching exactly with what he'd put on the résumé. Bryant had graduated in the top five percent of his class at Stanford, and had worked for four other Silicon Valley tech companies at steadily increasing pay grades and levels of expertise prior to joining Moonola. I didn't recognize the names of any of the four other companies, but I assumed they all had colorful fonts and probably some anthropomorphized animal as part of their logo. A financial check showed he had no significant credit card debts at that time, and that he didn't appear to owe anything but a sizable mortgage on a property in Palo Alto. Was there such a thing as a non-sizable mortgage, these days?

That led smoothly into an evaluation of his personal life. Again, no obvious red flags. Married for four years at that point to Jasmine Mary Bryant, a thirty-one-year-old botanist whom he'd met while at Stanford. They had one child: a four-year-old girl named Alyssa.

The one question mark was over a six-month gap in his résumé. Bryant had taken a sabbatical from the company he was working for at that point, picking up early the following year just before he moved to another company. The report noted that when questioned about it at the Moonola interview, he said they had briefly relocated to Seattle while Jasmine's mother was undergoing chemotherapy for breast cancer. When the mother-in-law got the all clear, they came back to Palo Alto.

Aside from that, there was absolutely nothing out of the ordinary. A stable, ordinary, professional guy. So what had gone wrong?

I remembered Stafford mentioning that Bryant had split from his wife. Actually, he had thought Bryant was single at first, then remembered "something about an ex-wife." I wondered how recent that was; thought about calling Stafford and then decided it was unlikely he'd have paid enough attention to Bryant's personal life to know. Besides, there was an easier way to check.

I leafed back to the personnel details and checked the address. The house in Palo Alto was there as the initial home address from the time of his recruitment, but there was an amendment about six months ago. Bryant had moved from what Google informed me was a good-sized three-bedroom detached house in an affluent suburban area to a one-bedroom condo in Monte Sereno. Still a nice place, in a desirable Silicon Valley commuter town within a half hour's drive of Moonola.

So six months ago, something had happened that had meant Bryant had moved out of the family home and into a place of his own. The cops had already given the condo a once-over, according to the report. I wondered if they had checked out the previous address. Given the lackadaisical approach Stafford had complained about, I thought it was worth the cab fare to Palo Alto to find out.

I picked up the sheaf of papers, tapped them square, and tucked them back into the plastic wallet Stafford's receptionist had provided. I finished my coffee and took my phone out. I tapped into recent calls and scrolled to a number saved under the letter *C*. I tapped again and listened to the electronic ringtone. It would be midafternoon in Florida, and I wondered if Coop would be in the bar already.

There wasn't really an accurate description for what Coop did, but *agent* probably came closest. Or perhaps *broker*. He was the guy people talked to when they wanted something done. He was the guy who could contact people like me, or whoever was most appropriate to the job at hand. Our relationship was based on a carefully balanced combination of mutual trust and "don't ask." I didn't know too much about him or how he came to be so well connected, and he didn't ask too much about me. He had no more than a vague idea about where I hung my hat, and I was supposed to know only that he was based somewhere in Florida. It had been Coop who had referred me to Stafford, for his usual modest commission.

The ring cut out, and I heard distant traffic noise.

"How'd it go?"

I smiled. Straight to the point, as always. "Good. I think I have somewhere to get started."

"Glad to hear it," Coop replied, his already-gravelly tones betraying the onset of a cold. "I'll process the up-front, and you can let me know when you deliver."

"Your confidence in me is inspiring."

He chuckled. "I don't think this is going to be one of your tougher assignments, Blake. A computer nerd on the run? What's the worst that could happen?"

I shook my head. "Stop it."

"Stop what?"

"Tempting fate. You know what I say: There's always—"

"'Always something you don't know,'" he finished. "Anyone ever tell you you're one of life's pessimists?"

"You know what the Russians say about that?"

"About what?"

"They say that a pessimist is a well-informed optimist."

"Cute."

I smiled. "Take care of that cold, Coop. It's chilly out there."

"Not in Florida."

"Even in Florida."

We exchanged goodbyes and I hung up, looking back at the file photo of Scott Bryant. It was an upper-body shot of an African-American man in his midthirties, slightly overweight, with close-cropped hair and a neat beard. He wore rimless glasses and a burnt-orange short-sleeve shirt and was flashing a wide grin for the camera. The impression was someone who was pleasant and friendly and a little nerdy. The picture was as unassuming and nonthreatening as the information in the background check.

But the background check had reinforced an entirely false impression. I wondered if the photograph would, too.

SEVEN

South of Portland, Oregon

IT WAS TORTUROUS, keeping to fifty in the slow lane, but Scott Bryant knew it was worth the frustration to make sure he wasn't stopped. The car itself—a blue '07 Pontiac, bought cash via a pseudonymous eBay account—wouldn't give the highway cops cause to stop him, but if he was pulled over for speeding, he would be forced to show his driver's license, or claim he didn't have one with him. Either one would spell trouble. So although the pace was frustrating, it was necessary.

He still had plenty of time, anyway. The buy was set up for tomorrow morning at eleven. A little less than twenty-four hours, now.

After that it would be over and he'd be on his way to…someplace else. He hadn't decided where yet. That wasn't due to a lack of planning. He had been meticulous about every detail of what he needed to do from now until tomorrow morning at eleven.

Getting into the server room to swipe a copy of Me-Time and then leaving without being challenged had been the most difficult part. Unfortunately, it had been impossible to cover his tracks for long. It was inevitable that they would have discovered his crime by now. He wondered if they had gone to the cops immediately. He had a hunch that Stafford wouldn't want to, but even if he did, he had cleared the apartment in Monte Sereno out a week ago. The only other connection he had in California was Jasmine, and she wouldn't be able to tell them anything useful.

The thought of her triggered a nauseous feeling of guilt in the pit of his stomach. He had thought about calling her to tell her about what he was going to do. He had wanted to, but deep down he knew it was better this way. If this didn't work out, it was all on him, and that was the way it needed to be, for all their sakes. But a part of him wondered what she would have said anyway.

So far, everything was going to plan. He had tried to leave nothing to chance. He had cut his credit cards up and put them in the trash. He'd wiped the data on his old cell phone and then smashed it and tossed it into the storm drain at the bottom of his street for good measure. He had a new set of clothes, a new prepay phone, and enough cash for unexpected emergencies. He had food and bottles of water for the journey. He had twenty dollars for singles for tolls. He had planned out every detail from walking out of Moonola yesterday right up until eleven a.m. tomorrow at Wakey's Diner. At 11:05, he'd be leaving with two million dollars in cash, walking a hundred yards across the street to the bus station, and beginning his new life.

What happened after that was a mystery even to him. Deliberately so. It was as though it would be tempting fate if he made concrete decisions beyond the culmination of his plan. On a rational level, he knew it was dumb. He remembered how Jasmine had teased him about his superstitions: that somebody who worked with the hard and fast certainties of technology could be in thrall to such primitive instincts. Don't walk under ladders. Step on a crack, break your mother's back.

Never enter through the front door. Never count your money when you're playing. Never accept the winnings in fifties.

He knew superstition wasn't related to the part of him that was good at his day job. It was an intrinsic element of the other side of him. The one he had known to keep hidden from Jasmine until it was impossible to hide it any longer.

It was funny. For the first time, the two halves of his life had come together, because this was the highest-stakes gamble he would ever make in his life. The highest stakes he would ever play, for the biggest payoff.

For some reason he thought about the guy who had sold him the Pontiac last night: a short, nervous-looking guy who introduced himself only as "Bill." According to Bryant's instructions, Bill had delivered the car to an empty parking lot. After Bryant had checked the car over to make sure the tires and lights were all fine, Bill had accepted eight hundred and fifty dollars for the transaction—eight hundred for the car, fifty for delivery. After they had shaken hands, Bill had tapped his shirt pocket, just to make sure the money was still there. Just then, Bryant did the same thing, making sure the MeTime flash drive was still there.

In twenty-four hours…*less* than twenty-four hours, it would all be over.

EIGHT

New York City

"Close the door behind you," Faraday said without looking up.

She kept her eyes on the report on her screen as Murphy entered the office and took his time getting comfortable in the chair in front of her desk. He unbuttoned his jacket and sat back. He was too damned comfortable in her presence. The other men made sure to respect her position, even Usher in his creepy, monosyllabic way. But Murphy treated her as though they were equals. They were not.

"I think that went pretty well," he said, in the tone of a husband congratulating his wife after a successful dinner party.

Finally, she closed the window on her screen and let her eyes meet his. "I'm uncomfortable with this, Murphy."

"You were okay about it when it was Crozier."

"That was very different and you know it. That was reacting to a live situation—this is preemptive."

"Never heard that raised as a problem around here before."

She said nothing, just fixed him with a stare, until he smiled apologetically.

"You really do want to do things differently, huh? That wasn't just a hard-ass new boss act, was it?"

"I don't act, Murphy. And I think we're way past me being the new anything. I realize it's important for your ego to pretend this is still a boys' club, and that's why I indulge you, to a point. Drakakis was sloppy. He let men like Crozier and Blake run wild. I'm not going to make that mistake, but it doesn't mean I want to rush into anything."

"Who's rushing? It took us months to get this close. Without this new lead, we'd be chasing dead ends for the next year."

Faraday didn't rise to the bait. Murphy's reference to dead ends was a veiled dig. Faraday had wanted to focus on pinning down Blake's base before they made a move against him. From the painfully few confirmed sightings, there was a hypothesis that he was based somewhere on the East Coast. They had a few promising angles of investigation, but so far nothing had panned out. Not until one of the many lines they put out had been tugged, giving them a live and time-sensitive opportunity.

Perhaps Murphy had a point, though. In the year or so since she had taken over, she had been entirely comfortable with the vast majority of decisions she had made, the reforms she had implemented. She knew that she was grudgingly accepted by the men, even if none of them warmed to her personally. She couldn't care less about that, so long as they respected her.

But if she had a legitimate shot at the genuine threat and didn't take it... Well, then the whispers would start. Perception was everything, and she knew Murphy wouldn't hesitate to use that against her if he didn't get his way on this. She sensed he wanted Blake bad, for whatever reason. There was more to it than he was telling, she was sure, but that didn't change the fact that

Blake could be very dangerous indeed if the truth ever came to light. So on balance, it was worth going ahead, even if she wasn't entirely comfortable.

"This is the time," Murphy said again, a flicker of concern in his eyes suggesting that he was worried she might be changing her mind. "We remove Blake and that's it. No one will ever know what really happened to the senator."

Faraday bristled. Even now she couldn't quite believe it. That one of their own operatives had murdered a US senator and his wife in revenge for a botched deal to leak sensitive files. Drakakis, her predecessor, had acted quickly to protect the operation. An Iraq veteran with mental health issues named Evan Froelich had been put in the frame for the assassination and conveniently found dead by his own hand shortly thereafter. They had made efforts to track down Blake and his accomplice back then, of course, but luck and training had allowed them to slip the net. In any case, they had known that it was in the interests of both men to lay low and not make ripples. If that changed, they could be dealt with later. Later had finally come.

Jesus. If there was ever a need to demonstrate why a change in the regime had been necessary, the Carlson assassination had been it. Two dead civilians, a murderous loose end, and an extremely risky cover-up. She cursed Drakakis for putting her into this position, where the only tenable solution was to finish what he had started. It wasn't the way she worked, but it had to be done. Martinez had been dealt with already. Now there was only one remaining loose end, one last snip.

"I don't want any blowback on this, Murphy. Is that clear?"

He leaned forward in his chair, his expression suddenly serious, all business. "I have a good team in place for this. We do, I mean. Once we move on the connection in Orlando, we'll have everything in place no matter where Blake is hiding. It's going to be clean and quiet. Surgical."

The assurance given, Murphy sat back and smiled again, baring his teeth. All of a sudden Faraday decided Usher's dead-eyed stare wasn't so bad after all. To avoid looking at him, she glanced at her screen and clicked to open Cornell Stark's file. Two photographs at the top of the screen: one from his army days, one more recent. In contrast with Carter Blake, Stark had barely changed in the four-year gap between the images. He had close-cropped, reddish hair, dark, thoughtful eyes, and an identical, focused expression in both pictures. Giving nothing away.

She cast her eyes down the dashboard stats. Fitness tests, psych evaluations, after-action reports.

"Stark is lead on this operation, correct?"

Murphy nodded, his brow furrowing slightly, as though wondering if she was about to question the decision. "I think he's ready."

She looked back at him, fixing him with a cool stare. "I agree."

Murphy's smile seemed to falter for a second. Was that a slight tinge of jealousy? Faraday had been extremely impressed with Stark so far. He hadn't put a foot wrong. For the first time, she sensed that her approval bothered Murphy, and as soon as the thought crossed her mind, she knew why that was. Stark was neither one of the old guard nor a green recruit eager to be taken under Murphy's wing. He was his own man.

"Good to be on the same page, as always," Murphy said after a second.

After he left, Faraday thought about Drakakis for the first time in a while. About his last moments in this office. The carpet had been replaced, but she knew there was a large, tear-shaped bloodstain on the floorboards beneath the spot where she was sitting. She could have chosen any other office, of course, but this one had the best view and was closest to the ops room.

Faraday put her predecessor out of her mind and picked up the phone. She dialed a four-digit extension that put her through to a desk two floors below this one.

"Williamson," was the acknowledgment. The technician sounded bored with her own name as she said it. Faraday could hear keys tapping in the background, could picture Williamson staring at the screen, not breaking from her task, giving the call through her headset the minimum attention required.

"We're moving on Prodigal Two. I'll need you on shift tonight."

Faraday heard a tab snap open in the background and knew it was one of Williamson's ever-present Red Bulls.

"Good to know. So that means I can forget about working the flights?"

Faraday thought about it for a moment. "No. Keep at it."

Williamson's shrug was almost audible on the line. "You're the boss."

"That I am," Faraday said, and hung up. If stage one of the operation went well tonight, Williamson's work over the last few weeks would be largely redundant. But it was always advisable to have a backup plan.

NINE

Palo Alto, California

THERE ARE THREE ways to go on the run.

Actually, there are a million different ways. But there are three real options from which to choose before a person starts to think about the details. At one end of the scale, you stay close to home. At the other, you relocate to another country. The third option is midway between the two extremes.

The people who try to half-ass the whole thing stick around the area they're familiar with, maybe crashing at a friend's house where they convince themselves no one will think to look for them. Those people are generally the easiest to find. Then you have the opposite type: the ones who go for broke and leave the country, headed for Europe or, more intelligently, a nonextradition country in South America. This option makes a lot of sense, because if you're running away from someone or something, it's a natural instinct to want to put the maximum number of miles behind you to do that. The only problem is that in this day and age, it's very difficult to leave the country without your point of departure and destination being tracked on about a dozen different systems. Fleeing to a foreign country makes finding you a complicated and expensive task, but at least it gives the people who are looking for you a solid starting point. They know you're in Barcelona or Ecuador or Timbuktu, or wherever, and they know that without a support network, you're likely to behave in a certain way.

The smart people don't do either of those things. The smart people stay in the country, but get the hell away from whatever they're running from. They buy a used car for cash using a fake ID, or they take the bus or the train. Better: a few different buses or trains to big population centers. They take nothing inessential with them, they pay for everything in cash, they dump their cell phone, and they don't keep in contact with anyone. It's at once very simple and harder than it sounds.

Given that Scott Bryant was a Stanford grad who had already pulled off a successful data heist in a high-security data center, I was reasonably confident he wasn't an idiot. That meant he wouldn't stick around town, and he was smart enough to know the cops might have put a hold on his passport.

I hailed a cab outside of the coffee shop and gave the driver the address of Bryant's house. Depending on what happened next, it was worthwhile to rent a car, but I wanted to hear what Bryant's wife had to say first. Palo Alto was the next town to the north from Sunnyvale, so it was a short trip on the 101. The house was on Amarillo Avenue, a short distance from the exit off the freeway.

I called up the details of the house on my phone on the journey. It had commanded a hefty price tag when Bryant and his wife had made the down payment a couple of years before and would probably fetch even more now. Considering the asking price, it was curiously unimpressive—a wide one-story building with a covered parking spot, just three bedrooms, a stone patio, and a reasonably spacious yard. Most other places in the country, it would have been an unremarkable residence for a working professional. Here, thanks to inflated Silicon Valley real estate prices, it nosed into a seven-figure purchase price.

There was an old lady tending yellow roses in a garden across the street who watched me with interest as I got out of the taxi. I smiled at her and started up the front path. The door opened on a blond woman wearing jeans, a white blouse, and a polite smile. When she saw I wasn't anyone she recognized, or the mailman, she tilted her head and the smile took on a warier edge.

A voice came from behind her.

"Mommy, who's at the door?"

Before her mother could answer, a tiny four-year-old girl with her dark hair in a ponytail was trying to squeeze through the gap between the woman's hip and the doorframe to get a glimpse of me. I smiled down at her and looked up again as Jasmine Bryant asked how she could help me.

"My name's Carter Blake," I said. "I'm here on behalf of Moonola."

I left it deliberately short and to the point, because I thought the way she reacted to that sentence would tell me a lot. I was right.

The smile vanished and her expression took on an awkward, embarrassed look. "I'm afraid my husband doesn't live with us anymore."

Interesting. Either she was an excellent liar, or she had no clue what her husband had been planning. I didn't catch a hint of suspicion or guilt in her face or her voice.

"Mommy—"

"Just a *minute*, sweetheart. Sorry."

"No problem," I said. "If this is a bad time…"

"Is Scott all right?"

"Actually, that's what I'm here about. He hasn't been seen at work for a couple of days and, well, naturally there's some concern. I just wondered if you'd heard from him in the last week or so."

She shook her head. "We haven't spoken in weeks." She glanced down at her daughter and her voice went up an octave. "Sweetie, there's a pack of cookies in the kitchen. Why don't you go get one?"

The kid's head snapped up, suddenly serious. "Three."

"*One*. I'll count."

The two of them held a staring contest for a moment before the daughter relented and ran back into the house.

Jasmine Bryant watched her get out of earshot and then stepped out onto the porch, letting the door swing most of the way shut behind her. The polite smile had vanished.

"What did he do?"

"I didn't say he'd done anything."

"Cut the crap. If they're looking for him, it's because he's done something he shouldn't have done and skipped out, right? That's what he did to me. What are you, a private detective?"

"I'm a consultant. I'm helping them resolve the situation."

"So there is a situation."

"He's taken something they'd like to get back. If I catch up to him soon, I think they'll go easy on him."

The lie rolled off my tongue before I had consciously thought about it.

"I'd help you if I could. But we haven't spoken in weeks, like I said. I've seen him twice since I kicked him out of this place." She turned a little and looked up at the house, sighing. "And we won't be too far behind him."

"Do you mind if I ask?"

"He ran up debts north of two hundred grand in Vegas, and now all of a sudden we don't have the money I thought we did." She laughed bitterly. "Hell, we don't have the 'we' I thought we did. You know something, Mr. Blake? I don't think we ever really know anyone."

"You must be pretty angry with him," I said, feeling only a little like a heel.

"That's an understatement," she said. She was looking beyond me at something. I glanced around and saw the old lady across the street bending over her flower beds watching us. She hurriedly looked down. Jasmine Bryant kept her eyes on her for another couple of seconds before looking back at me. "You probably think you can persuade me to help you find him, just to get back at him, right?"

I thought carefully before replying. "I wish I could tell you it hadn't crossed my mind."

She nodded. "Well, you can't. I may be angrier than hell at Scott, but I wouldn't sic the police on him just to get even."

"I'm not the police." I held up my hands, palms out. "Look—I don't even have ID."

The corner of her mouth curved upward, and then she sighed. "He's gotten himself into a lot of trouble this time, hasn't he?"

"My guess? It looks like he made a bad decision on impulse."

"Did you mean what you said? That they'll go easy on him if you bring him back?"

I thought about Stafford's request for Bryant's balls on his desk. It wouldn't be easy. But for some reason, looking through Bryant's file, meeting his estranged family, I couldn't believe he was a genuinely bad guy. Just one who had made some bad decisions and was in way over his head. I knew Stafford's number one priority was getting the MeTime software back. Surely I could negotiate favorable terms in return for that.

"I think I can arrange it," I said. "As long as we put things right."

She stared at me for a minute, then opened the door. "You can look in his study, if you like," she said. "I don't know if it'll do any good. He left in kind of a hurry."

TEN

BRYANT'S STUDY WAS in the third bedroom, the one with the window that looked out on the backyard. It was small, and contained only a computer desk and a bookcase with three shelves, the top two lined with a mixture of mystery novels and coding manuals, the bottom containing magazine folders and ring binders.

Jasmine gave me the password for her computer, and I spent half an hour checking the usual things on Bryant's profile. Internet search history showed nothing out of the ordinary—no queries for flights to Timbuktu or research into how to effectively disappear. Either Bryant's crime hadn't been planned far enough in advance for him to have left a trail there, or he had been sensible about not leaving clues behind.

I browsed through the file space, not even attempting to look at everything. There were thousands of files, and it would take a team of people a long time to meticulously check each one. If I struck out on leads, it might be worth asking Jasmine if I could turn the computer over to Stafford's people, but I wasn't sure if she would go that far. Instead, I spent some time superficially looking at his file structure. He had been conscientious with his filing—keeping documents from previous jobs, along with a whole lot of stuff from his time at Moonola. I happened on a folder buried in the Moonola file called "Nevada" that held spreadsheets with dollar amounts with strange notations that I guessed were Bryant's way of keeping track of his gambling. Unfortunately, it hadn't helped him keep on top of his losses.

I was about to give up and start looking through the folders in the bookcase when I noticed a folder within the *Work* section with an unfamiliar title. All of the other titles were either easily understandable, or matched the names of companies I'd seen on his résumé. But this one stood out. It was titled "Aella." I clicked into the folder and found documents similar to the ones stored under the names of other companies he'd worked with: meeting notes, system requirement specifications, source code files, contracts. I took a break from that to Google the word *Aella*. It was the name of a software company based in Seattle.

I clicked back into the Aella folders and looked at a few of the files. Bryant's labeling convention as so diligent that it took me a matter of minutes to find information I needed. He had worked for Aella as a freelance consultant, managing on a project that had rolled out over a six-month period the previous year. The dates matched precisely with the time Bryant was in Seattle, supposedly because of his mother-in-law's chemo.

So for some reason, Bryant hadn't wanted to tell his then-employer about what he was really doing in Seattle, hence the sabbatical. It didn't take a rocket scientist—or a tech genius—to work out the reason. He didn't want his employers to know he was taking on a lucrative fixed-term project for a competitor.

I printed out a copy of one of Bryant's invoices, detailing the hours billed and showing Aella's address, folded it and put it in my pocket. I knelt down by the bookcase and started going through the binders and

magazine files, just to be thorough. I found some mortgage statements, family documents, birth certificates,
but nothing work-related. As I replaced the last binder
on its shelf, I felt a little resistance at the back. I pulled
it back out and reached in, feeling my fingers wrap
around a small lump of plastic. I pulled my hand out to
see that it held a small cell phone.

I came out of the study a minute later. From the doorway, I could see across the hall and through the open
kitchen door. Jasmine was sitting at the table with her
daughter, who was playing a game on some kind of
handheld device while Jasmine drank coffee. The sunlight was streaming through the venetian blinds, bath-
ing the room in golden stripes. For a brief moment, it
looked almost as though all was right with the world.
Jasmine heard the study door open and met my gaze.

"Any luck?"

"I don't know," I said truthfully. I held up the phone.
"Is this your husband's?"

She squinted at it before shrugging. "I guess so.
Maybe an old one. Do you want to take it?"

"It might be worth having a quick look, if it isn't
password protected," I said.

"Three-nine-one-one."

Both Jasmine and I looked down at Alyssa, who'd
chirped up without bothering to look up from her game.

"Excuse me?" I said.

"Three-nine-one-one. That's Daddy's pin on most
things, except the cable." She looked up and blinked at
me. "It's my birthday. I'm nearly *five*."

Jasmine and I exchanged an amused glance, and I
held the phone out to her. "Got a charger?"

Ten minutes later, I was scrolling through Bryant's

e-mails, looking for something that might confirm my suspicions about his direction of travel. I had been lucky that he had never bothered to wipe this old device when he upgraded, because it was still linked to his personal Microsoft profile, although not his Moonola account, by the looks of the e-mails. I was unlucky in that he didn't seem to have conducted any e-mail conversations about his plan to skip town with Stafford's software. That was hardly surprising.

But it's always worth checking to make sure the person you're looking for hasn't made the one mistake in among the hundred other things they've been careful about.

I gave up on the e-mails and thumbed through some of the photographs on the phone. I went back to the Seattle period and found some touristy shots of the Space Needle, the Pike Place Market and the zoo. Alyssa looking much younger, Jasmine and Scott looking much happier.

"Did you enjoy Seattle?" I asked.

"I liked it okay."

"And your mom's doing okay now?"

Jasmine studied me for a second. "Why do you ask?"

"Your husband told the company she had cancer. That's why you moved to Seattle for a while, why he had to take a sabbatical."

She sighed. "My mother hasn't been sick a day in her life. She lives in Ohio."

I nodded sympathetically and closed the photo gallery. I decided to look at one last thing: the calendar. Like the e-mails, it automatically backed up from the Microsoft profile. I didn't expect to find anything, so

I was surprised when I saw three recent appointments this week.

I tapped on the first one: it was a one-hour appointment at six p.m. the day before titled *Shopping*. There was no location or additional notes, but that matched exactly with the time Bryant had stolen the MeTime software from the server. The second one was three hours later. Again, there was no location, and the title of the appointment was simply *Car*. Could he have been saving vague-sounding appointments in his calendar as a way of making sure he kept to a timeline? Shopping could be a code for stealing the software. Car—picking up a rental, perhaps, or buying one second-hand in order to skip town without leaving a trace.

There was one final appointment in the calendar for eleven a.m. tomorrow. No location, just a vague title again. It said, simply, *Delivery—EWK*. For a moment I wondered if the three letters stood for an airport, or perhaps an abbreviation for a building. And then I thought about what I'd found out about his work for Aella, and I knew exactly what they stood for.

Bryant had made his one mistake, and with everything else I now knew about him, I was pretty sure it was going to lead me straight to him.

ELEVEN

New York City

FARADAY TOOK A break from staring at her computer screen and closed her eyes, massaging the center of her forehead with her thumb and index finger. She swiveled around in her chair and looked out at the skyline, wondering if it would snow tonight. The news said a major blizzard was coming later in the week, but for now the night sky was clear. That was good. It would be a late night tonight, and the last thing she needed was to make it later if her driver was delayed.

She swiveled back around when there was a knock at her door. She raised an eyebrow when Murphy entered, the usual ironic twinkle in his eye absent.

"Not like you to knock," she said.

"Stark's team is all set up," he said. "You asked me to let you know."

She nodded, noting that he had passed up the opportunity for a snappy comeback. Definitely not himself. Again Faraday thought about how different Murphy had been since the Crozier thing. Ever since they had gotten a lead on the man now calling himself Carter Blake, there had been a subtle change in him. When Faraday had been brought in to replace Drakakis, she had found Murphy a reliable asset, but one who never seemed to take things too seriously. He approached each task with an unflappable air, giving you the sense that he didn't really care about the outcome. The ongoing hunt for Blake was different. Whenever the subject came up, he was serious, focused. Like now.

Faraday got up and followed Murphy out. They crossed the corridor, and Murphy keyed in the daily code to access the ops room. It was a large, windowless room that felt a little like a cross between a movie theater and NASA mission control. There was a well-lit area up front, with chairs arranged around a horizontal table screen. After that there were four rows of computers, arranged on descending levels to the bottom of the room, where the far wall was taken up completely with a screen, divided up into nine rectangles. A different image could be shown on each one, or they could combine to display a single image. Right now the top six rectangles were showing what Faraday assumed was a live satellite feed. It displayed a series of buildings arranged around a swimming pool, the underwater illumination making it shine like a sapphire in the midst of the sprawl.

Although there was space for more than a dozen staff members at the computers, only three were occupied. Faraday walked past the closest two and approached the farthest station from the entrance.

"He's at home?" she said, addressing Williamson.

Williamson glanced around at her. Her eyes moved from Faraday to Murphy and then back to Faraday. Finally, she nodded. "As of twenty-eight minutes ago."

Williamson was in her early twenties. She had shoulder-length dark hair and a doughy, pale look about her that spoke of too many hours indoors staring at screens. Two unopened cans of Red Bull were sitting on her desk, ready for action. She lacked the slightly nervy, eager-to-please demeanor of her coworkers, but in a way that was completely different from Murphy's wry condescension. She wasn't attempting to undermine Faraday, or make herself look good; she just had no concept of wanting to impress other people. Faraday liked that about her. That, and the fact that she never failed to deliver, no matter how difficult the task.

"Stark only checked in at the forward base five minutes ago," she continued.

"What kept them?"

"Pileup on I-4. Bad one, couple of people dead." Williamson paused, picked up the nearest Red Bull and popped the tab. She took a long gulp and put it down, turning back to the screen. "That meant major slowdowns on the 408. Thanks to that, we're a half hour behind schedule."

"Okay, but aside from that?"

"Good to go."

Faraday turned to Murphy. "This is the best lead we've had on Blake in eight months. If this goes wrong, it sets up way back."

Murphy wasn't looking at her. He was staring straight ahead at the big screen on the wall. "It isn't going to go wrong. He won't be able to ignore this."

Faraday looked back at Williamson.

"Send the message."

FIVE YEARS AGO

New York City

WHY DON'T YOU tell me about Winterlong?

In retrospect, the senator's opening question to me was almost funny. It was a regular laugh riot. Because it turned out that Senator Carlson knew more than I did. A lot more.

The second manila folder on his desk had contained classified reports. Unedited after-action briefings. Photographs. It was a meticulously compiled history of an entity that was not supposed to have a history. Winterlong had no past; it simply had the here and now, and what had to be done.

It was a small, elite unit set up for maximum effectiveness with minimum footprint. We carried out the jobs that could not be done on the record. I was familiar with some of the operations recorded in the file. I had taken part in some of them. I knew some rules had been bent and broken from time to time and had broken a few of them myself.

In the early days, it had been easy to convince myself that those rules were breached advisedly and with necessity. We played a little rough sometimes. We went places where we weren't supposed to be. Places where there could be no negotiation, no admission of authorization, should we be captured. We specialized in off-the-books work. When going through standard channels wouldn't get the job done, that's where we came in. Invisible, unaccountable, deniable. Off the books.

Except that there was a book, and Carlson had it.

And it turned out I didn't know the half of it. Whether by luck or design, I hadn't been involved in any of the missions that had led to the worst things in that file. And as soon as that thought crossed my mind, I remembered a conversation I'd had with Drakakis a year or so back and knew it was by design.

We had been alone in his office following an operation in Karachi. I'd raised my concerns about another member of the team: one Dean Crozier. Crozier had an enthusiastic approach to the use of violence. It was more than a tool of the trade for him. It was an end in itself.

"You're uncomfortable with him," Drakakis had said after I described what I'd witnessed in Karachi. Drakakis was in his late fifties, tall with receding gray hair and the beginnings of a paunch. One of that missing generation of soldiers who had been too young for Vietnam and too old for Gulf War I. Who had completed a long career climb without ever serving in a real war.

"That's an understatement. He's a killer, sir."

He'd raised an eyebrow at that and started to make some wry comment, but I continued before he could get it out.

"He's dangerous. He's feeding an addiction out there."

Drakakis had nodded. "You're still fairly new, and perhaps I've been remiss in not explaining certain facts of life to you. Well, I'll make up for that now. You see, this is a team, and a team depends on chemistry. You understand that?"

I'd said nothing, having a good idea where he was going.

"Thing about chemistry, it takes the right mix of elements to get the result you need. Different sorts. Take you, for instance. You're good at what you do—that goes without saying. If you weren't good, you wouldn't be here. But you have something important in your character, too. You're..." He stopped and searched for a way to explain it. "You're one of the white hats, is what I'm trying to say. And Crozier? He's one of the black hats." He chuckled. "That boy just might be the blackest of the black, in fact." He paused and narrowed his eyes. "You know where I'm going with this, son, don't you?"

I considered my answer. "You're saying it takes white hats and black hats, sir."

His lips stretched over his nicotine-stained teeth in a wide grin. "That's exactly right. It takes both kinds. Of course, if I had my druthers, I'd use people like you all the time. Solid. Dependable. Upstanding. But it can't always be that way. Sometimes you need a black hat. Do you understand that, son?"

I had thought about it and nodded, even though I didn't truly know that I did.

After seeing Carlson's file, I knew for sure that I didn't understand. And Drakakis had known that I wouldn't, which was why he'd shielded me from it. Carlson's file confirmed all the worst misgivings and suspicions I'd had and then some.

Torture, for starters. Not just waterboarding and other examples of so-called enhanced interrogation, but the kind of thing that would have made the more enthusiastic members of the Spanish Inquisition wince. Indiscriminate extrajudicial killings, not just of legiti-

mate or gray-area targets, but anyone who happened to
get in the way when no one was looking. The instances
of abuse and murder trailed across the globe, to every
hot spot in which I'd been deployed, and more besides.

Worst of all, it wasn't restricted to confirmed or even
suspected bad guys. Civilians were fair game. Not just
as collateral damage, but deliberately targeted in order
to flush out another target, or worse, simply to send a
message.

As I leafed through the pages in the file, I passed
through skepticism to denial to horror. I had been blind.
I had accepted that we needed to operate outside the
system to get the jobs done that couldn't be done any
other way. I was okay with that. I knew where the line
was, and so far I hadn't had to do anything that crossed
that line. But in reaching that accommodation with myself, I had chosen not to think about what that principle
could lead to. The way that the lack of rules, the lack of
oversight could be abused by the wrong kind of men.
Men like Crozier, in particular, but he was only the most
extreme example.

The greater good. An old-fashioned, perhaps naive
concept. But it was why I had joined Winterlong. Or
perhaps that wasn't the whole story. I had been attracted
by the challenge, by the freedom. That we were stopping supposedly untouchable bad guys and unques-
tioningly saving lives allowed me to overlook some of
the compromises. Only now, looking at the seemingly
endless array of images in front of me, did I realize that
the same setup had been a lightning rod for those with
darker motivations.

I got about two-thirds of the way through the file

before I lost my stomach for it entirely. I closed the file and dropped it back on Carlson's desk.

"Eye opener, isn't it?" the senator said. "How does it make you feel, soldier? Are you proud of that?"

I'd been looking down at the floor, almost unaware there was still someone in the room with me, but at the sound of the disgust in Carlson's voice, I looked up at him, anger burning in my eyes.

"It makes me feel sick. This isn't..." I gestured at the folder, trying to form my feelings into words. I gave up after a minute and sat back in the chair. "How did you get this?"

Carlson was watching me with interest. "I kind of expected you to deny it all. Tell me these documents are faked."

I shook my head. "It's not fake."

"Exaggerated, then."

We locked eyes for a moment. Without breaking the stare, I reached for the folder. I looked down and leafed back through to a particular photograph. A photograph taken in a burnt-out bunker somewhere in Iraq. Crozier's work, from the look of the knife wounds inflicted on the handcuffed bodies.

"Senator?" I asked, turning the photograph toward him. "How the fuck do you exaggerate that?"

His eyes alighted on the photograph and looked away instinctively. He nodded in agreement and took the folder from me, closing it again.

"There's a pattern in this file," he said. "Certain names that come up again and again. Yours is not one of those names."

"And that's why we're having this conversation?"

"It's not the only reason we're having this conversation," he said after a moment's thought. "You asked me how I got this. You seem like a smart guy, so you probably already know the answer. I got this from the only place it could have come from."

"Inside."

"Exactly. I'm not going to tell you who, naturally, at least not until I know that you're willing to come on board with this. To be honest, going this far with you is a risk I'd rather not take."

A couple of faces flashed in my mind's eye, but I knew it would be pointless to start playing guessing games. I knew one thing: Whoever had leaked this file to Senator Carlson was the same person who had told him I would be approachable.

"Then why take the risk?" I asked.

"Because we need more. The evidence in this file gives us the men on the ground. That's not good enough for me. We need something on the people in charge, and I think you can help get me it."

I didn't know why I'd be in a better position to do it than Carlson's other mole, but I put that to one side for the moment, because I had a much more pressing question.

"What makes you think I'm willing to come on board?"

Carlson's lips widened a miniscule amount in an approximation of a smile. "Nothing much, soldier. Only the shade of green you turned when you started looking at those pictures."

AFTER LEAVING THE senator's office, I took the elevator back down to the ground floor and walked across the tiled lobby to the same door I'd used to enter the building.

I started to walk, not thinking about where I was going, just knowing I needed to walk. I needed fresh air—as fresh as it gets in Manhattan, at any rate—to clear my head, and I needed space to think. The sun was declining in the west, shining into my eyes along West Fortieth, so I turned in the opposite direction and headed east. I passed by Bryant Park and crossed Fifth and Madison and kept going until I was in sight of the East River. I looked across the water. The UN building rose high on my left. The traffic soared past on the FDR Drive.

The senator's proposition had been simple. He wanted me to do nothing out of the ordinary. He wanted me to carry on exactly as normal until the next assignment. But when that assignment came, he wanted me to keep my eyes open for an opportunity to get him the evidence he needed. I wasn't sure exactly what form that evidence might take. The senator had taken a big risk by reaching out to me. Maybe bigger than he knew. But then, he had been right. Because I wasn't considering whether to do what he wanted. Despite myself, I was already thinking about how.

The pictures from the files flashed before me. I tried to push them aside, but they kept muscling back in. I tried to focus on the cars passing on the FDR with their oblivious occupants, heading home after what they probably imagined was a hard day at the office.

I felt detached from the world. Like I had been standing on the deck of a ship on calm seas, and out of nowhere a wave had picked me up and tossed me overboard. I was nothing and nobody. I stood there for an hour, thinking that every certainty I'd thought I could count on had been washed away and now I was standing with no idea who I was or where I was going.

The shadows were growing longer, trailing the onset of evening. Suddenly, I remembered a voice from a few hours ago, and another lifetime.

Terradici's. Tonight. Eight o'clock.

I looked at my watch and saw that it was a quarter to seven. I may not have known who I was or where I was going anymore. But I knew there was somewhere I was supposed to be at eight o'clock. For now, that would have to do.

TWELVE

Seattle

IT WAS ALMOST four in the afternoon when I left Jasmine Bryant's house, which meant the first available flight was an Alaska Airlines service leaving San Francisco International at seven thirty and touching down in the Seattle-Tacoma airport a little more than two hours later. Ever since the Samaritan case, I'd been more hesitant than usual about flying, because it was the one mode of travel where you were forced to leave a trail. But then again, I hadn't encountered any problems so far, and by paying cash at the terminal and using a driver's license as ID, there was nothing to make me stand out from the millions of other passengers moving around the United States.

I climbed onto the plane on a mild, dry evening in San Francisco. A couple of hours later I stepped out into a cold, rainy night in Seattle. The temperature was just above freezing, and the wind chill drew gasps from the departing passengers as they adjusted to a new season in the space of seconds. The contrast felt like we'd jumped forward in time from early fall to winter. Only that wasn't an ideal comparison, because winter would never really come to California.

Sea-Tac was located ten miles south of the city proper. I took a taxi into town, looking out of the window for the familiar sights to orient myself: The Space Needle stood out, lit up brightly against the night sky. My first time in the Pacific Northwest, though I'd long enjoyed its influence on wider society in the form of good coffee and rock music from Hendrix to Cobain.

I knew that Scott Bryant's meet was set up for eleven in the morning, which gave me just over thirteen hours to work out where the meeting would be. Seattle is the biggest city in the Pacific Northwest. More than three million inhabitants in the metropolitan area, and probably around three million and one places to arrange a quiet meeting. I knew it would be a waste of time focusing on *where*, when I could get what I wanted by thinking about *who* instead. Aella had been the major thing that stuck out about Bryant's background, largely because it had been the one thing he had made the effort to hide from his record. A rival software company he had worked for in secret in a town he'd spent time in a year or so before. A town that was eight hundred miles away: the kind of distance it would take you most of a day to drive. Enough time to check into a hotel, get some rest, and arrive fresh for an eleven a.m. appointment.

When I had examined Bryant's documents stored from his time freelancing for Aella, one name came up repeatedly: Eric W. Kelner. It hadn't taken more than a couple of clicks to ascertain that Kelner was the CEO of Aella.

EWK. Sometimes it doesn't take much to lay waste to the best-laid plans. Sometimes it only takes three letters. My research also told me that the company name was taken from Greek mythology, belonging to an Amazon warrior killed by Hercules. Aella meant "whirlwind," and if Eric W. Kelner didn't play ball, that was exactly what he was about to reap.

Finding people who don't want to be found can be a challenge. The process often involves a certain amount of skill, the employment of certain tricks of the trade, and often most important, the ability to exploit the minor mistakes of your target. This particular job wasn't over yet, but so far it hadn't been difficult to pick up Bryant's trail, thanks to his mistake with the synced calendar.

The point is, finding someone who doesn't want to be found almost always involves effort. But finding someone who *isn't* expecting anyone to be looking for them? That's a breeze.

One of the advantages of living in a democracy is the fact that political donations, in theory at least, have to be transparent. Successful businessmen make political donations, sometimes to more than one candidate or party. They do this for the obvious reasons: They want their business to remain successful and unencumbered by bureaucracy. Federal law requires that they register their donation on a publicly accessible database, providing the name, place of residence, and the amount and party they donated to. It's a stalker's dream—in the time it takes to hit a few keys, you can find the home address of any individual with a political consciousness. There are a couple dozen other effective techniques for snagging a home address, but this is one of the easiest, and it doesn't even require subterfuge.

Ninety seconds on the portal told me that Kelner had donated the maximum two thousand dollars to the GOP in the run-up to the last election, and that he resided at 1232 Forest Avenue, in the affluent West Mercer Island neighborhood. Twenty minutes and a taxi ride across the Lacey V. Murrow Bridge later, I was standing on the sidewalk outside. I gave the driver twenty bucks and told him to circle the neighborhood for ten minutes. I didn't think I would need longer than that.

The rain had eased off, so I waited for the noise of the engine to die away before I turned to look up at Kelner's place. The three-story home built into the hillside was in darkness except for one window, and water dripped from the eaves and ran in streams down the sloped driveway.

The door was opened a few inches by a tall woman in her midtwenties with red hair cut in a bob. Not a natural red, more like the color of a London bus. She had obviously decided her natural color wasn't exciting enough and had opted for something more eye-catching. It was striking in contrast to her very pale, almost pure white skin. She held the door open six or seven inches in a way that categorically did not invite me in, while her gray eyes looked me over in a politely questioning way. I wasn't anyone she recognized, and it was too late in the day for a Jehovah's Witness.

"Yes?"

"I'm sorry to drop by so late," I said. "I wondered if Eric was home. It's kind of important."

She held the door in position and kept her eyes on me as she called Kelner's name. A muffled acknowledgment came from within the home. I couldn't make out the exact words over the sound of the rain, but I assumed Kelner was asking who it was.

She widened her eyes, prompting me.

"Scott Bryant," I said without hesitation.

"Scott Bryant," she yelled, still not taking her eyes from me, or moving her hand from the door.

I heard hurried footsteps on polished floorboards, and another hand appeared at the edge of the door, pulling it open as the redhead released her grip.

Kelner was in his fifties: bald, thirty pounds overweight, and wearing a blue shirt over jeans. He was too old for his partner and way beneath her league. His expression was irritated as he started speaking, obviously spouting the line he'd arranged in his head on the way to the door.

"I told you not to—"

He stopped dead as he realized I wasn't who he was expecting. Then his lips started to form into the start of a question. I was guessing it would have been, *Who the hell are you?* But he stopped himself. I watched him process through the unexpected development with a knowing smile on my face. I wanted him to think I knew absolutely everything. I wanted him to pin his hopes on being able to cooperate with me as fully as possible to extricate himself from this situation.

"Everything okay, hon?" the redhead asked after glancing from his face to mine and back again.

"Yes. Yes. Give us a second, okay?"

She shrugged, gave me another look up and down, and moved back into the house. Kelner stepped out into the night and closed the door behind him.

"What do you want?"

"I want to make a deal."

"I don't know what you're talking about."

"Really? You want to mess around with something like this?"

He pressed his lips together, clearly deciding he

wasn't going to make this any better by doing more talking.

"I'm looking for Bryant. As you've probably guessed, I'm working for his employers."

He took it in, still keeping his mouth tight shut.

"My instructions are very specific. Mr. Bryant took something and they want it back. They're only interested in him. If you help me out, this conversation stays entirely between us. I don't get paid any extra for making trouble for you."

He opened his mouth to make some sort of angry denial. I cut in before he could build up a head of steam. "Having said that, if you *don't* help me out, I'm going to have to use what I know about you to find him another way. And I know it all, Eric. All about you and Bryant and MeTime."

I'd played my hand, and I was relieved to see he stiffened at the mention of MeTime. I probably could make some trouble for him, if it really came to it. If nothing else, I could let Stafford know exactly who had tried to buy his stolen software and let him focus his considerable resources on digging up the proof.

I kept my face entirely impassive and watched Kelner's eyes: narrow and seething. I could imagine his brain working feverishly away back there, weighing up the sacrifice of billions of dollars in future income against losing everything he had tomorrow. His jawbone stood out as he gritted his teeth. His whole body was tensed, as though he was barely suppressing the urge to attack me, our physical mismatch notwithstanding.

But then something clicked into place, and he came to his decision. His jaw unclenched and he seemed to lose a couple of inches in height, nodding after a moment.

"I don't know what you're talking about, of course. I've never heard of Scott Bryant. And I assume you won't be relaying this conversation either to him or to his employers. Whoever he or they may be."

I pretended to think it over for a second before nodding in agreement. "You assume correctly."

"I don't have much of a choice, do I?"

"I don't see that you do."

"Eleven a.m. Wakey's Diner. First Avenue. It's across the road from the bus station."

I took out my phone and tapped the address in. It existed, which was a positive sign.

"What if he doesn't show?" Kelner asked.

I answered without looking up from the screen. "Then I guess I'll just have to think of something else. But I think he'll show. That is, unless anyone tells him not to."

His lips straightened into a thin, humorless smile. "I don't think there's any danger of that."

"Good. Then we having nothing to worry about."

He put a hand on the doorknob and twisted it down, pausing before opening it again. "I won't see you again, will I?"

I affected a look of polite confusion. "Won't see who again?"

He nodded understanding and opened the door, stepping back inside and closing it firmly without another word. I looked down at the address I'd typed in. The date and the time tallied with what I knew, and the location across from the bus station made sense. Bryant would want to make the exchange and get as far away as he could, as quickly as he could, and leaving as little trail as he could.

I walked back down to the main road and waited a couple of minutes until my cab appeared at the corner. I got back in and told him to take me back into the city, to the nearest hotel to the bus station on First Avenue. I was looking forward to a night's rest before I attended my appointment with Mr. Bryant.

Halfway into the journey my phone rang and turned the prospect of a restful night into an impossible dream.

THIRTEEN

THE CALL SHOWED up as a withheld number. I toyed with the idea of ignoring it and then decided to pick up. It was Coop. That idea surprised me, because we both liked to keep communications to a minimum. At first I thought he had some new information on Bryant, but I knew it was something else when I heard his voice. There was a tone I had never heard from him before, and it took me a second to work out what it was: confusion.

Coop had received an e-mail a half hour before. The sender's address was a generic Gmail account. The subject line read simply, *For the attention of J. Cooper.* That got his attention right away, because this was the e-mail address through which prospective clients contacted him. Without exception, those clients knew him only by pseudonym. He told me he had opened the e-mail and found a very brief message and a PDF attachment titled *Martinez.* I felt a tingle at the base of my spine at the mention of a name I hadn't heard in years, but I kept listening as he relayed the content of the message:

WHAT HAPPENED TO JAKE MARTINEZ?
CARTER BLAKE WOULD WANT TO KNOW.

And that was it. No sign-off, no instructions, no hints as to the identity or motives of the sender. Coop had double clicked to open the PDF and had known immediately that he would have to tell me about this.

"What is it?" I asked, though I had a pretty good idea already, and I knew I wasn't going to like it.

"It's a scan of an Interpol black notice," he said. He didn't need to translate the lingo: I knew all too well what a black notice was. "Looks like it was circulated three weeks ago on a male Caucasian body found dumped just outside of a town called Tyumen in Siberia. No identification, but the labels on his clothing were mostly American and European, and he was carrying a pack of Marlboros. No ID on his prints, and no one locally has come forward to claim him."

I cleared my throat and tried to keep my voice level. "Cause of death?"

"You knew him, didn't you?" Coop said. "I can hear it in your voice."

"How did he die?" I repeated, annoyed at Coop despite myself.

"Executed. Two nine-millimeter bullets in the head, one in the gut. They beat him first, by the looks of this. Broken fingers. Dog bites, too."

I closed my eyes and rubbed the bridge of my nose, picturing the body in my mind's eye.

"You still there?"

"Yeah. Send it over."

"Yes, sir."

"Sorry. Yeah, I knew him. We worked together."

"I guessed that. That isn't good, is it?"

"Certainly not for Martinez."

Coop forwarded me the e-mail and the attachment. There were two pictures at the top of the Interpol document. The first was a computer-aided composite of a man in his mid-thirties with brown eyes and dark brown hair. The second showed the same person, apparently. It was a graphic close-up of a dead man lying on a blood-stained patch of snow. Evidently, he had been there long enough to freeze solid. The two holes in his head looked like black marks, as though he were the victim of some kind of medieval plague. The face was distorted by the gunshot wounds and the cold, but it still looked human enough for me to be sure that this was Jake Martinez. What was left of him, anyway.

I remembered something Martinez had said, the last time I saw him: *All we're doing is delaying the inevitable.*

There were a lot of reasons why Martinez, or anyone in our former line of work, might show up dead. There was only one reason why somebody would have gone to the trouble of contacting me through Coop to tell me about it.

Winterlong.

Martinez and I had come to an arrangement with them five years ago. A mutual understanding that we would leave each other alone. The picture of Martinez dead in the snow told me two things: That arrangement was now null and void, and they would be coming after me next.

FOURTEEN

Seattle

SOMETHING HAD CHANGED.

I thought about an abandoned house in the Santa Monica Mountains. The man with glasses. The eerily calm face I'd seen several times since my nightmares. What he'd said:

Drakakis isn't here anymore.

Perhaps I had been fooling myself for the last few years, thinking that if I only kept my head down and stayed out of their way, they would let sleeping dogs lie. Even as I thought about it, I knew I had never truly believed that. The Samaritan case had put me back on the agenda for them, as I had feared it would. Covering up Dean Crozier's history with Winterlong would have been expensive and resource-intensive. They wouldn't risk having to do that again, particularly with two loose ends who might decide to start talking at any moment. Better to tidy up quietly, on their own terms.

Our low profiles and the probability of us maintaining our silence had kept us safe until now, but Martinez's face on the Interpol black notice told me that period of détente was over. There was no doubt in my mind. The mention of my name in the accompanying e-mail could mean nothing else. It was them, and I was next.

The only question was, how long did I have?

No one in the world knew where I was, since I hadn't known I would be going to Seattle until a few hours previously. My name would show up on the passenger manifest flying from San Fran to Seattle, but that would be a needle in a haystack unless they knew where to look or were prepared to bring in other agencies. I didn't think they would want to do that if they could avoid it.

That brought me back to thinking about the reason I was here: I had a job to do, and I was close to completing it. I had the time and place of the buy, and in a matter of hours, I would leave Bryant. After that? Once I had returned the stolen software to Stafford and secured the balance of my fee, I could go to ground.

I would head east, to the place I was keeping the very thing that Winterlong wanted.

I thought about Martinez, an unidentified boy in the Siberian wastes. I thought about the small suburban house where I'd last seen him, about our agreement. We hadn't expected to hear from each other ever again. I thought about why Coop had received the e-mail and knew that they expected it to flush me out. Did they expect me to come after them? Charge blindly in to get revenge for Martinez? If so, they had the wrong guy.

I dialed Coop's number again.

"Trouble?" he asked, not wasting time on a hello.

"You could say that. How did they get your e-mail address?"

"I don't know, Blake. And I can't say I like it."

"I'm sorry. It might be a good idea to clear out, lie low for a while. And after this call—"

"Don't worry, I'll get rid of the phone. And I think

you're right. I think I'll make arrangements to be some-place else as of tomorrow."

"That's a good idea," I said. "E-mail when you get settled. We'll work out the Moonola thing."

"You on the right track?"

"I'm getting there."

"Always a pro, no matter what."

I smiled. "I'll talk to you soon. Be careful, Coop."

"I always am."

I hung up and stared at the screen of the phone. It wouldn't hurt to take the same precautions I'd advised Coop to take. I switched the phone off, removed the battery, and put it back in my pocket. A second later I changed my mind and asked if the driver minded if I opened a window. I tossed the phone out as he turned the next corner.

It was after midnight when the cab drew up in front of a budget hotel on First Avenue.

"You in town long?" the driver asked. I figured he was making a last-ditch effort for a good tip, having been unable to lure me into a conversation for the length of the trip.

I shook my head. "Not long." I handed over the fare, plus ten. As I stepped out of the car, the rain began again.

THURSDAY, JANUARY 7TH

FIFTEEN

Orlando

COOP'S EYES OPENED gradually. It was still dark. He had fallen asleep facing the digital alarm clock on his bedside table, so he didn't have to move a muscle to know that it was 3:57 a.m. He didn't think he had been having any kind of disturbing dream, and he hadn't woken naturally before eight o'clock in any of his fifty-nine years, as far as he was aware. So what had woken him?

He kept his eyes on the luminous digits and listened. The low hum of the air-conditioning. The distant hum of the traffic on the 408. Too early in the year for crickets. A dog barked somewhere, blocks away.

But then...something else.

A scratching noise coming from the hall. From the front door. From the lock of the front door.

Coop, still hazy from the deep sleep, snapped fully awake. He hopped out of bed with a dexterity that belied his years and physical condition and moved quickly across the carpet to the partially open bedroom door. There was a lock on the door, activated by a twistable knob on the inside. One of the many benefits of living in a hotel suite rather than a place of his own. He used to keep the door locked at night, a precaution he had neglected recently. But then, if the door had been fully closed, he would never have heard the scraping from the front door.

He closed the bedroom door, holding down the handle so that the catch wouldn't make a noise, then gently released it and twisted the lock. Assuming whoever was working on the exterior door knew what they were doing, this one wouldn't trouble them much, but it would buy him another few seconds.

Just as the lock clicked softly home, he heard an answering click from outside as the front door finally surrendered. He stepped back into the room, circumnavigated the bed, and took the Colt .45 from the top drawer of the bedside table. He clicked the safety off and then opened the sliding glass door that led out to the balcony. No time to get dressed, so as he stepped out onto the concrete in his shorts and vest, he gave thanks that he lived in Florida and not in New Hampshire.

The balcony was a solid chunk of rough concrete, with a four-foot-high wall guarding the two-story drop. The balcony extended along the front of the building, and all of the rooms and suites had doors that opened onto it. This time of the year they would likely all be closed and locked, but perhaps he'd get lucky.

As he calculated his next move, his mind was working on the identity of the person or persons who had just infiltrated his suite. He was a couple of decades past being as careful as he used to be, but that didn't mean he could afford to write this off as a simple burglary. After all, he maintained contacts that many people would kill for. He had in excess of three million dollars in his various bank accounts, not counting the transactions he held temporarily for some of his contractors. There were plenty of reasons why this home invasion could be very personal. And then there was Blake. That e-mail he'd sent him earlier. The dead man in the snow.

Coop moved quickly along the row, trying his neighbors' sliding doors one after another. All were locked, and all were in darkness but one, the last on the row— Tom Mitchell's place—was casting the flickering blue light of a television onto the balcony. Tom was forever falling asleep in front of *The Late Show*. Coop heard a *click* from behind him that he knew was the sound of his own sliding door being unlatched, and prayed to be lucky. He reached out and grabbed the handle of Tom's door.

It was open.

He darted through the gap and slid it closed, knowing he was too late to complete the action without being heard. Sure enough, Tom was passed out in his armchair in front of the wall-mounted plasma screen, his head rested back, his throat issuing a mucous-strangled croak. He coughed himself awake as Coop stepped in.

"What the—"

Coop opened his mouth to respond, to tell him that they both needed to get the hell out of there, when he saw movement reflected in the glass of one of the picture frames on the wall. He ducked and ran for the open door into the hall as he heard a series of rapid cracks as bullets fired from a silenced pistol penetrated the glass door. He heard thuds as they punched into the drywall, following his path across the field of fire. Tom Mitchell's blood splashed his arm as he made the door and tumbled into the hallway. Definitely no random home invasion.

Don't think. Don't look back. Just move.

Coop unlocked the front door and swung it open,

diving out into the corridor, gun pointed back along the corridor in the direction of his own door. Whoever they were, they had extinguished the hall lights, but in the moonlight spilling out from his own open door, he could make out a dark-clad figure pressed against the wall outside. He didn't bother to take aim, just fired three quick shots as he fell back in the opposite direction. The noise was deafening, shattering the silence of the night. He hoped it would wake the place up, get them all dialing 911.

If they had someone covering the door, they'd likely have people on the standard front and back exits from the hotel. He just had to hope whoever it was didn't have the inside knowledge to be covering the sole remaining exit as well. He ducked through the door to the stairwell, wondering if he had managed to take out the man outside his door, at least. The bullet hole that appeared in the wall next to his head answered that question.

"Shit."

Coop barreled down the stairs barefoot, keeping the gun trained at upper-body height as he rounded each corner. He hit the ground floor and kicked the door to the lobby open, before passing it by and continuing down to the basement.

As he descended the last of the stairs he thought about the fact Charlie would be working the front desk. His final night shift of the week. They would kill him if he got in the way, like they'd just killed Tom. Maybe they'd kill him even if he didn't get in the way.

Can't think about that now. Just run.

The keypad lock on the door at the bottom of the stairs delayed him for about a second and a half. Charlie had supplied him with the four-digit code months ago, in return for half a bottle of Jim Beam. The basement was lit by fluorescent strip lights and cluttered with stacked boxes of catering supplies and sacks of dirty laundry. Coop closed the door behind him as quietly as he could and spent a second with his ear to the door listening, trying to keep his breathing steady.

He heard footsteps reach the ground floor and the lobby door bang open again. They'd bought it—for the moment.

He moved fast across the space to the east wall. There were long, narrow windows at ground level looking out onto the alley alongside the hotel. The windows were wire-mesh glass to thwart people from breaking in, but thankfully there was nothing to keep people from opening them from the inside.

Coop forced himself to stop as he reached the windows. He scanned the narrow field of view. He saw nothing, but it was difficult to tell since the alley was lit only by the overspill from the streetlights out front. It didn't really make a difference: This was it, his only chance.

He unlatched the nearest window and pushed it up. It creaked and complained as it swung up. He placed the gun on the ground outside and hauled himself up and out, scraping his bare legs badly on the steel frame.

He gripped the gun again and maneuvered himself with some difficulty to his feet, breathing heavily now, the blood pounding in his ears. No time to think about heart trouble, just time to run. He forced himself to be still for a moment, letting his eyes sweep over the darkness of the alley, confirming he was alone. When he was as satisfied as he could be, he edged toward the street and flattened back against the wall when he reached the corner. He paused another second and then risked a glance around the edge.

He could see lights on in some of the rooms. The results of the shots he had fired a minute ago. With any luck, some of the neighbors had already called the cops.

The hotel entrance was sixty yards away, beneath a red awning that stretched out over the sidewalk. There was no one outside the entrance, which meant if he was in luck, there were only two of them, and they were still inside. Maybe they'd worked out that he'd headed for the basement. If so, that locked door wouldn't hold up to a bullet. No matter what, he didn't have long. Where the hell were the cops?

Suddenly, he was aware of the ridiculousness of his situation: standing outside at four in the morning in his shorts, holding a gun and trying to work up the guts to make a move.

The street was empty, so he heard the engine before the car made the turn two blocks away. Coop shrank back into the shadows but kept his eyes on the headlights as they approached. It was a taxi, the FOR HIRE sign lit up.

He felt a surge of hope and suppressed it, reminding himself he still had to convince the guy to stop for an old guy in his underwear. Waving the gun was a no-no—even if he actually tried to use it to force the driver to stop, it would likely have the opposite effect. Too many cabdrivers had gotten shot in Orlando for the driver to take the risk of cooperating with a carjacking. For the same reason, he couldn't try to conceal the gun behind his back. It would be a dead giveaway. The way he was dressed was enough of a strike against him.

But the vehicle was only a half a block away now, just

passing the hotel entrance and the red awning. He was out of options, and this was it. In another thirty seconds, the men with guns would come from the front door or through the basement window or from somewhere else.

He made the decision. He dropped the gun and stepped out onto the street, raising a hand as the taxi approached.

The taxi slowed and pulled in. Coop got in close and quickly opened the back door.

"Warm out tonight, huh?" the driver said without looking back. So much for him not noticing.

"Yeah," Coop grimaced.

"The husband came home early?"

"Something like that."

Coop asked to go to a cheap, anonymous hotel he knew on International Drive and hunched down in the seat, keeping an eye out the back as they pulled away. As he watched, a figure appeared at the door, staring intently at the taxi as it pulled away.

Shit. Had he gotten the license plate? How long would it take them to get to their cars and follow? He turned back to face front, addressing the driver.

"Actually, I've changed my mind. You know O'Shaugnessy's Bar?"

The drive made no indication that he had heard. Through the half-open window next to him, Coop heard sirens at last. Thank God. That would give the bastards something to keep them busy. Just as Coop as about to ask the question again louder, the driver answered.

"You got an address?"

"You don't know it? It's on Poinciana Boulevard."

Jimmy O'Shaugnessy's establishment officially closed at two, but it was a rare night Jimmy didn't stick around until dawn shooting pool with the regulars behind locked doors. Coop would be able to borrow clothes and money. That was another point—his wallet was still in the back pocket of his pants in the hotel, which meant he had no way to pay for the ride. This driver was going to have to continue to be understanding, and Jimmy was going to have to be in.

He kept glancing at the road behind them as he tried to plan his next movements, at the same time as trying to process the ordeal he had just narrowly survived. It had to be something to do with the dead man in the snow. It had to be. And that meant it had to do with Blake. He had to get ahold of Blake. Blake would know what to do.

So many competing thoughts crowded his head that he didn't notice the driver was headed in the wrong direction for a good couple of minutes. He didn't snap out of his own thoughts until the cab made a sharp turn down a blind, unlit alley. The headlights lit up a seven-foot-high corrugated iron fence as the car slowed and stopped. And then the driver switched the lights off, plunging them into darkness.

"Hey, what are you—"

Coop froze as the silhouetted man in the driver's seat turned around and raised a gun, a pistol, elongated by a suppressor. He was still thinking about the gun he'd left behind, thinking that he wouldn't have had to reach for it anyway, when the muzzle flash lit the interior of the car up.

The last thing he saw was the cold disinterest in his killer's eyes.

SIXTEEN

"Did you have to kill him?" Stark hissed as soon as he got close enough.

He holstered his weapon as Abrams opened the door and got out of the taxi, still holding the Glock. He glanced at the corpse in the backseat as though confirming the veracity of the complaint before responding and then shrugged. "Kill or capture. Wasn't me who let him get away, Stark."

Stark let that one pass. He had been concerned that a three-man team was insufficient for this assignment. Not that there was any question of the target getting away for real, of course, but with more men they could have achieved their goal without killing anybody. Of course, if Usher hadn't taken so long on the goddamn lock, it might have helped, too.

Instead of taking the bait, he leaned down so that his eyes were level with the nearest window that looked in on the backseat. He surveyed the aftermath. The old guy was definitely out of competition. He was sprawled across the seat, his still-open eyes staring upward. There was a neat circular hole in the center of his forehead. Blood and chunks of gray matter were splattered all over the back window.

Stark shook his head. The guy was in his underwear, for Christ's sake. It was…undignified. He couldn't help admire the old guy. He had made a solid attempt at giving them the slip, and from a standing start, too. They should have brought more than three of them to cover all exits. If Abrams hadn't been circling the block…

A horrible thought occurred. "Jesus, what did you do with the real driver?"

Abrams looked up, his eyes narrowing. "I wasn't supposed to kill him *either*?" He held the look for a moment, then chuckled. "Shit, Stark, lighten up. I took it from a gas station two miles away. We'll be long gone before the cops think to look in this particular alley."

"You better hope so. This isn't Mogadishu, Abrams. Rein it in."

"Whatever you say, boss," Abrams said evenly. Stark got the distinct impression he was enjoying this. Even knowing the importance of discretion, he was comporting himself with all the restraint of a drunk looter during a Super Bowl riot.

"Let's hope Usher got what he needed," Stark said.

They rendezvoused with Usher half a mile from the alley. He had brought the van and was sitting in the front, the light from a laptop screen illuminating his face. He glanced up at their approach and unlocked the doors. Stark and Abrams climbed in. In the distance, they could still hear sirens.

He looked at Stark and Abrams in turn. Stark had already brought him up to speed with the results of the chase via the in-ear comms equipment they all wore.

"Cleanup?"

Abrams gave a thumbs-up. "I left the car at the bottom of an alley. You'd need to go deep in there to even see it, and even then it's too dark to see the body until you get up close."

Usher nodded and looked back at the screen as the

progress bar completed, the screen double-reflected in the lenses of his glasses. "The man I killed in the hotel will keep their attention for a while."

Stark didn't comment on that. More collateral damage. If this was their idea of restraint, he hated to think what these two had been like going after Martinez in the ass-end of Russia.

Usher had connected a portable hard drive to the USB port of the laptop and was watching another progress bar at about two-thirds of the way to completion.

"How long do you need?"

"Another minute. He left this." He handed Stark a cell phone. "Last call was two hours ago, and an e-mail a minute later."

"The black notice?"

That had been Murphy's idea. The action had two aims: to flush out the target and to spook him. Stark hadn't been sure about it for that very reason. All else being equal, he preferred his targets not to know when the wolves were on their tail until it was too late. But then, Murphy had an extra insight into this target. Besides, every other suggested method of tracking down Carter Blake would take a lot longer. They couldn't be certain that Cooper, or his files, would lead them to Blake, but they could rely on Cooper contacting him.

It had already taken them months following the revelation that Blake was still active to identify this one link to him: Jefferson Cooper, a specialist agent in this field who brokered deals between those with difficult assignments and those willing to undertake them. Cooper— Coop to his close contacts—was ex-CIA. Cooper had left the agency in the late nineties, spent some time as a consultant for some civilian military companies, and was now earning a nice little living as a man who knew people. He was careful, both to stay below the radar himself and to ensure he didn't keep anything to tie him to the various contractors he was in touch with. His address book, if he had one, would be full of ex-spooks for hire. But Blake was something a little different.

Stark thumbed through the recent calls on the phone. None of them had names. Some were saved in the phone book as single initials and numbers. The last call in the log was to a number saved as "B2."

"What was the e-mail address he sent it to?" he asked Usher.

"Very generic. He made that call, and then he forwarded the picture. No additional text from him in the e-mail."

It had worked. The name and picture had triggered Blake's curiosity.

"It has to be Blake, right?" Stark said. "He calls him, tells him about the black notice, and then Blake asks him to forward it. That means we have his cell number."

"Which means we have him, in about two minutes," Usher agreed.

"What are you gonna do, call him?" Abrams asked.

Usher's eyes narrowed, as though he couldn't work out if the other man was making a joke. He tapped away on the laptop, paused, then tapped a few more keys in. "He's switched his phone off, but we have the last ping from a cell tower a couple of hours ago."

"Where?" Stark asked.

"Seattle."

"Figures. Around the corner would have been too convenient." He looked through the windshield. "Let's get the hell out of here. We know where he is. Now let's clip his wings."

Usher went around into the back. Stark followed, while Abrams jumped into the driver's seat and twisted the key in the ignition. They rolled out onto the road and headed toward the freeway.

SEVENTEEN

Seattle

STARK'S TEAM WAS in the air before the blood had dried.
A chartered jet waiting on standby took them directly
to Seattle.

Thanks to Abrams, they had no need for the equipment
they had in place for the restraint and sedation of a prisoner, which at least removed one potential headache. They
touched down at Sea-Tac a little after seven a.m. local time.

Stark had managed to sleep for most of the flight,
jolting awake only when the wheels hit the ground.
He was grateful—he had made good use of downtime,
while avoiding dwelling on the fact of being thirty-six
thousand feet in the air in a metal tube. The chartered
flight was faster than a commercial service and just as
quick as a military jet would have been, with the advantage that there was no need for an official paper trail.
Faraday was keen that this operation, like the Crozier
op, attracted as little attention as was possible. Stark
suspected Abrams hadn't received that memo.

They disembarked from the jet and Abrams picked
up a rental car. Stark sat in the back as they headed for
downtown, watching the sun come up over the Emerald
City. Blake was out there somewhere. The last ping from
his cell had been around midnight local time, not long
after he had spoken to Cooper.

Fifteen minutes later, Abrams pulled into the basement garage of a downtown Marriott. They took the elevator straight to the tenth-floor conference suite. The entire floor had been booked for three days, at what Stark assumed was great expense. But again, it was off the books.

They joined the forward team, who had flown in a couple hours earlier. They had already fully established the field ops room. Laptops, maps on the wall, strategic area priorities already mapped out in neat bullet points on one of the wall-mounted whiteboards.

Dixon looked up as they entered. The big man made a show of standing to attention.

"Welcome to Seattle," he said. "Business or pleasure?"

Stark ignored that, eyeing the whiteboard. "Anything on his cell? Any e-mails back to Cooper?"

"That's a negative," Dixon said. "Let's hope he's still here."

Stark was certain he would be. They had let Blake know they were onto him, but he couldn't know just how close they were. And he would find it more difficult than expected to leave town, in any case.

"All right. First thing, somebody needs to point me in the direction of the coffee. Second thing, he's not going to find himself." Stark looked at the whiteboard again, mentally prioritizing the locations and dividing them between the ten men in the room.

EIGHTEEN

Seattle

BY TEN THIRTY, Wakey's was in the quiet lull after the breakfast crowd and before the lunch crowd. It had an old-time feel that set it apart from the chain places. Parquet flooring, lots of dark wood and red leather upholstery on the booths. There was a lunch counter running the length of the place, facing windows that looked across First Avenue to the bus station. I wondered if Scott Bryant had bought his bus ticket already.

I assumed the deal was a cash buy. Anything involving bank transfers would be too traceable for either party. Industrial espionage had come a long way in the past century, from folders pilfered from locked filing cabinets to gigabytes of data on a piece of plastic smaller than your thumb, but the preferred payment method hadn't evolved at all in that time.

I took one of the stools at the lunch counter and looked at the menu printed on boards above the window. I had gotten there early to make sure I was in place for Bryant's arrival, but it would be an efficient use of the time to eat as well, since I had skipped breakfast. Ever since Coop's phone call at midnight, my appetite had taken a leave of absence. On my way to the diner, I had stopped at a coffee shop to check my e-mail. The coffee shop had tablets bolted to each table, so you could browse the Internet over a cappuccino. There had been nothing from Coop.

A burly cook wearing a white short-sleeve shirt and a backward ball cap approached and asked for my order. I ordered a steak sandwich and a black coffee and watched as he prepared the sandwich filling on the griddle in front of me. As he mixed peppers and onions into the pile of chopped steak, I savored the aroma and turned on my stool so I could survey the rest of the clientele. Six other people besides me. An elderly couple taking their time over their food, chatting to each other; three teenage girls, all with heads down, staring into their phones; and a big guy in a plaid shirt occupying one of the booths on the far wall.

I wondered if this diner had been selected for the meet because it was quiet. Maybe Kelner had picked it, or perhaps the choice had been Bryant's, drawing on the experience of his sojourn in the city.

I turned back around just in time to see the cook plating up the sandwich. He slid it in front of me in a smooth, practiced motion. While I ate, I kept a discreet eye on the three areas I'd selected my spot to ensure I could see: the door, the street immediately outside, and the entrance to the bus station across the road.

I finished the sandwich and started on the coffee. The old couple finally finished up and asked for the check. One of the teenage girls looked up from her phone long enough to tell her friends she was leaving. Her two compatriots glanced up from the screen for a second to smile their goodbyes. Two guys in suits came in, took the next booth down from the plaid shirt guy, and opened their respective MacBooks.

At five to eleven, I asked for another coffee and the

check, in case I had to move quickly. The cook came back with both at the same time. I laid cash down on the plate and was starting on the second coffee when a familiar face passed by. Scott Bryant was on the street outside, glancing into the diner and straight through me as he walked. He paused a second at the door, as though psyching himself up, and then pushed it open.

Bryant stopped again inside the door and surveyed the interior. He had made some effort to alter his appearance. He had shaved the beard and ditched the glasses. He wore a long black overcoat and one of those hats with flaps at the sides. A good choice: It covered his hair and his ears, and it was certainly appropriate to the climate—I had seen a dozen passersby wearing hats like that in the time I'd been in the diner. He gripped the handles of a canvas laptop bag in his left hand. The bag also fit right in, but I knew it was functional. Nobody was going to hand over a substantial amount of cash for a five-dollar flash drive without first making sure it contained exactly what they expected it to.

He let his gaze sweep around, taking in the guy in the plaid shirt, the remaining two girls, the MacBook guys, and me, and deciding none of us was a threat. Satisfied, he made his way to the booth nearest the door, which was unoccupied. He took the seat facing the door and removed his hat, keeping the coat on. From my position behind him, I was able to watch him for a while, enjoying his nervous mannerisms as he drummed his fingers on the table and hesitantly ordered a beer, before changing his mind and asking for a mineral water.

I gave him a couple more minutes, just to let him really start to worry that no one was going to show up. I was about to make him wish nobody had.

I drank the last of the coffee and got up. I walked across the parquet floor to Bryant's booth. His head snapped around as he heard me approach. He couldn't have looked guiltier if he'd had the word *thief* scrawled across his forehead in marker. Before he could make a move, I put my left hand on the back of the seat and my right on the table, positioning myself so he would have to get physical if he wanted out of the space.

"You're really not very good at this, are you, Bryant?"

He backed a couple of inches further along the booth seat. The leather upholstery squeaked as he moved. He looked up at me, barely concealed panic in his brown eyes. "Who the hell are you?"

I let the question hang for a moment, then indicated the seat opposite him with my hand. "If I sit down, you're not going to do anything stupid, are you?"

He thought about it, glanced past me at the door as though considering making a break for it, then shook his head slowly, keeping his eyes fixed on mine. I believed him.

I dropped my arms and slid into the seat across from him. We watched each other across the table for a minute.

There are a lot of ways it can go when you finally come face-to-face with a subject, dependent on a number of variables. If at all possible, you want to close out the business in hand without any kind of physical confrontation, although for obvious reasons, sometimes that's impossible. I try to plan the encounter out in advance, but in most cases you don't really know how it's going to go until you see the whites of the subject's eyes. Sometimes not even then.

I was looking at the whites of Scott Bryant's eyes now, and I knew I was in a good position. If he had been inclined to use violence, it was likely he'd have done so immediately. If he had a plausible get-out-of-jail-free card, he would have been talking it up already, or at least acting confident. The man across from me looked like he knew it was all over, and I had barely spoken to him.

That's why I knew silence was the correct technique. He didn't have a clue who I was, how I'd found him, or what I was about to do. He knew why I was here, of course—to intercept him before he sold MeTime to Kelner or one of his staff. Beyond that, nothing. He didn't know if I was a cop or a federal agent or a bounty hunter. He didn't know if I was carrying a weapon. He didn't know if I had orders to take him to jail, or to put a bullet in his head. I wanted all of these possibilities to swim around his head for a while before I got down to business.

Eventually, he broke the silence.

"You're not…"

"Kelner?"

"Who I was expecting."

"That's pretty clear."

He let out a sigh that had an uneven timbre, like he was trying not to shiver. "So what now?"

"Do you have the software?"

He said nothing for a moment, perhaps hoping I would give more away, and then nodded when he saw I wasn't going to. He reached into his inside pocket and removed a small white envelope. He tore the top off and put his hand inside, removing a small blue flash drive between his thumb and forefinger. He took his eyes off me for the first time and looked at it like an alcoholic regarding a drink he'd just been ordered to pour down the drain.

"Any other copies?"

"No."

I didn't believe that, but it wouldn't make any difference.

"Put it down."

He hesitated, then did as instructed, gently laying the drive on the polished wood of the tabletop. I left it there, sitting back in my seat as though the main business was concluded and we could both relax now.

"Stafford?" he asked.

I nodded. "You must have known he would come after you."

"I didn't think I had made it that easy. Who told you?"

"No one told me," I said. "I do this for a living."

He stared at me for a moment, as though trying to decide whether I was lying.

"I don't suppose you're going to let me just walk out of here."

I shook my head. "It doesn't have to be as bad as you think, though."

He almost smiled. "What, he's going to give me a slap on the wrist and say no more about it?"

"Probably not," I admitted. "But you're in luck. No harm done yet, so if we go back now with the software, it doesn't need to mean jail time."

He shook his head firmly. It was the first decisive movement I'd seen him make since I laid eyes on him. "Uh-uh. No way. I'm not going back."

I reached over and plucked the flash drive from the table, holding it up to the light. "Amazing things, aren't they? Twenty years ago you'd have needed a half-ton of floppy disks to store this much data. Now you can keep it in the watch pocket of your jeans."

"Do you have a name?" His tone had gained a little

steel, now that he was resigned to losing his meal ticket and, in all probability, his freedom.

"When it suits me."

"Okay. Mr. Man-With-No-Name. You got Stafford's data back. I'm sure he'll be very pleased with your work. What do you need me for?"

"You know what I need you for. The data isn't enough. He needs to make sure you can't sell this to somebody else from the copy I know you've made."

He said nothing, waiting for me to continue. I explained my proposal: Stafford would get the software back, plus a signed statement admitting to how, when, and why Bryant had stolen it, and confirming he hadn't given a copy to anyone else.

"It's the only way he can be sure MeTime's protected," I finished. "If anybody hits the market in a few months with a reverse-engineered version of the software, he can prove exactly where it came from."

The resigned look in Bryant's eyes had changed while I'd been talking, because now he saw the out for himself. Now he was thinking, calculating.

"But he would need me to cooperate. Testify, if it came to it."

"That's right," I said, sensing I was getting through to him. "But only if you already gave a copy to someone else. Did you?"

He shook his head.

"But you made a copy."

The corner of his lip curled upward a little, despite himself. "Of course I made a copy."

"So, by a stroke of luck, you're in a reasonably advantageous position. In return for no jail time, you sign a sworn statement saying the software has gone no further. He knows you're on the level, because you'll go to jail if it shows up somewhere else. But he needs that guarantee. If he presses charges, you have no reason to cooperate."

Bryant picked up the glass of water for the first time. He tilted it back and drank it in one, his throat muscles working as the liquid went down. When he was finished, he wiped his mouth and stared back at me.

"And what if I don't believe you? What if I just get up and walk out of here?" He glanced from side to side, taking in the rest of the clientele. "You going to stop me, with all these people about? I'll yell 'kidnap.'"

"Go ahead. They can call the cops. I'll explain the whole situation to them. What'll happen then?"

He was silent for a minute, trying to think of every way out and knowing there was only one possibility.

"You can make this happen?"

I nodded.

"Why should I trust a man with no name?"

A fair question. "My name's Carter Blake. You bring MeTime back with me, and there's no jail time."

I was making a promise that I hadn't cleared with Stafford, of course, but I know Stafford was a pragmatist, and he wouldn't be able to dispute the logic. The only reason for him to turn down this deal was pure vindictiveness. And a man would have to be pretty vindictive to jeopardize two billion dollars.

"Okay, Blake. You have a deal."

He held his hand out. I shook it.

"I wish I could say it was nice to meet you," he added.

FIVE YEARS AGO

New York City

GIVEN THE WAY our conversation had been occupying my every waking thought over the last couple of weeks, I was surprised by how much I wasn't thinking about Senator Carlson. Carol and I were in Central Park, walking at a leisurely pace through the zoo on the Park Avenue side. The leaves of the trees had already started to turn brown and drop, but a sudden upswing in the temperature had arrested the onset of fall for a brief moment. We had both removed our coats, and Carol smirked as I draped hers over my arm along with mine.

"An officer and a gentleman, huh?"

I stopped midstride and affected a concerned look. "You're right. How sexist of me. Here."

Carol ignored the coats offered in my outstretched arms and kept walking. "I'll let it slide just this once."

"Very understanding of you."

"That's me, very understanding."

An officer and a gentleman. The choice of words hadn't been accidental. I thought about our first date: the way she had held out to the end of the main course before really starting to question me, guessing a little too accurately about my background.

"You're definitely military," she'd declared, after I'd politely evaded another of her questions about what I did for a living. "My dad was in the military. It's difficult to hide it completely, though you do a pretty good job."

I just smiled. "Interesting. Tell me more."

"Why don't you tell me yourself?"

"I'm more interested in your version."

She had pouted her lips theatrically and risen to the challenge. "You're recently back from overseas."

"But I already told you that."

"I haven't finished. You shaved when you came back. I can tell from the tan line."

I'd taken another drink and motioned for her to continue.

"So your hair's a little long, too. That and the fact you had a beard tells me you're not regular army or navy, which means...some kind of special ops?"

I grinned. I remember being surprised at how much I was enjoying her company and how much I didn't mind the interrogation that would normally make me uncomfortable.

"I can see why Carlson keeps you around."

"How'd I do?" She looked serious, like the competitive part of her really had to know.

"Not bad. But I'd rather talk about something else, if you don't mind."

She cocked an eyebrow. "And what's that?"

I held her gaze for a moment. "Coffee or dessert."

She didn't hesitate. "Both."

She had been content to let me keep my cards close to my chest on that first night. Maybe she had even enjoyed the mystery. But I could tell from her periodic digs—like the officer and a gentleman crack—that my reticence was beginning to niggle her.

We walked in silence for a couple of minutes, soaking up the unexpected warmth of the November sun and watching the other people doing the same: the joggers and the families and the nannies with high-end prams walking the offspring of some of the residents of the rarified apartments that overlooked it all. This was the fourth time we'd been together since my first meeting with Carlson, and we had already established that neither of us was the type to be concerned by a lull in conversation. Fourth date, but all of a sudden I realized there was a different feel to this one. For the first time, we hadn't arranged to go to dinner or a movie or any other approved date activity. This time we had just decided to go for a walk because spending time together seemed to be what we did now. I wondered if that subtle difference had occurred to Carol.

The realization felt good but quickly brought with it a stab of apprehension. Because the more time we spent together, the more she and I became "we," the quicker we would reach that point where we had to talk about where this could go, rather than just enjoying the moment.

And just like that, I was thinking about Carlson's office and Winterlong. I had made it the best part of an hour. Definitely a new record.

I was still awaiting the next assignment. My phone had been quiet for weeks, and I was beginning to wonder if the unease I was feeling about that was more than just paranoia. I had been thinking about what would happen after I made my move, if and when the opportunity arose. There would be no question of me sticking around waiting for Winterlong to hunt down their turncoat. I would have to disappear for good, leaving everything behind. Everything and everyone.

"What are you thinking about?"

Carol was looking up at my face as we walked, and I realized my expression had given away the fact I was brooding on something.

"Nothing in particular," I lied. "Just thinking."

"Thinking about when you're going to tell me what you've been talking to the senator about?"

That caught me by surprise. She had asked me about the meeting over dinner on the first night, and I had deflected the inquiry with something vague about my work overseas being of interest to Carlson. She hadn't pressed me that night, and she hadn't asked again. Until now. And the way she said it revealed she knew the senator and I had spoken on more than one occasion.

"Don't look so worried," she said, while I was still trying to come up with a response. "Need-to-know, huh?"

"Something like that," I said. "He'd have to tell you himself." Not exactly a lie, but a disingenuous response. I knew there was no way Carlson would share our conversation with Carol or anyone else. Not yet, anyway.

"I figured," she said. "Hey, isn't that creepy?"

"What?"

Carol had stopped walking and was looking up at the little animatronic figures emerging from the clock tower above the three archways that lead out of the zoo and back into the park. The clock was chiming while an off-key tune tinkled away.

"It is creepy," I agreed, grateful that she had chosen to change the subject.

She kept looking at the clock for a moment as the song played and the tourists and the nannies and joggers passed us by.

"It's getting late," she said.

We left the park and got the subway at Fifth and Fifty-Ninth, heading down to Carol's apartment in the East Village. It was a one-bedroom walk-up, which would have been a cheap place to rent for a folk singer or a poet in the sixties, but I guessed nowadays it would absorb the bulk of her salary.

We'd talked on the way about where to eat, then decided it would be fun to stay in and cook. Carol wasn't much of a homebody. This was her first day off in three weeks, and she apologized that she wouldn't have much in the cupboard. We picked up some supplies at the Italian grocery store on the corner and took everything up to her place.

Her apartment was small and neat. You could tell a lot about the occupant with a cursory glance: It was a place to sleep and occasionally relax, but it didn't feel quite lived in. The only real personal effects were a large bookcase taking up one wall of the living room and a television in the bedroom. I recognized the spare, utilitarian ethic from my own place and wondered for a second if this was another reason we were unconsciously drawn to each other. As though to prove the point, she picked up a remote control from the coffee table, pressed a couple of buttons, and a Sam Cooke song started up from hidden speakers somewhere. "Wonderful World." My favorite soul singer, and something else we had in common without knowing. Chemistry is a funny thing, just like Drakakis had said.

"I like to put on music when I come in. More relaxing than just turning on the news, you know what I mean?"

I nodded at the other door leading off the living room.

"Kitchen in there?"

She nodded and then looked at the bag of groceries. "Yeah, but just put them down here."

I did as she asked, and all of a sudden she was in my arms, her right hand on my cheek, pulling me in for a kiss. When we broke for air a minute later, I smiled.

"I thought you were hungry."

"There's more than one way to be hungry," she said playfully.

We kissed again, breaking earlier this time as she grabbed my hands in hers and tugged me back toward the hallway, quickening her steps as we fell into the bedroom. We tumbled onto the bed, her pulling my shirt out from my belt and fumbling with the buttons as we kissed some more. She pulled her T-shirt over her head before putting her arms around me again.

A patter on the window distracted us for a second as the rain started up out of nowhere. I looked back at her, wondering if this was a good idea when so much was still in question. She seemed to sense my hesitation and nodded.

We kissed again.

NINETEEN

Seattle

I HAD BEEN alert for the possibility of Bryant making a run for it when we got outside the diner, but he played along, resigned to the new itinerary. There was nowhere to run, not really. He knew it as well as I did. He had already proved he wasn't the type of person who could disappear without a trace. Now he was without resources, friends, or even the chance of a payoff. He would last a week on the run, tops. All he could do was delay his arrest, and sacrifice the chance to cut a deal with Stafford that might keep him out of jail.

"So do you have the plane tickets ready?" he asked as we got into a cab headed for Sea-Tac.

I shook my head. "I always buy them at the airport."

"More expensive that way."

"In some ways."

The journey passed in silence for a couple of minutes as the cabbie negotiated the surface streets and turned onto the on-ramp for the Alaskan Way Viaduct.

"Should be a smooth trip this time of day, fellas," he called back as we merged into southbound traffic. "Twenty, twenty-five minutes."

The mention of time reminded me that I had really expected to hear from Coop by now. I made up my mind to call him right after we bought the tickets.

"So I guess we're gonna be traveling companions for the next few hours," Bryant said after a minute, settling into the seat and seeming to relax for the first time since I'd seen him.

"Looks that way."

"It doesn't have to be awkward, does it?"

I looked over at Bryant. His demeanor surprised me. He seemed to have accepted the reversal of his fortunes with good grace and was content to sit back and enjoy the ride. I didn't know if he was putting up a front, either for my or for his own benefit, but I had to admit I kind of admired his attitude. It made me think I'd made the right choice offering a deal to Jasmine Bryant, and to him.

"Not on my account."

"I guess you do this a lot, huh?"

I thought about it. "'This,' tends to be different on every job. But yeah, I find people. It's what I do for a living."

"You're an expert, then. So how'd I do?"

"What do you mean?"

"How close did I get to getting away clean?"

"From me?" I asked. "No offense, but not very. As soon as I knew where you were headed and that you hadn't made the sale yet, I knew I could get you."

"And how did you find that out?"

"Trade secret. Let's just say everybody makes mistakes."

He shrugged and looked out at the cars coming the other way on the other side of the barrier.

"Great. I wanted to make the sale last night. Kelner put me off. Said it would be better to let things cool down a little."

I didn't say what I was thinking: that Kelner had been playing it safe; waiting to see if Bryant was going to get caught. And he had been right to do so.

He shook his head at his bad luck. "I could have been long gone."

I didn't say anything to that. I knew better than most that it's more difficult to truly disappear than people realize. If the sale had gone through before I had tracked Bryant to Seattle, it would have made things a little more difficult to me—not to mention a lot more difficult for Kelner—but I would have found him sooner or later. And besides, he had already left enough of a trail to lead me to his prospective buyer. In that sense, Bryant's loss was Kelner's gain. Since the deal hadn't gone through, there was nothing concrete to tie him to any of this.

I was grateful to be thinking about the work, about something that was largely under my control. The traffic on the highway started to bunch up a little at the exit for Sea-Tac. Bryant was still staring out of the window, watching a 737 take off, headed out over Puget Sound. I knew he was wishing he were on that plane, and not the one we were about to catch.

"Why did you do it?" I asked quietly, so as to be sure the driver would not overhear.

Bryant turned, and I saw a flash of embarrassment in his eyes that I had caught him gazing at the plane and guessed what he was thinking about.

"Did Stafford pay you extra to provide counseling? Why do you think I did it? For the money. Same reason you took this job. What's the difference?"

Money isn't the whole story for me, and I doubted

it was for him, either. I shrugged. "I guess one difference is, I knew what I was getting into."

He stared back at me for a moment and then turned back to watch the airport buildings as they passed. "You know what, I've changed my mind. Let's skip the small talk."

TWENTY

THE DRIVER LET us out at the drop-off lane in front of departures. I paid him and grabbed Bryant's laptop case from the seat between us. He didn't object. As we passed through the doors into the terminal, he looked at the case and realized it was the only item of baggage I was carrying. He spoke to me for the first time since the cab.

"You travel light, huh?"

I had left my stuff at the hotel. Retrieving it before we flew back to California would have meant a delay I didn't feel I could afford. With a bird in the hand, I decided I could afford to replace the clothes and the travel toiletries, and the laptop was clean. I wasn't just thinking about not giving Bryant more time to change his mind about cooperating. I was starting to get more than a little concerned that I hadn't had an e-mail from Coop yet. I knew he would be busy, but I had expected to have heard something from him by now, even if it was just to tell me he hadn't received any more e-mails with photographs of unidentified dead bodies. That made me think of something I had forgotten to ask Bryant.

"I take it you have ID?" I asked.

He patted his coat pocket. "Driver's license and passport, right here. Be prepared, huh?"

He looked so rueful that I almost wanted to apologize for catching him. I reminded myself that he had brought this misfortune entirely on himself, not caring about the fact he might bankrupt his boss and put his coworkers out of a job.

He shook his head. "I thought I was being so smart driving up here. Staying off the grid. Flying is too traceable these days, you know? Not that it matters now, I guess."

Bryant couldn't know that he was starting to make me nervous. He was right. Flying was too damn traceable. Right now my priority was to get Bryant back to Stafford, get paid, and get clear. I had been reasonably relaxed about how much time I had the night before. Now I wasn't so sure. A two-hour flight to California would probably be okay. After that, I would heed Bryant's advice and get the hell off the grid. I knew where I had to go, and I realized now I would have to do it the long way.

I told Bryant I had to make a call and we found a solitary phone booth, tucked away in a corner beside the restrooms like a forgotten heirloom. He raised an eyebrow, obviously surprised I wasn't using a cell phone, but said nothing. He stood a couple of feet away from the booth as I picked the handset up. I hadn't used a pay phone in a while, but probably not as long as most people. Pay phones still have their uses. One of these days they'll rip out the last one and put it in a museum, and there will no longer be any such thing as a truly anonymous call.

Given that my phone was at the bottom of Lake Washington, it was helpful that I have a good memory for numbers. My first call was to Coop's cell. It went directly to voice mail. No personalized message, just the operator's default request to leave a message or call back later. I hung up before the message ended. The low-level anxiety I had been feeling had increased. The next call was to a number I hadn't memorized, but hadn't had to: It was the direct dial on the business card Stafford had given me the day before.

"Why the hell is your phone switched off?" was the first thing he said.

"It's been giving me problems," I said, before cutting to the chase. I told him I had made some progress and that there was a very good chance I could get the MeTime software back to him, its secrets intact. The hook baited, I laid out my suggestion. Bryant and I would return to Moonola with the software. Stafford could confirm no more copies were in existence, and in return for a detailed and signed statement from Bryant, Stafford would agree not to press charges. His response was immediate.

"Not a chance. He's going to jail; that was the deal."

"The deal was I do whatever I need to do to find your guy," I reminded him. "I couldn't have gotten this far without making certain assurances to certain people, and I can't go back on that now. If you're willing to compromise a little on this, you get everything you want. No harm, no foul."

Stafford was quiet, thinking it over.

"The other option is easy. I return the fee and maybe Bryant sends you the software back by mail. Or maybe he doesn't. This is a good deal, Stafford."

His reply sounded like it came from between gritted teeth. "How soon can you be here?"

"This evening. Say, five o'clock at your office?"

"All right, Blake," he said. "I guess it'll have to do."

I hung up and looked at Bryant, who had caught

enough of my end of the conversation to know whom I'd been speaking to.

"He went for it?"

"Another satisfied customer?" I said. "Just about."

There was a nearby ATM, and I withdrew another five hundred dollars for the tickets. The blond attendant on the United tickets desk gave us a glassy smile as we approached and asked us how she could help us. I asked for two tickets on flight 468—the next plane to San Francisco International. She looked down and tapped rapidly on the keyboard in front of her. She checked the screen, and her fixed smile took on a sympathetic cast. She inclined her head sadly.

"I'm afraid we only have seats in business left on that—"

"Business is fine," I said.

"Might as well go out in style," Bryant said.

All of a sudden, I was on edge. I don't like flying at the best of times. It's the only type of travel where you have no option but to go on record: You have to provide your name and use photographic ID. Like Bryant had just said—too damn traceable. But I needed to get him back to California and get moving. It would take only a couple of hours by air; and by the time anyone wanted to check up on it, all they would have would be San Fran as a starting point of where to look. The alternative was to drive, which would take most of a day.

The attendant hit some more keys and turned to face us again, the smile dialed back up to full wattage. "That'll be six hundred and seventy-two eighteen including tax. May I take your credit card please, sir?"

"Can I pay cash?"

Back to sympathetic. "We no longer accept cash, I'm afraid."

I sighed. This was a recent innovation at the larger airports, designed to create a faster and more efficient airport experience for customers, or something like that. But I knew I was leaving a trail anyway, so one more bread crumb wouldn't make it any worse. I handed over the Amex card I keep in my wallet as a last resort.

"Thank you, Mr...." She paused as she read the name on the card. "Blake. And I'll need photographic identification for you and your traveling companion, too."

We handed over our driver's licenses, and she deftly arranged the credit card and the DLs on the desk in front of the keyboard like a croupier dealing a hand. *Two hours*, I reminded myself as she started to tap our details into the system. *Just two hours.*

And then the attendant's demeanor changed absolutely. In the course of our conversation she had modified her smile as appropriate to the information she was giving us, but suddenly the bulletproof customer-service facade had vanished like fine mist on a summer's morning. She was reading something on the screen she was not used to seeing, and she was frowning. I felt a thousand needlepoints dance up and down the length of my spine as her eyes moved away from the screen and back to us. She remembered to smile only at the last moment, but her attempt was brittle, fake in a very different way before.

"I apologize. We're having some problems with the system. Do you mind waiting here while I contact my manager?"

You idiot, I cursed myself. *So much for two hours.*

"Actually, I'll come back. We'll go get a coffee." I held out my hand for the cards. The attendant didn't move. Bryant was looking at me, a bemused expression on his face—so there was a technical glitch, so what?

"I need to keep your identification until…until the technical issue can be resolved. If you could please just wait here a moment, I'm sure it won't take long."

There was no point wasting any more time. I grabbed Bryant's arm and started walking away.

"What's wrong? She said it would only take a minute."

I could hear the attendant calling after us, her *Excuse me*'s gaining in volume and urgency. People standing in line at the other ticket desks were starting to turn and stare at us.

"We're getting out of here," I said. "Now."

"But you said… What do you mean we're getting out of here? Why?"

"Because I'm on the No Fly list, and that's very bad news."

TWENTY-ONE

IT WAS BAD news for more than just the obvious reason.

Appearing on the No Fly list doesn't exactly make you a VIP in and of itself—there were about six thousand names on the list last I heard, and it was growing every year. So in terms of notoriety, it's not quite the same as hitting the FBI's Ten Most Wanted. But it's not a good sign. You don't get on the list by jumping bail, or committing a run-of-the-mill crime, which was how I knew it was my name and not Bryant's that had set off the alarm bells.

It means that you've made it through a number of filters of persons of interest and have been designated as a live risk: someone who should not be allowed to board an aircraft. That my name was on the list meant that they were more serious about getting me than I'd appreciated. It meant somebody had pulled strings with the FBI. If I know anything about the feds, it's that they're not exactly ultra-compliant, no-questions-asked types. So not only was Winterlong on my trail, but they wanted me bad: bad enough to create some ripples. Right about now, someone was receiving a phone call to let them know that someone by the name of Carter Blake, answering my description, had just tried to buy a plane ticket at Sea-Tac. The only question now was, how close were they? Did I have time to get Bryant back to San Francisco by alternative means, or should I just cut my losses and go?

I glanced around as we walked. The terminal was a high space bounded by sixty-foot-high windows. There was a raised mezzanine level accessed by stairs and escalators and a food court and stores beneath. There were lots of people crowded around, waiting for their gates to be announced, saying their goodbyes to friends and relations. I decided that heading immediately for the front entrance would just make us stand out more. Instead, I made for the busier area around the stores at a quick walk. Bryant was keeping pace with me. That made me realize that he really did understand his best chance was to stick with me. If he had decided to stay at the ticket desk, there would have been nothing I could have done about it.

"Blake, what's going on? I thought I was the master criminal here."

I ignored him. I glanced behind me and saw two burly security guys in white shirts and navy chinos approaching the United desk. The woman was pointing in our direction. Fortunately, we were already obscured by the crowd. I hoped there was another way out through the food court.

"Seriously, tell me what's going on, or you can forget me going any further. I'm not getting mixed up in some terrorist thing."

A lady with white hair and pink-tinted glasses gave a sharp intake of breath at the mention of the T-word as we passed.

"Keep your voice down," I hissed. "This isn't a terrorist thing."

"Then what?"

"I used to work for some people. They don't like me very much."

"I can buy that, and I've only known you for an hour."

"We need to get out of here."

"No, sounds like *you* need to get out of here." He sounded vaguely amused. I guess I would have in his position, too, if I had no idea how much danger we were both in.

We passed a Starbucks, and one of those generic airport bar and grills. I saw a sign for the restrooms and a fire exit. It was better than nothing, though I expected the door would be alarmed.

"We," I repeated. "If airport security gets ahold of us, they'll put us in one of those little rooms for a few hours until they hand me over to my people and you over to the cops."

"Why are you saying all this like it's my fault?"

"Bryant—shut up."

He opened his mouth again before deciding to take my advice. I looked over my shoulder, glad to see no sign of the security twins just yet. I glanced around the stores again, seeing a clothing store. That gave me a better idea than hoping there was a back exit we could sneak out of.

"Give me your coat," I said.

"What?"

"Just do it."

He shrugged the overcoat off and handed it to me. I removed my own coat and draped both over my arm, heading for the clothing store. The space within was full and cluttered, thanks to the spatial limitations of an airport concession. Folded T-shirts and sweaters were stacked on shelves around the walls, and heavier garments like coats and dresses were hung on racks crammed together across the modest floor space. The cashier was serving a customer, an old man in a gray fedora. I made my way to the farthest rack and hung the coats up over a pair of turquoise dresses, before making my way to the front again. On the way, I passed a couple racks of coats. Glancing at them long enough only to make sure I didn't select anything too small or too large, I plucked two raincoats from the rack—one green, one blue—and made my way to the register.

The cashier had finished serving the guy in the fedora, but a large woman was now approaching the register carrying a plastic-bagged T-shirt. We were about equidistant on our approaches, and the cashier glanced at both of us with an indecisive smile, as if to say, "You two figure out who's next."

Seeing the look, the woman quickened her pace pointedly. I did likewise. I didn't have the time to wait in line, and I definitely didn't want to attract even more attention by shoplifting the coats. I beat her to the counter by a nose.

"Listen, I hate to do this, but I'm running really late. Do you mind?"

The woman pursed her lips, stepping in front of me and actually physically butting into me. "I most certainly do. You should have arrived in better time, shouldn't you?"

I glanced at the price tag and took two hundreds from my wallet. I dropped them on the counter, with a look of apology to the cashier. Mission accomplished, I brought the coat back out and handed one to Bryant. His face wrinkled up at the sight of the cheap raincoat I'd just overpaid for.

"I liked that coat."

"Well, now you can like this coat instead," I said. I pointed back out at the main terminal space. "Walk straight across there. Don't run. I'll meet you at the taxi stand in three minutes."

He rolled his eyes but nodded assent, walking out in front of me. We'd be exiting through the front as two lone men in raincoats, rather than sneaking out through the back as the pair the United check-in woman would have described to the guards. I hoped that would be enough of a diversion.

I gave Bryant thirty seconds and then followed him. As I cleared the ring of travelers hanging around the food court and the shopping area, I saw the two big security guys again. They were scanning the faces in the crowd, speaking into their radios and wearing the unmistakable expressions of people who are trying to identify someone they've never laid eyes on from somebody else's description. Of course, the place was scattered with security cameras, which would make it easy to track our movements and our escape method later, but not in enough time to stop us.

I saw Bryant exit through the revolving door ahead of me as I passed within ten yards of the nearest security guy. He was talking calmly into his radio, eyes darting around the crowd. I looked around and saw three other security officers closing in on the shopping area. All I needed was ten more seconds to reach the exit, and safety.

And that was when I saw the man in glasses.

TWENTY-TWO

I HAD SEEN his face only once before, but I knew I would never forget it as long as I lived. However long that turned out to be.

It was a face that promised nothing good. The face of a tax inspector interviewing a suspect about a discrepancy, or an uncaring doctor about to give a patient bad news. The blue eyes behind the round lenses seemed to study everything that passed before them like a predator dispassionately regarding its next meal. Pitiless countenance aside, the rest of him blended in to his surroundings, from his neat haircut to the black overcoat worn over a button-down shirt, black pants, and polished shoes. If he had had a briefcase, he would have looked like an executive on his way to or from a meeting. But he carried nothing. Nothing that wouldn't fit beneath his coat.

Our eyes met and it was too late already—the flicker of recognition flashed behind the glasses, and I pictured the last time I'd seen this man, pointing a gun at the head of an LAPD detective named Jessica Allen.

It felt like we stared at each other for an hour, though it couldn't have been more than a split second. I turned away and started walking quickly, following in the direction Bryant had gone. I quickened my pace to just short of a run as I approached the exit doors, not daring to look back and not even worrying about the airport security anymore.

It had been too late the moment Coop had sent Martinez's black notice; I knew that now. That had been the reason for the e-mail: not just to rattle me, but to find me. They must have known my general location for hours, were probably staking out the airport as one of the most likely places to find me. That phone call about the No Fly list had probably come directly to the cell phone of the man in glasses.

As the automatic doors gave way at my approach, I saw the people behind me faintly reflected in them. The man with glasses was a dozen paces back, another man now walking alongside him, watching as he pointed me out. The second man was around the same height, short, reddish hair, dressed similarly.

I passed through the doors. The rain had started up again, harder than before. Bryant was there, poised to climb into the open back door of cab at the front of the stand. I glanced around. It was less busy than I had been hoping at this exit. Most people had scurried for cover from the downpour. There were only a few people making their way to the public pickup points farther on. That was bad: Fewer people meant fewer witnesses.

"Are we good?" he asked, completely oblivious to how much more trouble we were now in.

"Get in," I yelled, running toward the front passenger side.

"Carter Blake!" I heard the shout from behind me, knew it was either the man with glasses or his friend, whom I hadn't gotten a good look at. "Police. Stop where you are!"

I ignored it and yanked the door open, sliding in. Bryant was already in the backseat.

"Maybe we should…"

"That's not the police," I said as I heard the voice again. Closer, louder.

"Stop or I'll shoot."

The taxi driver was looking over the head restraint, past Bryant and through the back window at the two approaching men he assumed were plainclothes cops. He turned to look at me, alarm in his eyes. "What is this?"

"We have to get out of here," I said. "They're not cops."

I glanced back and saw the man in glasses pointing the gun straight at us. I yelled, "Get down," as I ducked. Bryant reacted quickly. The driver, not quickly enough.

Three shots shattered the back window, safety glass spraying over the interior. I heard a flesh impact as the driver took a bullet in the side of this throat. He slumped over, his eyes rolling back in his head. His body was held up by the seat belt as a torrent of blood coursed down the front of his shirt.

Staying down, I slammed the car into drive and lunged headfirst into the driver's footwell, slamming the palm of my hand down on the gas pedal with my left hand while I gripped the wheel with my right and yanked us out into the lane. The wheels spun and then caught, jerking us out onto the road. I corrected the steer blind, hoping we wouldn't hit one of the concrete pillars outside of the terminal.

Two more shots punched into the car, one of them passing through the back window and exiting through the windshield, the other hitting the driver's side wing mirror. I gritted my teeth as we sideswiped another vehicle. A glancing blow, not enough to slow us down. I risked putting my head up in time to avoid plowing into another car and course-corrected enough to keep us on the straight before ducking down again as I heard two more shots.

Bryant's suddenly high-pitched yell came from the back. "What the fuck, Blake?"

I ignored him and stabbed my finger at the button to release the driver's seat belt, taking my other hand off the wheel long enough to scrabble at the door handle and push it open wide. I grabbed the wheel as the car started to list to the left and yanked it hard right. The driver's body tipped over and out onto the road. I took my other hand off the gas, shuffled across into the driver's seat, and stamped my foot down on the pedal to bring us up to speed again. The exit road curved around on itself before leading out, but there was a line of low bushes directly ahead that offered a shortcut. I floored the gas and braced myself as we hit the verge and plowed through the line of bushes, swinging onto the road that led out of the airport in front of a shuttle bus. I felt impact as Bryant slammed into the back of my seat, face-first, with a yell.

"Seat belt," I yelled, daring to glance in the rearview for the first time. The shuttle bus had slewed into verge to avoid us, neatly blocking the exit road behind us. That was good, but I knew we wouldn't get far in a shot-up stolen taxi.

We passed under the freeway bridge, took the curving on-ramp at sixty, and merged onto the freeway. The cold air sucked through the bullet holes in the windshield and breezed through the smashed rear window. Bryant was looking back out of the window in disbelief.

"They shot at us. They just shot at us. Why would they...?"

I kept my eyes on the road, looking out for signs for the next exit. The real police would be on our tail soon enough.

"I told you. They're not cops."

"Well, who the hell are they? They can't just start shooting at us. Can they?"

"They're people who don't give a shit if you think they can't start shooting at you. They're people who won't stop until we're dead." I thought about that. Bryant was as deep in as I was now. Marked for death by association. "I'm sorry."

"Where are we going?"

"You'll know as soon as I do."

TWENTY-THREE

Seattle

STARK WALKED OVER to the driver with the idea of checking for a pulse. He realized there was no point when he got within ten feet of the sprawled body. His head jerked around as he heard a scream. A large woman in a raincoat looked out from the shelter of the parking structure across from the taxi stand.

"Oh my God, is he dead?"

"Please stay back, ma'am," Stark commanded, waving her and the other people who were emerging from the shelter to gawk away. They were very lucky that these bystanders had been too busy getting the hell out of the way to pay close attention to what had happened.

He returned to where Usher was standing. The pair of them holstered their weapons and waited patiently in the rain, keeping their hands visible. With any luck, Blake's name triggering an alert moments before would mean the cops could be quickly persuaded they were on the tail of a dangerous fugitive. Still, it was a hell of a mess. Faraday would be pissed.

"Was that a good idea?" Stark asked. It was Usher who'd started firing first. Stark had backed him up only reluctantly, aiming for the tires. By that time, Blake had gotten the car out of effective range.

"We'll take care of this."

"That wasn't what I asked," Stark said. "You killed the driver."

Four airport security guards were approaching them, guns drawn. Stark was pleased to see they didn't look scared or tense, just wary. The way he and Usher were dressed, their demeanor, and the fact they'd put their guns away was enough to put the cops at something like ease, as far as was possible in this kind of situation. The two of them looked like feds of some variety, so they got the benefit of the doubt. How different from the reaction they might have gotten in other parts of the world.

Usher turned to look at him, speaking quietly. "Blake killed the driver." The combination of the intense stare and the calm, flat voice, put Stark in mind of a hypnotist. He knew Usher wasn't trying to convince him it hadn't been his bullet that killed the driver—that would imply he cared. No, he was just making sure Stark knew the official story. Of course, an autopsy and ballistic tests would eventually confirm that the driver had been killed by a bullet fired from outside the vehicle, but that would take several hours. By the time that was confirmed, they would both be long gone, never to be seen by local law enforcement again. Questions would be asked, demands would be made, but nothing would reach the unit, or Usher. The blame would be filtered up through various government agencies until it evaporated entirely.

"Keep your hands where I can see them and identify yourself," the closest security guard called out. He was a tall black man in his forties, gray hair at his temples. Calm, experienced-looking. He obviously sensed they were authorized personnel of some kind, because he hadn't yelled at them to lie on the ground yet. Stark was glad they weren't dealing with an unpredictable rookie.

"Officer, I'm going to produce my identification, okay?" Usher said.

The officer nodded. "Slowly. Left hand. Right hand where I can see it."

Usher did exactly as ordered, moving carefully and deliberately. He produced an ID wallet and held it up for the cop to look at.

"We're with the Department of Homeland Security. I'm Agent Black; this is Agent Burrows."

The lead cop stepped forward, his body language already relaxing. The other three kept their guns on the two men while he examined the ID. It would pass muster, because it was indistinguishable from a real DHS ID.

He handed the ID back to Usher. "Okay. What's going on, Agent?"

"Thank you," Usher said. "We've been tipped off that a couple of terrorist suspects were about to board a domestic flight. Sure enough, one of them was flagged on the No Fly list about ten minutes ago when he tried to buy a ticket. We made a visual on the suspects but before we could make the arrest…" He paused and gestured at the body lying on the road fifty yards away. "They killed a cabdriver and stole his vehicle. We need to run them down as soon as possible. These men present a live risk."

A dozen more security personnel had arrived while they'd been talking. Two paramedics were examining the body of the driver with no great urgency, one of them shaking his head.

"They won't get far. Any particular reason we

weren't informed of your operation today, Agent?" the cop said, a hint of sarcasm in his voice.

Stark pitched in, deciding Usher's matter-of-fact condescension was not the ideal tool to extract themselves quickly from this situation. "I'm sorry, Officer. We had people at various locations across the metropolitan area. We couldn't be sure they'd be here until United's database triggered the No Fly alert."

"We'll need the pair of you to wait right here."

"I'm afraid we don't have time, Officer," Usher said. "This is a matter of national security. We'll be pleased to cooperate once..."

The officer shook his head and held a hand up to stop Usher. "I've got shots fired in my airport and a dead civilian. Nobody's going anywhere."

Stark sighed inwardly, although he'd been expecting this. He turned to Usher. "Do you want to make the call?"

Usher kept his eyes on the officer. His eyes had narrowed and his tone was even frostier than usual. "I'll make the call."

TWENTY-FOUR

Seattle

WE LEFT THE freeway and I pulled off the road at the first opportunity, which turned out to be the entrance to a business park. We passed several rows of units: I saw a tire place, an auto repair center, and a bunch of different wholesalers. Nobody was out front of any of them, apart from a guy in coveralls stacking tires with his back to us. I slowed down a little and took a few random turns until we ran out of open businesses and found ourselves surrounded by boarded-up units. I found a blind alley between two derelict units, just wide enough to admit the taxi, and nosed it in as far as it would go. There was an opaque roof of corrugated plastic sheltering the alley, and by ramming the car straight into the junk at the far end, I managed to make sure its full length was under cover. I got out and gave myself a once-over. Some of the taxi driver's blood had gotten on my left side, but thankfully it wasn't obvious against a dark suit. Some of it had soaked into my shirt cuff, so I rolled both shirt sleeves up so they weren't visible. When I saw Bryant had made no move to join me, I opened the back door.

"Come on."

He was staring straight ahead, looking a little sick. He hadn't spoken since the freeway, and I wondered if he was in some kind of delayed shock. I didn't have time for that. While I felt bad that events hadn't exactly gone to plan, my sympathy for Bryant had limits.

"Bryant, *now.*"

He broke the thousand-yard stare and looked up at me before nodding slowly and sliding out from the backseat. His nose was bleeding a little from the collision with the head restraint, but it didn't look broken. I headed back for the mouth of the alley, not wasting any more time on persuasion. Bryant followed behind, not needing to be told a third time. He had retrieved his laptop case from the backseat. There was a bullet hole through the dead center. When he saw it, he looked like he was going to throw up.

"Could have been worse," I reminded him. "Is there anything saved on that? Search history? E-mail password?"

Bryant shook his head. "It's brand new. Just for the demo."

"Good. Leave it."

The rain had abated for the moment, but from the look of the sky, it was temporary. We turned the corner, and I looked up and down the road between the row of units. All were shuttered or boarded up, and there was nobody else in sight. I knew we had to keep moving, but there was something I had to do first that couldn't wait. I asked for Bryant's phone and he handed it over.

"It's okay," he said. "It's clean—no contract. Untraceable."

"Nice idea," I said. "If you hadn't synced it to your personal Microsoft account."

I turned away from him as his jaw dropped. The ID we'd left at the United desk meant that our pursuers knew Bryant's name. Eventually, they would be able to trace devices registered to his online account and probably be able to use that information to locate this phone. But that would take them a while, and I'd make sure we left it here after I made one last call.

"Everybody makes mistakes," he said quietly, repeating my words from earlier.

"Goddamn right they do," I said, more to myself than him.

I didn't call Coop's cell phone this time. Although it was part of our understanding that we didn't know where each other was based, old habits died hard. I had spent some time a while back tracking down the specific hotel in Orlando in which he resided, even managing to pin down the name he stayed under.

I found the number of the Sunset Apartments on Google and hit the button to call. The voice that answered sounded harassed, impatient. At first I mistook that for standard-issue snooty concierge behavior. But when I asked to speak to Mr. Gray in room 204, there was a full two seconds of silence.

"Excuse me a moment, sir."

There was a pause as the receiver was cupped with a muffling hand, hushed voices relaying the information of whom I'd asked for. It sounded as though he was asking for direction.

The voice was artificially bright when it came back on. "May I ask who's calling, sir?"

"Tell him it's Mr. Kubert."

Bryant was watching with interest, and mouthed *What's up?* I ignored it.

Another pause, phone muffled again. I heard a scuffing sound as the phone was passed to someone else.

"This is Detective Mike Malone, Orlando PD Homicide. Who's speaking?"

I felt as though I'd been delivered a gut punch. I hung up, turned the phone off, and removed the SIM and memory cards. I dropped the phone on the ground and stamped down on the screen with the heel of my shoe. Bryant opened his mouth to protest, then thought better of it when he saw the look on my face.

All of a sudden, it looked like the clock was running down.

THE DRIZZLE BEGAN again as we walked, lighter than it had been at the airport. We made our way back through the maze of units, taking a different route than the one we'd driven in by. As we got nearer the entrance, we found more places open for business: a cake supplies outlet, an auto parts store, a remaindered books warehouse. I was hoping there might be a used car lot, but no such luck. Finally, we found our way back to the main entrance just in time to hear sirens on the freeway a quarter mile back. I froze and watched as two police cars flew over the bridge crossing the road we were on and continued past the exit. That was a break: Either no one had seen us leave at the first exit, or the information hadn't been conveyed to the cops on the ground yet.

In truth, I wasn't concerned with the kind of cars that announced themselves with sirens and flashing lights as I was about the anonymous black SUV that might appear at any moment. The men at the airport had much more information about who we were and why we were running than the cops, and that would mean they'd stand a better chance of catching up with us.

The road we were on was quiet, but I could see

steady traffic passing at the next intersection, about another two hundred yards away in the opposite direction from the freeway bridge. We covered the distance quickly. All around were vacant lots and low buildings. Too open, too exposed. As we reached the corner of the intersection, I saw what I thought was a bus stop on the other side of the road. As we got closer, I realized it was a light-rail stop on the airport line and—a break at last—a northbound train was approaching. The sign above the windshield told me it was headed to downtown Seattle. Back to square one. I avoided eye contact with the driver, who paid almost no attention to either of us as we paid cash for two tickets into the city. Bryant sat down first, taking the closest empty seat to the front. He glanced around warily at the other passengers, as though expecting another attack.

When the doors closed and the train suddenly moved off, he finally spoke.

"So, what now?"

"Now we get the hell out of town."

"We? You think I'm going anywhere with you after you almost got me killed? No way. Deal's off."

I sighed. "This has nothing to do with the deal. They're looking for us both now."

"What the hell do you mean? I never even met you before this morning. They don't even know who I am."

"They saw you with me. That means you're a potential lead to me. You don't want to hear about what they'll do to find out what you know." He opened his mouth to protest, but I kept talking. "And they know exactly who you are now. We had to leave our ID at the ticket desk, remember?"

He looked like he was trying to think of another argument, before shaking his head in frustration. "Shit."

"Tell me about it."

"This is your fault, you know. I'm going to get killed because of you."

"Don't look at me, Bryant. If you hadn't swiped Me-Time, they'd be shooting at me in an entirely different state right now."

The train slowed for the next stop. A couple of streets from us, we saw a police car run through an intersection, lights on. Bryant and I exchanged a glance.

"So where do we go until the heat's off?" he asked quietly once we were moving again.

"The heat's never going off."

"Goddamn it, Blake. Do you have *anything* good to say?"

"Sure. The good news is, I have a plan."

FIVE YEARS AGO

New York City

CAROL HAD ARRANGED to pick me up at one o'clock that afternoon, but there was a conversation I needed to have with her boss first.

I contacted the senator via the prepay cell phone I had been using for this purpose, and asked for a meeting. He paused, then said he would shuffle his diary around a little and suggested meeting in Battery Park in a couple of hours. I got to the meeting point at Pier A ten minutes early, but Carlson had beaten me there. He was dressed in a long winter coat and hat. For a guy able to project his personality so forcefully on television, he was doing a creditable job of blending in.

I didn't waste time on pleasantries. "I want out."

Carlson stared back at me, his face betraying no emotion. After a second, he nodded his head to the side, indicating that we should walk and talk.

"What do you mean?" he asked after we had walked a few paces.

"I mean out of all of it. You, them, everything. I'm not going back."

He took a moment to let that sink in. The temperature had plummeted in the last few days, and the wind blowing off the harbor was freezing. Small groups of tourists and couples wandered past, on their way to the Liberty Island ferry.

"Are you going to say something, or are you just here for the exercise?" I said when we had covered a couple hundred yards without him saying anything else. Carlson stopped and looked across the harbor.

"Seems to me that choice isn't one that's open to you."

"How do you figure?"

"You told me yourself. People don't leave Winterlong. My other contact tells me they're starting to get suspicious."

"What makes him think that?" I had long since stopped trying to get a name out of Carlson.

"Little things. Nothing dramatic. They're taking a few more precautions. Codes being changed more regularly. More meetings of the senior staff."

"Does your guy think they're onto him?" I caught myself just in time before I had said "us." I still wasn't sure there was an "us."

Carlson shook his head. "No. He doesn't think they know anything specific. But that doesn't alter my point—you don't just walk away from Winterlong."

"I've made arrangements," I said. "Not because of this. On some level, I think I've been preparing for this for a long time."

Carlson turned his head to look at me, saying nothing.

"I have an apartment where I can lie low for a while. I know a guy who can set me up with everything I need. Driver's license, employment and financial history, passport if I need it."

"You would need money."

"I have money. I could walk away from you right now and five minutes later I wouldn't exist. Winterlong helps on that. Everything about me is classified anyway, from my record to my medical history to my fingerprints. They've done the work for me: I'm no one. Easy enough to be a different no one."

"Is it?" He turned away again. "I need you on this."

"You have another guy."

"And what do you think will happen to him if you disappear? That kernel of suspicion is going to pop. Best-case scenario, his hands will be tied. Worst case…"

"It's not my problem."

He paused and started walking away again. I thought about turning and walking in the other direction, but in the end I followed.

"You've been seeing Carol, I understand."

"She told you that?"

"Not directly, but it's obvious to anyone who knows her she's seeing someone. She's…happier. Are you going to walk away from her, too?"

"Who says she can't come with me?"

He gave me a look of disappointment. "You aren't really that naive, are you? Besides, it wouldn't be much of a life for her. Leaving everything behind, always looking over her shoulder. I believe you when you say you could do it, but Carol?" He shook his head.

I said nothing. After a moment, Carlson continued.

"And if you leave her, how do you know they won't try to trace you through her?"

"Because nobody knows about me and her." The second it was out I realized that wasn't true. Carlson knew, and if he knew, maybe other people did, too.

"How sure are you about that?"

CAROL ARRIVED AT one o'clock on the dot, in a car she had rented for the weekend. Her idea—she had taken a couple of rare vacation days, and we decided it would

I WAS ROUSED by the buzzing of my cell phone. Reluctantly opening my eyes, I saw that it was still dark outside and the rain was still falling. The buzzing continued. I knew what the call meant. Very few people had my number. In a second I would have to break this spell and go back to the world. Back to Winterlong. I looked at Carol, still dozing, her head on the pillow beside mine, a lock of blond hair trailing down over one eye, the corner of her mouth curled up in a smile as though she was having a pleasant dream. More than anything, I wanted to let the phone ring out. I wanted to hurl the phone out of the nearest window and forget all about Winterlong.

It buzzed again. I moved my arm out from under Carol's head gently. She opened her eyes partway and murmured a sleepy, "Hey."

"Hey back."

I got up and dug the phone out of my pants pocket. The screen showed a withheld number, of course. I walked across to the window and hit the button to pick up.

"What's going on?"

"This is your wake-up call. Do you require a newspaper?" The voice belonged to Murphy. My voice must have given away the fact that I had just woken up. I sighed.

"Just tell me when and where."

"Three hours, the usual place. Pack your toothbrush."

I looked back into the bedroom. Carol was sitting up in bed, smiling back at me. "Everything okay?"

I hung up on Murphy. Nothing was okay. Nothing at all.

TWENTY-FIVE

I HAD TOLD Bryant I had a plan. In retrospect, maybe "a plan" was stretching it. Plans rely on detail, reflection, the weighing up of risk. What I had was a goal: to keep moving and to stay out of my pursuers' way long enough to retrieve the one thing I might be able to use against them.

I began to tense up on the ride back into the city as more and more passengers joined the train. So far none had given us a second look, but I wondered if our faces had been released to the news. There was no way to access the Internet to check. All of a sudden I was really feeling the lack of a phone—it was hampering forward planning in a strange city, giving me no way to look up maps or transit options as we traveled. I consoled myself with the thought that, had I not ditched the phone, my forward planning might have been hampered permanently. Briefly I thought about Stafford—he would not be pleased when I failed to deliver Bryant at the appointed time. I reminded myself that an aggravated client was pretty close to the bottom of my worry list.

As a precaution, we sat apart for the last few stops, so as not to present a matched pair. The next step was to make some effort to alter our appearances. In particular, I wanted to ditch the two raincoats as fast as possible. The only reason I hadn't already was that we would be far more conspicuous not wearing any coats on a typically rainy Seattle afternoon in early January.

We left the train at University Street, the second-from-the-last stop. We turned onto Third Avenue, and I spotted a branch of Macy's a couple blocks away. A department store was ideal for our purposes, and not just because of the range of goods. There would be lots of different exits, lots of ways to thwart surveillance.

I asked Bryant if he was carrying any cash. He was, since he had already been on the run for a day longer than I had, and with more prep time. I gave him instructions and told him to meet me at the exit at the opposite side of the ground floor in fifteen minutes. The in-store signs told me those doors would bring us out on Fourth Avenue.

He nodded, and we split up. I realized that this was the first time I'd given him a real option about whether to stick with me or pull a fade, and wondered if he'd be dumb enough to run. In all honesty, it would make things easier for me. Who knew—perhaps my pursuers would leave Bryant alone, correctly assuming that he knew nothing. Then I thought about the gun pointed at Jessica Allen's head in LA. The man with the glasses didn't like loose ends. He might try to get information out of Bryant, or he might simply put a bullet in his head to tidy up. Either way, they would find him, and he would have no chance to defend himself, if he even saw them coming.

The ground floor was mostly taken up by the cosmetics department. I crossed the floor through an atmosphere composed of a thousand mixed scents, noting the positions of the store cameras. Another good thing about a department store of this kind: the building had been renovated, extended and refitted time and again over a century or so. Plenty of camera blind spots. I found a perfect such blind spot in an alcove that led into a choice of two routes. I pulled the coat off, balled the light fabric up in my hands, and stuffed it behind a large potted plant in the corner. I waited a few seconds for a group of senior citizens to pass by, and then tagged along with them as they headed for the elevators. It would be far from impossible for someone to piece together my movements from the different cameras later, but it would take time. I left the group at the elevators and took the stairs to the sixth floor, which I noted from the store directory held both the menswear department and customer restrooms.

I passed through the AV department on the way. Some of the display televisions were showing news channels, with footage from the airport. I tried not to stare at the screens, but was reassured that I didn't see my own face or Bryant's. The on-screen text looked pretty vague: SHOOTING AT SEA-TAC.

I selected jeans, a flannel shirt, a winter coat, gloves, and a pair of boots, together with cheap hair clippers, batteries, and a pair of nonprescription glasses. I paid cash and headed for the restrooms. There was one guy washing up at the row of sinks, taking his time. I waited for him to leave, then took his place at the sinks. I took a second to examine myself in the mirror, running my fingers through my hair. It had been getting a little long, anyway. I inserted the batteries into the clippers and set the cut length to a number one—just short of an induction cut. I got to work.

Five minutes later I'd flushed the clumps of my hair down one of the toilets and changed into the new clothes in the cubicle. I stood on the toilet seat and lifted one of the ceiling panels. I stuffed my suit, shirt, and shoes into the crawl space. I tried not to think about how much I had paid for that suit.

I put the glasses on, unlocked the door, and made for the stairs again.

When I reached the Fourth Avenue exit, I thought at first that Bryant had taken the option to run. Then I realized that he had done a pretty good job of changing his look himself. He wore a long black overcoat, a green sweater, and a beanie hat.

I thought again about John Stafford, expecting the two of us in California in a couple hours' time. He was going to be waiting a while longer.

"What now?" Bryant asked.

I looked across the street and saw a road sign directing traffic toward King Street Station. "Now," I said, "we get the hell out of town."

TWENTY-SIX

New York

FARADAY DRUMMED HER fingers on her desk as she waited for the connection.

She disliked waiting for a call to be put through to one of her operatives at the best of times, and this was far from the best of times. And then the quality of the silence on the other end of the phone changed subtly and she knew he was there.

"Tell me what the hell went wrong at the airport, Usher."

"I don't think anything did go wrong."

"David Mendez begs to differ."

Usher mulled over that for a second, as though it were a trick question. "Who's David Mendez?"

"The taxi driver who wound up dead in the middle of the road."

Usher didn't continue along that line of discussion. "We located the target. He could have been anywhere in Seattle, but one of our surveillances paid off. I'd say we made very good progress. Had we had a little more notice…"

"Then what? You wouldn't have shot up a civilian airport and still managed to let your target escape?"

"I decided—"

"This was supposed to be sub rosa, Usher. I'm not

popular with Homeland Security or the Pentagon right now. Seattle PD are pissed, and I expect the FBI will be, too, when they find out they can't touch this. I'm investing time and favors keeping a lid on something that should have been taken care of quietly. I thought you were good at quiet."

There was silence on the other end of the line. Faraday could feel herself beginning to lose her grip on her temper and wondered if there was anything she could say that would rattle Usher. In many ways he was the model operative. He followed instructions to the letter, always doing exactly what was asked with single-minded, sometimes brutal efficiency. But for some reason, Faraday worried about him. She wondered what would happen the day they gave him an order he didn't like. Most of the men in the unit were killers—they had to be—but she could honestly say that Usher was the only one who made her uneasy. And that was unacceptable.

She made a mental note that a tougher line would have to be taken with him. He would have to be kept on a tighter leash in the future. But not until Carter Blake was in custody, or in the ground.

"Usher? Are you still there?"

When he spoke again, his voice was level, reasonable. "We had a shot. The decision was made to take it."

The decision was made. Like it was out of his hands. Faraday sighed.

"I don't want to have to clean up any more messes, all right? There's only so far you can push need-to-know. When they autopsy that driver, they're going to want to know why they can't speak to the shooter." Usher said nothing. Faraday sighed inwardly, wondering what so-

lution she'd expected him to suggest that would make
this all better. "Okay. You're in touch with the rest of
the team?"

"We've rerouted everyone back to base." He was referring to the temporary operations center they'd set up
in a Marriott hotel downtown. "We're IDing potential
search zones right now. News says the police have no
trace of the taxi."

"Thank God for small mercies."

"If they do pick up Blake, we'll need to extract him
from custody, of course."

"We'll cross that bridge when we come to it, but not
without my authorization. Is that clear?"

"It's clear."

"That's good. Now, tell me you're making better
progress than our friends in the police."

"Blake is still in the area. He can't have stayed on the
freeway long in that car, so we're working off the first
couple of exits as a starting point. I think he'll try to lie
low. If he wants to get out of Seattle, he has limited options. He can't rent a car without his license, and he certainly can't fly. That narrows down the options a little."

"Good. It's just unfortunate that he knows how close
we are now."

Usher said nothing.

"Okay," she said after a minute. "Get to it. And,
Usher?"

"Yes?"

"Try not to kill anyone else."

TWENTY-SEVEN

Seattle

IF I HAD been in any doubt when I received the e-mail showing Martinez's body, the shoot-out at the airport had cleared it up. I was on Winterlong's kill list, and it didn't look like they were choosey about when or where it happened. Or who got in the way.

I knew why they wanted me dead. It was because I possessed something that could, perhaps, take down the whole organization. Five years ago, that had been my bulletproof vest. Now it seemed it was no longer enough to protect me. Martinez had had the same bargaining chip after all, and it hadn't kept him alive. That meant they had found him and somehow forced him to give up what he had. Or maybe they had taken a gamble, decided he wouldn't have trusted anyone else with knowledge of where he had stashed it. It was the same problem I had faced: As soon as anybody else knew about it, it lost its value.

One thing was clear: I needed to get my hands on that bargaining chip. If I couldn't stop them from coming after me, I could make damn sure they'd have too much on their plate to worry about me. The only problem? The Moonola assignment had taken me about as far away from home turf as it was possible to get without leaving the country.

Flying or renting a car were both now out of the question. Stealing a car would only make it more likely we'd be picked up by the cops—which almost sounded like a good idea, except that the police would hand us over five seconds after somebody waved the Patriot Act in their faces. I needed a way to cross the country as quickly as possible without having to show identification or otherwise draw attention to myself. We didn't have time to hitchhike, so that limited our options to the bus or the train. A bus would be too small, with too few passengers and nowhere to hide. That left one option.

Amtrak ran seven long-haul routes out of King Street Station every day. The eastern-bound service, which was called the Empire Builder, ran over two thousand miles to Chicago across the Rockies, taking almost two full days to reach its destination. Chicago would get us close to where I needed to be, and perhaps even allow me to get Bryant to something like safety.

The plan wasn't perfect, by any means. The unavoidable fact that my travel options had been so curtailed meant that this mode of travel could be predicted. I just had to hope that the man in glasses and his friends would be spread thin enough to give us a chance. The train would give us some important advantages over a bus or any other kind of mass transit: personal space. We could hole up for the two days, eat meals in quarters, and be on the lookout just in case.

King Street Station wasn't far from Macy's. Its hundred-year-old redbrick tower stood out from the more modern skyscrapers that towered over it. We were in luck: The Empire Builder's single departure for the day was scheduled for four forty, in just over half an hour.

The ticket desk stretched around one corner of the large, high-ceilinged waiting area. There was a bank of screens in the middle of the concourse, some of them displaying departure and arrival times, one tuned to a news channel. I gave in to my curiosity, slowing my pace a little as I passed. I tried not to look too interested, but then again, there were plenty of other travelers grouped around the screens. Some were watching the news with interest. Just as many were more concerned with whether or not their train was going to be delayed.

There was no sound, just the same few camera angles refreshed in a cycle. I guessed some were live, and some, like the footage of an ambulance hurriedly leaving the scene, were from earlier in the day. The views alternated between some stony-faced cops guarding crime scene tape, a wide shot of passengers staring resignedly at departure boards, and a shot of the airport drop-off area from farther away. Thanks to the restricted airspace around the airport, the only image missing was a helicopter view of the crime scene.

The ticker along the bottom of the screen provided the basics of a story on a loop. The heading had changed to, TERROR AT SEA-TAC?

I liked the question mark—it suggested that nobody knew exactly what had happened. Nobody who was cooperating with the media, anyway. The bullet points scrolling by hadn't been updated much in the last hour: *One dead in shooting; Police seeking two unidentified male suspects; Air traffic disrupted.*

I watched the updates and the images for long enough to be satisfied that, even if the police knew our identities, they had not released them to the press. Otherwise there would be names and pictures on the screen. Winterlong was keeping us to themselves for the time being. I didn't know whether to be grateful or not.

The news changed to another story then: the weather alert in the Northeast. There was a big blizzard due to hit New York State and the surrounding areas at some point in the next two days. Emergency planning was in full effect. I hoped that wouldn't cause me any problems.

I examined the ticket desk. I could see security cameras covering each of the stations. The one at the far end was a little smaller than the others, and a cluttered shelf meant there was a partial obstruction in front of the cam. I picked that one, and asked for two Chicago-bound tickets on the Empire Builder. The bald, bespectacled guy behind the desk barely glanced at me, tapping away at his keyboard.

"Coach seats?"

"Do you have any cabins left?" I wasn't sure of the exact terminology, but I needed a door I could lock at night.

He didn't look up at me, just said, "A Superline Roomette?"

"Does it have a door?"

"Yes."

"Okay, then."

He kept tapping away and then told me how much it would be. I got a reaction at last when I slid nine hundred-dollar bills across the desk. I waited for him to tell me they only accepted credit cards, like the woman at the United desk, but then he shrugged and counted the bills out, before pushing my change back along with the tickets. Cash purchase, no ID. Maybe I would travel this way in the future. If there was a future.

I made my way back to where Bryant was waiting.

"So where are we going?"

"East," I said.

"Specific. Nice."

"We're headed to Chicago first. I know someone there who might be able to help."

"Chicago's cold this time of year."

"Well, we have two days to acclimatize."

We waited until the last possible moment to board the train, climbing on to the coach car next to the front locomotive, three cars ahead of the one we were booked onto. The hum of the idling engine kicked up a notch as soon as the doors closed. Brakes hissed and metal squealed as the lumbering behemoth slowly started to break free of its inertia. The train swayed as it picked up speed and we crossed through the next couple of cars: the first fully-seated, the next containing sleeping roomettes. The cars were double-decked. I checked the number on the ticket as we passed into the next one and found our roomette, in the middle of the lower level. The door opened onto a small space, no more than four feet deep by seven wide. There were two seats facing each other that converted into a bed, along with another bed, which folded down from the wall for the top bunk. A picture window almost the full width of the room showed the last of the platform passing by as we moved out of King Street.

I heard Bryant whistle skeptically behind me as he caught up and surveyed the roomette. "Tell me you don't snore."

"Don't worry about it," I said. "We won't be sleeping at the same time."

I ducked under the low doorframe and stepped into the tiny space. It would be a long two days. I had no gun, no phone, and virtually no money left. But at least I was reasonably sure that nobody besides Bryant and me knew exactly where we were. Dusk was already beginning to fall. I sat down on the nearest seat and watched as the train passed by the towers of Seattle, headed east. Into the cold.

TWENTY-EIGHT

WE ROLLED ON at a steady fifty miles an hour. Once we had cleared the city, Bryant announced that he could use a nap. He pulled down the top bunk and climbed up into it, grunting as he adjusted his body into the tight space. I sat down on the seat underneath, watching as the world rolled past outside.

It was the first time I had just sat and looked out of a window for as long as I could remember. I had no laptop to work on, no files to read, no phone. I didn't even have a book to read. I had no easy way of checking on the news or anything happening in the outside world. In a way, I savored it. Of course, the circumstances were not of my choosing, but it felt like a gift: an opportunity to take stock, to plan my next move.

I like to work alone. It's not just part of the sales pitch—I'm at my best when the only person I know I need to rely on is me. However, there are times when you need someone else to help out, and my current situation dictated that this was one of those times. I needed to get Bryant somewhere safe, and that somewhere had to be away from me. The question I kept asking myself was, was it right to endanger yet another person—one of the few people I cared about—even if I needed their help badly? I counted the people who had died already, either because they could provide a lead to me, or just because they'd gotten in the way. Martinez. Coop. The

taxi driver at the airport. I didn't want to add another
body to the list.

The suburbs of Seattle were soon gone, and then
we were out on what was once called the Great Northern Railway. We pushed east across Washington State,
passing through Edmonds and Everett as the sky became fully dark, reaching the long tunnel through the
Cascade Range sometime after six o'clock. Once we'd
passed through nearly three miles of darkness at the
heart of the mountain range, we emerged into what
seemed like another season again. Snow blanketed the
ground, the rolling landscape of white seeming to emit
a soft luminescence in the dark.

I made up my mind. Our eventual destination was
serendipitous—it seemed like fate was offering an opportunity.

Bryant was still sound asleep in the bunk. I got up
and opened the door. The passageway was empty in
both directions. I checked I had the key and pulled the
door shut, listening as the lock clicked into place automatically.

The lounge car was five cars down. It was lined with
windows that curved upward into the ceiling, where
passengers could hang out during the day and take in
the view. At the far end was a wall-mounted pay phone,
which, naturally, didn't take coins. There was a small
shop, and I picked up sandwiches, two bottles of water
and some fruit, as well as a prepaid phone card. There
were some paperback novels on sale, so I bought the
latest Stephen King and a couple of other books with
interesting covers. Staring out of the window was all
very well, but I might as well take full advantage of this
impromptu vacation.

I used the phone card to dial a number from memory. I hoped the person I was calling hadn't changed her cell number. I smiled when the ringing stopped and a familiar voice answered.

"Hello?"

I cleared my throat and tried to sound as casual as possible. "Hey, remember me?"

There was an uncertain pause, and I wondered again if I'd made a mistake.

"Blake?" Special Agent Elaine Banner sounded surprised to hear my voice. I didn't know whether it was a good or a bad surprise. We hadn't spoken since I had helped her track down a prolific serial sniper named Caleb Wardell in Chicago. In the course of that job, I had saved Banner's daughter's life and Banner had saved mine. That's the kind of experience that builds mutual trust. Or so I hoped.

"How comfortable are you talking on this phone?"

"It's secure," she said, though she and I knew that was relative. It was secure only as far as the balance of probability said nobody looking for me would be tapping a federal agent's phone hundreds of miles away. After a second, she added, "But let me give you another number, just in case."

She read out what I guessed was the number of her personal phone, and I memorized that one as well before hanging up and redialing. A minute later we were talking again.

"So what do you need?"

Same old Banner—no time wasted finding out if this was a social call to catch up after all these months. I wasn't sure she'd have welcomed such a call from me, in any case.

"I'm in a little trouble," I said. I quickly explained the key events of the last few hours: the photograph of Martinez's body that told me I was being hunted. Coop's murder down in Florida. The shooting at the airport.

"That explains it," she said when I mentioned the airport.

"How do you mean?"

"The Sea-Tac thing. Homeland Security have a lid on it tighter than two coats of paint. Lots of speculation, no IDs on the suspects. Now I know at least part of the reason."

"Let me guess—need-to-know, national security, all that kind of thing?"

"That's about right. What the hell did you do, Blake? I mean, Homeland Security is after you?"

"No. Not Homeland Security. Somebody who can make a call to Homeland Security and has enough pull for some no-questions-asked cover from them. For the time being, at least."

"On second thought, I don't want to know. I mean, I can just about give you the benefit of the doubt that you're not a terrorist."

"Which is why you remain one of my very favorite FBI agents."

"Skip it," she said. "Just tell me what you need."

I did as requested, giving her the basics. No more information than she needed, and leaving out where exactly I was. Not because I thought Banner would tell anybody, but because it was in both our interests if she didn't know too much. Finally, I explained that I was carrying some excess baggage in the form of a two-hundred-pound fugitive software developer and that sticking together wasn't likely to result in a pleasant outcome for either of us.

She listened, not interrupting again after the airport part. When I finished, she was quiet for a moment. I wondered if she was thinking, or just considering whether or not to hang up and forget she had ever met me. To tell the truth, I wouldn't have blamed her if she had. I hated to ask her for help, but with Coop dead, she was one of the only people in the world I trusted to be able to help us without putting herself in harm's way. And she was certainly the only one within easy reach of any of the stops on the Empire Builder route.

"Bad luck seems to follow you around, Blake," she said at last.

"That it does."

And then she started talking and I realized she hadn't been considering not helping me. She had just been working everything out in her head. "Okay, I have an off-the-books safe house we might be able to use. Let me make a few calls. It'll only be for a few days, max."

"A few days is great. In a few days I'll have made this go away, or…"

"I get the picture. How close are you right now?"

I turned and looked out the window at the dark landscape rushing past. "We're taking the long way," I said. "We'll be there in two days: Saturday, evening time."

There was a pause, and I could tell she had already worked out how I was traveling. She had the grace not to mention it.

"That's good. Give me some time to set things up quietly. What number do I call you on?"

"You don't. This has to be our last conversation until Saturday night."

"All right. So you better tell me everything you need now."

I laid out what we'd need to safely stash Bryant away, plus a few more requests that would entail Banner breaking a few more state and federal laws and putting her career in jeopardy. At the end of it, she simply said, "Okay. Let's say seven o'clock. You remember the last place we saw each other?"

"Of course." I wasn't likely to forget, for a couple of reasons. This was going to be a different kind of meeting altogether.

"See you then," she said, getting ready to hang up. I stopped her.

"Banner... Thank you."

"I'll see you on Saturday."

The line went dead. I held the handset for a moment before replacing it. The odds were still stacked against me. Even if everything went to plan in Chicago, I still had a long way to go to get clear of this. A hell of a long way. But for the first time in twenty-four hours, it felt like I'd managed to wrestle back some small measure of control over my destiny.

FIVE YEARS AGO

Kandahar, Afghanistan

IT HAD BEEN hotter the last time I had visited Kandahar. The daylight hours were still relatively warm, even in November, but the nights brought bone-chilling temperatures when it was clear, and sometimes snow. We had passed the wrecks of old Soviet-era armor on the way in: tanks and BTR-60s, lying abandoned in the desert like a warning. It had been less than three weeks since I had received that unwanted call from Murphy, but it seemed like a lot longer.

In truth, I'd been keeping too busy to think about Carol all that often. I hadn't even thought too much about my conversations with Senator Carlson. Because so far, the job we had been assigned had reminded me of why I did what I did.

It was one of those operations for which Winterlong was perfectly equipped. A bomb maker building his notoriety through a series of deadly coordinated attacks across Afghanistan and across the border into Pakistan. All the indications were that he had the skills and ruthlessness to escalate to worse—and potentially on US soil. His nom de guerre translated as the "Wolf."

The trouble was, that was virtually the only thing that was known about him. Whereas the US military's other high-value targets had their images and vital statistics plastered over posters and printed on cards carried by troops in the field, the Wolf was an enigma. The local CIA operatives and others had been trying in vain to identify the Wolf for the best part of eighteen months. Along the way, some had speculated that there was no Wolf, that it was a propaganda exercise capitalizing on a general upswing in the professionalism and effectiveness of the Taliban insurgents. But the investigation teams clearing up after the many suicide attacks credited to the Wolf showed that there was a consistent signature. A hallmark to each of his atrocities.

A bomb disposal tech who had defused one of his efforts in downtown Kabul had given him another name: "the Michael Jordan of bombers." The guy was good. There was a seemingly inexhaustible supply of angry young men willing to drive his bombs into military checkpoints or crowded marketplaces, and it was difficult to do anything about that, short-term. But if the source of the lethally effective car and truck bombs could be traced and eliminated, it would save a lot of lies.

But it had been eighteen months, and nobody could find the Wolf's lair. The best intelligence we had suggested his base of operations was Kandahar, in the south of the country. Cross-referencing the bombing locations had suggested that, as did an intercepted message that suggested the Wolf made his home somewhere in the city.

So as time went by with no results, the sense of frustration began to reach higher in the command pyramid, until somebody made a call and six men were chosen. The assignment was standard: Go in with a small team and as much time as we need, build the intelligence, zero the target, put him out of action. Throwing man-power at the situation hadn't worked, so the powers that be had decreed that it was time for a subtler approach.

There were two shooters: Dixon, two hundred and fifty pounds of muscle with a penchant for using knives, and Murphy, the oldest member of the team. Murphy was a little less physically imposing than Dixon, but more than made up for it in understated intelligence. There were two signals intelligence specialists: Martinez was tall, a little younger than the rest of us, and either aloof or just quiet. Collins was smaller and more wiry, with premature gray hair. Collins was in operational command, but by the nature of the setup, that didn't mean much from minute to minute. It just meant that he had final say when more than one potential course of action presented itself.

That left myself and Ortega on front of house, as well called it. Meaning we handled hum-int, or human intelligence: the people part of the equation. Ortega was a little shorter than average, with a straight scar down the right side of his face and a mean streak a mile wide.

I had worked with only two of the other five men before, and I didn't particularly like either of them. Murphy was a skilled operator, and amiable enough, but I knew I could trust him about as far as I could spit him. As for Dixon... From our brief encounters, it was clear he was one of Drakakis's black hats. In a unit as secretive as this one, with every mission hermetically sealed, there was a whole lot I didn't know about the guy. But the rumors fit well with my impression of the man and with the file Carlson had shown me in New York. Something was broken inside him, and I was starting to think it was the character trait that made him most useful to our superiors.

But we had a job to do, and until I figured out an exit strategy and a way to give Senator Carlson what he needed, this job was one that needed doing. After two weeks of painstaking work building on the existing intelligence, I had finally shaken loose a promising lead. The only problem was, I was required to follow up on it alone. Sneaking in someone else as backup simply wasn't worth the risk, in terms of the mission.

Moving around the city in daylight hours was never the preferred option, so I was still unsure that I'd made the right decision as Murphy dropped me off at the street corner my contact had named. I hadn't written the directions down, but I knew where to go from here.

"Keep your phone on," Murphy said quietly as I stepped out of the car onto the street. The omnipresent smell of dirty car fumes assaulted my nose. "I'll see you back at the safe house at fourteen hundred."

I nodded. I certainly hoped I would.

The street corner was at the far end of a bazaar, beside a fruit store with its freshest and most colorful wares displayed outside to tempt passersby. I walked to the farthest of these and pretended to examine a mountain of pomegranates, then turned and raised my eyes to the second floor of the building across the way. There was a row of small windows, each one above a door on the ground level. I counted along the row. Three windows from the right-hand side of the building, there was a red vase in the center of the ledge. My eyes dropped down to the door immediately below.

I patted the right-hand side of my chest gently to reassure myself that my Beretta M9 was still there, and waited for a gap in the traffic to cross the road. The door was plain and unadorned, apart from a circular handle. I twisted the handle and found it unlocked, as expected. It opened onto an unlit passageway: stone floor, stucco walls. I closed the door behind me, as per my detailed instructions, immediately glad to be off the busy street.

There was another door at the far end that was ajar and let in just enough daylight to see by. There were two closed doors on the left-hand side of the corridor. I ignored them and made for the one that was open. As I got close to the sliver of daylight, I felt an unfamiliar tightness in my chest. I hesitated at the door and listened, not sure what I expected to hear. If I was walking into a trap, whoever was out there wouldn't be making any noise. Up until this moment, I had been sure enough that this offer was legit. I was happy with the risk-to-benefit balance. But now, standing in front of this door, I suddenly felt a great unease. I swallowed it down and forced my mind to work on a purely operational level. I drew my weapon, clicked the safety off, and held it down by my side. I held my breath and pushed the door open all the way.

It gave onto a small, dusty courtyard. The sun was directly overhead. My eyes darted to cover the space, finding no one at ground level before catching movement above. I raised my gun, then quickly dropped it again when I saw a woman in a burqa hanging brightly colored laundry over the railing of her balcony. I turned my body to the side to conceal my gun as she glanced down and eyed me briefly with disinterest.

I let out the breath and passed quickly across the center of the courtyard to the doorway on the opposite side. This one was just a gap in the wall. Bare, rusted hinges told me there had once been a door there, but not for a long time. Through that, there was another unlit corridor with an unlocked door at the end. This one let me out on a narrow alleyway.

For the first time since I had left the car, the miasma of smog was blotted out by an even more pungent aroma. An irrigation ditch ran down the edge of the alley, filled with raw sewage. I remembered the instructions—turn left, then knock on the fourth door on the right.

The fourth door was a slab of featureless steel with one unadorned keyhole and a narrow slit-hatch. No handle. I knocked softly four times. The hatch opened after a second.

"Yes?"

I answered in Pashto, telling him I was a friend of Karim's. I had no idea who the hell Karim was, but it was what I'd been instructed to say.

There was a pause. If this really was a trap, I was about to know about it.

"Do you have a gun?" he asked, in English.

I hesitated and then took the Beretta out again, holding it up slowly by the muzzle, taking great care not to point anywhere near the hatch.

"Pass it through. The butt first."

I did as I was asked, adding my own wordless condition by removing the magazine first. The gun was pulled inside, and then there was silence for almost a minute. Long enough for me to start wondering if I'd been had.

But then I heard the rattle of a big key turning in the lock, and the door swung silently outward on greased hinges.

A tall, bearded Arab man stood before me, dressed in the standard dishdasha. He held a Colt .45 pointed squarely at my midsection. He looked me over and then he jerked his head back.

"Come in."

I entered a small, enclosed vestibule. I wasn't surprised when the tall man immediately gripped the back of my shirt and pushed me against the wall, frisking me for a second weapon. He didn't find any—I was traveling light. When he was satisfied, he lowered his gun and told me to go through into the building. I entered what I now realized was the back room of a store. DVDs in plastic wallets were stacked high on shelving units lining each wall, mostly pirated Hollywood blockbusters and porn. There were boxes of cheap phones, too. I would know where to come next time I needed a supply of burners. In the far corner was a small office desk with a laptop and one of those banker's lamps with the green shades. It seemed oddly out of place.

"Have a seat," my new friend said, indicating the swivel chair in front of the desk.

I did as asked, and looked up expectantly. He lit a cigarette, taking his time, and inhaled deeply.

"I am Ahmad," he said finally, offering his hand.

I shook it. "Call me Smith," I said. I saw his brown eyes flicker with amusement. We had picked equally anonymous pseudonyms. It was almost a sign of mutual respect: neither of us wanted to insult the other's intelligence by even attempting to pretend we were using our real names. Each of us knew that Ahmad and Smith would cease to exist the moment this meeting was over.

"The money is okay?" Ahmad asked, meaning, had I gotten it authorized?

"It is. All I need is the name. Who is the Wolf?"

"Better than that, my friend, I have a name and an address."

I was intrigued. "That would certainly make my job easier."

He smirked. "I don't think so."

"I don't understand."

He handed me a slip of paper with some Arabic script at the top. Below it was an address translated to English, printed in small, neat capitals. "The man you are looking for is currently at this house. He goes by the name Ajmal al Wazir."

I recognized the name, and started to get an inkling of what the smirk a moment ago had meant. The only rich people in Afghanistan are the politicians. The reason for that is they get to skim from any money that comes into the country for infrastructure. If twenty million comes earmarked for building schools, each level of the establishment takes a cut along the way, so that perhaps a few hundred thousand makes it to the school-building program. In Kandahar, many of the top levels of that tree of corruption held the name Wazir.

"The al Wazirs are hiding the Wolf?"

He shook his head. "Not hiding. He is one of them. And now you see why this was so expensive?" He studied me, as though expecting me to challenge him on the information.

"Give me two hours. If this checks out, you get the bonus."

"Okay," he said after a moment, and handed me back my gun. "A pleasure doing business with you. When you go back out there, turn right instead of left, and the alley will bring you out on Shafakhana Sarak."

"Thank you."

"Good luck, Smith."

I holstered my weapon, then left the way I had come in. I took the right and emerged onto the bustling thoroughfare of Shafakhana Sarak. I watched the people walking to and fro, as heedless of anything else as any Western pedestrians going about their business in the big city. I wondered how they could do that, when the risk of being suddenly blown to pieces was exponentially higher than in New York or London or Berlin. Because of men like the Wolf.

If my target really was member of the house of al Wazir, it explained why it had taken so much effort and money to get his location.

The safe house was just under two miles away in the Zoar Shar area of the city. Old Kandahar. It wasn't hard to navigate through the back alleys by recalling the map in my head.

As I walked, I returned to the other question that had been keeping me awake nights, when the hard work of the mission took a break from distracting me. What the senator had said hadn't exactly surprised me—that was the worst thing about it. I had been wondering for the last couple of weeks whether Carlson's mole was with us on this mission, and if so, which of the other five he was. I almost didn't care. I wanted to do the job, go home, and disappear—forget about Winterlong and Carlson. All of a sudden, the quiet, building urge I'd had for the past few months to get out of this organization had become an imperative.

Up until my meeting with the senator, it had been a job I'd enjoyed, been good at, and thought was worthwhile. We kept operations separate and secret out of necessity—because that was the way it had to be. But some of the rumors I had heard, some of the things I'd seen with my own eyes, had had me calling everything into question. The senator's file had provided the other pieces of the puzzle.

Why hadn't I quit before? For one thing, I knew deep down it wouldn't be as easy as that. For another, I didn't have anyone or anything giving me a compelling reason to quit. But that was the other thing that had changed in New York. Now there was someone. I realized at that moment that that was why I had suddenly felt so uneasy walking into that courtyard. Things were different now, and not just because of what the senator had said.

Things were different because I had something to lose.

FRIDAY, JANUARY 8TH

TWENTY-NINE

Idaho

THE MOTION OF the train slowing roused me from a half dream. From the bunk above me, I could hear Bryant snoring softly. I looked out of the window and saw a single-side platform and an old station building with a covered waiting area out front. The blue sign above the door to the station building said, SANDPOINT, ID. I checked my watch. It was two thirty-five a.m., which meant that we were still on schedule. I stared out at the platform. Aside from a Pepsi machine casting out its blue glow, there wasn't a lot to see. Nobody getting off, nobody getting on. The train pulled out, and I settled back in the seat, closing my eyes. It would be three hours until we stopped again, after we'd passed into Montana, and I looked forward to getting a couple hours of uninterrupted sleep.

After twenty minutes, I gave up on that idea and sat up, gazing out the window as the freezing night passed by, thinking about what was behind and what was ahead.

If we were lucky, all we had to do was stay put until Saturday and Chicago. Leaving Bryant behind in Seattle would have made some things easier, but it hadn't ever been an option. Winterlong would have found him, and as soon as they figured out he had no useful information, they would have killed him. If Banner could get Bryant to relative safety, it would be one less thing for me to worry about. But I would still have a long way to go from there.

The people who were pursuing me knew that eventually I would have to go back home. The only question was how long it would take them to nail down the location of home.

I thought about the precautions I had taken over the last five years and knew there were a few areas where they had been less than perfect. Inevitable compromises I'd had to make that could be exploited with the right information, the necessary skills, and a little luck. In truth, I knew I could have pulled off a perfect disappearance, if I had really wanted to, but that would have required a total withdrawal from the world.

From day one, I had known I was never going to open a repair shop or man the pumps at a rural gas station. The obvious reason was that I needed an income to live off the grid in relative comfort, unless I wanted to go the mountain man route. But it was more than that. When you find something you're good at, it's not so easy to walk away from it.

So, the best part of a year on from what had happened in Afghanistan, I began to test the waters. I contacted people I knew of who could put me in touch with the right clients. People like Coop, who specialized in finding work in the private sector for people like me. Beyond assessing that I had the requisite skills and experience, he didn't ask about me and I didn't volunteer anything. That wouldn't have made me any different from the vast majority of his clients: former CIA and NSA and military intelligence types whose ex-employers might frown on their taking all of that expensive government training and putting it to uses that may or may not be approved of by Uncle Sam.

For a while I told myself that I was a needle in a haystack. In the second decade of the twenty-first century, the subterranean market for secondhand spies and special operators was booming like never before. I knew it would be impossible for me to work without leaving any trail at all, of course, but that trail would lead back to Carter Blake, not who I was before. And Carter Blake was a cypher, a dead end. I hadn't counted on my cover being blown by a run-in with the past.

I tried to think about how *I* would find me. I knew that air travel was the big hole in my cover. I had had no choice but to fly unless I wanted to drive everywhere, which wasn't practical. The kind of jobs I was offered spanned the country: Florida one day, California the next. I had resisted the offers to work overseas so far, so that I didn't need to worry about a fake passport. Because no one could tie the name Carter Blake to my previous life, I decided keeping the same ID for flying was within the realm of acceptable risk. If things got out, I could discard the name and find another just as easily.

What I didn't bet on was being nailed on national TV: my picture and my name broadcast across the country in association with a case in which Winterlong was already taking great interest, because it concerned another of their former operatives: Dean Crozier, latterly known as the Samaritan.

So now someone with the right skills and the necessary level of tenacity and access to data protection overrides could start to map the movements of Carter Blake over the past few years and begin to build up a pattern. I had made a point of varying the airports I used within reach of home. I had been careful, but I hadn't been *obsessively* careful.

I realized now that I should have dropped the Blake identity after Los Angeles. Laid low for a while. But I had been complacent, relying on the fact I had leverage, or thought I did. I thought I would see them coming. In the end, it probably wouldn't have made any difference. It would have been closing the stable door after the horse had bolted.

Again, I wondered what had changed. I had taken steps to make sure I was a hard man to track down, but my strongest precaution was my deterrent: the Black Book. Drakakis knew if he made a move on me and screwed it up, it would be the end for him. For some reason, whoever had succeeded him had decided the risk of leaving me in the game outweighed the risk of eliminating me.

But the reason they were coming for me was academic, when it came down to it. The stalemate of the past few years was over. The personal cold war between me and Winterlong had burst into life, and the next move had to be mine.

THIRTY

Seattle

THE TEMPORARY OP center in the Marriott had been a hive of activity all night, but Stark could sense the frustration building in the room as dawn began to break with no new leads since the airport. Where the hell were they? It seemed as though Carter Blake and Scott Bryant had dropped off the face of the earth after slipping the noose at Sea-Tac. Stark wondered what Blake had decided to do: stay put, or get out. After hours of monitoring the police search and chasing up fruitless leads throughout the city, his hunch was that it had to be the latter. Seattle obviously wasn't home turf for Blake— he had only been there in pursuit of this Bryant guy.

In the absence of any better ideas, catching Bryant was their strongest lead for the moment. Blake would probably part company with him as soon as possible, and he would be easy enough to run down. He might be able to give them some idea of where Blake was headed. He surveyed the other three men in the room: Ortega and Usher, plus a relatively new addition to the team named Travers, who was monitoring police communications and keeping in touch with the four men they had around the city. For the moment it felt like he and the others were spinning their wheels.

Stark snapped out of his thoughts as he saw Travers

stop whatever he was doing on the laptop and put a finger to the earpiece of the headset. He listened intently, nodding when he was sure of the message.

"The found the taxi."

Stark crossed the room and stood next to him expectantly. "The police found it?"

"Yeah. It's coming through over the scanner."

"Finally. Where the hell did they dump it?"

"They're saying…" Travers called up a satellite shot on the laptop screen and indicated a spot on the screen. "Here. About four miles from Sea-Tac. It was concealed. No sign of the suspects."

Stark shook his head. "That's just off the damn freeway. How the hell did they miss it for this long?"

"You know how it is—lot of ground to cover," Travers said.

"No way they're still in the city now," Ortega said. "Blake's in the wind."

Ortega had an old, white scar down the right-hand side of his side. The scar wasn't so noticeable when his features were composed, but it distorted his expressions a little when he smiled or frowned, as he was doing just now.

Travers looked up from the screen, looking at each of the two older men in turn, as though expecting a solution. "So what do we do now? Wait for another shot at him?"

Stark sighed. "That's going to be difficult."

"We tracked him down once," Ortega reminded him.

"We used a one-time-only tactic. We'd been onto Cooper for weeks, waiting for the right time. We don't get to do that again, for obvious reasons. We had one chance at the airport—we could have done it quietly, tailed him until he was cornered, but Usher had to start shooting."

Usher, who had kept quiet until now, chose this moment to speak. "I told you," he said quietly. "I had no choice."

"Really?" Stark said, turning to look at him. "All he was doing was getting in a cab. We could have dealt with that differently, is all I'm saying. We could have tailed him. We could have waited and got a drop-off address from the cab company. But instead we were left behind explaining a dead civilian to Deputy Dawg while Blake left us in his dust."

"He's right," Ortega said. "Blake was careful before. Now he's going to be invisible. We had precious little on him as it was: a name, an MO, and, for a few hours, a cell number. Now the phone's gone and he'll ditch the name, too. He's completely off the grid. We don't have any fucking clue where he could be going."

Stark slapped his palm down on the desk in front of Travers in frustration. He walked over to the wall where they'd hung the map of the city, finding the spot where the taxi had been dumped and placing it in the context of the whole area.

"Okay, let's go back over it. At least now we know he didn't drive out of the city, at least not right away, and we know where he was at about one o'clock yesterday afternoon. Cops are searching the vicinity, but if he's smart"—he caught himself and gave a wry smile—"which we know he is, he'll have gotten out of there immediately."

He stood back and looked at the spot on the map, letting his focus creep out to the surrounding geography.

"There's a stop for the light-rail airport link close by. That would take him right back into the center of town."

"Doesn't mean he used it," Ortega said.

"Doesn't mean anything at all," Stark said. "But he was off guard. Improvising. It's likely he would go with the flow. I think he headed back into the city, and there's nothing else around there. We still don't know if he's holed up somewhere, or if he managed to get out of town." He turned away from the map and looked at Travers. "Find out if the light-rail has cameras."

Travers nodded and looked down at his laptop. Ortega joined Stark at the map, glancing in turn at the circled locations where they'd spread their resources. The air was closed to Blake, and he didn't have a car. He couldn't easily procure one, either—not without being unsure of whether he'd just tagged himself once again. Rental was out, and either stealing or buying one cash would leave another person with the knowledge of his mode of transport, if the link was made. That left public transportation, assuming he didn't decide to walk or hitchhike. Because of Seattle's isthmuslike geography, most of the transportation routes in the metropolitan area passed through the heart of the city. Taking the highways out of the equation, that left bus, rail, and ferry. With no trace of Blake since the airport until now, there had been too many options to narrow down in too long a time period.

With a little luck, that was about to change.

THIRTY-ONE

New York City

AFTER NEARLY TWENTY straight hours of dead ends, Faraday received the latest update from Seattle with cautious optimism. Her first instinct had been to help the information along a little by releasing Blake's picture to the FBI, with strict orders not to share with the media. They would be able to call on the superior manpower of the bureau in locating their target, after negotiating that it would be them who made the final engagement, naturally.

But then Murphy had asked to see her in private, away from the noise and bustle of the ops room. And much to Faraday's chagrin, he had a very good reason for not risking giving the FBI some help.

"Why didn't you tell me about this before?"

Murphy was standing by the floor-to-ceiling window, looking out over the city. The late-morning sky was dark, heavy with clouds. Faraday stayed on her feet, too, sitting back against the edge of her desk.

"You're right," he said. "I should have told you. I just thought…"

"That I didn't need to know," Faraday finished for him. "Is that what you thought?"

He didn't respond to that, but his lack of a response

was confirmation enough. Eventually, he said simply, "I'm sorry, okay? I thought we could handle it quietly."

"Join the club. When this is done, we're going to have a talk about some of the men. Particularly Usher."

He nodded, taking the scolding like a contrite student. It made Faraday dislike him all the more.

"So what exactly does this son of a bitch have on us, Murphy?"

"Specifically?" He shook his head. "I can't tell you that, because I don't know. Nobody really knows why Blake killed the senator, but we think it was a deal gone wrong. Carlson wanted dirt on Winter—" Murphy stopped dead as he saw the look on her face. He knew full well how much she hated the way some of them still used that old code name. Apart from anything else, it was a flagrantly unnecessary security risk. Code names changed for a reason. "Carlson wanted inside information on the organization," he continued, using Faraday's preferred nomenclature. "Blake liberated some potentially damaging information. A Black Book from an operation in Kandahar."

A Black Book. Now she understood. That could be damaging indeed. Murphy saw the recognition in her eyes and continued.

"He was going to sell it to the senator. Something went wrong, and Mr. and Mrs. Carlson wound up on a slab. And we wound up with a hell of a cleanup job. You think Usher shooting up the airport was bad? Walk in the park."

She ignored that. The previous twenty-four hours had not felt like any walk in the park. "So what's our potential exposure?"

Murphy shrugged again. "I don't know any more

than you now," he said. "But I know Drakakis was worried. And I don't think we want to risk the feds finding out before we do."

He was holding something back, Faraday thought. Or perhaps she was just wired to suspect that by this point; maybe he was on the level this time.

"So what do you suggest? Keep them in the dark and hope we find Blake before he has a chance to do us some damage?"

Murphy nodded. "Exactly."

"And how do we know he hasn't sent a copy to his lawyer or his favorite aunt? Instructions to release it if anything happens to him."

"Those drives are protected by sunset scripts. Every time you view the data it gets closer to erasing—makes it very difficult to copy, and I don't know if he could trust anyone to do the job. It's useful as a deterrent, that's all. I don't think he's ever thought about leaking it, because it wouldn't do him any good."

"I hope you're right."

Murphy turned away from the window and looked at her. She had a bad feeling about what he was about to say, and she was proved correct.

"I'm going out there."

"Absolutely not."

"Look, Faraday, Stark, and the others are making progress. I hope they'll get a line on where he went soon. But if anybody can track this bastard down, it's me. I worked with him. I know how he thinks."

Faraday circled around the desk and sat down in her chair. She looked him up and down appraisingly. "You scored two seventy-five on your last PFT, as I recall, Murphy. Are you sure you're still cut out for the field?"

He moved across the room and put both hands on the desk, flashing one of his cocky quarterback smirks at her. "Minimum is two sixty."

Faraday considered. Whether she liked it or not, Murphy had a point: He did know Blake. And perhaps someone closer to the action could keep a tighter rein on Usher.

"All right," she said finally.

Murphy nodded and straightened up. Faraday spoke as he was turning to leave.

"This isn't kill or capture anymore," she said. "Is it?"

Murphy was all business again. "Blake isn't going to be taken alive."

"I have no doubt you'll make sure of that."

THIRTY-TWO

North Dakota

WE KEPT TO the roomette for the most part as the train wound its way east, crossing through Idaho and then into Montana during the night. I had had a restless sleep, partly due to the compactness of the accommodation and partly due to the fact I had been rousing myself every hour or two to watch the platform at each stop. It was dark again by the time we crossed into North Dakota, and an announcement over the train's speakers reminded me to wind my watch forward to Central time.

By the evening, we had both begun to succumb to cabin fever. I read the books I had bought and thought a little bit more about what we would do when we reached Chicago. Bryant had napped frequently and, just as frequently, complained about the confinement. I had given in around five o'clock and let him walk the length of the train and back. Twelve cars plus two locomotives at either end. It had killed half an hour.

Neither of us had talked much about the reality of our situation. It was as though we were in a temporary bubble of relative security, and neither of us wanted to burst it. As the clock ticked on and the miles slipped away, I began to feel like we were getting closer to safety. I reminded myself that there was a long way to go yet.

I left the roomette a little after nine p.m. to buy us

dinner: our fifth prepacked sandwiched feast of the journey. I bought another book and a deck of cards, deciding it would be something to break the monotony. As I was paying, I felt the train begin to slow on the approach to the next station. I took the sandwiches and moved across to the windows at the platform side of the lounge car. The snow was no longer falling, but it looked pretty inhospitable out there. The station signs told me we were in Minot, North Dakota. I watched the platform as it rolled by at a gradually declining speed. I saw a handful of passengers waiting patiently: a young backpacking couple, a group of older people, a family with a little girl clutching her mother's hand, and a baby strapped to the father's chest in a BabyBjörn. Everybody in warm clothes, packed for a trip. Nothing out of the ordinary, once again.

When I got back to the roomette, Bryant took me up on the suggestion of a couple of hands of poker. We didn't have any chips, of course, or indeed much in the way of cash, so we played using a pile of individual sugar portions I'd liberated from the lounge car. It didn't take long for me to be glad we weren't playing for real money, as the pile of individually wrapped sugar on Bryant's side of the table began to grow.

"I'm breaking one of my rules, here," I said.

"What's that?" Bryant asked, looking puzzled.

"Never take on an expert in his field."

Bryant looked like he wanted to laugh out loud for a second, but then he composed his features and shook his head. "Not quite an expert. In fact, that's the reason I'm here."

I didn't say anything to that as I swept the cards up from the table and tapped them into shape. I remembered speaking to Bryant's wife back in California. *You never really know anyone.* I decided not to press him on it.

Bryant stood up to stretch his legs. He put a hand on the edge of the top bunk and ducked his head to look through the window. There was nothing to see but darkness and snow. The last stop, the one after Minot, had been Rugby. In another few hours and another few stops, we would cross into Minnesota. Bryant grew tired of watching the darkness go by and turned back.

"I'm going for a walk," he said.

I shook my head. "You already had a walk. I told you, we stay put unless absolutely necessary."

"I thought you said the police didn't release our names or our pictures yet. Who's going to recognize us?"

"I told you, the police don't have anything to do with it," I corrected. "The people who want me have suppressed our names and pictures. That's only because they don't want to involve anyone else unless they absolutely have to. If they get desperate, they might just decide to release them, and all bets are off."

Bryant sat down on one of the seats. Then he changed his mind and got up. He looked like he wanted to pace. The problem was, the spatial dimensions of the room restricted him to about one and a half paces, max.

"You know what, Blake?"

I squared the cards and slid them back into the pack. Then I looked up at him. "What?"

"This is fucking *bullshit*!" He slammed a fist off the door for emphasis.

"Calm down."

"I will not calm down. All I wanted was a new start.

Okay, I stole something that didn't belong to me. Sue me. Put me in fucking jail, okay? I didn't sign up for this. I don't deserve to be shot at and dragged halfway across the goddamn country before probably having to sleep with one eye open the rest of my life because the guy they sent to get me is public enemy number one, okay?"

I looked up at him, keeping my expression impassive. This had been building since the day before, ever since the immediate adrenaline rush of the chase had begun to subside. I knew he needed to get it out of his system.

"What do you want from me?" I said after a moment. "An apology?"

"Yes! Yes, I want an apology. This is your fault, Blake, all of it."

I opened my hands and shrugged. "All right. I'm sorry."

"That's it?"

"What more do you want? I'm sorry you're involved in this, and I'm doing my best to get you uninvolved. Believe me, I didn't choose this situation either."

"What more do I want? How about telling me exactly who's after us?"

"It's better—"

"'Better you don't know.' Save it. I want to know who's going to kill me. I have a right to know."

It was my turn to look out of the window at the darkness. All being well, we had another eight hundred miles and seventeen hours with Bryant in this kind of mood, so I supposed a little candor was worth the price. I hadn't given him any of the details partly out of a lifelong habit of never giving anybody any more than the minimum necessary information and partly because it wouldn't do him any good. It might make him even more afraid. But now I was reconsidering. For one thing, he was right; he did deserve an explanation for why his life was suddenly in danger. For another, perhaps a little scare was good. If he was more scared, he'd be more careful.

"All right," I said at last. "I guess we have some time to kill."

THIRTY-THREE

Seattle

"GOT HIM!"

The jubilation in Travers's voice was palpable. Stark
remained cautious.

It had been a long day, piggybacking on the police
and FBI investigations, relying on the key information they had withheld to ensure those other agencies
couldn't make a breakthrough before them.

Others had come to the same conclusion as Stark following the discovery of the taxicab at the business park.
The whole area had been locked down and searched
carefully, but too much time had elapsed for anyone to
hold out much hope of finding the airport fugitives in
the immediate area. They looked at the proximity to
the light-rail and the absence of any other nearby travel
options or reports of carjackings, and investigated the
possibility that one or both of the suspects might have
taken that option to head back into the city.

Travers had beaten the FBI to the punch in calling
Sound Transit, the light-rail operator. Yes, they did operate CCTV on their services for passenger and driver
security, and yes, they were only too happy to help the
authorities with their investigation into the shooting at
the airport. Was it some sort of terrorist thing? Travers
gave the standard noncommittal responses and barely

had to pretend to be from a government department for the guy to enthusiastically agree to send all video files from all of their services between twelve noon and two.

Twenty minutes later, their contacts said the feds had made the same request, except that they asked for all footage from the entire day. Typical FBI—thorough to the point of procrastination.

The compressed video was sent within a half hour. Stark instructed Travers to begin by focusing on city-bound services between twelve thirty and two. There was a service every ten minutes during the day, which gave them nine videos to look at. It didn't take long for them to find Blake and Bryant, getting on the train at 13:08. They both kept their faces down, but they were easy to spot, given the fact there were hardly any other passengers. The pair separated and took different seats during the journey, before alighting at University Street.

It would be almost two hours before the FBI video analysts matched up the two men on the 13:08 footage with the suspects from the airport.

From there, it had been tougher. It was difficult to move through a major city without leaving a trace on camera, but finding their two targets would take coordination and manpower that they didn't have. It would take the FBI time to do the donkey work, to access all of the street cameras and store security cams and anything else they could find. As Stark saw it, there were two options: Wait for the feds to piece together Blake's next movements, or try to hurry things along. He had contacted Faraday, asked for the latter. He wanted to release Blake's name and picture and give their worker bees something more to go on. Although Stark didn't say it out loud, he questioned why this had not been done already. The answer had come back after a short interval, and it was in the negative. There was too much of a risk that Blake would be arrested before they got a clear shot at him.

Reluctantly, Stark backed off. It was a fine balance. They needed to help the FBI just enough but make sure they didn't get too close to finding Blake by themselves.

So they tried to work a step or two ahead. The feds were just following the trail of two unknown suspects. They lacked the crucial insight into who Blake was, where he might go. There were three major transport hubs within easy walking distance of the stop at University Street. Security footage from there might let them cut to the chase.

But now, after hours of mind-numbing tedium, it sounded like Travers had made a breakthrough. When Stark saw the close-up of Scott Bryant's face, he knew that the excitement in Travers's voice had been earned.

"This is King Street?" he asked. You couldn't see much in the background, but they had spent so many hours looking at footage that they had become experts in identifying locations in downtown Seattle.

"King Street," Travers confirmed. He had been working through the multitude of video feeds from King Street Station for the past couple of hours. It was laborious work because there were so many: platform facing, waiting areas, ticket desks. One of the cams had a shelf that jutted frustratingly into the frame, meaning that if a customer stood a little way back from the desk, his face was obscured. When they had noticed that, they'd groaned. If Blake had picked this departure point, he would likely have used that one. But it looked as though his traveling partner hadn't been so careful.

Finally, they had nailed down Blake and Bryant's exit route from Seattle: aboard a train out of King Street. But going where?

"Good job," Stark said, his eyes moving to the time stamp in the corner of the screen. "Now let's find out which train they took."

FIVE YEARS AGO

Kandahar, Afghanistan

I LOOKED UP as Collins said my name.

"You didn't give up comic books when you hit puberty?"

I looked back down at the Batman trade paperback in my hands. I liked to read in my downtime, and comic books are one of the English-language imports you can still usually get in most places around the world. I was reasonably sure Collins had never read a book of any kind.

I glanced at Dixon, who was sitting across the main room of the safe house, sharpening one of his knives. The end of his tongue was jutting out from between his teeth in concentration.

"What can I say? The high culture in this place intimidates me."

Collins followed my glance and shrugged, conceding the point. "Come on over. Martinez has an update."

I tossed the Batman book aside and got to my feet.

The safe house was two rooms on the second floor of a derelict building in the district of the city called Zoar Shar. It was Spartan accommodation—gray walls, concrete floors, rusty bars on the glassless windows. An interpreter had found six thin mattresses and some multicolored blankets, which helped in the freezing nights.

The sleeping area was the smaller of the two rooms, and we kept our equipment and computers in the other. We hung blankets across the windows by day, but spears of sunlight made their way in through the gaps, making the dust motes shine in the air. The walls were covered with old graffiti in black spray paint, all in Arabic. One of the walls functioned as a bulletin board, where we had pinned maps and visuals relating to the mission. There was a new picture in the dead center: a smiling headshot of our target, Ajmal al Wazir, scion of Kandahar's first political family. The fortunate son.

Martinez had his tech nest set up in the corner of the second room. Over the three days since we had identified the Wolf, I had occasionally attempted conversation with him as he led the work on developing that intelligence. I had concluded that he liked to keep himself to himself. That was fine by me, and in fact it would have been nice if a couple of the others had followed his example.

Martinez was examining satellite images of an urban location that I assumed was somewhere in Kandahar on one of his two screens. Murphy, Collins, Ortega, and I were arranged around him as he translated the bird's-eye view into identifiable locations.

The only one who showed no interest whatsoever was Dixon. He remained on the other end of the room with his back to the wall, still sharpening the hunting knife. Everybody had something, I reflected: I read comic books, Collins and Murphy played cards, and Dixon sharpened his knife collection. In our line of work you need a certain appreciation for the tools of the trade, but in my book, and out-and-out fetish for blades is never a promising character trait. As the rest of us watched

Martinez's screen, the metal on metal would issue a distracting *sssshhhhhnnn* noise every few seconds. You could just about block it out, after a while.

"How sure are you about this intel?" Martinez asked, turning to direct the question at me.

"When are we ever sure?" I said. "But I think so, yeah."

His response was a frown. "I was afraid of that. If he's here, then we're in trouble. It's a fucking fortress. Twelve-foot-high walls, barbed wire, guards around the clock. Cops seem to be on the payroll, too—there's a drive-by once an hour."

I had expected as much. As soon as I had discovered the Wolf was a member of one of Afghanistan's richest families, I had known we were up against difficult odds. It was like discovering you needed to make a citizen's arrest on Tom Cruise, against the wishes of the police.

"We'd need a battalion to attack this place," Martinez confirmed. "That's the bad news."

It was a rhetorical suggestion. Politically, there was no way that was going to happen. We would have to find some way to get to the Wolf quietly.

"So there's good news?" I asked.

"If you're right about this, I think he's working off-site."

"What do you mean working?" Collins asked.

Martinez indicated the screen. "Every morning, two cars leave the south gate of the compound..." He brought up a closer image with a time stamp of yesterday at eight o'clock local time. It showed two Jeeps passing through the gate. He zoomed out of the first screen and traced a line across the city with his finger before zooming back in.

"They drive two miles southwest to this neighborhood." The close-up showed the Kotali Murcha area.

I nodded. It was a journey of riches to rags—Kandahar's most exclusive neighborhood, Shahri Naw or "New City," to a virtual slum built along the trail leading out of Kandahar City proper to the upper Arghandab valley. Martinez found the right spot on his zoom and framed it so we could see a row of black squares in what looked like a residential street.

"What are those?" I asked, and then it came to me before Martinez could answer. "Garages?"

"Yes. The two Jeeps park around the back, and he goes in. He spends hours a day there. They post a guard out front, one at the back, probably more in the Jeeps."

"Heat sig?" Murphy asked.

"Thermal imaging shows some major heat in which-ever garage he's working. I think he's putting together a goddamn fleet."

I counted the row of garages. "So if he has a vehicle in every one…six car bombs?"

"If this is the only location, six minimum. Looks like he's planning another coordinated attack."

If he were right, this would be the biggest attack yet.

"How long until he's ready?"

"Could be a week, could be tomorrow. We've only had eyes on him since you got the tipoff."

"So we have to move on this," I said, turning to Collins.

He watched the screen for another couple of seconds and nodded. "We do. Okay, let's hear some pitches."

"First off," Murphy said. "We have to take him at the garages. Not even up for debate. The house is too secure. Plus we have to deal with the car bombs."

Collins turned to direct his voice at Dixon, irritated. "Dixon, get off your ass and get over here."

Dixon didn't move, but put his knife back in its sheath and looked up at Collins as a partial concession to his notional position of authority.

"Tell me how long you need to put six VBIEDs out of commission."

Dixon rolled his eyes at the clumsy acronym and for the very first time, I empathized with him. Vehicle-Borne Improvised Explosive Device—why use two words where five will do? He thought about it for a moment.

"Easiest way is don't. Just set them to blow. No more car bomb."

"No more *neighborhood*," Martinez cut in. "This spot's right in the middle of the civilian population. Fucker knows what he's doing."

Dixon shrugged almost imperceptibly, kept looking at Collins.

"Man has a point," Ortega said. I wasn't sure if he was talking about Dixon or Martinez.

There was a tense silence. Martinez was looking at Dixon in disbelief. Collins had a neutral expression, as though he was giving the pitch due consideration. Murphy was hanging back for once, watching the others to see where we would fall on Dixon's suggestion. It was simple—it had that much going for it. Looked at objectively, it was the plan that stood the greatest chance of success.

It was also a suggestion that could only be cooked up and executed by a full-fledged psychopath.

"No fucking way," I said. "Forget it."

Ortega stood up, looked at me, then over at Dixon, who was sitting back against the wall, the hint of a smile on his lips. Whether it was in contemplation of the oncoming mayhem he was about to create, or the confrontation he had sparked, I didn't know. Perhaps it was both. "Dixon is right. We go in at night, take out any guards, then rig the whole thing to blow up in the Big Bad Wolf's face. It's clean."

I couldn't help myself. "Clean? You think blowing up a bunch of families is clean? You think you can get away with that?"

Collins was listening to us both, his expression unreadable. "Technically, there'll be nothing to get away with. Ajmal al Wazir had to be a deniable assassination. You've been here long enough to know the score."

Ortega was warming to the fight now. "It's better. We do it this way, no one even knows Wazir was clipped. It looks like an accident. Bomb maker's working someplace he shouldn't be, there's an accident, and he takes out himself and a few of the locals—boo-hoo. Maybe they'll be more careful who they let set up shop in the neighborhood after this. It sends a message."

Martinez was shaking his head. "I don't know, man. We can do this another way. Clean."

"Damn right we can do it another way," I said. "Ortega—you know there's a term for people who deliberately kill civilians to send a message, right?"

Ortega's scarred face went through a few contortions of disbelief while he came up with a response to that. "Fuck you," was his considered rebuttal. "Collins, you didn't tell me we had fuckin' Yoko Ono on the team."

I ignored him and addressed Collins. "We stake the place out, let him get inside, and then take out the guards and the Wolf. We don't even need to decommission the car bombs. Kandahar's finest may not be a shining international example of law enforcement, but they're going to notice a firefight first thing in the morning."

"More risk this way," Collins said, his eyes pointedly sweeping around the room to take in the five of us. "You know that."

"More certainty this way," I countered. "What if it isn't the Wolf who shows up? We'll never get another shot at him if we don't make sure."

Collins thought about it. He looked at Ortega, who was rolling his eyes at my suggestion. Then he looked over at Dixon. Dixon was watching us all with amusement. I think it was his grin that made Collins's mind up.

"Okay. No pyro this time."

Ortega walked away from the screens in disgust. Martinez and I shared a relieved glance. Murphy nodded, as though either plan sounded okay to him. Dixon shrugged and took his knife out again, keeping the amused look on his face.

"We'll do it your way," Collins said. "Don't make me regret it."

THIRTY-FOUR

North Dakota

BRYANT WAS TIRED and he was scared. After a day and a half in this cramped box, rolling east at a leisurely pace, he was also frustrated. It felt like being confined to a mobile death row cell. He thought about Jasmine and Alyssa again. If only he had dismissed the stupid idea of stealing MeTime, he wouldn't be here, wondering if he was ever going to see, or even speak to them again. But the more he thought about it, he knew that was only the last straw. There were many if-onlys in the chain before he had made that final disastrous decision.

And now Carter Blake was about the tell Bryant why they were being hunted. He doubted the explanation would do much to lift his spirits.

He watched as Blake considered what he was going to say next. He didn't speak for a long minute, just looked down at his hands, deep in thought. Bryant began to wonder if he'd changed his mind. But then he lifted his head and spoke.

"It's called Winterlong."

"Excuse me?"

"The organization that's taken an interest in me. The one I used to work for. Actually, that's not quite accurate. Winterlong was a short-life code name that stuck. They prefer not to call themselves anything."

"I knew it," Bryant said. "CIA, huh?" He had guessed as much, both from the skills Blake seemed to possess and the fact that their pursuers seemed to believe they could operate with absolute impunity.

Blake shook his head, as though correcting a slow student. "No. It was…is, actually, a small, entirely self-contained operation. Absolutely classified. We specialized in the jobs nobody else could do. Either because they required our unique approach, or because they were too politically sensitive."

"Which means the dirty jobs."

"Sometimes," Blake agreed. "We were separate from everything else, but we could call on…mediated support when necessary. As in some CIA operative would get a phone call telling them to cooperate, or an air base in Kabul would be told to get ready for an unscheduled takeoff, no questions asked. No questions asked was basically the mantra."

"So you were like…a secret SEAL team?"

"No. It was the whole package—signals, asset-handling, all the stuff the CIA usually does combined with strike capability. They dropped us into a hot zone with instructions of what they wanted done, and then they let us get on with it. We got established wherever it was, set up our own infrastructure. We had signals guys, human intelligence guys, shooters. For those types of jobs, that's all you need. From the moment we touched down, we went dark. We completed the mission, and we did it our way."

"And what was your involvement?"

"I did pretty much what I do now. I was a tracker. I found hard-to-find targets. I located new assets. I found out how to get close to people with nineteen layers of personal security."

"And then you did what with them?"

"It depended on who it was and what the mission was."

Bryant smiled sarcastically. "Sure it did. You were a hit squad. You kill any world leaders I might have heard of?"

"It wasn't that glamorous, Bryant. Like I said, we weren't there for the noticeable stuff. We were there for the behind-the-scenes work that keeps everything on the level."

"You sound like you're okay with this stuff."

Blake seemed to stop and consider for a second. Like he had fallen into an old trap of justifying the actions of these people, even though it was likely they were about to end his life. After a minute he shrugged. "Do you like sausages?"

"I know, I know," Bryant said. "Don't go see them being made."

In his time with Blake, he had gone through a whole range of reactions to the man: first fear, then resentment, then a grudging respect. Eventually, he had begun to realize that he liked the guy a little, despite himself. But right now all of those emotions were sidelined. Right now all he felt was anger. The man in front of him was no different from the men who had shot at them at the airport, who had killed that driver. Just like them, Blake had taken the money and he hadn't asked questions. Or not the right ones, at any rate.

Bryant's voice took on a harder edge, and to his surprise, he found himself not caring about the potential repercussions. "That doesn't answer my question."

Blake looked taken aback for a second, and then his gaze hardened.

"Do you know what kind of people I had to find? Bomb makers. Drug kingpins. Al Qaeda cells. People the world was absolutely better off without. Maybe you don't have to think about all of that nasty stuff in your cozy little Silicon Valley womb, but somebody has to deal with it."

Bryant was undeterred. "You're telling me you never had to do anything you weren't okay with? Who are you trying to convince, man? Me or you?"

That seemed to bring Blake up short, because he stopped what he was about to say and looked down at his hands again. Then he sighed and continued speaking, without looking up.

"Toward the end of my tenure I started to get uncomfortable with some aspects of our work. That's why I left, and that's why I work for myself now."

"So what made you leave?"

Blake gave a little smirk, as though that was a long story, and stood up, stretching his arms to kill a cramp. He put a hand on the edge of the upper berth and leaned against it as he looked out of the window of the train.

"A lot of little reasons. And one pretty big one."

"What happened? The good little soldier started thinking for himself?"

If he noticed the barb, he gave no indication. "The opposite, actually. I didn't change—their opinion of me did."

"How so?"

"They brought me in because I filled a skills gap, but perhaps I wasn't ever a perfect fit. I think every member of the team went through a kind of unofficial probation. I lasted as long as I did because I got results, but I always felt like I was being kept out of the inner circle. It was about being willing to do what it took, no matter what."

"And you weren't willing?"

"Sure, within my own limits. Turned out my limits were incompatible with the team. I was approached by someone powerful. Someone who made me believe I could help to make things right. But he was wrong, and it cost him his life."

He sat back down opposite Bryant. Neither of them spoke for a while. Bryant watched the other man, absorbing what he'd said, while Blake stared out of the window. There was nothing to see out there in the night, but Bryant had a feeling the other man wasn't thinking about here, or now.

Finally, Bryant prompted him to continue. "What did you do?"

"I acquired some information that they were eager to avoid falling into the public domain."

"Evidence?"

He nodded, and then a smile suddenly appeared on his lips, like he had thought of an amusing joke. He reached into his pocket and removed the flash drive he'd taken from Bryant earlier, the one that held the MeTime software. He examined it in the palm of his hand and looked up at Bryant. "Incredible, isn't it? What you can find on one of these."

Bryant said nothing, waiting for him to continue.

"Every operational commander received a full mission spec and orders on one of these. Couldn't be done any other way, since we couldn't guarantee secure Internet access. It was called the Black Book. It was the bible—everything we did, who did what to whom, when, where, and on whose orders. It was updated during the mission with the raw notes for after-action reports. Operational commanders had orders to destroy the book if necessary. It had a fail-safe: built-in software that wiped the data clean if you tried to access it more than a predetermined number of times."

Bryant nodded, realizing that finally, here was something that fell within his own area of expertise. "A sunset script," he said. "Smart. But not impossible to get around."

"I never thought I would have to," Blake said. "I just needed the threat. I used it to keep them off my back. And it worked, for a while."

"Until now?"

"Until now."

"So what changed?"

"The guy I made the deal with is gone. I think there were people who never wanted me running around. They wanted to finish the job. Only I did a good job of hiding from them for years. Right up until last year. A case I was working brought me into contact with them, and I guess somebody decided it was time to tie up this loose end."

"What about the flash drive—the Black Book? Do you still have it?"

"Of course I still have it. I keep it somewhere safe."

Bryant indicated the dark landscape passing by them out of the window. "Someplace east of here, I take it. And you need to get to the drive before they get to you."

Again, Blake didn't respond right away. He looked like he was thinking something through. Making a calculation.

"Listen," he said after a minute. "There's a good chance I may not be able to get there before they catch up with me. If you make it out, you might need to know this. I have a place in Upstate New York. It's an old farmhouse, miles away from anywhere."

Bryant was confused. If one of them was going to make it out of this, his money was firmly on Blake.

He continued. "There's a concealed vault in the basement: That's where I keep everything important. It's a bookcase. The vault opens when you pull two particular books in sequence: *The Great Gatsby* and then *All the President's Men.*"

"Why are you telling me this? Don't you—"

"I'm not telling you everything, not yet. But when we get to Chicago, I'll give my friend the name of the place. Between the two of you, you'll be able to find it."

There was a hollow look in Blake's eyes that Bryant knew was more than just fatigue. From the experience of the last day and a half, he understood two things: Blake knew how to handle himself, and he was pretty adept at evaluating any given situation. If Blake was this worried that he wouldn't make it out of this alive, it did not bode well.

Bryant said, "Why didn't you make a backup? Give it to somebody you trusted?"

"It was copy restricted. I'm sure you can get around that, too, but the data would have wiped on another view. And there was another guy."

Bryant took a moment to understand the significance of the word *was*. "Oh. What happened to him?"

"He was found executed in Russia four weeks ago. They sent me a picture. Partly to threaten me, partly as a means of finding me."

In the pit of his stomach, Bryant felt a growing nausea that had nothing to do with the motion of the train.

He reached up and massaged his forehead with the fingers of both hands.

"Fuck. We're dead, aren't we?"

"We're still breathing right now," Blake said.

"But for how long? You just told me these people specialize in hunting down fugitives and al Qaeda and whatever—you think I'm going to be a problem?"

"We have an advantage—I know what we're up against. I was one of them."

"Can you get me out of this?"

"I think so. My friend in Chicago will keep you out of harm's way while this goes down."

"What makes you think he'll be able to hide me from them?"

Blake smiled. "Two reasons. One: *She's* good. Two: I'm going to try to give them enough to worry about that they forget all about you."

THIRTY-FIVE

"YOUR TURN," I SAID.

Bryant shrugged. "You already know everything about me."

"Not true. I dug up enough to track you down. I don't know anything else about you. I almost got you killed. Least I can do is take an interest in how you got yourself in the position for that to happen."

He shrugged. "Not much to tell. I live alone. Worked for Moonola for a year and a half. I was bored. I saw an opportunity and I took it."

"Bet you regret it now."

"You can say that again."

"Why did you do it?"

"I already told you: the money."

I shook my head. "Nobody does anything for the money."

"What the hell are you talking about, Blake? Do you work for free?"

"On this job? Starting to look that way." I had barely given Stafford a second though since Seattle. Idly, I wondered how many increasingly pissed-off messages had built up on my voice mail.

"I'm serious. Everybody wants to get paid. Me, you, everybody."

"Money's just a means to an end," I said. "What did you really want?"

He sat back and looked out the window again. It was snowing again. The landscape around us was an ocean of white in the dark. "I wanted my life back," he said quietly.

He let that sit for a while, and I thought it over.

"A lot of people would say what you did guaranteed the opposite. You'd have been on the run. You would have had no choice but to start fresh. A new place, a new you."

"That doesn't sound so bad."

"You might be disappointed. Take it from me."

He kept talking, still looking out of the window, as if talking to himself, rather than me. "I had a wife— you know that? What am I saying, of course you know that. Jasmine. We met at college. Got married in Hawaii. Little girl, too."

"Alyssa."

He turned his head to look at me, surprised. "You met them?"

I nodded. "Cute kid."

He turned to look back out at the passing landscape again. "The cutest. Two months since I saw her."

He didn't say anything else for two full minutes, so I prompted him. "What happened?"

"You want the short version? Roulette, Texas Hold'em, blackjack. I always liked gambling. Ever since I was a kid. It was never a problem. Card game here. Weekend in Vegas there. Fifty bucks on the horses once a week. You're expecting me to tell you about some big blowout, right? One night where I lost everything. But it wasn't like that. It was gradual, so you wouldn't notice. I *didn't* notice. One day I came home and I thought the house was empty. Then I heard Jasmine upstairs, crying. She was sitting on the bed, holding a letter. She'd been laid off at work, came home to tell me, and then she saw a letter from the credit card company. She opened it and found out we were two hundred grand in debt and rising at seventeen percent. I know. I'm an idiot, right?"

I didn't say anything. I couldn't talk. I'd been in denial myself for the past few years. A problem of my own I had ignored, tried to forget about. Winterlong.

Bryant shook his head again. "I knew it was mounting up, of course. I just…"

"You thought you could handle it. You thought you could wait it out."

"Exactly. You said I'd have to leave everything, that I couldn't be me anymore. Blake, that's exactly what I wanted."

"What were you going to do?"

"I hadn't worked out the details yet. I was going to go somewhere nobody would think to look for me. Somewhere far from the coasts, a hundred miles from anywhere with a population above four figures. Some little town in Iowa or North Dakota or Kansas. I was going to rent a little apartment, get a job fixing computers or painting houses or whatever. Two million buys some time to think, you know? Once I got established, I'd come back for Jasmine and Alyssa. I'd be able to give them everything back."

I didn't say anything. It was a modest dream, as the dreams of multimillion-dollar techno-criminals went.

"You've gone quiet, Blake. What are you thinking?"

I smiled. That had been one of Carol's stock phrases, asking me *What are you thinking about?* whenever I'd been quiet for a little too long.

"I'm thinking that sounds like it would have been nice."

"You think she'd have come?"

I shrugged. "I don't know. I don't know your wife. But I can tell you one thing from experience—there's no such thing as a fresh start."

"No?"

"No. You can run away from everything, you can take a new name, a new job…but there are some things you take with you, no matter how much you wish it wasn't so."

"And there's always people who remember you, right?"

"Right."

Bryant gathered the discarded cards from the table, squared them, and put them back in the pack. "On that note, I think I'll turn in. How long until Chicago?"

"We'll be there around four tomorrow afternoon."

Bryant gave an exasperated sigh and climbed into the top bunk. I heard the springs in the mattress settle. Less than ten minutes later, he began to snore. I wondered if the act of talking about how he came to be here had been a weight off. It had been the opposite for me.

I sat back and looked out of the window again. I thought about the odds of me making it to my destination. And then I thought about the longer odds of the two of us getting out of this in one piece.

I would have to try to get some sleep in a while. But not before the next stop.

SATURDAY, JANUARY 9TH

THIRTY-SIX

Minnesota

THE LOCKHEED JETSTAR was buffeted by a cross-stream of chill northerly winds as they began their descent. Stark glanced out the window again, but there was nothing to see. Even if they were over a population cluster, the lights would be cloaked by the blanket of moonlit clouds below. He glanced up at the sound of the hinges creaking on the cockpit door as Ortega appeared from within and gave a nod.

"Ten minutes to touchdown. Pilot says it will be bumpy."

Stark nodded and fastened his seat belt. He looked at the other two men seated nearby: Usher had done likewise, yanking the strap on the belt tight. Kowalski smiled and slouched in his seat, making no effort to fasten the buckle. He was slightly too big for the seat to be comfortable, but then, Kowalski's size was the reason Murphy had suggested him, rather than Abrams, for the advance team. Given the probable location of their target, close-quarters combat was a distinct possibility.

"Long as nobody's shooting at us on the approach, I'm happy," Kowalski said.

Stark swallowed at the first of a series of dips as the pilot began his approach. He had never been a fan of flying, and five years of regular air travel, sometimes into enemy territory, hadn't made him like it any more. He guessed it was one of those things you didn't get used to; you just learned to put up with it. Stark almost preferred it on the few occasions he had been aboard a plane under enemy fire—it took his mind off the flying.

The pilot had been reluctant to make the trip, back at the little airfield south of Seattle. He had pointed to FAA guidance suggesting not to fly unless necessary. There were pockets of storms all the way along the flight path. Farther east, it was getting even worse: They were planning for a full shutdown of all commercial flights in the Northeastern states if things kept going the same way. But then, as Kowalski said, they'd all made trips in conditions worse than these.

Another steep dip flipped Stark's stomach, and he thought about the mission to keep his mind off the descent. There would be a car waiting for them at the small provincial airport. If, as predicted, they were on the ground inside of ten minutes, they would actually be slightly ahead of schedule. It was a short drive to the Amtrak railroad station at Detroit Lakes on night roads. Local forecast said snow, but nothing that would shut the roads down. The Empire Builder—still on schedule according to Amtrak's website—would roll into the station at three ten.

Another dip and they dropped below cloud cover. Clusters of lights spread out below marked out the small towns of Minnesota. Freezing rain streaked the Plexiglas windows, blurring the lights, and the jet lurched a little to the left as another gust of wind butted into them.

Focus on the mission. Was Blake still aboard the train? Stark supposed it could have been a bluff, a way to send them off on a wild-goose chase while Blake laid low or took another route out of Seattle. But he thought not, on balance. Too many variables. Travers had gotten lucky finding Bryant on the security tape. There was a good chance they would never have found it.

Once the four of them were aboard the train, they would have time to find him. It would be a full hour to the next stop at the small town of Staples, and it would be easy to spot him if he tried to leave there. After that, there was only one stop for the next three and a half hours. Of course, this was all based on the assumption that Blake was still on the train and hadn't gotten off at any of the intermediate stops between Seattle and Detroit Lakes, but again, on balance of probability, it was likely he was aboard. Faraday seemed to be convinced that Blake's base of operations was on the East Coast, and the Empire Builder would take him most of the way there.

The rear wheels thumped down on the tarmac, actually surprising Stark. He tensed as the front wheels contracted a moment later and skidded slightly on the snow. He let out a breath as the plane straightened up and the reverse thrust kicked in, slowing them down.

The four of them stood up and grabbed their packs from the overhead lockers. Stark removed his shoulder holster from the pack and strapped it over his chest, then checked the Glock 19 before sliding it into the holster. Lastly, he grabbed the black parka from the locker and put it on. The other three men went through a similar routine as the pilot brought the jet to a stop. A minute later, the co-pilot was unlocking the hatch and swinging it open. A gust of wind and snow blew in at them, the temperature abruptly dropping in the cabin. Stark checked his watch again. Thirty-two minutes until their rendezvous with Carter Blake.

THIRTY-SEVEN

Minnesota

I HAD FALLEN asleep in the seat, but the change in the motion of the train stirred me as we approached a station. I opened one eye and glanced out of the window—Detroit Lakes, Minnesota. If we were on schedule, that meant it was a little after three in the morning, which explained why the platform was so quiet. Not quite deserted, though. As our car rolled by the waiting area, I saw a lone figure in a dark-colored hooded parka watching the train pull in, hanging back in the shadows.

I opened the other eye to get a better look before the figure passed out of my line of sight. I was pretty sure it was a man, and I was also pretty sure he intended to get on the train. He had a small backpack strapped on. He was on his feet, ready to move once the train ground to a halt. It was odd that he wasn't standing farther out on the platform, getting ready to board. But he wasn't Amtrak staff, and there was no other reason to be at the station in the middle of the night unless he was picking somebody up.

I got up and reversed my position to the other seat, trying to see back down the platform. Bryant grunted in his sleep in the berth above me.

Maybe it was nothing. Maybe the guy in the parka was just picking somebody up, backpack notwithstanding. Maybe he had some other reason for not approaching the train. But I don't like maybes, so I pressed the side of my head against the glass and squinted down the floodlit platform. The snow had started falling again, the flakes lazily drifting across my field of view.

I saw a couple get off from the next car, the woman was shivering in a leather jacket. Just about okay for Seattle in January, not so much for Minnesota. The man wrapped an arm around her and they walked quickly to the exit, lugging a pair of suitcases, their breath making clouds in the night air. Mumbled, indistinct sounds of conversation from the pair managed to penetrate the glass before they moved out of range. I heard a couple of brief yells from one of the train staff, answered by a station-bound coworker. I kept watching. No more disembarkations. Those were the exception, rather than the rule, particularly at this time of night. The majority of the passengers were on for the whole trip. A second later I heard a shout from the guard, signaling that we were good to go.

And then I saw the man in the parka cross the platform, moving quickly and purposefully toward the doors about two cars down from us. And he wasn't alone. Three more men, dressed similarly in parkas and hoods, with packs, emerged from the shadows and followed.

The guard yelled again, and the pitch of the engine rose and the Empire Builder began to roll out of the station at Detroit Lakes.

With four new passengers.

FIVE YEARS AGO

Kandahar, Afghanistan

MARTINEZ WAS GONE.

He had simply disappeared in the night, in a way that should not have been possible. Standard protocol was, two men on watch at all times. Martinez had offered to swap with Dixon to take the two to six shift, along with Ortega. But Ortega was notorious for sleeping on the job, and this time had been no exception. He had sat at the north window, brim of his hat over his eyes, and positioned himself so that it looked like he was watching. If anything happened in the night, he would wake soon enough. But whatever had happened, there hadn't been any noise loud enough to wake him. Instead, he'd awoken as the full moon broke through a patch in the cloud cover a little after five, the brightness rousing him. He had known something was wrong right away. He checked the back room and found the rest of us sleeping, but no sign of Martinez.

Ortega immediately woke us and said he had dozed off for a few minutes. When this was met with skepticism, he'd admitted Martinez could have gone at any point in the previous two hours. No sign of him, no note, no warning. We tried to raise him and got nothing. He had taken his pack and his weapons. The possibility that an unfriendly had infiltrated the safe house was discussed and quickly discarded. There was no sign of a scuffle, and if the building had been compromised, either we would all have known about it, or we'd be dead.

No, for whatever reason, no matter how little sense it made, Martinez had picked up his belongings, unlocked the door, and walked into the freezing Kandahar night.

The others tossed theories around while we decided what to do and whether to delay our raid on the Wolf's lair. I remained quiet, thinking about the look on Martinez's face the night before. I left the other four debating courses of action in the south room and walked through the bare doorway into the back room where Martinez's equipment had been set up. Collins was at the desk, checking through the contents of the drawer.

"Lost something?" I said.

His head jerked up, and I saw something like panic in his eyes for a split second before he composed himself. He shook his head. "Just looking for…"

"Looking for…" I prompted, when he didn't continue.

"For an explanation, I guess. Where the hell has he gone?"

I held his gaze for a moment before shrugging. "I don't know. You want to call off?"

Before Collins could answer, Murphy appeared at my side.

"Vanished like virginity on prom night. Any ideas, hoss?" he said, addressing Collins.

Collins looked back at him, like there was something he wanted to say, but then just shook his head.

"You want to call off?" I asked again.

Collins though about it. "No. No, we go ahead. Martinez can take his chances, wherever the hell he is."

AN HOUR LATER, we were on the road. The sky was still dark, but the dirty yellow sodium streetlights were extinguished: one of the city's frequent rolling blackouts.

We took two vehicles. Murphy, Collins, and Dixon were in one car. I rode in the other with Ortega, both of us very conscious of being a man down. We took separate, prearranged routes. I watched the early-morning sidewalks pass by, the locals not giving us a second glance. There was no reason to; we were riding in a beat-up Citroën, not a Humvee, and our dress did nothing to make us stand out as Americans. We crossed through the main city boundary and into the Kotali Murcha neighborhood. The line of garages we had spent days watching from above was four blocks ahead when Ortega pulled off the road. We backed into the alley that we had chosen as the best retrieval point, and Ortega switched the engine off and killed the lights. Mid-November, so the sun wouldn't start to rise for another half hour.

I called in our location to the other car, which was circling the area until we got a confirmed visual on Ajmal al Wazir—the Wolf. Ortega and I left the car and moved quickly toward our positions. Ortega crouched just inside the mouth of an alley diagonally across from the line of garages while I moved a little farther down the street. My assigned role was observation and recon, and I wasn't going to get involved in the rough stuff unless I was needed. Because of that, and especially because I had to avoid attracting attention, I was armed only with my Beretta, which I kept holstered underneath my jacket. Ortega and the others had MP5s, and wouldn't be making their presence known until the time for stealth was over.

Martinez's satellite surveillance had suggested that al Wazir traveled light, normally with only three or four men. They had been making this trip for days with no trouble, so I hoped the level of trouble we were about to bring would come as something of a surprise.

I crossed the street, keeping my eyes on the stretch of road headed east, the direction from which we expected the Wolf to approach. I glanced at my wristwatch as I reached the other side: 07:13. I stepped underneath one of the awnings sheltering the stores that lined this side of the road. From this position, I had sight of the line of garages down the street and also of the spot I knew to be Ortega's position at the mouth of the alley, not that he was allowing himself to be seen.

The line of stores was varied. Most were still closed, but two were already open and another—a butcher's shop—was in the process of opening. I watched as the owner began hanging the day's carcasses on a rail that overhung the entrance and the sidewalk. Next door was a café. It was open, but the three small tables outside were unoccupied this early on a winter morning. On the other side was some kind of junk store—it was hard to tell what exactly it sold, other than clutter. A tall, skinny man was sweeping the sidewalk outside. He glanced at me, nodded, and looked back down at his work. I turned the other way and spoke just loud enough for my voice to be picked up by the mic.

"This is two. I'm in position."

Ortega's voice immediately answered, crystal clear through the tiny receiver nestled in my right ear.

"One, in position. Picking this up, six?"

"Copy that," Collins replied. "In position. No visual on Big Bad."

"He's late," I said.

I looked up and down the street. Traffic was almost non-existent on this particular stretch of road, but all around I could hear the sounds of a city slowly rising to meet the day. From far off, I heard the whine of a motorcycle. The man with the broom was still working away. I glanced at the hanging carcasses outside the butcher's shop, swaying slightly in the breeze. Nothing that looked appetizing, even if I had been at all hungry. I raised my eyes and looked through the window of the store. An older man within was smoking a cigarette, regarding me with suspicion.

I moved along to the next unit, the café. I glanced up and down the street again: still nothing. I positioned myself where I could pretend to be regarding the menu in the window while still keeping a good view of the street.

"What's the matter, you skip breakfast?" Ortega's voice in my ear. I smiled and said nothing, because the owner of the café was coming out to see me. He regarded me with the standard level of caution. He spoke in Pashto.

"Coffee? You want something to eat?"

I glanced back at the road, which was still empty.

"Coffee," I agreed. "No milk."

He held his hand out toward the door, but I pulled out one of the chairs outside.

"I'll sit out here."

He looked like he was about to question me, and then shrugged and disappeared back inside to fix the coffee. A customer was a customer, even if he was crazy enough to want to dine al fresco in November before the sun came up. I sat down, feeling the comforting weight of the Beretta settle on my chest.

"This is two. What's happening?" I said quietly through gritted teeth.

"This is six. Stand by," came Collins's response.

Where the hell was he? Not a break in the routine in days, and we knew the cars hadn't been moved from the garage. Had the Wolf decided to take a day off? Or had he been tipped off? I thought about Martinez and immediately dismissed it. I had a good idea why he'd split, and if I was right, it had precisely zero to do with the mission in hand.

Collins spoke again. "This is six. We have a visual."

I held my breath. I barely even noticed as the café owner placed the cup of coffee in front of me. The scent drifted up to my nose in the cold air.

"Okay?" the owner said, glancing from the coffee to me, a concerned expression on his face.

"Tashakor," I replied.

If they had a visual and they were still in their designated position, that meant the Wolf and his entourage were seconds away from rounding the corner.

I counted the seconds. Ten. Fifteen. Nothing.

I cleared my throat loudly and spoke under my breath. "This is two. Update?"

"Wait one," Collins's voice said.

Just to keep my hands occupied, I picked up the cup and sipped the coffee. As I swallowed, Collins spoke again.

"Target is turning back. Something's wrong."

I cursed under my breath, hearing a similar noise from Ortega. A second later, Ortega was in my ear again. "Two, get the fuck out of there."

I was on my feet already as I acknowledged. "Say again?"

"Just get to secondary position. *Now*."

I didn't know what the hell was happening, but I guessed it couldn't be good. I turned and jogged toward Ortega's alley. What the hell was happening? Whatever it was, getting me to cover was more of a priority than explanations. I hustled across the road and into the alley, expecting to see Ortega waiting for me.

The car was still there, but Ortega was gone.

The narrow alley stretched forty yards between two stucco buildings. At the far end was a main road.

I put a finger to my ear. "This is two, at secondary. Where the—"

I stopped as I heard a whisper of movement behind me, from the direction of the street. I started to turn and felt a sharp pain in the side of my neck. My vision started to blur, and I felt arms around my upper body. And then the walls seemed to be flowing around me like stone waterfalls and everything went gray and finally black.

THIRTY-EIGHT

WITH NO SMALL amount of difficulty, I roused Bryant and told him I was going to check something out.

"What's wrong?"

"I don't know yet. Maybe nothing. Stay in here and don't answer the door to anybody. When I come back I'll knock five times."

"Blake, that doesn't sound like nothing."

I didn't reply. I opened the door and stepped out into the corridor, closing it quietly but making sure the lock clicked home. Quickly, I moved down the corridor. The main lights were off this time of night, but the thin light strips along the floors provided enough illumination. I crossed into the next car, which was coach: all seated. Lighting at a minimum in here too. Sleeping passengers hunched in most of the seats, a few night owls watching movies on their laptops with headphones plugged in, or reading books using little page lights. From my excursions to the lounge car, I knew the rest of the train was just as full as this car. It would take them a while to search the train, particularly at night.

I passed through to the end and exited through the sliding door into the join area between the cars. In the next car, there was a restroom area, the pod sticking out into the corridor and blocking the line of sight ahead. I hesitated a second, hoping none of the four men were heading this way yet—if we ran into each other at the door, there would be no going back. I stole a glance around the corner and saw nobody coming. Emboldened, I stepped forward and proceeded. This one was seating also. Most people sleeping, some on laptops and reading. I slowed as I approached the doors to the next car and peered through the window. At the far end of the next car, there were two men standing in the aisle.

I pulled back before either of them happened to look in my direction. I thought about how I would run the search. Four men searching a train packed with hundreds of people. Twelve cars, two locomotives at either end. A mixture of coach and sleeping, plus two baggage cars and the lounge. Their odds were improved by the fact they could visually ID both me and Bryant. They had to anticipate I'd taken one of the roomettes, for exactly the reasons I had done so. But there was still the possibility that I might be among the seated passengers, and those would be easier for them to check, particularly at night. Just quietly walking up and down the aisles, checking the sleeping faces, would allow them to eliminate a large portion of the passengers with relative speed.

But all four of them trying to do it all at once would likely attract the attention of the Amtrak staff. So they would probably take turns. One at a time, taking maybe one or two cars, then a break. Then another of them checking another two cars. They'd still be able to eliminate everyone traveling in the seated cars reasonably quickly. They had almost an hour until we reached the next stop. I thought about waiting until then and then trying to leave the train undetected, but quickly dismissed the idea. If I were them, I would put a man out on the platform at every stop. Two men leaving the train at a small-town station at four a.m. would be just as no-ticeable as four men boarding. And even if we could slip past them, we'd be stuck in the middle of nowhere in the middle of the night with no transport. If we were going to stand a chance at leaving without being no-ticed, it would have to be later, with a crowd. St. Paul, perhaps. Even then, it was unlikely they would miss us.

I chanced another look and saw one of the men had sat down while the other had disappeared. They would have had to buy designated seats, so I guessed they had split the team over multiple cars. They'd attract less at-tention as a group that way, and they could keep an eye on four different locations without leaving their seats.

I made my way back to the room and knocked softly, five times.

Bryant opened the door at once, like he'd been wait-ing behind it. He was wide-awake now, his eyes betray-ing the strain of the last few days and hours.

"Problems?"

"I think so. They must have traced us to the station back in Seattle. Four men got on at the last stop, I think they've already started making the rounds."

"Shit."

"My thoughts exactly."

"So what do we do?"

THIRTY-NINE

New York City

A QUIET KNOCK at the door awoke Faraday from a light sleep. Her eyes snapped open, and she needed no time to orient herself or to remember why she was sleeping on one of the ready cots. She got up off the thin mattress and stood up. Although it was freezing outside the building, the room was overheated and dry. She opened the door to see Williamson. Williamson's half-lidded, disinterested stare could have been blamed on the hour, were it not the expression she affected at all times.

"Did they get Blake?" she asked immediately.

Williamson shook her head. "Uh-uh. Or at least, not as far as I know. They intercepted the train at Detroit Lakes, Minnesota, on schedule. Nothing since then, but there are a lot of cell black spots out there."

Faraday nodded. After checking in at the station, they wouldn't contact central command unless there was something to report. When there was something to report, they could use the satellite phone.

"Did Murphy rendezvous with the second team yet?" The second team was shadowing the route of the Empire Builder by road, as closely as possible. Murphy was going to rendezvous with them at the next available point.

"Still en route. Weather held him up."

"Then what do you have for me?"

"Not an address yet, but I think I found Blake's neighborhood."

"Seriously?"

Two minutes later Faraday was back in the ops room. The giant screen on the south wall was divided into different windows: one was a live satellite view of the operation area. Fully a quarter of the live screen was obscured by clouds. The weather was starting to close in. Faraday hoped that wouldn't cause delays on the track—it would be one more variable to consider.

A larger window on the big screen showed a clear view from earlier in the day of the same geography. A barely discernible thread crossing the middle of the screen horizontally was the Great Northern Railway. Superimposed lines and labels marked out the state boundaries and population centers currently invisible on the live feed. She knew the weather was another factor Blake might be able to exploit. As things stood, it would be easy to check the handful of people leaving the train at night stops. Less so if the train was forced to come to a halt between stations, or canceled at the next stop. She just had to hope Blake was operating under the illusion he was in the clear.

She shelved those considerations for the moment and turned her thoughts toward the promising new avenue that had opened up. There were three banks of monitors, but only one station was in use. Williamson sat down in her chair and unlocked the screen.

"Talk to me," Faraday said, as her eyes scanned the screen. It displayed an array of times and dates and numbers. It took Faraday a second to realize what she was looking at.

"The flight records?"

"That's right. You told me to work with the known and suspected dates and locations Blake has been over the last five years. We didn't have much to go on. We started out with Crozier in LA, and looked at everything around that. Lucky for us, the FBI had already done some of the work for us. When Blake was briefly a suspect in the Samaritan thing, they looked into him, as far as they could."

"Which would have given them nothing, right?"

"Right. But they did ID the flight he took into LA. He came in from Fort Lauderdale with a stop-off at Fort Worth."

"Cooper was in Florida. Does that mean Blake—?"

Headshake from Williamson. "I think he was on a job down there. He appears on another flight inbound to Lauderdale, this one from Newark."

"Okay."

"Then we go back to October of the previous year—and this is what really put me on track. His prints were run by the police in Fort Dodge, Iowa."

The date and location chimed in Faraday's head. "The Wardell case—it *was* him." The Wardell case had been one of their possibilities for Blake's involvement. Officially, the FBI had tracked down the deadly serial killer, but given what they knew now about Blake's operations since leaving Winterlong, it was highly likely the case bore his fingerprints. And now, it appeared, it literally did.

"How the hell did we miss this?"

"We didn't. Homeland Security flagged the request, hit the local cops with a DR-17 and passed it onto us."

"Who was it escalated to? Drakakis?"

"That's right. The trail was almost purged from the system."

"Almost?"

Williamson answered that with a low chuckle. Under normal circumstances, Faraday would have answered with a barb to tell Williamson not to be so cocky, but she let it go. She was far more preoccupied with who had purged the fingerprint hit, and why.

But that would have to wait for the moment. She listened as Williamson carried on talking, too absorbed in the pleasure of finding the discrepancy to care about the whys and wherefores. "Anyway, Wardell was caught and killed November 2nd. Blake evidently stuck around a couple of weeks, or he came back for some reason—he flies back east on the 16th."

"Newark again?"

"JFK."

All roads seemed to lead back to New York, or at least somewhere on the East Coast. This was the one chink in Blake's armor—he couldn't fly without leaving a trail, and he had to use a consistent name for ID, unless he wanted to take the risk of maintaining multiple identities. And up until recently, there had been no real need: They didn't know he was calling himself Carter Blake until LA, and even if they had, it wasn't exactly a unique name. Only now that they had been able to build up a picture of his movements could they make the connection that suggested an area of home turf. And even then...

"Okay, New York area, that's good. Cuts it down to millions of locations rather than hundreds of millions."

"Definitely in the area," Williamson said. "And his

record says he had an apartment in the city when he was with us."

Faraday massaged her temples. New York City? Was Blake really headed in their direction? Something told her that wasn't quite right.

Williamson continued. "So you're an ex-operative with no past, and you're looking for a place to stay. Somewhere you won't be found. What's important?"

"No paper trail. Rent, mortgage, insurance," Faraday said. And then she thought about something else, something that would be hard to come by in the city. "Privacy."

"Right. So I'm looking at cash buys over the period. These are getting rarer, particularly when you cut out the millionaires."

"He won't be in the city," Faraday said. "Someplace quiet. Rural or small-town."

Williamson thought about it. "Makes sense. Cuts the job down a little, if you're right. So do you want me to stay on this or go back to monitoring the ever-enthralling police bands of Seattle?"

She considered it for a moment. "Stay on this, Williamson. And keep me posted."

FORTY

Minnesota

I TOLD BRYANT why I was pretty sure they were on the train because of us. With no weapons and few places to hide, I came to a simple conclusion—somehow, we had to get off the train before they found us.

"Can't we just stay in here, wait it out? I mean, there's no way for them to know we're in here, right?"

"We could try," I said. "But if it doesn't work, we would have nowhere to go. Besides, if I were running this search, it wouldn't help. I'd check the easy options first—give the seated passengers the once-over. My guess is, that's what they're doing right now. Then I'd move on to the sleeper cars."

"They couldn't get in without breaking the door down. And like I said, they don't know which room we're in. They're not going to break down a hundred doors."

"They don't need to," I said. "They just need to knock on a hundred doors. Law of averages says not even that many. They'd get to us sooner or later. They could say they were Amtrak staff, that they're looking for a missing kid or something. At three in the morning, nobody's going to argue; they just want to get back to sleep. Of course we would stay quiet and ignore the knock, but by the time they've finished, they would have narrowed it down to a few rooms they haven't managed to eliminate. Then they watch those rooms and wait us out. By that time, it's too late to do anything but sit and wait for the inevitable."

"When you put it that way…"

"Doesn't sound so good?"

Bryant nodded. "Okay. Then how the hell do we get off this train?"

I estimated the time since the last calling point. "Next stop is in about forty-five minutes, give or take."

Bryant nodded at the window. "I'm not so sure about that."

I looked outside. The snow was flying past much more thickly now. And was it an optical illusion of the swirling flakes blowing past, or were we moving a little slower than we had been? I could see ice on the window outside our climate-controlled bubble and knew it was well below freezing out there.

We had one advantage at least: minimal time required to pack. I stood at the door and listened for a second, and twisted the handle. I stuck my head out in the corridor and looked both ways. Empty. The noise of the train rocking back and forward was louder out here.

We turned left, because it was the opposite direction from where I knew the four men had joined the train. There were four cars that way against nine in the other direction, and if nothing else, I wanted to get us in a position where we could be attacked from only one direction. We made it to the far end, where there were the same transparent sliding doors leading into the join between cars and then another set of the same doors with an airlock to keep the noise and the cold out of the interiors. We passed through the first set of doors and the temperature dropped twenty degrees. I stepped across the join and hit the button to open the next door. It was another sleeping car, like ours. A narrow corridor about a foot and a half wide, with doors along the left-hand side, windows along the right. The snow outside whirled and sparkled in the dim light from the strips along the floor.

Bryant spoke behind me, keeping his voice low. "What do we do when we run out of train?"

"I'll let you know when we get there."

I was heading for the front of the train because I knew there had to be a staff-only area near the driver's cabin. It would be a better place to hide out than in the passenger areas, and it might provide some other options. I didn't relish the idea of leaving the train while it was in motion at fifty or sixty miles an hour, so it would be nice to evaluate alternative courses of action. Then again, maybe the front of the train would be full of Amtrak staff who would turn us back the way we came. I hated having so little idea of my next move, but as I had told Bryant, doing something was better than doing nothing. Or so I hoped.

One car down, three to go, I thought as we reached the next set of doors. We passed through another cold spot and this time into one of the seated cars. We walked quietly through the dozing passengers, the occasional light sleeper or reader glancing up curiously as we passed. Another set of doors. We stepped over the join and into the next car. Another sleeping car. Same row of doors on the left side, same windows on the right, same floor lights. Everything the same, except one thing.

There was a big guy in a black parka standing half-way along the carriage.

FORTY-ONE

HE WAS AROUND six two with a wide, muscled frame. He had short blond hair. He had his back to us when we entered, but turned fast at the sound of the door opening. For a nanosecond, both he and I froze.

And then we sprang into motion. I charged down the narrow corridor, yelling at Bryant to get back to the room. I didn't have time to glance behind me to check he was doing as he was told, because I was focused on the man in front of me going for his gun. It took him a split second longer to reach for it than it would have done had he not been wearing the bulky parka, giving me just enough time to cover the three strides between us and slam into him before he had a chance to aim.

A stray shot escaped as I fumbled for his wrist, going for the gun. It pierced the floor of the car without much fuss, just a muzzle flare and the thump sound as the attached suppressor did its job. He used his free hand to grab for my throat as I forced his gun hand down again. I ducked backward, grabbing the wrist of his gun hand with both of my hands, pulling him off-balance, and then used his momentum to beef up a head-butt. He grunted in pain and got a couple good shots into my ribs with his left while I twisted his right hand until the gun dropped to the floor.

Slipping out of my grip, he hit me a couple of times hard on my left side again, while bringing his right around toward my head. I blocked it with my forearm and then another from the left. He was fast—had already gotten in several blows to my one. I ducked under another swing and wrapped both arms around his midsection, slamming him hard against the wall and down to the floor of the car. His head cracked off the surface, and as he was lifting it again, I planted the palm of my right hand in the center of his forehead and slammed it back down again, hard. I gripped as much of the short hair on his scalp as I could and tried the same again, but this time he managed to twist his head and I lost my grip midway to pounding his head against the floor one more time.

Before I knew his hand had moved, I felt his balled fist slam into my stomach, knocking the wind from me. It was followed by his knee, jutting up. I folded, and he planted a foot in my gut, pushing me backward. Already off-balance, I was lifted almost into the air as he kicked me back from him and started to scramble to his feet. I landed on my back and got to one knee.

The door between us cracked open, and a man in his seventies, with bedhead and bags under his eyes, started to step out into the corridor, his mouth open. It was like the referee had stopped the bout. Both the blond man and I paused. We finished getting to our feet as our eyes flicked between each other and the old guy, waiting for him to make a move. The old guy looked at me, then the blond man, then closed his mouth, quickly retreated back inside, and closed the door firmly.

Suddenly, there was a blade in his hand, the moonlight from outside glancing off steel. I remembered the gun. I couldn't see it in my field of vision, and since we were in a very confined space, that meant it had to be behind me. I took a step back, glancing behind me for the split second I needed to locate the pistol. It was ten feet from me, but my sparring partner was already rushing me with the knife. Split-second decision: I could either retrieve the gun or prevent him from gutting me. Not both. I fell back another step and timed my action to match his approach speed. I spread my arms to balance my weight, pivoted on my left foot, and slammed the heel of my boot into the side of his face as he bore down on me. I kept moving on the follow-through, twisting my body so the blade plunged through the space where my upper chest had been a split second before.

He staggered off-balance, and his momentum took him past me on my right side like a bull sweeping past a toreador. Without thinking, I curved my left arm and swung it back hard, driving the hard point of my elbow into the base of his skull. It connected hard enough that I felt the jolt in my fingertips.

I spun around in time to see his legs carry him another couple of paces before he slammed facedown on the floor, his limp arms not even twitching forward to break his fall. If it was an act, it deserved an Academy Award, but I was taking no chances.

I crossed the space between us and stamped down on the fingers that were still wrapped around the hilt of the blade, then kicked it away from him. I stepped quickly over the body and retrieved the gun: a Glock 19. I held it on him for a moment, watching for any movement, and then I crouched down next to him. Keeping my finger tight on the trigger, I gripped a handful of the collar of his parka in my left hand and hauled him over onto his back. His nose had been broken in the fall, but he was still breathing through his open mouth.

Gradually, awareness of my surroundings drained back into me. The strobing light of the moon filtered through trees and snow. The rattle of the wheels on the track. I looked behind and ahead, saw no one. The old guy in the roomette wouldn't open that door again until we got to Chicago, if then.

I turned back to the still form of my opponent. He was wearing a communicator: a slender earpiece and mic so subtle that I hadn't noticed it in the fight. I pulled it off him and examined it: lightweight but tough, bone conduction technology for superior sound quality. There were two buttons, marked with a circle and a square. Pressing the square would let you talk to the rest of the team, the circle put you in touch with the base. I put it to my ear and heard only dead air.

I checked it was turned on and attached it over my own ear. The earpiece was custom-molded so the fit wasn't perfect, but it stayed in place. Then I patted him down. I found three different forms of fake ID—all in different names—including a Department of Homeland Security special agent badge that looked legit. I reminded myself it probably was legit, at least in the sense that it wasn't counterfeit. DHS was a nice, convenient cover—the spaghetti dinner of government agencies that had been scrambled together to form an umbrella initiative to tackle terrorism on US soil was a very broad church. The badge brought with it a level of power and a lack of accountability that other domestic law enforcement agents would kill for.

I took another few seconds making a thorough search, knowing I needed to move fast. I found a couple of spare magazines for the Glock and pocketed them. Finally, I found a cheap push-button cell phone. I didn't have the time to examine it, so I switched it off and pocketed it, too. I stood up and turned back toward the doorway, hoping that Bryant had made it back to the room. I gripped my purloined Glock and held it low as I approached the next car.

As I passed into the next car, I saw passengers sleeping on either side. I thought about tucking the Glock into my belt, but the attached suppressor made it too cumbersome. In any case, I didn't really want it to leave my hand. Instead, I held it down by my side, trusting that the matte black finish wouldn't be noticed against my dark clothing in the dim light. I moved quickly down the aisle. I made sure to glance at the occupant of each seat as I passed, on the off chance that Bryant had taken a seat. Another thought occurred to me: What if one of my pursuers was in here, hiding in plain sight? If so, they would have me at a lethal disadvantage by having the ability to recognize me. A teenage girl wearing Beats by Dre headphones glanced up as I passed, probably wondering why there was so much traffic all of a sudden. I gave her an amiable smile and continued toward the next car.

This was the last one before ours. Another sleeping car. I was a third of the way along the corridor when a voice spoke from right beside me.

"Kowalski?"

I tensed up and started to raise my gun before I remembered I was wearing the downed man's headset. Bone conduction. There hadn't been a burst of static, and the sound quality was good enough to fool me that the speaker was whispering in my ear. I froze midstride, holding my breath in case it gave me away.

"Kowalski, you there?" The voice sounded tense, on the verge of being concerned.

I cleared my throat and tried to keep my voice as neutral as possible. "Copy."

There was another pause, and for that instant I was certain the speaker knew what had happened. But then he started talking again. Excited, eager to convey whatever message he had.

"We've got one of them—Bryant. We think Blake's up ahead. Any sign? What's your location?"

Shit. I swallowed and took a step back. "Negative."

There was a pause, a longer one this time.

"Kowalski? Is that you?" Obvious suspicion in the voice. And then a single word. "Midnight."

The word required a response. I turned and started running back to the previous carriage as fast as I could.

"Rambler," I guessed, figuring I might as well launch a Hail Mary.

I was hopelessly off target. The volume of noise rose, saying, "Who is this?" even though I was pretty sure he already knew the answer to that.

"Kowalski's out of action," I said quietly. "Walk away now, or I can arrange a reunion."

FORTY-TWO

STARK'S INDEX FINGER was pressed against the bud of the earpiece, trying to get a clear read on the other man's voice over the clattering of the train. He activated the mute switch as he turned to Ortega and Usher. Ortega was jamming Scott Bryant up against the wall of the room with one hand. An entirely unnecessary precaution: one, because Bryant's hands were securely cuffed behind him, and two, because the terrified look in his eyes said he wasn't taking an off-beat breath without their say-so.

"Kowalski's down," Stark said.

Usher simply nodded, entirely unaffected, just processing the new information. Ortega's face twisted into a pissed-off grimace, and he pushed down hard between Bryant's shoulder blades, mashing his face harder into the wall.

"Where the fuck is Blake?" he hissed in Bryant's ear. "I swear to God…"

Bryant closed his eyes and gritted his teeth. Stark sighed.

"Think about it, Ortega. This was their room. We caught Bryant coming back from the front of the train. What does that suggest?"

Ortega shrugged. "Blake's tricky. You don't know him like I do."

"I don't know him at all, and I'd just as soon keep it that way." Stark opened the door a crack and glanced up and down the corridor to check it was still clear, then closed it and turned back to the others. "Ortega, stay here. Make sure he doesn't go anywhere. If Blake shows up, put a bullet between his eyes. Kowalski made a mistake."

Ortega nodded and put the barrel of his Glock against the base of Bryant's neck. "Make a sound and I'll paint the fucking wall." His voice was matter-of-fact. He nodded at the other two to go ahead.

Stark opened the door again and stepped out into the dark corridor, Usher close behind. He walked quickly down the corridor, keeping his eyes on the doors. There were four cars ahead. Kowalski was in one of them, perhaps dead. And in that same car, or close by, would be Carter Blake, armed and ready to do whatever it took to survive.

FORTY-THREE

THE MOST IMPORTANT quality in my line of work is adaptability. Control what you can, but don't expect to control everything. Make plans, but don't be surprised when you have to tear them up and start from scratch. Don't waste time on wishing things were different; deal with them as they are.

The last couple of days had tested that maxim to the limit. Forget about plan B. I was shifting on to plan E or F by the time I picked up the transmission from Kowalski's friend. So they had Bryant. I guessed there was an outside chance that whoever I was speaking to was misdirecting me, that he had known whom I was speaking to as soon as I acknowledged the call, but I doubted it. If there was anything I could still do to save Bryant's life—and I wasn't entirely sure there was—it would have to wait until I'd extracted myself from this situation.

Five seconds after cutting the communication off, I was at the far end of the second-to-last car. I passed through the first set of doors and found what I'd expected to earlier in the night, when the odds of survival had seemed ever so slightly less impossible. There was a STAFF ONLY sign on the second door. Passing through it, I found that the space in the forward locomotive was truncated, to make room for the driver's cabin up ahead. It was laid out similar to the sleeping cars, but with fewer doors. Staff quarters. Had it not been for the encounter with the man I now knew was Kowalski, I would have tried to find an empty one and hole up until we hit the next station. But it was too late for that now.

The train swayed and the wheels clattered on the tracks. Already, I had a pretty good idea of what I had to do next, and I wasn't happy about it. I glanced out of the closest window and tried to estimate our current speed. It was difficult, in the dark, with the snowflakes dancing across my field of vision on the diagonal. I thought we were moving a little slower than we had been earlier, but not much. Maybe forty-five, fifty miles an hour, down from sixty. And then I thought about who was behind me and closing the gap. They would be here within a minute. I had Kowalski's Glock, so taking my chances in a gunfight was an option. It would be three against one, of course, but at least they would be hampered by the tight space. On the other hand, I could try to bargain, but that would be futile when it was so obvious I had nowhere to go.

Nowhere to go, except one place.

I stepped toward the door and examined the controls in the side panel. There were two large buttons: one to open, one to close the door. Both were inactive while the train was in motion, of course. It was an identical setup to the exit doors at the equivalent positions in all the other cars. I had spent a little time examining them earlier, making sure I knew where everything was, all while not really admitting to myself that I might find myself having to take this course of action. Above the button was a glass box with a button inside, like a fire alarm. The bold text beneath it said, EMERGENCY

DOOR OPEN—DO NOT USE WHILE TRAIN IN MOTION. It was good advice.

I unscrewed the suppressor from the Glock and put the gun inside my coat. Then I wrapped my sleeve around my fist and smashed the panel. The glass fractured smoothly and dropped out, leaving the emergency button unguarded.

Out of the corner of my eye I saw movement. I glanced back through the doors to see the doors at the far end of the next car opening and closing; at least two men were silhouetted against the light between the cars.

I hit the button and the doors sprang out and open. I felt the sudden blade of a freezing fifty-mile-an-hour slipstream bite into me.

FORTY-FOUR

As THE DOORS OPENED, the exterior footplate, tucked in to increase aerodynamics, automatically folded down. There was no time to contemplate the stupidity of what I was about to do. If I hesitated, my pursuers would be upon me.

Gripping tight onto the edge of the doorway with my right hand, I put one foot on the plate and reached my left hand out for the handle on the outside. The wind slammed into me like a wall of ice. As I gripped the handle, I was grateful that it was coated with smooth plastic—had it been bare metal, the cold would have stripped the skin from the palm of my hand.

Snow-covered pine trees whipped past. I looked down at the ground rushing past and estimated we were doing fifty, minimum. If I jumped now, I would likely be killed. But if I hung around waiting, the men with guns in pursuit would make that a definite. About a mile ahead of us, I could make out the beginning of a gradual incline—the train would have to slow a little for it, maybe enough to make jumping a better bet. But it would take a minute or longer for that to start happening, and I didn't have that long.

I stepped fully out on the footplate and switched hands on the exterior handle. The wind, catching the entirety of my body now, pulled at me, trying to cast me out into the slipstream. The noise of the wheels on the track was deafening, and I tried not to think about being thrown under them.

I concentrated on keeping at least three points in contact with the train at all times. Even so, I felt the ache in the muscles of my right arm as I gripped the handle tight while reaching around the edge of the car. On a freight train, I would have had lots of options. There would be a clear gap between cars where one was coupled to the next, and I would have been able to sit atop the coupling, sheltered from the full force of the elements. But this was a passenger train, so there was a flexible cover to provide a passage between cars. I prayed for a handhold on the back of the car. I gritted my teeth as my fingers fumbled up and down the small, unseen area within my grasp and found only bare, freezing steel.

I risked a glance back. The snow strafed my eyes, but there was no one at the doorway yet.

I brought my left hand back around so I was gripping the handle with both hands, adjusted my grip, and moved both feet as close to the edge of the footplate as I possibly could. The car rocked toward me as the train entered the start of a long curve—a minute adjustment for hundreds of tons of train, but one that almost hurled me from my perch. I held my breath and gripped until the train settled into the curve and then reached around the back again.

This time my fingers found something. I felt around the protrusion—it was rectangular with rounded edges: a rung. Just what I was hoping for, as long as there were more.

Just then, a face appeared at the door. Gun raised. Without thinking, I gripped the rung, let go of the handle, and swung around the edge, gripping the rung with my right hand as soon as my feet had left the footplate. The wind caught me straight-on and tried to fling me into the air again, but I held firm and swung into the narrow gap. I heard a muffled curse from the doorway as the man who had seen me realized what had happened.

There were three more rungs above the one I was hanging from with both hands. Their purpose was to provide access to the roof for maintenance workers. No big deal to scale a stationary train safely parked off-line and undercover. Quite a big deal on a moving and rocking train with snow coating the rungs, making them slippery. I glanced down and found a bottom rung, catching it with one foot and gratefully stepping the other foot onto it. Back to four points of contact.

I reached up and grabbed the next rung, then one after that, pulling myself up so my line of sight was above the edge of the roof. The wind hit me full in the face once again, the oncoming snow streaming into my eyes. I squeezed them into slits and located a vertical rung on the roof, more by feel than by sight, and started to haul myself up.

Then I felt fingers close around my right ankle and dig into my flesh. Too slow. I gripped the rung on the roof with both hands and put my weight on the other foot, trying to kick the hand free. The fingers held firm, so I shifted my weight onto my left side and tried another tack: dragging the hand with me, hoping the owner would either quit or lose his balance. At first the hand held tight, but then I felt the fingers release a little, shift to the leg of my jeans. I kicked again and suddenly I was free. I scrambled onto the roof, my knuckles whitening on the roof rung as I braced myself against the full onslaught of the oncoming wind. For a moment all I could do was kneel and hold on.

A barely audible sound from behind me, carried to me on the wind, reminded me I didn't have the luxury of time for a coffee break. It was the sound of my first pursuer's foot on the bottom rung at the end of the car. I gripped the roof rung tightly with both hands and lifted my feet, bracing them on the surface of the roof in a crouch. I squinted at the track ahead. The incline was closer now, but still some way off. Shifting my focus to the immediate foreground, I saw more balance rungs jutting up from the center of the car's roof. The middle section was a flat strip about two feet wide before the downward curve became more pronounced on either side. This was no simple and steady path, though, because the rungs were spaced at least fifteen feet apart, with nothing else to grab on to in between. But then, they hadn't been designed for this activity.

I braced myself like a runner on the blocks, put my weight on my right foot, and launched myself straight ahead. I made it two strides toward the next rung before the biting wind slowed my momentum, trying to steer me off the edge. I angled my body toward the next rung and dived for it, just catching hold with my right hand. I brought my left hand up to it, braced myself, and then risked a glance over my shoulder. Through a tunnel of flying snow, I saw the upper body of a man reaching out over the end of the car, one hand on the rung. As I watched, I saw what he was doing with this other hand. Muzzle flare flashed twice, the suppressed noise of the gunshot utterly lost in the cacophony of the train and the wind. Instinctively, I ducked, pressing myself down against the roof. One of the bullets smashed into the surface of the roof ten feet from my hands; the other was lost in the night. I had a minor advantage now, because his visibility facing ahead was worse than mine looking behind. I braced my legs and knees on the roof until I was confident of letting go of the rung with one hand, then reached into my coat and pulled out Kowalski's Glock. Another muzzle flare and a third bullet hit the surface of the roof five feet from me this time. Getting closer, I trained the gun on the end of the car and fired four shots in as tight a grouping as I could manage, with the motion of the train and the wind spilling my aim all over the place.

The upper body of the man vanished. Had I hit him? Absolutely no way to know, but I had forced him to duck back down at the very least. I turned my head and squinted into the oncoming snow, finding the third rung sticking up another fifteen feet away; just past the idle of the car. After the experience of getting from the first rung to the second, it looked a hell of a lot farther.

Changing tactics, I positioned myself on the far side of the rung, my feet jutted forward, my hands reaching behind me to hold on. I took a breath and let go with my right hand. Another breath and I let go with my left again, lunging forward. This time, the wind knocked me down on my first stride. I felt myself being blown off course again so I dropped flat to the roof, spreading my arms and legs and making myself as small a target for the wind as I possibly could. Now I was spread-eagled on the roof, halfway between rungs, with no way to hang on but by the friction of my hands on the rough surface of the roof. Keeping my face down to the roof, I inched forward, praying I had taken out the first guy and that his compatriot hadn't worked up the nerve to follow yet.

I risked raising my head a half inch to look ahead and saw the next rung was almost within reach. Just another three pushes ought to do it. One...two...

A bullet hole appeared in the roof next to my right elbow. I yelled a curse and ignored the urge to recoil. Then I gritted my teeth and inched along the rest of the distance, grabbing the rung and pulling myself along again.

I heard the snap of another shot passing by my head. With all of the noise, it had to have been pretty close for me to register it at all. When I looked back, I saw that both of them were there now: one was on the roof already, the other maneuvering himself up from between the cars. I raised my gun and fired three more times in their direction. Again, impossible to tell for sure, but if I'd hit anything, especially from this distance, it was pure luck. Which was true for them, too, of course. But with two guns, they had twice as many rolls of the dice.

I glanced behind me, squinting my eyes into the direction of travel. We were almost at the incline, and I knew the train would be slowing a little, even if it didn't feel like it from my current position. Waiting for the optimum jump window wasn't an option. There were two more rungs before the end of the car. I had to try to cover the distance in quick succession. The more space I could put between myself and the two men behind me, the better.

I tucked my Glock into my belt. Then I got my feet in position again, trying to ignore the fact there were probably bullets in the air around me, and launched myself toward the next rung. The journey to this one felt easier, either because I was getting the hang of this, or because the direction of the wind happened to stay constant for that particular five-second span. I gripped the second-to-last rung and took a breath, not bothering to look back this time.

I focused on the final rung, telling myself that all I needed to do was get to it and I could slide down between the cars and give myself the best possible chance of surviving the jump.

I let go of the rung and took one stride, two…

And then my foot slipped. Maybe it was a patch of ice, or maybe I had misjudged the edge of the flat section of roof in my haste to complete the last lunge. I would never know the exact reason. All I knew was that suddenly I found myself tumbling toward the right side of the roof. My right foot twisted as it hit the more pronounced slope, and I tried to go flat again, anything to keep myself on the roof. And then the wind caught me full on and flung me toward the edge like a rag doll.

My left shoulder jammed off the edge of the roof, and then I was in the air. White above and black below. Then black above and white below.

FIVE YEARS AGO

Kandahar, Afghanistan

MY FIRST THOUGHT was that I had the worst hangover in the world. As I started to pick up the feed from my other senses, I began to realize that this was something worse than just a hangover. I was lying on a hard surface, on my side with my arms around my back. Nearby I could hear the sound of somebody moving, working on something.

I started to open my eyes a crack and immediately closed them again as the light stabbed into them. With an effort of will, I opened them and realized that the dazzling light source was nothing more than morning sunlight cast through the gap between the bottom of a panel door and the concrete floor. For some reason, the fact it was a panel door brought everything back to me. The stakeout on Ajmal al Wazir's garages, the sudden alert from Collins, the empty alley, and then... I was guessing the "and then" was the source of my headache. A stinging ache in my neck told me I'd been injected with something that had knocked me out for a while. The garage. I was in the Wolf's lair. And I wasn't alone.

Trying not to make any noise, I turned my head. I saw wooden crates and cardboard boxes full of parts and junk. I saw that there was only one other person with me. His back was to me, as he leaned over the sidewalls of a flatbed pickup truck. He wore combat pants, an olive-green T-shirt, and a pocketed assault vest. He almost looked like...

"Murphy?" I said out loud, before I had a chance to think it through.

Murphy turned and squinted at me through what, to him, probably felt like half-light. When I saw the guilty expression on his face, I knew I had been too quick to speak. I also knew why I was lying on my side, and why my arms were in such an unnatural position. I didn't need to try to separate my wrists to know they were cuffed, but I tried it anyway. Sometimes I hate it when I'm right.

"How long you been conscious?" he asked. I noted the word he had used: conscious. Not awake.

I started to speak, but no sound came out. My throat was as dry as the desert. I swallowed to try to moisten my mouth and tried again.

"What the hell is going on?" I said, intentionally slurring my voice a little.

Murphy picked up a rag and wiped his hands. I was suddenly aware of the smell of the place. My nose isn't up to sniffer dog standard, but I'm familiar with the distinctive aroma of C-4 in large quantities.

With an effort, I managed to haul myself up into a seated position. My eyes were getting used to the relative light now, and Murphy's features had come into focus enough so I could see an expression of genuine regret on his face. I knew exactly what was happening, and why.

"I'm sorry, man."

I jiggled the cuffs again, the chain clinking against the concrete of the garage floor.

"Take the cuffs off," I said.

He shook his head. "No can do, compadre. Orders."

"What the hell are you talking about?"

He shrugged. "No point in playing dumb, not now."

I stared back at him, waiting for him to continue.

"You and Martinez. We know about it. He got away, for now. We can't make the same mistake with you."

"I don't know what—"

"You know, all right. Maybe you didn't know we knew, is all. Your little meetings with the senator. Getting pretty friendly with those folks. Especially that little blonde. Nice work, by the—"

"Don't fucking talk about her."

He shrugged. "Fair enough. We're not interested in her. Not unless you were stupid enough to tell her anything, which, personally, I don't reckon you would have been. Or am I wrong?"

I quelled the anger rising up in me, stamped down on the urge to haul myself to my feet and rush him. With my hands bound behind me, it wasn't like he would let me get close enough to tear his throat out with my teeth. That didn't stop me from thinking about it, though.

"You're not wrong."

He nodded, looking pleased. "So. Here we are. I guess you know what happens next."

"You're making a mistake. I didn't even speak to Martinez. I didn't even know he was the one."

"Ain't my mistake to make. This comes all the way from Drakakis. He wants to cut the cancer out. And unfortunately for you, that includes present company."

"Killing me won't make any difference. The senator has—"

He cut me off. "We're taking care of the senator,

too." He held his wrist up to the light and squinted at the dial on his watch. "You might just outlive him, in fact."

"You can't do this."

"Do what?" Murphy asked, affecting confusion. "This never happened."

He walked around the back of the truck and slammed the tailgate. I knew the flatbed would be packed with explosives, together with whatever extras Murphy had just finished hooking up. I wondered how long he would give himself to get clear of the scene.

He cast his eyes over the flatbed again, just to make sure he hadn't forgotten anything, and then walked back across the garage. He crouched down, gripped the edge of the panel door, and yanked it up. The panels continued up into the space above, letting the full glare of the morning sun in. Murphy took a step outside, paused, and turned back to me. He was silhouetted against the glare, his face unreadable.

"Sorry, hoss. You know this is nothin' personal."

And then he took another step back and hurled the door back down again. I heard it rattle again as he padlocked it behind him.

I didn't waste any time on a comeback. I needed every iota of energy I could muster. With all purpose in my life reduced to the basic survival impulse, my head cleared and the aches in my body seemed to vanish. I knew the odds of me making it out in one piece were slim, so I didn't think about the big picture. Break it down into stages and focus on one thing at a time.

Stage one: Get my hands into play. I tugged on the cuffs again to check the give and thought there might just be enough. I sat back on the chain, worked it down as far as I could manage on the backs of my thighs, and then brought my knees up to my chest, straining until I managed to pass my wrists under my feet. With my hands in front of me, I took a second to get a look at the cuffs and confirmed I wasn't doing anything about them in here. There were no hacksaws in sight, and even if there had been, the high-tensile steel would take me twenty minutes to cut through. I was betting Murphy had left a lot less than twenty minutes on the clock.

Stage two: I crossed the room to the back of the truck and brought my hands up to open the tailgate. I saw exactly what I had expected to see. Blocks of standard-packaged C-4 explosive and a detonator. If it had been a movie, there would have been a helpful digital clock with red numbers telling me how long I had to defuse it. Instead, I had a small black detonator wired up to a smaller block of C-4 and a gut feeling for how long Murphy would have given himself to get away. Two minutes, max. I wasn't sure I could do anything helpful in that time.

I angled my body over to look at the device, forcing myself to be thorough. It didn't look like there was anything fancy, no booby traps. This wasn't my area of expertise, but I had a rudimentary knowledge of demolitions. I tried the most obvious thing first, disconnecting the wire that fed from the battery. The lights stayed on, meaning that, as I'd expected, there was an integrated battery backup. I glanced around, hoping to see a screwdriver, or anything with a point small enough to fit the screws in the back, and came up with nothing.

Shit. This thing was going off any second now, along with the car bomb and the bombs in the adjacent garages, and there was nothing I could do about it. The car bomb was overkill, of course. Just the block of C-4 attached to Murphy's detonator would be more than enough to...

And then an idea occurred to me.

I picked up the detonator and its smaller block of C-4 and ran with it over to the door. I jammed it in the farthest corner from the pickup, right at the half-inch gap where the door met the ground. It wasn't even half a chance. The likelihood was the blast would be enough to ignite the explosives in the car and level the whole garage, along with most of the neighborhood. But if I could shore up enough junk around the device, and if the panel doors gave away immediately...

I stopped thinking, started moving the crates of parts and any other junk I could lay my hands on in front of the device, hoping that the crates weren't full of anything explosive. I was hampered by the cuffs, and I had to put all of my weight on my hands to push the crates across the floor. At the back of my head, I started to calculate how long since Murphy had left. There were a couple of layers of crates in front of the door now, and it looked hopelessly inadequate. I'd started to push the final crate over when I heard a short beeping sound.

I scrambled to my feet and hurled myself across the garage as the gaps between the beeps reduced to a single monotonous tone. I slammed myself to the ground behind the rear tire of the pickup. I covered my ears, opened my mouth, and jammed my eyes shut. I had a split second to note the irony of taking cover behind a giant car bomb when time ran out.

I registered a wave of fierce heat and blinding light before the pressure wave hit like an express train.

When I opened my eyes again, the world had gone silent this time, instead of dark, but I was comforted that there still appeared to be a world. The entire opposite side of the garage had disappeared—a loose flap of corrugated iron hanging down where there used to be a wall and a door and a pile of crates and assorted junk. I got to my feet and circled the pickup. It was blackened on the other side and the windows had all blown out, but the explosives hadn't detonated. Obviously.

I started to move toward the hole in the wall. I had to get the hell out of there. Murphy wouldn't be coming back to inspect his work, but that blast would be attracting plenty of other attention, and I didn't relish the idea of explaining to the first responders what a dazed American was doing setting off a bomb in a suburban garage. And then I felt a stab of pain and realized there was an even more pressing problem. There was a deep gash in my right side. A sharp wedge of wood, shrapnel from one of the crates, was embedded in my side.

I reached down and moved it. It hurt like hell, but it didn't seem to be in too deep. I hoped that meant it looked worse than it was. I took a grip and started to pull it out. A couple of inches of crimson-stained wood slid out of a hole in my side. I bit down on my bottom lip hard enough to draw more blood in an effort to stifle the yell as I pulled the wooden blade out of my stomach.

Pressing my still-cuffed hands hard against the wound, I headed for the hole in the wall and out into the light.

FORTY-FIVE

Minnesota

BRYANT KEPT HIS mouth shut and his eyes focused dead ahead on the sign two inches in front of him that said NO SMOKING. This was it—this time, it really was it. He was going to die in a cramped airless box, looking at a fucking no smoking sign.

But then the man with the scar on this face started talking. He pressed the barrel of his gun a little harder against Bryant's neck first, and chuckled as he winced.

"I bet you hadn't planned on this when you got out of bed yesterday," he said.

"No kidding," Bryant said.

The man with the scar drew the gun back a little and yanked Bryant around by gripping the collar of his shirt. He nodded his head at the seat by the window, indicating that he should sit down. The whole time, he kept his pistol trained on Bryant.

Bryant took two careful steps across the small space and sat down, keeping his eyes on the gun. He was no firearms expert, so he had no idea what make it was. He had seen enough cop shows to know that the cylinder on the end was a silencer, meaning that the man with the look of sadistic amusement in his eyes wouldn't need to worry about making too much noise. He could empty the gun into Bryant's head while the passengers mere inches away on either side continued their peaceful dreams uninterrupted.

Bryant was as scared as he had ever been in his life. Even as this crossed his mind, he realized that the exact same thought had occurred to him at least three or four time in the previous twenty-four hours. Each time, it had been no exaggeration, but each time, that level of terror had been quickly superseded.

When he had passed through the doors and seen the man with the gun approaching, the man who so clearly recognized him, he thought he was dead. When he had been forced to identify the roomette he and Blake had shared and then been bundled through the door, he'd assumed that his stay of execution would expire as soon as they caught Blake. He had remained convinced of that during the brief questioning. They had asked him where Blake was, and he had replied that he didn't know.

And then the other two had left: the one with the close-cropped reddish hair and the creepy one, the one with glasses who had stared at him the whole time without saying a damn word. But now the demeanor of the one with the scar had changed slightly. He had been the most aggressive around the others, but now he was sharing a joke, letting Bryant sit down.

"Did he tell you who we were?"

Bryant nodded slowly. "He told me he used to work with you."

The man with the scar on his face smiled, as though Bryant's phrasing amused him. "That's right. He was good at his job, too. Damn good. He used to help us track down targets. I guess he's still doing that, although…" He looked Bryant up and down appraisingly. "Probably easier targets these days, huh?"

Bryant said nothing. They sat in silence for another couple of minutes. The man with the scar relaxed his posture a little, though his eyes and the barrel of the gun never wavered from Bryant.

"Did he tell you why we're looking for him?"

"He told me you're trying to kill him."

The man shrugged. "That's sort of up to him."

"Didn't seem that way at the airport."

He smiled. "Sorry about that. You were just in the wrong place at the wrong time. Although... I guess you wouldn't have been in that wrong place if you hadn't taken what didn't belong to you, would you?"

Bryant swallowed, decided to ask the question. "Are you going to kill me?"

The man with the scar seemed to consider that. "Depends how cooperative you can be."

"What do you mean?"

"How much did Blake tell you about where he's going?"

"I don't understand. Your friends have gone to get him, right?"

"Right."

"You don't think they'll catch him? He has nowhere to go."

"You'd think, wouldn't you?" he said. "Trouble with Carter Blake is, he's a hard man to pin down. And believe me, this is from personal experience. We should know soon either way, I guess. Either my two friends are going to come back with Blake, or they'll come back with his body...or they're not gonna come back."

"You don't sound like you care either way," Bryant said.

"No point trying to second-guess fate. By the way, I noticed you didn't answer my question."

Bryant hadn't answered the question because he'd been trying to give himself time to think. This guy clearly thought there was a possibility Bryant could be of value to him, and that might be the reason he was still breathing. He had asked where Blake was going. That could be for the reason he had given: just in case they didn't manage to catch him. Or it could mean the information was valuable in itself. The Black Book.

He thought about Blake's remark about the flash drive. These people didn't just want Blake dead; they wanted a threat neutralized. If he could make the man with the scar believe he could be of value in finding Blake's planned destination, perhaps he could keep himself alive a little longer. Another gamble, this one with life-or-death stakes. But what choice did he have?

"He told me he's headed back east."

The man with the scar shook his head and pointed at the window with his free hand to remind Bryant of their direction of travel. "That's pretty obvious."

"He told me he needs to pick something up."

"Is that right?" An interested tone in his voice now.

Bryant nodded. "A flash drive." He paused and considered his words carefully. *Just a bluff. You've done it a thousand times at the card table.* "He didn't tell me what was on it."

The man's gray eyes narrowed. "That's very fortunate for you." He paused, and was about to say something else, when he was interrupted by a rap on the door.

"Midnight," he called out.

"High noon," came the response from the other side of the door.

The man with the scar nodded, and Bryant surmised it was some kind of countersign, to make sure he was opening the door to the person he expected. The man with the scar got to his feet, keeping the gun on Bryant, and locked the door with his left hand.

The man with glasses was in the corridor, along with another one Bryant recognized as the man Blake had fought a couple of cars down. The big, blond-haired guy. He had come away from that confrontation with a broken nose, the blood smeared across his top lip. He assumed this was the Kowalski he had heard the others talk about. Two things were obvious to Bryant right away: the redness of the skin on their faces and the flakes of snow on their coats told him they had somehow been outside, despite the fact the train was still very much in motion. The other thing was, Blake was not with them. Kowalski stayed in the corridor while the man with glasses squeezed into the roomette.

"Where's Stark?" the man with the scar asked.

"Stopping the train."

"Blake?"

The man with the glasses didn't answer right away, his brow furrowed in consternation. When the one with the scar prompted him, he shook his head. "I don't know."

"You don't know?"

He gave him a look that betrayed a hint of irritation, but when he spoke his voice was perfectly controlled. "Not for sure. Probably dead."

The man with the scar's eyes widened. He glanced at Bryant for a second, as though about to share a joke with him, then thought better of it and looked back at the man with glasses. "Probably," he repeated.

"I think we might have hit him. He fell." He jutted his head in the direction of the ceiling. "From up there."

"You call it in?"

He nodded. "Within two minutes, giving our coordinates. Should be enough to locate the body, if he is dead."

"If."

The one with the glasses gave no response. Instead he turned to Bryant, looking at his cuffed hands. His expression said Bryant was just one more problem that had to be dealt with.

"We'll have to take him with us."

FORTY-SIX

THE ONLY REASON I knew I wasn't dead was because I was pretty sure I would have ended up someplace warmer.

I lay still for a few seconds waiting for the pain in my back and arms to die down and for the world to stop spinning. When I started to be able to breathe normally again, I rolled over from where I had landed and wiped snow off my face. It felt like I had lost some time, but the lights on the back of the Empire Builder a few hundred yards away told me it had been only a minute or so since I had fallen. The lights disappeared as the track curved into the trees and the sound of the engine and the wheels on the tracks slowly died away to nothing. All of a sudden, it was very dark, and very quiet. With some trepidation, I put weight on my arms and raised myself off the ground a little. Everything seemed to be in working order, nothing broken as far as I could tell.

So how in the hell had I managed that?

I drew myself up to a sitting position and looked around. I blinked a few times to acclimate my eyes to the darkness, until I could make out my surroundings more clearly. I was about ten feet from the tracks, in a pile of snow that was a little deeper than the rest of the surrounding area. I looked above me and started to piece together what had happened. The track was lined here by tall pine trees. The one directly above me had

had most of its snow knocked off. I guessed that when I'd fallen from the roof, I had smashed into the soft branches of the pine tree. Lots of give, lots of kinetic energy absorbed. From there, I had fallen through the branches, which had absorbed more of my momentum, and landed in the deeper patch of snow beneath the trees. All told, it had been just enough to save my neck.

I patted myself down and found I still had the phone I had taken from Kowalski, but not the gun. I remembered I had tucked it back in my belt before making the final run and wondered if I had lost it before or after I left the roof of the train. I looked around me and saw no trace of it.

I got to my feet, giving myself another once-over for any injuries that might have remained unnoticed while I lay on the ground. Other than the ache along my right side where I had hit the ground, I was fine. I reminded myself that, for a couple of reasons, that was likely a temporary condition.

For one thing, I probably didn't have long before company arrived. Ordinarily, leaving a moving train at a random point cross-country in the dark would have been an excellent way of making a clean escape. But not with these guys, not with the resources they could call on. The men who had followed me onto the roof had seen me plunge from the train. They would be open to the possibility I'd been killed in the fall, but they wouldn't be close to satisfied until they saw a body. The only thing in my favor was the thick clouds would make live satellite surveillance impossible. But that only reminded me of the other immediate danger.

I was in the middle of God-knows-where at four in the morning in the middle of a blizzard. I cursed myself for leaving the gloves I had bought in Seattle in the roomette. Now that the immediate threat to life had passed, I realized how cold it was. I buttoned the coat and yanked the collar up to protect my neck from the freezing air. I rubbed my hands together to get the circulation going. From my extremely limited knowledge of the geography in these parts, I tried to work out exactly how dire my situation was.

The last stop had been Detroit Lakes, scheduled for three ten. The luminous dial on my watch read just after three forty. Half an hour at roughly fifty miles an hour was twenty-five miles, which meant that the next stop was another twenty-five miles down the track. That information was academic anyway, even if it had been two miles. I couldn't follow the track unless I really wanted to make changes easy for my pursuers. I knew there were small cities and towns dotted throughout Minnesota, and I just had to hope I was within range of one of them.

The tall pines lined both sides of the tracks. On my side, I could see lines of trees marching back until the darkness became absolute. On the other, I could make out slivers of snow between the trees. Open ground, perhaps somewhere I could see more of the lay of the land. I spent a few seconds kicking loose snow over the depression I'd left in the ground, knowing I could do nothing about the noticeably snow-free branches of the pine directly above it. Perhaps enough fresh snow would have fallen to disguise it by the time anyone else found the spot.

When I had made my landing zone blend in as closely as possible to its surroundings. I climbed the slight incline back toward the tracks, scuffing my feet to obscure the footprints. I stepped across the tracks and jogged down the incline into the woods on the opposite side. The air was slightly warmer in the shelter of the trees, but my breath was still visible in clouds. The stand of pines extended about a hundred yards or so, and then I emerged at a field that sloped upward gently. I stopped before I hit the open, snow-covered ground at the far side of the wood and jogged along the line of the sheltered patch for a couple of minutes. There was no way to avoid leaving footprints, but it wouldn't do any harm to prevent my entrance and exit points lining up.

When I had gone as far as I thought would make any difference, I stepped out into the field. It was hard to orient myself in the darkness, with the snow falling all around, but then a gap in the cloud cover passed under the moon and I got enough of a glimpse of my surrounding to get me started. The field was bounded by pines on three sides. On the fourth, it sloped upward to a near horizon.

I started up the hill, the deep snow making each step ten times harder than on the dry ground in the forest. The effort of lifting my feet and the all-pervading cold seemed to sap my energy the way driving a car with the pedal to the floor will drain the gas tank. What had looked like a five-to-ten-minute hike to the top of the rise seemed to be taking me all night. The ache in my side faded into a painful stiffness as the bruising started to set in, making the going even tougher.

Finally, as I got closer to the crest of the hill, I saw my first promising sign of the night. There was a slight orange glow in the night sky: the reflection of streetlights on low clouds. The sight was like a shot of adrenaline. I redoubled my pace, forging ahead to the crest of the hill. A couple of minutes later I'd made the crest and my hopes sank again. The land dropped into a wide valley. All around were fields and lines of trees. There was a town ahead—I could make out the small cluster of lights—but it had to be at least ten miles away. I estimated it had taken the best part of half an hour to cover a mile to this point, and I hadn't been as cold or as tired when I had started out.

But the town ten miles away was all there was. So I crossed the crest of the hill and started walking down toward the valley, keeping the distant glow of salvation within sight.

FORTY-SEVEN

Minnesota

WITH BLAKE GONE, there was no need to maintain their anonymity on the train. As soon as they had gotten Kowalski back on his feet, Stark had simply walked to the head of the train, knocked hard on the driver's door, and demanded, with the help of his Homeland Security ID, that the train be stopped.

The driver, a small, dark-haired woman in her late forties, was so surprised and intrigued by the break in the routine that she had gone along with the order with only the most minor of questions, questions that Stark answered easily and with an authoritative air of irritation. They were hunting a pair of suspects who had been passengers on the train. They had already taken one into custody, but the other one had managed to jump from the train, and they needed to go back to the right spot.

He covered all of this in the time it took the train to slow to a gradual halt, probably a couple of miles down the line from where the driver had started applying the brake, and four or five from the area where Blake had jumped. That was all right, though. Others were on their way.

"Does this thing back up?" Stark asked.

The driver grinned indulgently and shook her head.

"Not unless you have a couple hours to spend, Officer. And you'd have to make the call to my boss. And no offense, but you'd need more than that little ID card."

Stark left her and turned to head back down the train to Ortega, Usher, Kowalski, and their prisoner.

"Whoa, hold on there," the driver called after him. "What do I do about this? Who do I call?"

Stark shrugged. "We're good here. You can get on your way."

She looked suddenly suspicious. "What department did you say you were from again?"

"Thank you for your cooperation," Stark said with finality, and headed back to the others.

They left Bryant's hands free, on the understanding that any attempt to run would only result in a bullet in one of his kneecaps, and the five of them disembarked the train and started to backtrack. It took them a few minutes just to draw level with the rearmost car of the train, which still showed no signs of getting underway again. Getting everything reset to start up again was probably a job for twenty guys, Stark thought, knowing that the driver was probably cursing him right now as she thought about explaining to her boss why she had stopped the train for a random guy waving an ID card.

Usher checked the GPS coordinates and informed them they had a five-point-two-mile walk ahead of them in the snow. Ortega grabbed his phone and checked in with the second team, who had been en route to the next stop. They were thirty minutes away from the location where Blake had jumped or fallen, maybe a little longer, depending on how much the weather slowed them down and how far off-road they had to go to reach the exact spot.

The snow on the ground alongside the track was shallower and lay on top of gravel, so it was relatively easy going. They moved at a quick clip, just below a jog. Bryant moaned about the pace a couple of times, before Ortega slapped him across the back of the head and reminded him he was low on options.

In the end, they made the coordinates only ten minutes behind the second team, who had had to backtrack a significant distance to find a route through the woods. Their two cars were parked alongside the tracks, the headlights dazzling in the darkness. Stark heard the barking of the dogs from a couple hundred yards away as their handler finished removing them from the off-road vehicle. As Stark and the others approached, the passenger door of the nearest vehicle opened and a tall figure in a long coat got out. It took Stark a second to recognize Murphy, silhouetted against the lights and the falling snow.

"What kept you?"

"I like to be fashionably late."

The second team had already identified the landing area: one of the tall pine trees at the side of the track had its snow cover noticeably depleted, as though a very discerning gust of wind had hit it hard recently, while ignoring all of its brethren. With that signpost, they found that the snow directly beneath showed signs of impact and of an attempt to cover tracks.

There was no blood.

The pair of black Dobermans strained on their leashes, their eyes on the woods across the tracks.

Murphy watched the dogs with interest. He bent

down to look one of them in the eyes, baring his teeth in a grin. The dog emitted a low, pissed-off growl. He straightened up and looked across the track to the woods beyond.

"Let's run this rabbit down."

FORTY-EIGHT

I HAD BEEN walking for about an hour when I reached the stream. It bounded a line of trees ahead of me, cutting diagonally across my path. It was too wide to jump, and I didn't relish the idea of wading through the freezing water. I was shaking underneath my coat as it was. My hands were jammed into my pockets, but I had lost the feeling in my fingers. I knew I was in trouble. If I gave into the screaming urge in my joints to stop walking, to sit down and rest, it would be fatal.

So I started to walk along the bank, in the direction of the flow. Perhaps the stream would narrow farther along. Or maybe there would be a bridge. Where there was a bridge, there would be a road.

How far had I come? It was impossible to say. The snow continued to fall, making it difficult to judge the ground I'd covered. The only sounds accompanying me for the last hour had been my breathing, the sound of my footsteps in the snow, and the noise of my pulse thudding in my head. When a new sound echoed across the landscape from far behind me, I thought it was my imagination at first. A trick of exhaustion. But then I stopped and listened.

Barking. Not the barking of a single guard dog at an isolated farmhouse. Hunting dog.

I looked at the water. It would be freezing, would

hasten the onset of hypothermia. But I didn't have a choice.

I tensed and jumped in, barely feeling the cold as the water covered my legs below the thighs. I splashed through the stretch of deep water until I reached the shallows on the other side. I started along the edge of the water. There were enough loose rocks and branches that the snow had fallen unevenly, making any tracks I left indistinct. My steps became more faltering as the freezing dampness bit into my legs, and a couple of times I almost stumbled heading back into the water. When I had gone a reasonable distance from the spot I'd crossed, I started to look for a place where I could climb onto the bank. And then I saw the bridge.

It was a narrow hump-backed bridge, its walls covered with snow. I hurried to the edge of the bridge and climbed up the bank. A narrow road led out from the woods, turning into a plain strip of white as it emerged from cover. I stopped at the side of the road for breath and listened. I could still hear the barking. It was a ways off, but getting closer. I hoped the stream would give them trouble following the scent, but I wasn't betting on it. I steeled myself to keep going, but just as I was about to start walking again, I heard a sound. Different from the barking, more regular. A low, droning noise. An engine.

I shrank back into cover behind the parapet and watched the road, considering my options. Could it be more of them? A pincer movement from the opposite direction? Anything was possible. On the other hand, I wouldn't last much longer out here. A moment later headlights appeared through the trees. The engine was louder now. It sounded a little rough, in need of tuning.

As I watched, a pickup truck appeared out of a bend in the road fifty yards into the woods. I could stay behind the bridge, or I could take my chances. The biting-cold wetness around my legs made the decision for me. I stepped out onto the road and walked forward, raising my hand as the headlights washed over me.

FORTY-NINE

THE PICKUP ROLLED to a stop beside me, the wipers working hard to clear the snow on the windshield. In the
rainbow-shaped gap over the driver's side, I could see
an old man behind the wheel. He was the only person in
the vehicle as far as I could make out. I approached the
passenger door and glanced inside, seeing no one else
in the car. The old guy nodded at the door impatiently.
I pulled the handle and swung the passenger door open.

"Thanks for stopping," I said, hearing my voice stut-
ter through shattering teeth.

"Well, don't just stand there, son. You're letting the
cold in." I was reassured when I heard the unmistakable
Minnesotan accent—lots of long vowels.

Gratefully, I slid in beside him. The heat blasting
from the dash felt incredible. I was chilled to the bone,
so I wouldn't feel full the benefit for some time, but
already my face was beginning to regain some of its
feeling.

"So what the hell are you doing out here on a night
like this?" he demanded as I shut the door. His voice
was caught between annoyance and curiosity. I guessed
he was in his early seventies. He was wrapped up warm,
and his wrinkled face was covered by a straggly gray
beard.

"Car broke down." Three words at a time was about

all I could manage, which was good, as it saved me coming up with a more elaborate excuse.

"Jesus," he remarked. "Ain't you heard of Triple A?"

I grimaced and shook my head.

"Flat tire?" he asked. "I got a jack if you need. How far down the road you parked?"

I shook my head. "Think I broke…axle. Go back in morning. Can you g…" I kept stuttering around the *G*, but he caught my drift.

"Give you a ride?" he nodded. "Reckon I can do better than that, son. Maybe only a little better, but better. My place isn't too far. Hell, I let you out up in Stockton right now, might as well put a bullet in your head. No place to shelter this time of night. First bus doesn't leave until seven on a Saturday, and that one don't come back this way."

"I'm grateful," I said.

"Name's Preston. Sam Preston." Sam took his right hand from the wheel and held it out. I took it with some difficulty. He shivered at the coldness of my hand, and his brow ceased in concern. "Damn, son."

"Jerry Robinson," I said.

Sam turned in the road and started back the way he had come. After we'd gone a little way and I'd started to regain the power of speech and warmed up a little, I asked him what he was doing up this time of night.

"I'm a light sleeper, son. Don't sleep much these days. And I heard those dogs."

Sam asked me a few more questions about my breakdown as we drove, and I answered as nonspecifically as possible, hoping he wasn't trying to catch me out. He lived in an old farmhouse a couple of miles from the bridge. As we got out of the car, I heard the barking of the dogs again, from much farther off now. I tensed at the noise. I saw Sam watching me with interest. I covered my reaction by rubbing my arms, pretending they had stiffened during the car journey.

He told me I was welcome to use the shower and found me some of his old clothes to borrow, both of which I received gratefully. The fit wasn't perfect—he was an inch or two shorter than me and a little thicker around the waist—but all in all I'd been very lucky. It was only now, in the stove-heated warmth of the house that I realized just how lucky. If Sam hadn't happened by at that moment, it was a dead cert that either the cold or the dogs would have done for me.

"You can rest up on the couch tonight, I reckon," he said, indicating a well-loved brown leather couch that had been patched multiple times. "Tomorrow we'll call Dave Marshall over in Stockton and see about getting you towed."

The couch looked inviting, but I knew it wasn't to be. I had a rendezvous in Chicago in a little less than fourteen hours, and I didn't want to miss it. I would need Banner's help if I was to get back home before Winterlong caught up with me.

"Actually, Sam, I'm in kind of a rush. I'm grateful for the offer, but I need to get back on the road."

He said nothing, waited for me to continue. As though I would need a better excuse than that.

"Kind of a life-or-death thing, in fact."

He said nothing for a minute, his eyes unwavering in the flickering light from the wood burner. "You know, that road hits a dead end half a mile from the bridge. A hundred years ago, it used to go all the way to Greenville, I guess, before the railroad cut through. No way to get onto the road coming from that direction. Your car didn't really break down, did it? And your name's not really Robinson."

I shook my head slowly.

"I'm sorry I misled you."

"I may be old, but I'm not senile. Who's chasing you, son?"

"How do you know somebody's chasing me?"

"It's the only reason you'd pass up a warm couch on a night like this. And besides, I told you I heard the dogs. A pack of 'em. Trained, hungry. Huntin' dogs. Not much to hunt out there in weather like this. Not anything really. 'Cept maybe for you."

I smiled ruefully. "I'm sorry, Sam. You're right about the dogs. Somebody is chasing me, somebody I don't want to risk leading to your door. It's not the cops, if that's what you're thinking."

"Figured that. Nearest prison is fifty miles away, and you don't got the look of an escaped con. I wasn't sure at first, but…" He looked me up and down again. "Well, when I saw the shape you were in, I decided I was on the side of the man runnin', not the men huntin'. Does that make sense?"

I nodded.

"And, truth to tell, I make up my mind about a fellow pretty quick, and I've decided you're an okay guy, Robinson. Or whatever your name is. But that doesn't mean I'm about to let you walk back out there."

I opened my mouth to protest, but he waved a hand to stop me. "Stockton's ten miles away. There's a bus station. Can you get to where you're headed from there?"

"I think so."

"All right. The bus for Saint Paul leaves at seven.

You take my truck, you'll have plenty of time to make it. Just park it by the general store and put the keys through the mail slot. I can get them back from Eppie Davis in the morning."

He tossed me the keys and I caught them. I stared down at them in my palm, still red from the cold. "Why?"

"Because Eppie delivers my groceries on a Sunday, and she can take me back into town."

I shook my head. "Why are you helping me?"

Sam looked as though he hadn't considered the question until now. He thought on it for a second and then shrugged. "Good to be neighborly. And like I said, you seem like an okay fella."

Two hot cups of coffee later and I was behind the wheel of Sam's pickup. He'd told me the road only went one place, so I followed it at a steady thirty miles an hour, taking care in the snow and constantly checking the landscape for men with dogs and flashlights. I saw nothing for the whole ten miles. If I was lucky, the dogs would have lost my scent at the river. Perhaps the men chasing me would think I'd fallen in and been carried downstream. Either way, if the dogs picked up the scent again, it would be lost at the point I got into the pickup, and the tree cover meant there were no tracks in the snow. Sam's house was outside any realistic search area for a man on foot, so I didn't think he would be troubled tonight. Later, I would make sure they knew I was out of the area, but for tonight it would be better if they thought I was dead.

I made Stockton at half past six. It was a one-stoplight town. The bus station was a bench at the side of the road with a schedule fixed to a post. I kept going and found the general store a little farther ahead. I turned into the log, parked the truck, and wiped the steering wheel and the gearshift down. Then I locked up and put the keys in the mailbox of the general store as Sam had asked.

Thirty minutes later, I boarded the bus to Saint Paul. The only other passenger was a teenage girl with a backpack who kept her headphones on and her eyes pointed out of the window at the dark predawn landscape. The heating was lousy, but it was a lot better than being out there. I wrapped my coat around me like a blanket, put my head against the window, and let myself drift off to sleep with the motion of the bus.

FIFTY

BRYANT DIDN'T KNOW how long he had been locked in the small, dingy motel room. He was exhausted, but the combination of the hard plastic chair and the flickering fluorescent light seeping through the blinds conspired to deny sleep.

He didn't know exactly where he was. All he knew was that somehow, his situation had actually gone downhill since the point where he was facing a lengthy jail sentence. After the forced march back along the railroad tracks, he had been handed over to another two men with clothes and demeanor similar to that of the four on the train. He was bundled into a black SUV with one of the men sitting in the back with him while the other drove them cross-country until they hit a dirt track. The track led to a small country road, which led to a larger country road, which led to a highway, which eventually led to a town, and then another.

From the signs they had passed, Bryant knew they were still somewhere in Minnesota. They sped through a series of small towns, before slowing their pace and pulling into the parking lot of a beat-up motel. Before he had time to draw breath, the door had been flung open by another man and he had been hustled inside. He only had time for brief impressions: an almost-deserted parking lot covered in a blanket of snow, a red, white, and blue neon sign with some of the letters missing. The rooms were arranged in a row facing the lot. The two men took him to the room at the far end and locked the door behind them. Boards had been securely screwed over the front-facing window, and even the small window in the bathroom.

And now he was alone with his thoughts, wondering how in the hell he was going to get out of this situation. Nobody in the world knew where he was. He realized with grim humor that this very same thought had comforted him just a couple of days before. But this was different. Now it was looking likely that no one would ever know where he was again. He wondered what Jasmine would think, as the months and years passed. Most likely she would assume he had simply disappeared with his illicit retirement bonus. Alyssa would grow up believing that her father hadn't cared enough to stick around, or even to contact her again. Thinking about that future scenario was more painful even than the contemplation of his imminent demise had been. Instead, he tried to focus on the here and now.

He considered the men in whose custody he suddenly found himself. He already knew they wouldn't hesitate to use lethal force. Blake hadn't been particularly chatty about these guys. Either because he didn't want Bryant to know too much for his own good, or because Blake just wasn't a particularly chatty guy.

Except for that brief period back on the train, of course, when he'd opened up a little. Bryant had been wondering about that. After keeping him well and truly in the dark for more than a day, Blake had given him a couple of interesting pieces of information about himself and his plans. He wondered now how far Blake would get. He found himself hoping that he would make it all the way.

The sound of a key in the lock startled Bryant, and he stood up from the chair. The door was opened and a man he hadn't seen before stood in the doorway. The man was definitely one of them, so he knew not to raise his hopes. He was around six feet. Older than the others, but a toned physique was evident beneath the suit and shirt.

"Sorry to keep you," he said.

Bryant guessed that was an attempt at humor.

The man in the suit stepped into the room and carefully locked the door behind him. Bryant tensed, his mouth suddenly dry. He tried to swallow, thinking of something to say. Was this it? He saw the next few moments in his mind's eye like some kind of grisly home movie, the man in the suit pressing the barrel of the gun to Bryant's forehead and pulling the trigger twice. His body being discovered in the morning by some maid, hours after the men in the dark clothes had vanished into the night, as though they had never existed.

The man was watching him with amusement, seeming to read his thoughts.

"Relax. We're not going to kill you yet."

"Yet? Is that a joke? That's a joke, right?"

The man ignored the question. He examined the duvet on the mean single bed carefully, swiped his hand across it as though removing dust, and sat down opposite Bryant. "We didn't find Blake yet."

"Okay."

"I am sorry about the rough treatment," he said, sounding almost sincere this time. "My boys get a little overzealous sometimes. My name's Jack Murphy. We're going to need to keep you around for a while."

"I told your men, he didn't tell me where he was going. Believe me when I say I wish I'd never met the guy. Two days ago I was set up for a two-million-dollar payoff and a sweet retirement. Thanks to Blake, I've been shot at, dragged halfway across the country, and now I'm being held who-the-fuck-knows where by a CIA death squad or something." He paused and reconsidered. "No offense."

Murphy waved away the comment amiably. "The man's got a way of endearing himself to people. I'll give him that."

"What did he do, anyway? You people have to want him bad, to go to all this trouble."

"You could say he broke a promise," Murphy said. "Or…he broke a confidence, at least. The other thing is, he took something that didn't belong to him, and I'd like to get it back."

He was talking about the Black Book. The flash drive Blake had told him about. Bryant made sure not to show any reaction, but he picked up on the way Murphy had said "I," rather than "we."

He shrugged and held his hands up. "So what do you need from me?"

Murphy considered the question. He put his hands on his knees and leaned forward. "Blake left you behind on the train."

"I noticed."

"I mean, it's not like he had much option. But if I know him like I think I do, that's going to bother him."

Bryant snorted. "Hardly. Blake doesn't give a shit about me. He was going to turn me in to my old boss."

Headshake from Murphy. "That may be the case, but

he went to an awful lot of trouble to keep you with him. He wanted to keep you alive, is what I'm guessing."

"He wanted to keep his chance at a paycheck alive," Bryant shot back, though he knew Murphy was right.

Murphy straightened up and folded his arms, staring at him appraisingly. "Ortega said you mentioned an item that we're interested in. A flash drive Blake has stashed somewhere."

Shit. Bryant had completely forgotten he had let that slip. He said nothing, and Murphy waited a minute before nodding.

"That's right, so he did tell you something. But what else did he tell you?"

"That was it. He said you wanted some files he took, nothing else."

"You're sure about that?"

"I'm sure."

Murphy looked at him for a long moment, the good-humored smile slowly draining from his face until there was nothing but a dead-eyed stare. "That's disappointing. I wonder if we can jog that memory, Bryant."

Bryant shivered involuntarily and opened his mouth to say something. He closed it again when he realized his mind had gone utterly blank.

Murphy got to his feet and took a step toward him. "You've probably heard stories. 'Enhanced interrogation' is the official term. It's got its uses, I have to admit. But I'm kind of old-fashioned."

Murphy reached into his coat and then there was a pistol in his hand. With one smooth motion, he raised it and pressed the barrel against Bryant's forehead.

"You're scared, right?"

Bryant nodded.

"But your head's clear. No pain distorting your thinking. No physiological desperation to tell me exactly what you think I want to hear. Just the certain knowledge that I will pull this trigger if I think you're lying to me."

Bryant's eyes met Murphy's. His expression was calm, patient. It was Bryant's turn to talk now.

FIFTY-ONE

New York City

FARADAY SAT DOWN in front of the monitor screen and clicked on the icon to pick up the video call. The little clock in the corner told her it was 8:56 a.m., and an hour earlier in Minnesota. More than four hours had passed since they had lost Blake, and with each minute, it became less likely the news from the team was going to be positive. The screen went black for a second, and then Stark's face appeared. He looked tired and pissed-off, his face reddened from the cold.

"We lost him."

She kept her face composed. Another setback, just when they thought they were in the endgame. "What happened? He had nowhere to go."

He shook his head. "He definitely survived the fall from the train. The dogs picked up the scent clear at the jump point. We tracked him a couple miles cross-country until they lost the footprints and the scent. Like he vanished into thin air. He could still be out there, holed up somewhere—there's a lot of woodland about. Weather's still a mess; otherwise we could get a bird in the air with thermal imaging. Until that changes, we're working old-school: dogs and flashlights. And we've already taken a casualty."

"What do you mean?"

"Ortega ran into some trouble in the woods. He slipped on a concealed verge, broke his leg. He'll be fine, but we're a man down."

Faraday said nothing. She trusted Stark could guess her thoughts on this latest disaster.

"Anything on Kowalski's phone?" Stark asked, keen to change the subject.

Faraday looked over at Williamson, who was tapping away on her keyboard, working on her third can of Red Bull with two empties standing at attention. Faraday turned back to the screen and shook her head, noticing how tired she herself looked in the smaller rectangle at the bottom right.

"He switched it off on the train. If he still has it, he'll be too smart to turn it back on in range of a cell tower."

"I guess it was worth a try," Stark said with zero conviction in his voice.

"We have another complication, which you may not be aware of," Faraday said. "There's a chance Blake may have some leverage over us."

She explained about the Black Book, not mentioning that she had only become privy to this information a few hours before. Stark took the information in without comment. It didn't really change things from his point of view—they still had to find Blake.

Faraday thought for a minute and then came to a decision on something she'd been mulling over for the last couple of hours. "We're going to release an image of Blake to the FBI. Not a photograph. We'll go with a facial composite. We need some more eyes on the ground."

"That's an excellent idea," Stark said at once. He had been pushing for her to release more information on Blake all along.

"I'm glad you approve," she said, not overdoing the sarcasm. "Now, what's happening with Bryant?"

Stark considered the question and shook his head. "I don't think Blake would have told him anything useful."

"So what the hell do we do with him?"

Had it been Usher or Ortega she was having this conversation with, it would have been a question she would never have asked, because she probably wouldn't like the solution they would come up with. In reality, there was no need to do anything drastic. Bryant could probably be debriefed and safely dumped at a bus station with a warning not to talk. If Stark was right, if Blake had told him nothing, he would have no idea who they were. He would have no proof even if he did. Her instinct said it was too early to make any firm decisions in that direction, though. Stark's expression seemed to say the same thing.

"Murphy's talking to him now. He thinks we can use him."

Faraday was confused. "Use him how?"

"He thinks Blake will deal if we let him go."

"You don't sound convinced."

Stark nodded. "That's because I'm not. This guy was a target. A job. Why would Blake give a shit about him?"

She thought about it. It would certainly have been easier for Blake to cut Bryant loose back in Seattle. Why hadn't he?

"I don't know, but Murphy might have a better insight. See where it goes. We're working on the big picture back here. There have been some…promising developments."

"Oh yeah?"

"When you need to know, Stark. When you need to know."

FIVE YEARS AGO

Kandahar, Afghanistan

THE MAN WHO was not called Ahmad opened the door.
When he saw my face, his dark brown eyes filled with
anger, turning to shock when he saw my bloody, handcuffed hands clutching the hole in my side. He glanced
around the alley outside the door and then jerked his
head to tell me to come in.

A minute later, I was in the same back room where,
just a few days before, I had exchanged money for information. It was too uncomfortable to sit down, so I
leaned against the desk while he gave the hole in my
side a cursory inspection, shaking his head.

"I'm going to patch you up so your insides stay in,
but after that I don't ever want to see you again. Is that
clear?"

"Don't worry about that. I'll make it worth your
while. This—" I said, indicating the wound with my
free hand, "and one other thing."

"You push your luck, American. Whatever else you
want, we discuss after we deal with that little scratch."

I shook my head firmly. "No. First."

He persisted for a minute, insisting that my wound
needed immediate treatment. He was right, but I knew
the hole in my side could wait just a little longer. At last
he shook his head and gave me what I wanted, leav-

ing me in the back room with a fresh burner cell as he went to fetch his first aid kit. I dialed the number from memory. Carol's personal cell, not her work one. I held my breath as I waited for the call to connect between continents and then held it a little longer as I heard one ring, two, three. The pain in my side was utterly forgotten. The only thing in the world for me was that crackly electronic buzz.

On the fourth ring, the call was picked up.

"Hello?"

"Carol, it's me."

There was a pause, and I realized I hadn't thought through exactly what I was going to say. While I was coming up with something, she spoke again.

"Where are you?" Her voice sounded a little strange, out of it. Then I remembered it was late in New York, going on midnight.

"I'll tell you later. This is really important. I need you to get out of your apartment and—"

She said my name, and all of a sudden I realized that it wasn't the time zone or the quality of the connection that made her sound off. She had been crying.

"I'm not in my apartment, I'm on my way to… I thought you were calling about…about…"

"About what?"

"Haven't you seen the news?"

"The news?"

"It's on every channel. The senator's been shot. His wife's dead. He's in surgery, but it doesn't look… Wait a minute. What do you mean I need to get out? Why were you calling if you didn't know?"

The words caught in my mouth. I didn't know what to say or how to say it.

"Are you still there?"

"I think I know the people who did this. I think you could be in danger, too. There's a—"

"What the hell did you do? Who are you?"

"Listen to me. I'll explain later, I swear. The people who did this just tried to kill me, too. They know about you and me. I don't know if they'll come after you, but we can't take the risk. You have to disappear. Just for a little while."

"This is your fault. Oh my God. This is..." She sounded dazed, like she'd been hit a second time while reeling from an initial blow.

"Carol!" I yelled. "Listen to me. You can hate me later, but right now we've got to get you someplace safe. Where are you right now?"

"I'm with Clare, from the office. We're on Eighth, headed down to the office. It just seemed like—"

"Have her drop you off. Tell her to go home."

"What are you talking about?"

I gave her the address of an apartment building in Hell's Kitchen, made her repeat it back to me.

"Get into the lobby. The mail slot at the far right on the bottom row is unlocked. There's a key taped to the roof of the slot. The key is for apartment six-two. Are you getting this?"

"What are you—I'm not going anywhere. John would—"

"You can't help him right now. I need you to listen to me. The people who did this are very dangerous, and the office is the last place you should be right now."

I thought about Carlson's file. The pictures, names, and dates. They would make sure that disappeared, coordinated with the hit. They had probably visited the office already, but I wasn't taking the chance.

Carol started to protest more, and I cut her off. "You don't ever have to see me again. You don't ever have to speak to me again. But do this one thing for me."

There was a long pause. I heard a female voice in the background. *Are you okay?* Carol didn't answer. With an effort of will, I gave her time to think without saying anything else. Eventually, she spoke.

"Okay, this one thing."

I felt a surge of relief. "Thank you. Tell your friend to stay away from the office too—get the police to clear it first. You remember the address?"

"I've got it."

"Tell me again."

"I've *got it*."

"Good. Get rid of your cell and go there now. Try to stay put until I get back."

"Back from where?"

"I'll tell you—"

"No." Her voice suddenly lost its dazed quality, and I felt the full force of her anger directed at me. "Not later. Tell me now. Where are you? *Who* the hell are you?"

I took a breath. "Afghanistan. It'll take me a few days to get home."

She made a noise that sounded like she was trying for a sarcastic laugh, but it came out more like a sigh. "You didn't answer my other question."

It was a good question. Who was I, anyway? "Maybe I don't know the answer right now," I said. "I'll see you in a few days. Stay safe."

There was silence for a moment, as though she was

thinking of something to say, and then she settled on a simple, "Goodbye."

As the line went dead, I took the phone from my ear and looked at the blank display. Then I glanced down at the bloody mess of my shirt, my left hand clutching the wound in my side. Now that the message had been delivered, the pain rushed back with a vengeance. I looked up and saw Ahmad had returned with bandages and disinfectant.

"You look even worse than you did a couple minutes ago."

I nodded. "Feels that way."

FIFTY-TWO

St Paul, Minnesota

THE BUS GOT into Saint Paul just before half past nine in the morning. I had managed to sleep for most of the journey, although somehow that had made me feel even worse than I had at the outset.

I got off the bus with the rest of the passengers who had accumulated during the trip from Stockton. After checking the options for the next leg of my journey, I put some distance between myself and the bus station. I was still four hundred miles from Chicago, and I had less than a hundred dollars left. I invested some of that in buying another pair of gloves and a baseball cap. Then I used the last ten bucks to buy coffee and a cheese-burger and fries at a bustling travel diner. The calories helped, replenishing my energy after the long night, and I started to go over the next few moves I had planned.

I would need more money. There was no getting around that. I didn't think Winterlong would have been able to make any link between me and the backup checking account I could access with an ATM card, but I wasn't a hundred percent certain, either. There was only one way to find out.

I had almost finished eating when someone changed the channel on the TV attached to the wall of the diner. I stopped chewing when a familiar-looking face appeared on the screen. The caption said SEA-TAC SHOOTING, and above that was a computer-aided artist's impression of my face. The pic had clearly used my driver's license ID photo as a starting point, but I knew they had deliberately not used the picture itself. That would have made it too easy for a helpful police or federal facial recognition expert to match it to my DMV record, get my name, and start to unravel the whole thing. With my newly close-cropped hair and three days of stubble, I didn't look a whole lot like my computer-generated avatar, but still, it was not an encouraging development.

After I finished eating, I crossed the street to a branch of Western Union and presented the card to the smiling clerk, asking how much I could withdraw in cash today.

As I watched her tap on the keyboard to call up my account, I had a flashback of the airline ticket clerk's sudden change of demeanor when she typed the name from my driver's license into the computer. It would have been safer to use the ATM outside, I guessed, but it would also have limited me to withdrawing a couple of hundred. At least this clerk wouldn't be typing the name Carter Blake.

"You can withdraw one thousand dollars standard today, Mr. Grant, or up to ten thousand with two forms of ID."

I shrugged as though that was no problem. "Go for the thousand," I said. "I don't have my license with me."

She smiled. "Certainly, sir," and quickly produced ten crisp hundred-dollar bills, sliding them under the glass partition.

Twenty minutes later I was looking at another face behind glass at another counter, this one at the Union

Depot Transit Center. This face was male, middle-aged, and unsmiling. He acknowledged my request with a curt nod and provided me with a one-way ticket on the Megabus to Chicago. I waited until the driver was behind the wheel before I got on, watching the bus ramp for anyone who seemed too interested in the other passengers. I took a free seat at the back and pulled the brim of my cap down low. The bus started to pull out exactly on time. Twenty-four minutes to eleven.

FIFTY-THREE

New York City

"YOU WANTED TO see me?"

Williamson hovered by the door, her eyes pointed at the carpet. She looked a little uncomfortable away from her natural element. Faraday didn't make a habit of inviting people into her office. Murphy was generally the only regular visitor.

Faraday looked up. "First of all, I wanted to thank you for the work you've been doing, particularly over the last couple of days."

Williamson nodded. "I'm making progress with the house. I just need—"

"This isn't about that."

Williamson stopped. She looked up for the first time, waiting for Faraday to continue.

"This is about something else, and it goes without saying it is not to be discussed with anyone outside this room. That includes Murphy." *Especially* Murphy, she thought.

"Okay."

"The fingerprints hit in Iowa that was deleted. Is there anything else like that in the system?"

Williamson looked confused. "Any other fingerprint hits?"

"Anything that's been purged."

Williamson smiled. "You're asking me to find things that aren't there."

"Is that a problem?"

Williamson thought it over. "It's a challenge. The DR-17 was a lucky break. I had to reverse-engineer the trail, go back to the deletion. I could only do that because I knew what wasn't there. So the first question I'd need to ask is, what else isn't there?"

Faraday considered. How did one find something that no one knew was missing? The fingerprint hit was an unusual event. It had allowed Williamson to trace the deletion, and that deletion had suggested a pattern of behavior. If Drakakis hid that, perhaps he'd hidden other things. "Look at the patterns. Eyes-only reports for the director. Look for anything different. Anything that looks like a gap."

"I don't have—"

Faraday typed a password into her computer and stood up, offering Williamson her seat. "You have full access now. Level twelve."

Williamson's eyes lingered on Faraday for a second and then dropped to the screen. She sat down and began to hit the keys.

TEN MINUTES LATER, Williamson sat back from the screen, her brow furrowed.

"Well?"

She shook her head. "If you need details, files, I can't give you anything."

"But you can give me something."

She shrugged. "Dates. File sizes. There was a sub-folder in AAR restricted to Drakakis's user ID. Someone with level-twelve access purged everything from it a year ago."

"When, exactly?"

"December thirty-first."

The date of Drakakis's suicide. It had been his last act—the opposite of a suicide note. Instead of leaving a last testament behind, maybe he had erased one.

"How long will it take you to recover the deleted files?"

Williamson shook her head. "Can't be done," she said firmly. Faraday was taken aback. She had never heard Williams say that before. Generally everything could be done; it just required time and resources.

"What do you mean? You retrieved the fingerprint hit."

"That was different. That came through the main server. It left a trail. This was completely local to Drakakis. Technology-wise, it's as close as he could get to keeping it in a notebook, then burning it. We're lucky he carried out the deletions in this office. Otherwise we wouldn't be able to see that there was once a folder. Everything's gone, purged." She hit a couple of keys and an exported CSV file appeared on the screen. Columns showing creation dates and file sizes and deletion dates. The date was identical in every row:

20141231 23:37

This was important. Important enough that a man who was about to die had cared about it.

"You say this...ghost folder was in the local AAR file?"

Williamson nodded.

After-action reports. It was customary for these to be edited, polished, before they went anyplace else, even at the classified level. But this was another level even more locked down.

"This is what really happened," Faraday said to herself.

"Excuse me?"

"Thank you, Williamson. That'll be all."

She nodded again and left. Faraday kept looking at the door for a minute after it closed, thinking about the tear-shaped bloodstain beneath the new carpet.

She opened the secure file space on her desktop computer and started going back through, comparing the dates of the deleted files with the final classified AARs on her system. Every one of the deleted files corresponded with a logged AAR. Which meant that the files she and her superiors could see were not the whole story. She looked at the list, identifying locations just by the reference number. Baqubah and Mosul in 2009. Kandahar, 2010. And then she noticed that one of the files did not have a corresponding record on the official list. But the date was within days of the Kandahar mission. The mission on which Carter Blake had gone AWOL.

FIFTY-FOUR

Chicago

THE BUS FROM Saint Paul to Chicago was scheduled to take a little more than eight hours. Despite the weather warnings, the snow had abated for a few hours. It was like Mother Nature was taking a deep breath in preparation for the storm to come. At first I was sure I would be too wired to sleep, but as the bus joined I-94 and headed east, I began to feel drowsy. With some time to kill, I didn't fight it. As I slept, we passed out of Minnesota and into Wisconsin. I awoke as the bus made a stop in Madison and then snoozed lightly for another hour.

I forced myself to wake up fully at five o'clock. The sky had been dull and gray all day, a kind of perpetual twilight that now began to darken as night approached. The snow began to fall again, and all around us the traffic began to slow. I glanced at my watch and hoped we wouldn't fall too far behind.

Just after seven o'clock, we came into view of Chicago. The memories surged within me as I saw the skyline rising up ahead of us. All at once, it seemed like years since I'd last been here, and like yesterday. We made it into the city only a half hour behind schedule. The final stop was at Van Buren Street, but as the bus passed the Willis Tower, I got up and made my way down the aisle to the front of the bus.

"Mind if I hop off here?" I asked the driver.

"I mind a lot, pal," he began, and then he turned his head and saw the hundred-dollar bill in my hand.

I hopped onto the sidewalk on South Wacker and glanced around the street to make sure nobody was paying me any undue attention. I bought a map and a large black coffee from a 7-Eleven and worked out that my destination was only a couple of miles away. A quick ride in a taxi, but I had spent way too long sitting down. The walk would let me work the ache out of my legs and get some fresh air into my lungs. I headed west and south, making my way down to West Roosevelt Road and crossing the park. I reached my destination with two minutes to spare. The name on the sign had changed since last time, but there was still a coffee shop there. It looked like it was in the process of emptying for the night.

The lights at the intersection turned red and I waited for the evening traffic to bunch up before I crossed the street and pushed the door of the coffee shop inward. I couldn't remember what it had been called the last time I'd been here, but it was named McGrady's now. The interior decor had changed: Dark wood was out; bright orange walls were in. I cast my eyes around the interior, seeing lots of empty tables. I breathed a sigh of relief when I saw a familiar face in the back of the shop. Special Agent Elaine Banner was sitting with her back to the wall, with a good view of the doorway and the window looking onto the park. She had spotted me first, of course, and was looking at me with an expression that was hard to read. It wasn't quite a welcoming smile.

A waitress called out a greeting. I nodded and pointed at where Banner was seated to let her know

I didn't need to be directed to a table. As I pulled out the chair across from Banner, the waitress asked if she could get me anything, and I ordered another coffee. Banner had a bottle of sparkling mineral water in front of her, half of it poured into a glass. We waited for the waitress to leave, watching each other over the table. I was smiling; Banner still wasn't quite.

"Hi," I said.

"Hi."

"You look great," I said, meaning it. Banner was thirty-two years old, five eight, slim. Shoulder-length brown hair, styled slightly differently since I'd last seen her. Incredibly dark brown eyes that gave you the nagging sensation that she knew what you were thinking. She didn't return the compliment, and although I hadn't looked in a mirror in a while, I thought I knew why.

"What happened to your friend?" she asked, her eyes flicking to the street outside and then back to me.

"We ran into some problems. We got separated. I'm trying to fix that."

Banner shook her head. "Jesus, Blake. Do I even want to know? Every field office got a want sheet today with a composite on it that looks very familiar."

She slid a sheet of paper in front of me. The same facial composite I had seen on the news in Saint Paul.

"No name?" I asked.

She shook her head. "Very vague. You're wanted for questioning in connection with the airport shooting, and there's a national security implication. You're not believed to be a live terrorist threat, which has to be the nicest thing anyone's said about you lately."

"I do my best."

"I thought I disappeared before and they found me. Because I was out there. Eventually, you have to stick your head out of the door and see the world again. I could hide for a while, but eventually I'd be back in the same position. I had a friend who thought he was safe. He went to the ends of the earth, pretty much literally."

"Des Moines?"

"Siberia. They found him and they put two bullets in his head, and now he's another unclaimed body that nobody misses. That could be me in a year."

"You do it your way and it could be you tomorrow."

"That's the difference, Banner. It would be on my terms."

Her dark brown eyes fixed on mine and held them for a long minute. This time it felt like the other way around. I knew what she was thinking: that she should volunteer to come with me, to help. But I knew she wouldn't, just like she knew I wouldn't let her. She had a daughter, a career. Things I wouldn't jeopardize even if I thought her coming with me would make any difference. She was putting her neck on the line enough as it was. We had spent only a short time together and hadn't spoken since, but all the same, we knew each other too well and respected each other too much to indulge in the meaningless bullshit of that phony discussion.

She lifted her hands from mine. I curled my hand around the key, palmed it, and slipped it into my pocket. I left the other key, the one for the safe house, where it was.

"Take care of yourself, Blake."

I felt a sudden chill. Elaine Banner didn't know that that was pretty much the last thing I had said to Coop, three nights ago. And I answered in the same way.

"I always do."

FIFTY-FIVE

Minnesota

STARK'S CELL PHONE rang just after eleven p.m. He and Murphy were in one of the two rooms in the motel. Ortega was in the adjoining room guarding Bryant. They had made the decision to stay put for the night, just in case they got a lead on Blake—or his body—in the vicinity of his last-known location. The rest of the Minnesota team had split. Half of them were headed for the biggest urban conurbation in the area: the Twin Cities of Minneapolis and Saint Paul. The others had gone straight ahead to Chicago. In the absence of any other information, it made sense to cover the intended destination of Blake's train.

Stark reached for his phone and looked at the display, his eyes widening when he saw what was on it. The number of the caller, the first few digits denoting a cell rather than a landline, plus a single letter: K.

Kowalski's phone.

Murphy looked up from the small desk, where he was in the middle of his tenth game of solitaire. A jack of spades poised in his hand, midway to the table. "Are you going to answer that?"

"It's him. On Kowalski's phone."

Murphy said nothing, but a satisfied grin appeared

on his face. He tossed Stark the compact digital recorder they had ready for this occasion.

Stark caught it one-handed and switched the recorder on. He turned away from Murphy, put the call on speaker, and answered with a curt, "Hello."

There was no immediate answer, but he could tell someone was there. While he waited for a response, he looked back at Murphy, who was tapping out a message on his own phone, no doubt telling central command that Blake was calling.

They would be able to pinpoint his location in real time. Unless Blake had done something creative, which was always a possibility. Either way, Blake had made a deliberate decision to contact them using Kowalski's phone, which meant he was doing it for a reason.

"Am I speaking to Mr. S?" the voice on the other end of the phone asked quietly.

Stark glanced at Murphy. The phones they used were burners: always discarded following a mission. They contained only the numbers of the other field ops, plus a generic number that automatically rerouted to central command. Because the numbers changed so frequently, there had to be a simple way of identifying them, so each was listed according to initial. Kowalski's phone would have contained four numbers: O for Ortega, S for Stark, U for Usher, and H for home. It wasn't exactly an impenetrable code, but it didn't need to be. He considered his next words carefully. Negotiation is easier when both parties have names.

"I'm here, Blake. Call me Stark. Where are you?"

"Bora-Bora. You?"

"What a coincidence, that's where we are. Buy you a drink?"

"Some other time. Who else is listening in, Stark? Anyone I know?"

Murphy smiled and spoke in the direction of the phone. "Long time no see, hoss."

"Murphy," Blake said after a second. Stark caught an undercurrent of cold burning anger in his voice that hadn't been there a moment ago. "Wish I could say I've missed you."

"Likewise."

Stark cleared his throat. "Thanks for calling. I take it you want to discuss terms of surrender? Smart move. It'll go easier for everyone."

"New on the team, huh?" Blake said, a hint of amusement in his voice.

"Not exactly."

"Then you've been around long enough to know why I'm not going to give myself up. I have an aversion to being shot in the back of the head."

"Come on, Blake. It doesn't have to go that way." In the corner of his eye, Stark saw Murphy smile as he said this. He ignored it, listening as Blake started talking again.

"Can I ask you something? Why now?"

"I don't have to tell you anything," Stark said.

Blake spoke again immediately, his voice breezy, as though politely dismissing a sales call. "Well, good luck. It was nice talking—"

"Wait," Stark said quickly. "Why did you call?"

"I wanted to make a deal."

The two of them exchanged a glance. Murphy's grin widened at the confirmation of his theory.

"No deals, Blake," Murphy said, his voice resolute, giving no hint that this was exactly what he wanted.

"You're coming with us. Your call if you want to be vertical or horizontal."

"It's not as simple as that, though, is it? You don't just want me. You want the Black Book as well."

Stark looked at Murphy again. The amusement had drained out of Murphy's eyes at the mention of the Black Book. So he did have it.

"I don't know what you mean," Stark said.

"Cut the bullshit," Blake said. "I don't have time for this."

"We're listening," Murphy said.

"Good. But before I talk about the Book, you're going to tell me why this is happening."

"No mystery about that, Blake," Stark said. "You're a rogue element. You need to be taken out of circulation. One way or another, just like you said."

"We had an arrangement."

"Change of management," Stark said. "We do things differently now. It doesn't look good to have an assassin running around, putting the unit at risk."

There was a long pause.

"Blake, are you there?" Stark asked.

"I don't suppose it would do any good to tell you whatever they told you about me is a lie? I'm talking to you now, Mr. S. I know Murphy knows it's bullshit. I didn't kill the senator."

Stark glanced at Murphy, who was rolling his eyes again.

"That's right, Blake. You're a poor innocent victim," Murphy said. "None of us are Boy Scouts, but you crossed the line and you're on the other side now. It's nothing personal—you know that."

Now it was Blake's turn to sound amused. "I've heard you say that before, remember?"

"You mentioned a deal," Stark said, cutting in.

"Let Bryant go, back off, and I hand over the Black Book."

Stark opened his mouth, but Murphy got in first.

"We can talk about Bryant. And maybe we'll give you a head start, if you tell us where the Book is."

Stark fixed Murphy with a stare that he hoped conveyed the message, *What the hell are you doing?* If Murphy noticed, he didn't acknowledge.

Stark said, "We'll discuss it, then call you back in an hour."

"I'll take that as a joke," Blake said. "Because if I didn't, I'd have to assume you're insulting my intelligence."

"Wait a minute. You can't—"

"New York City, Tuesday night," Blake said, talking over Stark. "Bring Bryant to Grand Central at nine p.m. Just one of you. I'll be able to pick your people out of any crowd. You know it; I know it."

"Blake," Murphy began.

"Grand Central, Tuesday, nine p.m. See you there."

The line went dead, and Stark and Murphy looked at each other.

"New York," Murphy said. "Fits with our intel. Looks like we're in the right neighborhood."

"What intel?" Stark said. It was the first time he'd heard the city mentioned in relation to Blake.

"I spoke to Faraday a couple hours ago. One of her pet cybermonkeys thinks they've narrowed down Blake's base to somewhere in New York, probably upstate."

Stark bit his tongue against the urge to make a comment about need-to-know. Instead, he focused on what this new development meant.

"If he's serious about making the trade, he'll need the Black Book first. If he told Bryant the truth, he's stashed it at home, which means he's going to need to swing by en route to the city."

Stark considered the new information. They had two locations: one a wide search area and one a very specific location, and a rough time frame in which Blake would need to hit both over the next three days. But in the meantime, they could both find out where he was right now. Stark dialed H, got the switchboard, and asked to be put through to Williamson. Murphy tapped him on the shoulder, and he remembered to put the call on speaker again.

There was a click, a couple seconds of silence, and then Williamson's bored Midwestern drawl appeared on the line. "Chicago."

"Chicago?" Stark nodded. So they had been right to cover the destination of the Empire Builder. If only they hadn't been spread so thin. There were only two men in Chicago, both stationed centrally, as near as possible to the main transportation hubs.

"Uh-huh," Williamson agreed disinterestedly. "Location is showing up bright and clear. South Lafayette Avenue."

"He's not running a bounce?" Murphy asked.

"No way. This is crystal clear. Hasn't moved in the last five minutes—I take it you just finished the call?"

Stark bit back the impulse to make a sarcastic response. What the hell else would they have done before calling Williamson? Go out for a leisurely breakfast?

Instead, he quickly asked, "How close are Markham and Kowalski?" He was unable to keep the excitement out of his voice.

"Kowalski is five minutes away and closing, Markham a little farther. Only I haven't sent him there."

"What do you mean?"

"There's a Greyhound station on West Ninety-Fifth a quarter mile from the location. Markham's headed straight there."

"Nice work. Call me back as soon as anything's confirmed."

Stark hung up and looked out of the window at the frozen fields outside the motel room window. He turned his head back to Murphy.

"This could be it."

Murphy wore a troubled expression, as though this was a setback instead of an opportunity. He shook his head. "He's not that stupid, Stark."

With that, he opened the door and headed across the hall to the other room. Whatever happened next, there was no longer any reason to stick around this place a moment longer.

Stark started packing his equipment, calculating how long it would take them to drive to the nearest airport. He knew Murphy was right to be skeptical, but he couldn't help wondering: Could Blake have finally slipped up badly enough to let them catch him? A Greyhound station made sense, after all—another form of anonymous mass transit. Cash, no ID. A direct bus leaving Chicago now would get Blake to New York by tomorrow evening. Blake knew they would be able to pinpoint the phone's location, of course, but perhaps he wasn't banking on them having any kind of rapid-response presence in that particular city.

Of course, there was no way Blake would be in the same place by the time Kowalski arrived at the location, whether he made it there five minutes or five seconds from now. But Markham... Markham might well arrive at the Greyhound station on Ninety-Fifth at the same time as Carter Blake. And then Blake's trip would be cut short, one way or another.

FIFTY-SIX

Chicago

As soon as I hung up, I put the phone down on the table and headed for the door, checking my watch: 11:17 p.m. I had picked my spot after careful thought: the back room of a bar within easy reach of the Greyhound station. I knew they wouldn't necessarily believe I was stupid enough to leave them a trail, but that wasn't the point. I wanted to give them some more loose ends they couldn't ignore, put some possibilities in front of them that would make them spread their resources more thinly.

I knew it was likely they would have somebody in Chicago—again, it was what I would have done. But unless that somebody happened to be standing right outside the bar, it wouldn't do them a lot of good. Even then, I wasn't leaving by the front entrance. That was the other reason I'd picked this spot.

Assuming they had started tracking the phone the moment they saw Kowalski's number flash up, I estimated I would have a matter of minutes before they arrived, depending on how close they were. I opened the fire door and stepped out into the alley outside. It was deserted, just as it had been half an hour earlier when I had timed my route. I closed the door behind me until it locked, and then I jogged down the alley to where it opened on West Ninety-Third Street. I waited for a gap in traffic, and then I crossed the street and entered the alley across the street, heading north via alleys for another two blocks until I hit Ninety-First, where the black Toyota sedan Banner had provided me with was parked at the side of the street. I took the key she had given me in the coffee shop from my pocket as I crossed to the car.

I unlocked the door and got behind the wheel. My watch told me that I had made it here in less than four minutes. I had already covered twice the distance I could have had I been driving. If it were me, in the absence of any other information, I would ignore Kowalski's phone and head for the nearest transportation hub, which was the Ninety-Fifth Street Greyhound station.

Misdirection. They would suspect it, but they'd have to check it out, just the same.

I twisted the keys in the ignition and the engine grumbled to life. I pulled out into a gap in traffic and headed south and then east, scanning the road ahead and the mirrors for police cars or black SUVs. As the second hand hit the twelve to make it 11:33, I was on I-90 headed east, matching the brisk sixty of the other cars in my line. The towers of Chicago reflected back at me in the rearview mirror. I hoped my pursuers would be there for a while yet.

FIVE YEARS AGO

Cleveland, Ohio

"How did you find me?"

Jake Martinez looked like a condemned man as he stood in the doorway of the unassuming suburban house on the outskirts of Cleveland. I simply stared at him for a while. I didn't want to admit to myself how much satisfaction I was taking in his discomfort. Eventually, I spoke.

"This isn't what you think," I said. "I want to talk."

He looked confused.

"I know about the senator. He sounded me out, too. I guess his mistake was to cast his net a little too wide. Murphy found out about it. I was marked before we shipped out."

"Why should I believe you?"

"Because you're still breathing?" I lifted my shirt from the belt, exposing the long, inexpertly stitched scar in my side. I winced as the fabric rubbed against the still-raw skin. "A retirement gift from Winterlong."

He glanced at the wound and then opened the door wider.

A couple of minutes later, I was sitting on the couch while Martinez brewed coffee in the small kitchen unit. I took my phone out for the millionth time and tapped into the new e-mail account I had set up: nothing. I didn't want to be here. I wanted to be in the apartment in New York, confirming that Carol was safe and well. I had e-mailed her as soon as I'd managed to get back into the country. I had told her that I would be there as soon as I could, but there was something I had to do first. Something that could keep us all safe.

The first few stages of the long journey home had been fraught with close shaves. Only once I reached the border with Pakistan did I let my guard down enough to start looking into what had happened stateside. On the plane out of Karachi, I had caught up on the stories via half a dozen newspapers, reading between the lines of each one. The senator had died a few hours after his wife, following a last-ditch attempt at lifesaving surgery. It had been a charity dinner: nothing particularly newsworthy. Until a concealed gunman took the Carlsons down with three shots: two in the senator's head, the other hitting Elizabeth Carlson in the chest, rupturing her aorta. It was assumed she was collateral damage, but I knew better. It was a message.

The hunt for the perpetrator hadn't taken long. An Iraq veteran with a long history of mental health issues named Evan Froelich had been found dead in his apartment shortly after his fingerprints were found at the scene of Carlson's murder. He had had some kind of grudge against the senator, as a file full of angry letters from him had attested. The story was he had lain in wait, killed the senator, gone home, and shot himself. Open and shut. And nobody seriously questioned it but the conspiracy nuts, who busied themselves blaming Mossad or the Lizard People.

I was looking at my blank inbox again when Martinez spoke from the kitchen. "So if you're not here to kill me, why did you take the trouble to track me down?" It was the first thing he had said since inviting me in.

"I didn't have that much trouble, Martinez," I said. "Which means after we finish this conversation, you need to get the hell out of here and go somewhere you didn't spend successive vacations in 2002 and 2003."

He nodded. "My grandparents lived out here. If there's a consolation, I know they'll be a couple days behind you. As usual." He came back out from behind the service island and put a mug of coffee down in front of me. "Black, right?"

I nodded. The mug was red, with a picture of Pac-Man on it.

"So why are you here?" he asked. "Not that I don't appreciate the warning, you understand. But I'm guessing this wasn't on your way."

I took a sip of the coffee. "I want to know what you took from the safe house. There was only one reason you would have vanished in the night, rather than waiting out the mission. You didn't know they were onto me, so the only reason you would have risked attracting attention was because it was the only chance to get your hands on something you needed."

"Interesting theory."

"Senator Carlson told me he needed evidence that would give him Drakakis and the others. That was what you took, wasn't it?"

He drank his coffee, considering. "It's over now. Carlson's dead. That's what happens to people who mess with them. We're not going to bring him back by risking our own necks, too."

"I know that. But we can split the risk. If Drakakis

knows we both have the goods on him, we can make a deal."

"What kind of deal?"

"The only deal open to us right now, as far as I can see. Forget we ever existed."

"It won't work," he said, shaking his head.

"So what's the alternative? Sit here and wait for them to come and get you? I'll do the talking. I'll make Drakakis understand. He's a pragmatist, and I'm not going to give him any choice."

Martinez stared out of the window at the quiet suburban street outside. A trio of kids sailed by on bicycles, wrapped up well against the cold.

"We're dead men, you know that?" he said, not looking at me. "All we're doing is delaying the inevitable."

"We're all delaying the inevitable, Jake," I said. "Doesn't mean it's not worth the effort."

When he didn't respond, I asked him the question that had been niggling me since Afghanistan. "Why me?"

"What do you mean?"

"It had to be you who told the senator he could trust me. What made you so sure?"

He shrugged, as though it was the first time he had considered the question, though I knew that couldn't be true. "I know people. You were the only candidate. And later, over there, when the others were discussing detonating those car bombs and you talked them out of it, I knew I had the right guy."

Martinez put his mug down. He got up and walked through to the hallway. I stayed put and listened as he ascended the creaking stairs. A couple of minutes later, he reappeared. He held out the palm of his hand, in which there were two tiny black flash drives.

"It's called the Black Book. Offline orders for operational commanders. There's a sunset script that lets you access it five times before it's wiped. One of these drives has two more access windows left, the other only has one. It may be technically possible to copy it, but it's beyond my skills, and I can't risk taking it to a third party."

"I take it you've viewed them?"

"Yeah, and I took screen prints, for what they're worth. Without the metadata, they don't prove anything. But it's more than I expected. Between them, they have the details of the hit on Carlson, together with a profile for Froelich, the guy they framed. Date stamps will confirm this was all planned out way in advance of the assassination. You're right. This is our ace in the hole."

He handed one of the drives to me.

"That's the one with the Senator Carlson material. It's also the one with two windows remaining—you'll need to use one when you talk to Drakakis, as proof."

"What's on your drive?" I asked.

"Everything else."

I held it between thumb and forefinger, wondering if this was the right thing to do, or merely the best thing to do in a bad situation. In the end I decided saving my own skin was better than going out in a futile blaze of glory. I told myself I couldn't change anything anyway. Even if Winterlong was shut down, it would only be replaced by something just as bad.

"Let's get out of here," I said.

SUNDAY, JANUARY 10TH

FIFTY-SEVEN

New York City

IT WAS FOUR O'CLOCK in the morning when the car dropped Faraday off directly outside the anonymous office building on West Fortieth. Hank was her driver again. Hank had three ex-wives and five kids. This was more personal information than Faraday retained about anyone else in her working life. Unlike the other two drivers, Hank liked to talk. He was entirely unintimidated by her and chatted away like a cabbie while he drove. Faraday had been irritated by him at first and had come close to having him reassigned. But gradually she had warmed to his constantly upbeat attitude. Occasionally, she even engaged him in conversation. But not tonight.

Tonight, even Hank had seemed to sense that silence was what was required. As he opened the door for her, he offered a smile.

"Hope you have a good day, Ms. Faraday."

She murmured a "thank you" and hurried through the main door to escape the chill wind cutting down Fortieth. She nodded to the security guard at the desk and swiped her pass to get through the barriers. She waited for the priority elevator and, once she was inside with the doors closed, withdrew a second pass, which allowed her to access the twenty-seventh floor.

She had been away only long enough to go back to her apartment, shower, change into fresh clothes, and consume part of an uninspiring meal of sea bass and wild rice delivered hot to her door by Dean & DeLuca. When she realized she was far more interested in the fact her phone had not rung than the meal, she had scraped the remainder of it into the trash and called for a car. As she waited, she thought about black books and black boxes.

Four hours on from the call from Kowalski's phone, and it had become abundantly clear that Carter Blake had managed to pull one more disappearing act. The phone had been found exactly where Williamson had pinpointed it during Blake's call. Kowalski had made the scene within minutes, eager for a rematch with the troublesome target who had broken his nose. It was a bar, quiet for a Saturday night. It had a back room that was empty of customers. On the table nearest the entrance was Kowalski's phone, placed carefully on top of a note that said, *See you soon.*

Naturally, there were no cameras. The barmaid looked up from her magazine long enough to answer a couple of Kowalski's questions. She vaguely remembered a guy in his thirties with a crew cut buying a coffee, but she couldn't say when he'd left. There was a fire door in back, which meant Blake could have gone that way, or just as likely, he could have left by the front door without the barmaid noticing.

Meanwhile, Markham had arrived on scene at the Ninety-Fifth Street Greyhound station. It was busy, but not so busy that he wouldn't have noticed Blake arriving in a hurry. The bus terminal was a long strip beneath a canopy. Markham had been able to position himself where he could see the passengers joining the various buses and the ticket booths. After twenty minutes had passed, there was still no sign of Blake. He called Kowalski, confirming he had retrieved his own phone from where Blake had discarded it.

On Faraday's instructions, Kowalski had gotten back in his rented Ford and made circuits around the streets near the bar, while Markham kept watching the bus station, gradually becoming more and more certain he was wasting his time. They called up a list of the buses leaving the station within the window before and immediately after Markham had arrived on the scene, just in case he'd narrowly missed Blake, and found only two possibilities, headed for Memphis and Columbus, respectively. Faraday arranged for men to meet the two buses at their next scheduled stops and give them the once-over, putting a four-man team on the Columbus bus as the most likely option. She suspected it was a red herring, but a bus would be considerably easier to check than a train, at least.

The elevator doors opened and she crossed the corridor, tapped the code into the keypad, and entered the ops room. Aaron Kent, one of the three deputies beneath Murphy, was staring at the main display, satellite feeds showing various areas of the country. He turned when the doors opened, and Faraday looked at him. She didn't need to ask a question. Kent shook his head. No developments. Had there been any, she would have been contacted.

She walked across to her office, leaving the door open so she could hear any changes in atmosphere from the ops room, and sat down behind her desk.

No developments, four hours on.

She had ordered all of the technicians except Williamson to access security cameras around the general area of the bar. Unfortunately, the neighborhood was camera-light, which was undoubtedly another reason Blake had selected it. There was nothing covering the front entrance to the bar, nothing covering the alley out back. With all of the resources at their disposal, the only thing they had established for sure was where Blake had been up until 11:17 p.m. Chicago time.

Where had he gone after that? Thin air.

Which was exactly the point. Of course he hadn't been stupid enough to tell them exactly where he was without first making sure he had a guaranteed exit strategy. But equally, he knew they would have to take the bait. They would have to waste time and manpower making sure. Meanwhile, Blake was in a stolen car, or hitching a pre-arranged ride, or in a taxi, already miles from the city. Or perhaps he was holed up somewhere safe in Chicago, knowing they were faced with a dead end on his movements. Perhaps the business about trading the Black Book for Bryant had been another ruse, another misdirection.

Faraday shook her head. She couldn't help admiring the bastard's tactics. She wondered if he was enjoying himself a little. Blake was a master of the meticulous art of unpicking the diversionary tactics of a wily quarry. Perhaps it was exhilarating for him to be on the other end of the equation for once. After all, Blake knew every trick in the book. But then, she reminded herself, it was they who had written the book.

And Blake would be too cautious to take this for granted, of course. He knew that they would have other, more indirect ways to track him down.

As though in answer to her thoughts, Williamson

appeared above her, an expression of barely concealed glee on her face.

"The house?"

Williamson didn't reply. She simply turned and walked back out into the ops room. Faraday followed, too excited to be irritated.

"This was not easy," Williamson said as she sat down at her computer. "I had to chase up every cash sale individually. I narrowed the list down to fifty potential properties purchased in Upstate New York in the last five years. Then I accessed power company records to look at billing patterns. Six of them show extended periods with minimal usage."

"Suggesting those are periods when the property's empty," Faraday said.

"Right. Only one of them shows drops in power usage around the times we know Blake was in other places. Utilities are billed to a John Kirby. And guess what? On closer inspection, there's one big difference between John Kirby and any of the other bill payers."

"Kirby doesn't exist?"

"Bingo."

Williamson punctuated the word by hitting a key that brought up a satellite image of a house set into a clearing, surrounded by dense woods on all sides. A narrow access road led out to a main road.

Faraday took a breath to steady herself and leaned in over Williamson's shoulder. "Where?"

"It's a few miles outside of a town called Wilson. About a hundred miles north of Albany."

For the first time in days, Emma Faraday smiled.

FIFTY-EIGHT

New York City

"WE GO IN, secure the house, find the Black Book."

Faraday looked up from the table screen in the ops room and raised an eyebrow. "You make it sound very simple, Murphy. What are you going to do with the rest of the day?"

"If your people have the right house, we'll do the rest," Murphy said. "So I guess the real question is, how sure are you?"

It was a good question. Faraday disliked issuing absolute guarantees, and Murphy knew it.

"Sure enough that we're having this conversation," she replied. "It tallies with your interrogation of Bryant, doesn't it?"

"That it does."

When Murphy had revealed what Bryant had told him about the house and the bookcase, Faraday had been skeptical. Why would Blake trust a petty thief with his secrets? But when it emerged that Blake had held back some key details, it started to sound more in keeping with his reputation as a strategic planner. This in itself was a matter of concern. It suggested Blake really was considering leaking the contents of the Black Book. Not for the first time, Faraday wished that she knew exactly what information was on that drive. She had a pretty good idea, but no specifics. When Murphy had told her about Bryant's description of a farmhouse in Upstate New York, she knew Williamson had found the right house. Too much of a coincidence for this not to be the place.

From the moment Williamson had pinpointed the farmhouse, Faraday knew they would have to move fast. Luckily, the objective was not complicated, even if Murphy was making it sound easier than it was. They had had months to make plans for an assault on Blake's home in the event it was located. All that was required now was to plug the new information into the plan.

Their first priority was to secure the location and ensure that any sensitive material in Blake's possession was reclaimed. It was likely Blake was headed for home, but the fact he was forced to travel by road meant they would beat him to the punch. The clock was ticking, though. With the knowledge of the location, they had narrowed down to several potential strategies, before deciding on an expedited ground assault timed to ensure they took the house before Blake could reach it.

_____ ___ ___ved: Murphy, Dixon, Usher, and Stark. Murphy and Dixon outlined the assault plan, while Usher and Stark red-teamed it, coming up with holes in the strategy. Somebody referred to it as Operation: Homecoming, and since nobody could come up with a more apt name, it stuck.

"Easier to come in on a Black Hawk, maybe two," Stark said. "I know you don't want to—"

"Helos are out," Murphy cut in, nodding at one of the screens, which was displaying weather predictions for the next forty-eight hours. "The blizzard is going to be bad and getting worse by the time we get out there."

"Which means satellite surveillance is out, right?" Usher said. "What about other comms?"

"I'm assured they should hold up," Faraday said.

Stark said, "What's Blake's ETA, assuming he really is coming home?"

"He's coming home," Murphy asserted.

Faraday tapped on a tab at the bottom of the screen to switch to a map showing the ground Blake had to cover. "We have a last fixed point of Chicago at midnight Eastern. Almost nine hundred miles, assuming he's able to take the most direct route. Even if he has a car—and not accounting for traffic, bad weather, or needing to sleep—the fastest he could possibly get there is two, three o'clock this afternoon. Realistically, we're talking tomorrow evening."

"By which time we'll be bedded in and ready to welcome him back," Murphy said.

Stark tapped another tab and brought the satellite image of the farmhouse back up. He examined the knot of buildings. "precautions he may have taken?"

"Nothing we can't handle. We've taken way more heavily defended places than this," Dixon said.

"What if he doesn't live alone? What if the house isn't empty?"

"Then we'll take prisoners," Murphy said smoothly. "Or we won't. Depends what the welcome is like."

Faraday looked at the group of buildings: the house and a series of outbuildings. They looked like Monopoly houses from above. She looked at the timeline. She looked at the weather reports. They would have to go soon, if they were going to go.

"Anything else?" she asked the four of them. "If somebody's thinking about something we haven't already gone over a dozen times, now is the time to say it." She looked at the four men in turn. Nobody said anything. Murphy was watching her with a weird intensity. Dixon simply shook his head. Usher was staring back at her impassively.

"Stark?"

He said nothing for a moment and then shook his head slowly. "I think we covered everything."

She turned back to Murphy. Once again, she wondered if he knew what was in those missing files Drakakis had purged. She had come close to calling him in to ask him about it, deciding against it. Whatever Murphy knew, it could wait.

"How many in your team?"

Murphy answered immediately. "Other than the four of us? We'll need Markham. Kowalski wants in on it—he owes Blake a bloody nose. Three more: One to set up on the main road and look out for Blake, two to babysit Bryant and the cars. Ortega's out of action, so I'll take Walker and the twins."

Faraday's eyes narrowed. "Abrams, Jennings, and Walker, then. And you're set on taking Bryant along?"

Murphy nodded. "He's on the level with what he's telling us."

"You think he could be holding anything back?"

Murphy thought about it. "I'm not sure. That's part of why I want him there. This thing with the bookcase is interesting. Besides, if Blake shows up, could be handy to have him around."

Faraday moved on. "Nine men. You don't think you need more, given how much trouble this particular subject has already caused us?"

Murphy put both palms on the edge of the horizontal monitor and leaned over it, as though surveying a pool table before a break. "You don't need an army for this kind of job. You just need the right team. Small footprint."

Faraday said nothing, surveying the four men as they waited for her word. She turned away from them and looked at the clock on the wall. The seconds ticked past, like a countdown.

"Then I guess you had better ready your team, Murphy. Let's all hope this goes as smoothly as you expect."

FIFTY-NINE

Upstate New York

THE NORTHEAST WAS bracing for the worst. The governors of New York, New Jersey, Massachusetts, Connecticut, and Rhode Island had ordered states of emergency in advance of what was being called a potentially historic blizzard. In New York State, a curfew of five o'clock was instituted. All vehicles had to be off the road or their owners would face arrest. All businesses, schools, and government offices up to the Canadian border were closing. Air traffic was grounded. Emergency services were on high alert. The entire region was on lockdown.

Emergency preparation plans had been put into action, the various services coordinated to respond quickly to weather-related incidents. Thousands of municipal workers dug in for a long shift, gritting their teeth and thinking of the overtime. Everyone else shut the doors, closed the drapes, and settled in to make the most of the unexpected confinement. There was a holiday atmosphere for most, a tense, game-time feeling for those who were working to maintain the most vital infrastructure. The freezing air sang with the invisible trails of a hundred million phone calls and e-mails and text messages and public service tweets.

Nobody paid much attention to the brief, three-sentence communication instructing all personnel to keep clear of a series of roads within a five-square-mile area of Upstate New York. If things hadn't been so hectic, somebody might have been curious enough to ask for more information. There might have been speculation about why a particular stretch of country with barely any homes and no obvious danger spots should be temporarily off-limits; and whoever was doing the speculating would probably conclude that there was some sort of military operation underway. Moving equipment or sensitive material from one secure location to another, maybe. Or perhaps some sort of drill. That would make sense, in the severe winter conditions, after all. But everyone was too busy to have time for such speculations, and so the road crew responsible for that particular grid sector simply shrugged and crossed one more problem off their list.

So it was that the team assigned to mount the incursion on Carter Blake's house found themselves entirely alone on the stretch of State Route 73 after the intersection with highway 9A. They traveled in two black SUVs. Each vehicle carried five men. Stark drove the lead car. Dixon sat alongside him, Usher, Kowalski, and Walker in the back. The rearmost car was driven by Abrams and contained three other operatives—Murphy, Jennings, and Markham—and one reluctant passenger, Scott Bryant.

The snow had been coming down on and off all day, and if the National Weather Service was right, it was about to get a lot worse. The storm front approaching from the east was about to drop up to thirty inches of snow across the area, with conditions being particularly bad north of Albany.

Stark glanced up at the darkening sky again. The sun had been concealed behind storm clouds all day, and night was on its way. The drive had taken much longer in the conditions. He was actually glad that an approach by helicopter had been ruled out.

The road conditions were getting worse and worse, not just because of the new snow falling, but because the farther north they got, the more severe the conditions had been earlier. At times the convoy had to slow to walking pace to negotiate the big drifts blocking the road.

Stark thought about the briefing back in the city, going over all the information they had on the house. It was another of the advantages about working stateside: They had a lot more data to work with than they were used to. This wasn't some compound in a war-torn corner of the Middle East, something that had been built in secret and had to be surveyed using satellite images and educated guesses.

The house had a name: Hamilton Falls Farm. It had been built at the end of the nineteenth century and owned by the same family until the last descendant had died in the nineties and the property had lain empty for a few years, quietly going to seed. It had been restored following a small fire in 2008. This was a lucky break for them, because it meant they had access to the architect's plans, lodged with the county before the refurbishment project began. There were even photographs of most of the interior rooms, albeit from a few years before, when the house was last on the market. There were full details of utilities and phone lines to the house. With one signal to central command, they could cut the house's life support: no lights, no phone, no Internet. But that would likely be a mere precaution. All avail-

able intelligence suggested that the owner of the house
would not be at home. Not yet, anyway.

There were two objectives to the incursion. The pri-
mary objective was to go in fast and secure the house.
With luck, and Bryant's help, they would find the Black
Book and Blake's one remaining item of leverage would
be gone. There were only two possible outcomes to that
objective: They would find it, or they wouldn't. Either
way, the secondary objective would be the same: to
dig in and wait for their unsuspecting target to make
it to what he almost certainly believed was the safety
of home plate. And then there would be nowhere else
to run.

They passed by the access road to Hamilton Falls
Farm and continued for about a mile. There was a logging trail that entered the woods off the main road. It
was just a dirt track, entirely covered by the snow. Stark
only found it because he was looking carefully and
identified the gap in the trees. The lead car made the
turn and bumped onto the track, the four-wheel drive
getting them over the initial snowbank and coping easily with the trail once they made it beneath the partial
tree cover. Even so, the snow was still finding its way
through the canopy. The black and white verticals of the
forest created a strobe effect in the headlights.

Running according to the plan, they followed the
trail for almost two miles, angling northeast away from
the house at first, before curving south to bring them
within a half mile of the house cross-country. The two
SUVs came to a stop at the prearranged drop point: a
clearing beside a ramshackle wooden bridge. The bridge
crossed the river marking the boundary of the land that
belonged to the house. Although they were reasonably

sure that Blake lived alone, no one had given any consideration to simply driving up to the main entrance. Even if, as they expected, the house was deserted, there was no telling what defenses or early-warning systems Blake might have put in place. And besides, if, as the intelligence suggested, he was headed back there, they wanted to extend him a surprise welcome.

They debarked from the SUVs and prepared to move. Abrams and Markham were positioned with the cars to guard Bryant until they'd secured the house, as well as to make sure no one else approached from this angle. Walker headed back out to keep eyes on the main road. The men pulled on white snow-camouflage winter combat jackets and gloves. They checked their equipment: night-vision goggles, AR-15 assault rifles, flash-bangs, and incendiary grenades. Stark checked the coordinates on his GPS tracker: across the bridge and then half a mile due south through the trees. When the preparations were complete, there was one last thing to do. Abrams opened the back of the second SUV, and Stark and Jennings collected two additional loads: backpacks weighing around twenty pounds. Stark grunted as he hefted the additional weight. He was grateful that this extra load would only have to be taken on a one-way trip.

Carter Blake had tried to leave the war behind a long time ago. Now it was time for the war to come home.

SIXTY

STARK HAD BEEN walking for five minutes when he saw the slivers of open ground between the trees ahead, and he knew they were in reach of their goal. The trek through the woods was hard going in the darkness, with the snowfall filtering through the branches above. The snow on the ground helped by amplifying the ambient light, but hindered by obscuring the deadfalls and, on one occasion, a small stream.

The men, although more used to enduring the heat and dust of desert warfare, adapted themselves quickly to the terrain, and they made swift progress. They had split into three two-man teams, approaching the target in triangle formation, with team one, Stark and Murphy, taking the apex of the triangle. They slowed as they reached the edge of the woods. Although it was just after three-thirty in the afternoon, it felt like dusk had already fallen. The buildings of the property lay ahead across a large expanse of level ground: a barn, some unused stables, and the house itself. The house was a sprawling structure: two floors and an attic with a sharp pointed roof in the center and a series of jutting outposts where the first floor had spread out for comfort. It was almost completely in darkness, except for a single light burning in a room on the second floor.

Stark hunched down and cast his eyes left and right until he saw the other two pairs get into position, equally spaced across the edge of the open ground. One by one, each man called in his position over the open channel on their headsets. Team two—Usher and Jennings, their signals up—were roughly west of Stark and Murphy's position.

Murphy addressed Jennings, not needing to raise his voice above a whisper, though the other man was thirty yards away: "Welcome mat?"

Stark could see Jennings's head was down, scanning the screen of the device in his hand. He responded in an equally quiet tone, his voice carried to the rest of the team crystal clear over headsets. "Motion sensors at twenty yards out. Looks clear otherwise."

"Can you jam the sensors?" Murphy responded.

"Already done."

Murphy turned his eyes to Stark and nodded. Time to go. "Okay, let's just hope the son of a bitch doesn't have land mines."

Stark didn't think he had been addressing that to anyone in particular, but Jennings responded anyway. "Negative on that. As far as we can tell."

As far as we can tell. The words echoed in Stark's head. Good to have certainties.

Jennings completed the sweep and reported no other security on the approach. Stark saw him tapping out a short signal back to base, knowing that he was sending a simple one-word message: *D A R K.*

Almost instantly, the solitary light on the upper floor winked out. The big house lay before them, as black and uninviting as a freshly dug grave. Stark suppressed a shiver that had nothing to do with the cold. Murphy told team two to be ready to provide cover, before signaling for team three's approach to begin. The pair of men east of them—Kowalski and Dixon—began the advance. Dixon hung back, covering the windows of the house with his rifle as Kowalski approached the house at a weaving run, his footsteps crunching softly in the deep snow.

You could lay the groundwork as well as possible, you could make sure your firepower was overwhelmingly superior, you could confirm to within a ninety-nine percent probability that there were no hostiles, but an approach over open ground to a target location was always nerve-racking. Spacing out to present distinct targets meant that you would get advance warning of any hostile action, but that was of little comfort to the unlucky one on the receiving end of that action.

Stark breathed out as Kowalski made the cover of the awning hanging over the north side of the house. Dixon covered the same ground just as quickly, and the two men paused before splitting and circling the perimeter.

Stark waited until both men had vanished around the sides of the building before looking back to the spot where he knew team two was. He saw Jennings quickly, but it took him a second to find Usher, who was almost invisible in his cover spot. He glanced at Murphy, who was staring straight ahead, intently focused on the house as though he expected it to start moving.

"South side clear," came Dixon's voice a moment later.

Murphy spoke softly into the mic on his headset, and a few moments later two more white shapes split off from the tree cover and began to approach the house.

Jennings and Usher gained the perimeter of the house quickly and moved into their assigned positions at the front entrance. As soon as the two called in their positions, Murphy and Stark left cover and approached the house. As the others had done, they split out in a widening V formation, headed for opposite ends of the north side of the house. Stark kept his AR-15 raised, his eyes on the window that had been lit. He knew it had been a security light to make the house look inhabited, but he had to focus somewhere.

Stark made the shelter of the awning, in front of the big picture window of the living room. Peering through it, he could see by the meager light still in the sky that the room was sparsely furnished. Couch, television, books lining the entirety of the opposite wall. A door in the bookcase wall was closed, and he knew from the floorplans it led into the central hallway.

Murphy joined him at the window, the two of them exchanging a glance that said, *So far, so good.* Murphy nodded toward the northeast corner of the house. They moved in single file toward the corner that would take them around to the front of the house, the side that faced the main driveway. When Stark saw a moving shadow, he called out the pass phrase in a low voice.

"Tango."

"Disco," came the reply, equally quietly. Stark rounded the corner and came face-to-face with Dixon. They passed by each other, and Dixon continued his circuit at the perimeter. When Stark and Murphy reached the wraparound porch and the front door, Usher and Jennings were waiting for them. Murphy tapped the square button on his earpiece again.

"Kowalski, Dixon? Are you in position?"

There was a pause before Kowalski answered in the affirmative. "Back door secure." Dixon had completed his circuit and was with Kowalski covering the back door, just in case somebody was at home and tried to sneak out.

The advance intel showed that the previous owner had installed an Axiom burglar alarm about a decade before. It was an expensive model. Battery backup, so it wouldn't be affected by the power cut. There was no reason for Blake to have changed the alarm, other than extreme caution. Jennings was prepped for the Axiom. They examined the door. It was solid wood, maybe with steel behind it. The lock was six-point contact. Nothing out of the ordinary, but certainly secure enough for a normal household. It took Jennings thirty seconds to pick it. On standard ops like this, they wouldn't bother with such niceties, but there was no need to blow the door, and this way would mean the house looked undisturbed. That would be important later. Jennings glanced at the others when he was ready. The others trained their weapons on the door as he turned the handle.

Before he had gotten it open two inches, the noise started. Deafeningly loud in the silence, a dog was barking within. Jennings's gun jumped up in his hand. The four of them exchanged quick glances.

"Nobody said anything about a dog," Stark said, eyeing the door.

"Shoot it?" Usher suggested indifferently. His gun was raised, and he was peering into the darkness within. The dog, wherever it was, had yet to come into the light.

Stark shrugged and nodded. He liked dogs. He didn't like them enough to get bitten trying to restrain one, or to waste time they'd need to deactivate the alarm.

Stark, Usher, and Murphy trained their guns on the door as Jennings pushed it open. Stark's eyes narrowed as they saw an empty hallway. But the barking continued, sounding as though it were right on top of them. It took a second to locate the source: a small speaker attached to the wall beside a keypad. The barking sound was obviously rigged to activate when anyone approached the door, or perhaps when the handle was turned. A cheap security device, more a novelty toy than anything else. The keypad beside it was the entry device for the real alarm, and Stark suspected that would be anything but.

Jennings was examining it, shaking his head. A wire led from the keypad to a sealed white box on the wall.

"This ain't an Axiom."

"Can you turn it off?" Stark wasn't too perturbed if the answer was no. If they could get in without leaving an obvious trace, so much the better, but the main thing was they now had access to the house.

Jennings nodded, not looking happy. "Of course I can." As he spoke he was shining some sort of black light over the keypad, presumably to check if Blake had made the classic mistake. He shook his head. "He taps the keys." Meaning Blake either changed the code regularly, or he made a point of periodically tapping all nine number keys on the pad so that an intruder would not easily be able to narrow down the specific set of numbers that composed the code.

Jennings reached into his pack and withdrew a couple of small handheld devices. Discarding one, he held the other up to the keypad and tapped a couple of keys. After a pause, the device beeped and a five-digit code appeared on the screen. Jennings's fingers danced quickly across the pad on the wall, the red light switched to green, and the low electronic whine that was barely audible under the barking cut out.

Irritated, Jennings reached up and yanked the speaker off the wall, silencing the barking noise. Absolute quiet descended, and the four of them took a moment to listen for any sounds from within the house.

After a couple of seconds, Stark heard a series of soft clicks as the others turned on their night-vision goggles. The intelligence all but guaranteed they were alone, but intelligence can be wrong. Safer to clear each level of the building without flashlights to ensure they had an edge over anyone who could be lurking within. Stark and Jennings slid their additional packs off and left them in the hallway. They would unload the contents later.

Relieved to be unencumbered by the pack, Stark slid his own goggles down over his eyes and clicked the switch at the side, blinking his eyes as they adjusted to the pixelated green wash that lit the darkened hallway up as bright as a summer noon.

He moved his head from side to side, taking in the surroundings in the amplified ambient light. His breath caught in his throat as he saw movement out of the corner of his eye, from a direction away from the other three men. He jerked his head around, raising his gun. A familiar figure duplicated his actions precisely. Stark smiled. He had been about to open fire on a hostile full-length mirror.

He lowered his gun and let out a relieved breath as he took stock of the layout, ticking off comparisons to the schematic in his head. The hallway was large, three doors to the left, the farthest of which had to lead to the attached garage on the west side of the building. Ahead were the stairs to the second floor. On the right was the door to the living room. The floor was wood, looked like the original floorboards. The walls of the hallway were unadorned. There were no furnishings, beyond a coat rail by the door that held a raincoat and a leather jacket.

"All right," Murphy said. "We secure the building first. Then we see what we can see."

Stark realized he was holding his breath again as he approached the stairs.

SIXTY-ONE

I MADE PRETTY good time from Chicago, spurred on by the apocalyptic tone of the weather reports on the radio. I drove five hundred miles straight through the night, knowing that the heavy flurries of snow were merely a curtain raiser for the main event farther east. I was dead tired by the time the sky began to lighten, and a near miss with an articulated truck outside of Buffalo convinced me that I needed a break and a lot of caffeine. I pulled into the next rest stop and went into the diner.

I took a booth and ordered French toast, bacon, hash browns on the side, and a large pot of coffee. While I waited, I wound my watch ahead for the hour I had lost on the trip: It was just after nine a.m. local time. I took out the phone Banner had given me and switched it on. It connected to the diner's Wi-Fi and checked the weather again. It wasn't looking good. I checked one other thing before the waitress returned with my order.

I drank the first cup of coffee so fast that it scorched my tongue and took it easier with the second one, feeling my senses sharpen as the caffeine started to do its work. I poured a third cup before I started on the food. Half an hour later, I was feeling just about comfortable with the idea of being behind the wheel again.

It was technically daylight by then, but not so you would know it from the sky. I had found a Coleman Hawkins CD in the glove box and listened to it on repeat for a hundred miles or so. As dark gray morning became dark gray afternoon, I switched back to the radio. The East Coast was on lockdown: All public transportation was to be suspended from five o'clock, all businesses closed. I took the news of the strict curfew after five with mixed emotions. It would keep the way clear for me, but it would also make it riskier to complete the trip. Then again, the curfew was focused on the big metropolitan areas, where a lone car on the streets would be far more noticeable. I had hoped to make my destination in daylight. Now I would be grateful just to get there.

It was after four when I hit the outskirts of Wilston, and it was clear that the Toyota Banner had provided me with was going to be a poor match for the incoming weather. An SUV would have been better, but I reminded myself that beggars can't be choosers. I pulled over and took Banner's phone out again. No 4G, not even half a G. Coverage was patchy at the best of times out here, but in these conditions, you could forget about it. It had been more than an hour since I had been able to access the Internet.

I pulled back onto the road, the tires spinning a little, struggling to get traction, and drove down Main Street. The deserted sidewalks behind the walls of plowed snow and the rows of shuttered stores on the main drag made me worry I'd left it a little too late. An hour ahead of the curfew, and barely one in five businesses on the street seemed to be open. I guessed most folks were headed home to batten down the hatches, or already there, relaxing in the warmth and watching the action on the news. I was starting to give up hope when I saw exactly what I needed—an outdoor supplies store. The only problem was, there was a guy outside pulling down the shutters. I pulled the car to the side of the road and parked. The five-foot-high frozen mound of plowed snow at the side of the road meant I was actually parking close to the middle of the road, but there wasn't enough traffic for that to be a problem.

I opened the door and yelled a greeting at the guy pulling down the shutters. When the figure turned around, I saw it wasn't a man at all, but a woman wearing a bulky gray coat. Her pink face peered out at me from within the hood. She waved the hooked pole she had been using to draw down the shutters in the direction of the door.

"Sorry. We're closed."

I shut the door of the Toyota and hurried around to where there was a dip in the snow drift, half stepping, half stumbling over it. She watched me as I approached, shaking her head vehemently and gripping the pole in one hand.

"I'm sorry…" she repeated.

"Come on," I said, smiling and trying to look cold and desperate. It wasn't difficult, a method performance, you might say. "It's kind of an emergency."

She didn't say anything. Her eyes looked me up and down from behind eyelashes that had caught some flakes of snow.

"I need to get to my mother's house before the curfew—she lives alone."

She remained tight-lipped.

"I just need a proper coat and a couple of other things, I'll be five minutes. If you want me to make it worth your while… Well, I don't have much extra money, but…"

She let out an exasperated sigh, and I knew then she was going to give me my five minutes. I hoped I could talk her into something else, too.

SIXTY-TWO

WILLIAMSON CALLED FARADAY over without looking up from her screen. "They're in. No resistance."

Faraday nodded. The update had to have come in on the sat phone. There had been a tense few minutes when the communications had gone offline on the team's approach to the house. The storm had knocked out cell towers across the region, so they had had an hour or so to get used to not having standard phones. It was frustrating. She had to run operations on the other side of the world with far greater real-time information than what she had access to this time.

"Is Murphy on the line?"

"Stark," Williamson replied.

"Put him on."

Williamson handed her the headset and she addressed Stark.

"Talk to me."

"House is secured. Security was as expected, and we've finessed it. Nothing bent, nothing broken. No welcoming committee."

"Excellent. Come back to me if anything develops."

Stark signed off, and Faraday handed the headset back to Williamson. The adrenaline rush of the approach to the house was over; it was a waiting game now. She would receive hourly updates unless one of two things happened: the team found the Black Book, or Carter Blake arrived home.

FIVE YEARS AGO

New York City

MARTINEZ AND I laid out a plan of action and each of us took one of the Black Books. We shook hands outside of the little house in Cleveland, and I knew I would never see him again.

On my trip back to the city, I prepared a short video presentation, which I sent by secure e-mail to Draka-kis's address. I laid out the salient facts in the video. The first point was indisputable: I was alive and well, and so Murphy had screwed up in his task of killing me. I knew they would suspect that anyway, given that no bodies had been found at the scene.

Second, I confirmed what I imagined were their own worst fears. Martinez had gotten out of Afghanistan, too, and we had been in touch. I didn't talk about where I was, where he was, anything like that. I simply held up the black drive Martinez had given me so the viewer could take a good look at it, and then I switched to a series of screen grabs from the data on the file. I had had to burn one of the two remaining view windows to take these, but that was unavoidable. I ran through various screen grabs as a slide show. I didn't talk over this part: The slides told the story for themselves. The real story of the Carson assassination.

I finished my clip with the camera back on me.

"I'll talk to you soon."

I gave Drakakis half an hour to sweat after I sent the e-mail, and then I dialed his number on the burner cell.

"I'm speaking to a dead man," he said, in lieu of a hello.

"I got that message back in Kandahar," I said. "Somebody ought to have told you that threats work better before you fail to follow through on them."

"I want that fucking drive back."

"Be more reasonable. Otherwise you get it back via the front page of the *New York Times*."

"You wouldn't dare."

"Why not? What have I got to lose?"

There was a pause, and his voice was more controlled when it came back. "What do you want?"

"You already know what I want. Forget I exist. Forget about Martinez, too. As far as you're concerned from this moment forward, we never came back from Afghanistan. Which is just the way you planned it, of course. As long as you leave us alone, we'll keep quiet. But if I get a hint that you're trying to come after either of us, or anybody else connected to us…"

"If that information comes to light, you'll be jeopardizing—"

"I don't think you realize the severity of this situation, Drakakis. You made a bad situation a hundred times worse. You turned a worst-case scenario of bad publicity and a career setback into a grade-A clusterfuck. You ordered the murder of a United States senator and his wife. I leak this file, and you and your friends aren't just fired or going to jail. Remind me, is it the gas chamber or lethal injection at Leavenworth?"

He didn't say anything for a minute, trying to calculate a way out of this that didn't involve him having to trust the word of a man he'd just tried to have murdered. There wasn't one.

"You're lucky I'm offering you this deal, Drakakis," I said. "You think this sits right with me? You think I want to let you get away with this? The only reason we're having this conversation is because I know the only course of action that makes sense is stalemate. Like the old days: mutually-assured destruction. Neither one of us is going to win this war. You walk away; I walk away. Clear?"

I heard the sound of Drakakis clearing his throat. When he spoke again, it was like he was spitting the words out through his teeth, with a gun to his head. In a way, he was. "You have a deal. And I take it it goes without saying you know what will happen to you if those files ever see the light of day? They won't find us all. They won't find me, no matter where I have to go. And I'll hunt you down to the fucking ends of the earth and cut your heart out."

"I'm glad we see eye to eye."

I cut the call and dropped the phone in a nearby trash can. I walked two blocks south and then flagged down a cab. I told the driver to take me to an address in Hell's Kitchen.

THE APARTMENT WAS a sixth-floor walk-up. I had leased it as a precaution after my first meeting with the senator, paying six months' rent in advance. I had a feeling I might soon be in need of somewhere in the city that was off the grid, held under a different name. I didn't know how right I had been.

As I approached the building, I tried to blank my mind, to not think about why there had been no e-mails from Carol. I had tried calling her cell several times over the last few days, as much to reassure myself that she really had gotten rid of it as anything else. Each time the call had gone straight to voice mail.

I checked the mail slot downstairs. The key was gone.

I climbed the six flights of stairs and took my gun out, holding it by my side. I stood to one side of the door and took my own key from my pocket and slid it quietly into the lock. I twisted it and pushed. The door swung silently inward on hinges I had greased two months before. There was a short hallway terminating in a window that looked out into the airshaft. Bathroom and bedroom on one side, combination kitchen and living room on the other. All three doors were closed. I stood in the doorway, listening for sounds.

No footsteps, no springs settling on the couch. No TV noise. No cooking sounds. Nothing.

"Hello?" I called. "It's me."

There was no response. Either nobody was here, or somebody was here and was deliberately keeping silent. I held my breath and turned the handle on the nearest door, the bathroom. It swung open and I brought my gun up, checking the tiny, cramped room and shower cubicle. It was empty, but there was a pink disposable razor in the trash that I was pretty sure wasn't mine.

Bedroom next. The small double bed was made up more neatly than I'd left it, but there was nobody on it, under it, or in the miniscule closet. So far, so good. Carol had made it here, by the looks of things, and there were no signs of struggle so far. But I still had one room to check.

I held my breath and twisted the handle on the living

room door. The door swung open and I stepped into the room, covering the space with my gun.

It was empty.

I breathed out at last. I had been worried about finding evidence of a struggle, or worse. Instead, the place was much as I'd left it. Couch, television, bookcase, all of which had come as part of the lease. The tiny kitchen took up the westernmost quarter of the room, separated from the living space by a breakfast counter with two high stools. There was a sealed cross-colored envelope on the surface.

I holstered my gun and walked across the room, in three strides. I ripped open the envelope, knowing in my heart of hearts what the letter would say. The message was briefer than I had anticipated, but I had guessed right. It was a single sheet of notepaper. Clear, concise. Carol had said it all with four words in her inimitable curling script.

Don't look for me.

I took it to the couch and sat there for a half hour, occasionally reading the note again to see if it had changed. It never did.

After a while I realized that the light in the room had changed as the sun sank below the skyline, and that time hadn't really been standing still after all. I had done everything I'd come back to New York to do, and it was time to move on. I went into the bathroom and took a shower. I found a pair of scissors and my own razor in the cabinet and started to work on the beard that had grown back over the past few weeks. When I was done I looked like a new man. A man with no past and an uncharted future. I examined the new man in the mirror as I toweled off my face. I wondered what his name was.

Then I locked up, walked back down the six flights
and out onto the street. I walked a couple of blocks west
and descended to the Fiftieth Street subway. I took the
E line south to Penn Station, and then I stood below
the departures board, watching the destinations flash
up on the screen and deciding where I wanted to start
my new life.

SIXTY-THREE

Upstate New York

IT TOOK THEM what felt like a long time to clear every room of the house. It was somehow larger than it looked from outside. Perhaps there was some kind of optical illusion where the vastness of the sky and the woods and the hills outside somehow diminished the house itself. But the layout conformed to the plans they'd studied ahead of time. Three bedrooms, only one made up, a study with every wall lined with books, a living room with even more books, a large dining kitchen, two bathrooms, one upstairs, one down, an attic that was entirely empty, and a large, cement-floored basement. On the south side of the building was a small garage that contained a battered ten-year-old Jeep.

The basement was accessed via a locked door and a set of stairs. There was a work desk and tools, some boxes full of stored junk, and a single, wide steel bookcase on the wall. Jennings examined the edges of it and knocked on the wall. He looked at Stark and Murphy, who were waiting for his verdict.

"Could be something back there," he said. "We can blow it to find out."

"Bad idea," Stark said, examining the edges of the bookcase. "We don't know if it's rigged to prevent forced entry."

Murphy nodded in agreement. Stark knew he wouldn't want to risk losing the contents within if there was another option. He tapped the square button on his headset. "Markham, bring our guest to the house."

Murphy's instincts had been right about Blake offering to deal for Bryant. Maybe he would be right that Bryant could help them open the secret door, if there was one. While they waited for Markham to escort Bryant from the cars to the house, Stark left Murphy and Jennings downstairs and made another tour around the above-ground floors, spending more time to take in the details, the little things about a dwelling that told you about the owner.

Books aside, it was striking how Spartan the house was. There were no pictures on the walls, no ornaments, no interesting kitchenware beyond the basic implements. It was so devoid of clutter that Stark might have described it as a show home, except that a show home would have been artfully dressed to suggest more of a personal touch. He supposed it made sense. Blake was a man used to being on the road. He had carried this aesthetic with him when he'd left Winterlong, maybe even without realizing it. This was a place to disappear from the world when he needed to. To relax and recuperate, hence the books. But not a place to live.

Before they found the bookcase, Stark had started to worry that Faraday and Murphy had miscalculated. They had banked on Blake's homing instinct bringing him back here, to where he would think he was safe. But what if they were wrong? Maybe Blake would simply drop off the face of the earth, cash in his chips, and start again with a new name. He had done it before, after all.

The next few hours would give them the answer to

that. Taking Blake's last-known position in Chicago as a starting point and extrapolating using various scenarios—excluding flying, of course—Blake would be getting here at some point in the next few hours. The weather and the official curfew might have chased him off the road, of course, but Stark doubted it. A little heavy weather wouldn't dissuade a guy like Blake, not when he had a self-imposed deadline at Grand Central on Tuesday night. The one unknown quantity was the Black Book—if Blake had it on his person, he could head straight to New York City, might be there already, in fact.

But that was unlikely. Something so valuable would be stored safely, not carried around on every job, where it could be lost or stolen or damaged. It made sense that it would be here, and the bookcase in the basement existed, just as Bryant had described. In a little while they would get their answer.

SIXTY-FOUR

BRYANT SAT IN the back of the SUV and watched the snow come down outside. The last of the daylight filtering through the tree cover had vanished. He had shelved any ideas of going anywhere long ago. The doors were locked, the safety mechanism engaged so they could not be opened from inside. Even had they been unlocked, he knew there would be a bullet in his head before he could fully open the door.

It had been more than an hour since the other men had left for the house. Again, he felt guilty for talking, for telling Murphy about the bookcase Blake had spoken about. But then, they'd evidently known about the place already. It wasn't as though Blake had given them an address. When he'd talked about the farmhouse in Upstate New York, he realized he was just confirming something they already knew. Providing that information had kept him alive, for now at least.

One of the two men who had stayed behind was in the driver's seat. He hadn't spoken more than two words the whole time, answering Bryant's early attempts at making conversation with a stony silence. The other one had drawn the short straw: He was outside in the cold keeping watch.

He thought about the house and what the men were going to find there. Did they have the right place? Was

Blake there already? Was Blake even alive? For the past hour, ever since the other men had headed for the house, his unease had been growing. Whatever they found in there, it meant one thing. They were about to find out how useful, or otherwise, he was.

Back at the motel in Minnesota, Murphy had seemed satisfied that Bryant was telling the truth about what Blake had told him. And it mostly was the truth. All about how Blake had some information on them on a flash drive and that he needed to retrieve it, and that it was stored behind a hidden door in a bookcase in a place out in the middle of nowhere. That was the trick to a bluff, though. You had to be believable, but you had to hold something back. Bryant had claimed he couldn't remember the names of the books that would unlock the door, couldn't remember if Blake had even told him. And therefore Murphy had decided he was just useful enough. Bryant assumed Murphy was the leader, at least on the ground. Although none of them seemed to wear insignias denoting rank, the other men seemed to defer to his authority.

As though to illustrate the point, the man in the front seat suddenly stiffened. Bryant could tell he was listening to instruction through the earpiece in his right ear. He had a pretty good idea of who was giving the instruction. After a second, he acknowledged, saying, "Copy," and turned around in the seat to look directly at Bryant for the first time.

Bryant's mouth went dry as he stared back at the man in the driver's seat, wondering exactly what he had just been instructed to do. After a second, he spoke.

"Looks like you got an invite to the party."

Ten minutes later, after a grueling hike through the woods at about twice the pace he was comfortable with, Bryant was standing in the basement of a big house that was almost entirely in darkness. All except for the flashlight beam playing over the wide steel bookcase that looked strangely out of place in the basement.

"This looks like what he talked about," Bryant said.

Murphy turned the beam of the flashlight toward him, deliberately aiming it in Bryant's eyes to dazzle him.

"You remember the books that open the door?"

"Why can't you just pull them all out until it opens?"

Murphy reached a hand out and tugged at one of the books; it came out an inch and then stopped, obstructed by something.

"They're all like that. The books have to be pulled in a particular combination. And you know the combination, don't you?"

Obliging, Bryant looked over the spines on the shelf. He felt Murphy's eyes on him and wondered if he could tell he was looking for specific titles. He tried on a confused expression.

"I'm sorry. It's difficult to—"

Murphy stared at him for a long moment. Then he shifted the position of his gun, bringing the barrel up a little closer to Bryant. He didn't point it at his head this time. He didn't need to. Bryant remembered what it had felt like, the cold metal of the muzzle against his skin.

"Need help jogging your memory?"

Bryant swallowed and shook his head. "I think I remember now."

Murphy smiled. Bryant stepped forward and regarded the books on the shelf. After a moment's thought, he selected one on the far left of the top shelf and one in the dead center of the middle shelf. *The Great Gatsby* and *All the President's Men.* He pulled out one, then the other. There was a click, and the door swung open, revealing an unlit cavity in the basement wall.

Even though he had followed the instructions perfectly, Bryant was surprised when the door opened. Blake had been on the level. He had really trusted him with this information, and now Bryant was selling out that trust for another couple of minutes of life.

Murphy turned his flashlight on the space so that they could see it was a space about ten feet deep and three feet wide. On either side, leaving just a narrow space in the middle, were stacked long white cardboard boxes. They looked like they might contain files. Murphy played the beam of the flashlight around and saw nothing but those boxes. Six on either side, a dozen in all. He exchanged a glance with the man who had brought Bryant from the cars.

Murphy touched a finger to his headset and said, "Stark, get down here." He looked back at Bryant and directed the beam of the flashlight over the nearest stack of boxes. "Bring them out."

Bryant hesitated a second, then selected the top box on the left-hand side and hauled it down, grimacing at the weight. He placed it on the ground. It was about two feet long. Murphy cleared his throat impatiently, and Bryant lifted the lid off the box. At first Bryant thought he had been right about files. The box was filled with small plastic-wrapped documents, all of them shaped the exact width and a little less than the height of the box. He knelt down and pulled a handful from the front. Murphy took a step forward and directed the beam of the flashlight. It took Bryant a second to realize what they were.

And then he knew they'd all been played.

SIXTY-FIVE

By FIVE O'CLOCK, it was full dark, and it had been a long time since I'd seen another set of lights on the road. I was pleased that the Toyota was just about holding up. I had been starting to wonder if the full force of the storm front was going to miss us after all, when the blizzard kicked up a notch. The snow started to come down in clumps, blotting out the windshield faster than the wipers could cope with. It was like attempting to drive through an avalanche. I slowed to ten miles an hour, then five. The road seemed to have been plowed a few hours before, which meant the car was having to contend with six inches of snow and building, rather than a couple of feet. At this rate, it wouldn't take long until the difference was academic.

I knew I was close. I had driven this road a hundred times in the past few years, but the snow turned it into an alien landscape. Everything in the lights ahead was snow: falling, flying, dancing in the air. Visibility was down to about twenty feet in front of me. I kept my foot on the gas, feeling the car skid occasionally as the tires began to really struggle under the snow.

Under my breath, I coaxed the old Toyota to carry on. It had brought me this far; it could take another mile or two. I once read that you should always name a car. It's good feng shui or something, means the car is more likely to treat you nicely. I had dismissed that idea at the time. Now I was wondering if I should have christened this old heap at the outset of the journey with a name like Ethel or Martha or something. Or Susanne. Maybe the car was a Susanne.

"Come on, Susanne," I said.

Perhaps sensing a lack of seriousness in my plea, Susanne picked that moment to give up the ghost. The tires caught on a deep drift of snow and started to spin. I shifted down to first gear and revved the engine. The car groaned and tried to lurch forward, but the wheels lacked any traction. I eased off, then slammed my foot down again, gripping the wheel, hoping this was just an uneven patch that could be surmounted.

Nothing. I eased off, tried again. Still nothing.

Leaving the keys in the ignition and the engine running, I opened the door and stepped out into the freezing night.

Immediately, I knew the car wasn't going any farther when the snow came up to my knee. The blizzard was so intense that I had to use my hands to make a tunnel around the hood of my coat in order to properly see the wheel that was two feet in front of me. The car had grounded in the snow. Looking back down the road for as far as I could see, which wasn't far at all, I could see twin grooves cutting deep into the snow. It was a miracle I had made it this far.

I climbed back into the car, savoring the dry warmth of the interior for the last time, and pulled the pack Banner had given me out from the backseat. I checked the contents one more time, partly because it was always good practice to make sure, but mostly because it would buy me another minute in the warmth before I had to abandon the car. In addition to the other contents, I had picked up a few items in Wilston: a thicker coat, variable-glare-resistant snow goggles, thin thermal gloves, and a six-inch serrated hunting knife. In all honesty, I had been prepared to have to walk much farther. Getting this close was a bonus. Finally, I took the gun Banner had given me from the glove box and placed it at the top of the pack before zipping it closed.

I pulled the hood back up on my coat, opened the door, and took a deep breath.

I left the Toyota where it had grounded and continued down the road on foot. The snow was coming down even harder and the wind was kicking up, turning the world into a howling white haze. I kept the line of trees on my left-hand side, the only way I could be sure I was still on the road. It was hard going, but at least this time I had the right clothes and equipment.

I had been walking ten minutes before I saw the first identifiable landmark, the twisted, lightning-struck tree that was only a half mile from the main access road to the house. The tree was thirty feet tall, black and twisted and gnarled like something out of a Tim Burton movie. I had seen it when I'd first come out to view the place, and every time I had driven past since then I couldn't help but glance at it. I stopped by the tree and wiped snow from my goggles.

The road dipped ahead of me, and I knew that all I had to do was walk straight on, turn left into the access road, and from there it was less than a mile to the house.

Home free.

SIXTY-SIX

"COMIC BOOKS?"

Stark had descended the basement stairs to find Bryant and Markham looking on in confusion as Murphy knelt down and started pulling out more and more of the bagged magazines from the box. *Amazing Spider-Man, Detective Comics, Sandman, Astro City.*

He realized that Bryant was staring at him, every bit as surprised as he was.

"That's not what I expected," Bryant said.

Murphy picked up the box and dumped it upside down, scattering twenty pounds of comics all over the basement floor. There was nothing else in the box. He ripped the firm cardboard apart and discarded it.

"It's not exactly what I fucking expected either." He stood up, and Stark thought the look on his face was a mixture of fury and admiration at Blake's ruse.

"He played us," Stark said. "He knew Bryant would lead us here."

They should have known. A secret bookcase? Too showy to conceal anything of real value. More misdirection from Blake. He had known all along that Bryant's capture and interrogation was a possibility. So he had given Bryant just enough information to make sure they had to keep him alive, but not enough to give them anything worthwhile. It had been credible, because they were already looking in this neck of the woods, but if Williamson hadn't nailed down the location of the house, the information would have been useless by itself.

Murphy started pulling out the rest of the boxes and dumping them on the floor. Multicolored covers from decades ago scattered across the floor. There was no flash drive in any of the boxes. When he was done, he went into the cavity and systematically knocked up and down every inch of the walls. Solid brick. Nothing. If the Black Book was in the house, it sure as hell wasn't down here.

"We're wasting our time," Stark said. "There's nothing here for us."

Murphy looked at him, cold determination in his eyes. "No. We're going to take this place apart. You," he said, turning and pointing at Bryant, "stay the hell down here. You do not want to give me a reason to shoot something."

Bryant swallowed again and nodded.

It wasn't a stealth search. They would make sure the exterior of the house remained undisturbed for Blake's approach, but the interior was fair game. The team worked quickly. It was a familiar task. They were accustomed to going into an insurgent stronghold under pressure of time, stripping out laptops and memory devices and checking the standard hiding places in any dwelling.

The task was complicated by the fact that the object of their search was so small. Barely an inch long, the flash drive was easy to conceal, and Blake would know of all the places not to hide it. There was no guarantee it was in the house itself, for that matter. But for now they focused on the house.

Stark took the office, clearing out the drawers, then pulling them from the desk and checking for anything taped underneath. He disconnected the desktop unit and placed it at the doorway, ready to be bagged and transported back to base along with any other laptops or phones or cameras they came across. The minimalism of the furniture and decor made the task a little more manageable. There were no pictures to conceal things behind, no pot plants offering soil to bury small items within.

Within forty minutes, they had given the main house a thorough search. They had removed a desktop computer, a laptop, and several assorted memory storage devices: a few flash drives and even some old CD-ROMS. Those would be taken back to base and the analysts could get to work on them to see if they would yield anything useful. But the thing they were looking for, the distinctive black drive, had not yet been found.

Over the headset, Stark heard Murphy communicate with Markham and Jennings downstairs, sending them out to the cars with the equipment they had gathered so far. Then he heard Murphy raise Walker, who was stationed at the mouth of the approach road to the house. The land rose to that point, giving him a commanding view.

"All clear on south," Walker said. "Saw some headlights ten minutes ago, about two miles out, but nothing since."

"All right," Murphy said. "Try not to fall asleep."

"Roger that. Anytime you want to swap that roof over your head for guard duty…"

"Enjoy the fresh air."

Stark took a moment to look out the window, across

to the outbuildings. From the way the snow was coming down, they would be lucky to get as far as Albany tonight, even in the SUVs. He doubted that they would find what they were looking for in the adjacent buildings. If Blake had indeed stashed the Book out here, keeping it in the stables wouldn't make it any less findable. It was worth checking, though. Difficult to search in the dark, but the exterior buildings would have to be crossed off the list when they were done with the house.

He descended the stairs and found Murphy in the living room. Murphy raised his eyebrows, asking the question, and Stark shook his head.

"We've taken the place apart. It's a damn needle in a haystack, and we don't even know if it's in the haystack to begin with."

"Needle in a haystack's easy," Murphy said. "All you gotta do is burn the haystack down and go through the ashes with a magnet."

"Should we start on the outbuildings?" Stark asked.

Murphy glanced outside. "Later." He nodded at the two twenty-pound packs Stark and Jennings had brought from the cars. "How long do you need to wire the place?"

It was Murphy's fail-safe. If they could not find the Black Book, they could do the next-best thing: destroy the house and everything in it. It wouldn't provide the certainty he wanted, but if the Book was concealed anywhere here, it would burn up along with everything else.

"Five minutes, probably less." Stark answered without hesitation. They had planned carefully, and the advance intelligence on the house had been entirely accurate: exterior dimensions, room layout, construction materials. They had brought exactly what they needed. "We'll get set up in the kitchen," he continued. He knocked on the solid wall of the hallway next to the doorway. "This is a load-bearing wall: Take this out and the job's done."

Murphy nodded.

"All right. After you get done, take Kowalski. Give the barn and the stables the once-over, just see if there's anything obvious. Easier to look properly in the daylight."

"Sir," Stark acknowledged, hiding his annoyance that they were here for the night now. He knelt down and grabbed the first of the packs to carry through to the kitchen.

The task was completed in four minutes, not five. It wasn't the most challenging demolition job he had ever been assigned. When he was finished, he synced the remote detonator. He looked at Murphy, who was gazing in approval at the small stack of C-4 set up at the optimum spot to level the building.

"Code is 4649, okay?"

Murphy nodded acknowledgment, and Stark locked the screen and slid the small remote device into a breast pocket. Both men turned to the door when they heard the sound of someone clearing their throat. Usher was standing in the doorway, staring back at him through those glasses. Stark hated the way he did that. The way he just appeared.

They waited for Usher to say something, but he just looked back at them, awaiting instruction. Stark detected an undercurrent of contempt in his gaze, a little seasoning to the usual bland blankness. Like he was tired of the lack of progress. Before this mission, Stark wouldn't have thought Usher capable of frustration.

"Anything?" Murphy said at last.

Usher shook his head. Glanced at the stack of C-4 and then looked back at Murphy, regarding both with the same quiet indifference.

Murphy ignored it and looked back at Stark. "Okay. Take Kowalski and give the outbuildings a once-over."

Stark met Kowalski in the hall, and they opened the back door. Stark activated his night-vision goggles, but with the way the snow was coming down, it was like staring at an old-fashioned television set tuned to static. He clicked the switch off again, and they moved quickly across the open ground to the barn. The structure was two stories tall, with a corrugated aluminum roof. The exterior wood was weathered and warped, but structurally it looked sound. The big double doors at the front were secured by a padlock.

Stark backed up against the door and surveyed the tree line as Kowalski clipped the padlock off using bolt cutters. A minute later they were inside. The space was all but empty, just some machinery in the corner covered by a tarp and a ladder to the hayloft. Stark was about to tell Kowalski to check the hayloft when Walker's voice sounded in his ear on the open channel.

"Murphy?"

Murphy's voice came in immediately. "Talk to me."

"I got headlights. Estimate one mile away."

Stark drew a breath. Was this it? Who else would be on the road?

"Is he approaching?" Murphy asked.

"Affirma—hold on. Wait one."

Murphy held his breath as he listened to the crackling. The sound had gotten so bad that he'd only just caught the last sentence.

"Walker?"

"He's stopped."

"Say again?"

"I said he's stopped."

"Stay on it, Walker. Stark, are you getting this?"

"Loud and clear," Stark said. "You want us back at the house?"

"Negative. Sit tight. You have a view of the access road out there?"

Stark looked back out the main doors. They had a clear line of sight to the road, but that would require leaving the doors open. He took a couple steps back, glanced up, and saw that the window in the hayloft looked out on the same ground.

He confirmed and nodded to Kowalski to close the doors. Murphy spoke over the channel again, addressing Abrams this time.

"All clear at the cars?"

"Affirmative."

"Okay. Remain in position. Jennings, Markham, drop the goods at the cars with Abrams and get back to the south tree line. Approach with caution. And this goes for everyone: Do not take the shot. Allow him to approach the house. We don't want to spoil the surprise party, do we?"

SIXTY-SEVEN

STARK HAD FOUND a broken board in the side of the barn where he could see the main access road without leaving the ground level. He heard the occasional creak from the floorboards of the hayloft as Kowalski shifted position.

It had been five minutes since Walker's last report: The headlights he had seen had stopped in the road before switching off. Walker had speculated that the car had grounded in the snow, and he was proved right a few minutes later when he called in a lone man walking north along the road. Stark knew it had to be Blake. This was the only house for miles around. Anyone abandoning a car at that place in the road would either have to be certain that shelter was close by, or would be embarking on a suicide attempt.

But Stark was surprised they hadn't heard anything more from Walker yet. Given the position he had reported, Blake should have been practically at the access road by now. When he had waited as long as he could stand, he reached up to tap the button on his headset. Before his finger reached the button, Murphy spoke.

"Walker, what the hell is going on?"

There was a long pause, and then Walker's voice. The sound quality was fine, but Walker was yelling to hear himself over the wind. "He's gone."

Murphy's voice sounded again in Stark's ear.

"What the hell do you mean he's gone? Where could he go?"

"He was there. Now he's gone."

Stark stared across to where the access road emerged from the trees. He slid the night-vision goggles back over his eyes and flicked the switch again. More green pixelated television static, but no sign of any movement from the road. What the hell was going on?

SIXTY-EIGHT

THE MOST IMPORTANT thing about a trap is, you better make damn sure you know who's setting it.

The second the picture of Jake Martinez's dead body showed up in my inbox, I had known trouble was on its way. When my name triggered an alert on the system at Sea-Tac, I realized trouble was much closer than I anticipated. After that close shave, I had resolved not to take anything for granted.

I was conscious that my erstwhile colleagues in Winterlong had two very important advantages. One: They were better than anybody else in the world at hunting down a running target. Two: They knew me, and it was likely they could dig up just enough intelligence to predict where I might go.

Five years ago I had done everything I could to make sure my base was somewhere off the beaten path, somewhere that would leave as small a footprint as possible. I had bought the house cash, posing as an agent for a client in Florida who wanted to acquire a summer place up north. I had paid enough to guarantee a quick sale, but I had selected a house that wouldn't attract much attention and didn't have any neighbors within miles. But there's only so much you can do to stay off the radar. Drakakis eventually deciding to renege on our deal had always been a danger, so I had thought about ways to make sure I had an early warning if they came for me.

And I had also considered the scenario that they might take the house in my absence.

I had taken all the usual precautions of a homeowner who leaves his house uninhabited for long stretches of time. Timers on the heat and lights. A top-of-the-line security system. Motion-activated cameras on a live Web feed. But those things all relied on power, and I knew that the first thing invading force would do would be to cut power.

Power outages aren't exactly unusual in that part of the world, particularly during the winter months, so the security system worked with battery backup, as standard. I got an alert by e-mail when the backup kicked in for any reason. It happened a couple of times every winter, and it didn't mean anything by itself.

But I also had a backup for the backup. A battery-operated motion sensor covering the front and back doors that sent a signal via GPS whenever it activated. Again, I would get an alert every so often when a particularly eager salesman or charity collector ventured down the access road, found the house, and rang the doorbell. In itself, it didn't mean anything. But when both things happened on the same night, within five minutes of each other—when the power cut out and, minutes later, somebody approached the front door—that meant everything.

The five minutes I had spent on the kindly store owner's computer in Wilston had confirmed my fears. Not only had the power cut out; not only had the motion alarm been activated; but the perimeter motion detectors I had set up around the tree line had been gamed. It had been done skillfully—barely a blip in the telemetry, but it was there if you knew when to check the history, in this case around the time of the power cut. The live cams covering the grounds of the house had gone offline simultaneously.

From the moment I had seen the picture of Martinez's body, I knew something had changed and that they were playing for keeps. And I knew I would have to show them the error of their ways. The house was a trap, all right. Now it was time to show them who the trap belonged to.

SIXTY-NINE

THE TWISTED LIGHTNING-STRUCK tree was a half mile from the access road, but it also marked the point where one of the old riding trails intersected with the road. I didn't think there had been horses stabled at Hamilton Falls for at least a couple of decades before I moved in, so the trail was overgrown and obscured under normal conditions. Under a foot of snow, it was invisible, unless you knew exactly where to look. The trail led west for a couple hundred yards until it met the stream that ran through the estate. There the path forked. Continuing west, it crossed a small wooden bridge. To the north, it followed the path of the stream, gaining height as it approached the ridge overlooking the rear of the house. The stream made it easier to follow the trail. Within minutes, I was at the highest point of the ridge looking down on the house.

There were no signs of life, but I knew they would be careful about that. They'd be expecting me, would probably have someone watching the main road. The snow had been coming down too hard for it to be obvious, but there were depressions in the snow leading from the edge of the woods to the house. If I focused, I could just make out foot trails, where three or more people had advanced across the open ground in front of the house. There were absolutely no signs of trails or tire tracks from the direction of the main approach road, and this was exactly as I had anticipated.

I kept low and back from the edge as I navigated the remainder of the ridge. The path forked again. Going right would bring me down to the flat ground, the trail coming out at the old stables. I ignored that path, because I wasn't ready to approach the house just yet. I bore left and kept moving. Five minutes later, I slowed as I approached a point where there was a small hill. I got down on my belly and crawled through the snow to the edge. I peered over the edge and saw the ground fall away through the trees. Beneath the snow, I knew that the trail continued down the hill before curving off to the west. Looking beyond the curve, I saw a thick stand of trees and a wide clearing where the logging road came out. Just as I had expected, there were two black SUVs parked there, facing the road back out to enable a rapid exit. The vehicles were already coated with snow, except for on the hoods above the still-warm engines.

I lay motionless and watched the area for a couple of minutes. I saw no movement, but I was certain they would not have left the position unguarded. It was difficult to see anything with the snow coming down so hard.

And then he appeared. A figure wearing white moved from his position at the back of one of the SUVs, circled around the vehicles, and stopped again. He moved the barrel of his assault rifle, covering the approach road, and then slowly turned in a circle. I held still, knowing the upper part of my head was visible, but trusting that he wouldn't be able to pick me out of the background unless I made it easy by ducking suddenly. I kept perfectly still, all except my eyes, which were taking in the rest of the area, making sure there was only one guard.

When he had settled into his new position, I waited another minutes and then started to circle around him, closing the radius until I was within twenty feet of him. As I watched his back, his head turned. I ducked down, but he was looking in the direction of the house. I guessed from his body language he was listening to a communication through a headset, like the ones the team on the train had been wearing. That was confirmed a moment later when he spoke out loud. Just one or two words, and one of them sounded like "negative." He was confirming it was all quiet at this post, which meant they wouldn't expect to hear from him for at least a few minutes, which in turn meant I wouldn't get a better chance to strike.

I moved a little closer, to the edge of open ground, and then quickly stepped out into the clearing and behind the nearest vehicle. The guy was just ten feet away now, his back to me. I knew what to do. Quick and quiet. The hunting knife was clipped to my belt. I put my hand on the hilt and thought the action out, breaking it into neat steps. Four paces. Wrap my left arm around his arms to stop him swinging the gun around. Cut the throat in one quick movement. No hesitation.

Except I was hesitating.

Now that I was contemplating killing a man in cold blood for the first time in years, hesitate was all I could do. The knowledge that he would do the same to me in a heartbeat didn't make any difference. He started to turn, and I ducked behind the SUV, keeping an eye on him through gaps in snow on the windows. He turned three hundred and sixty degrees again, before facing

back to the access road. Sloppy. Not varying his position or line of sight often enough. Clearly, standards had
slipped a little. I gripped the hilt of the knife, braced
myself...and then released it.

I took my gun from inside my coat instead. I waited
for the next turn in his predictable routine, and knew I
had all the time in the world to get behind him. I stood
up, walked the four paces, and put the barrel of the
Glock firmly at the base of his skull.

"One chance. Move and you're a dead man."

A sharp intake of breath, and then he froze. Slowly,
he released his grip on the AR-15. It hung around his
shoulder on the strap as he raised his hands.

"Blake?"

"Good guess," I said. "Who are you?"

"Abrams. You don't have a chance. You know that,
don't you?"

"If they told you anything about me, you know I like
a challenge. How many?"

He shook his head, his voice calm. "I'm not telling
you anything."

I hadn't expected him to, and I wouldn't have believed anything he told me, anyway. I kept the pressure
on the back of his head while I started to lift the AR-15
off his shoulders with my left hand.

And then I heard the others. My eyes flicked to the
source of the noise, and I saw two more men in white
emerging from the forest, carrying transparent plastic
sacks full of equipment. Abrams heard them at the same
time and started to yell.

"He's here!"

SEVENTY

"BLAKE IS OUT HERE, at the cars. I need backup."

At the end of Markham's sentence, Stark heard a rapid clicking sound, which he knew was the communicator dampening the sound of a close-up burst of automatic fire. He heard the delayed echo of the burst out of his other ear from the north. They had heard another burst moments earlier, and he was already in the process of trying to work out from which direction it had come. Now he knew. The son of a bitch had gotten past Walker somehow.

He wondered what Blake's strategy was. Perhaps Blake had deliberately engaged the three men at the cars, trying to draw more of them away from the house. Somehow he had second-guessed them, or there was some extra warning system they'd missed. Either way, he was still one man against nine. Now was not the time to panic and start playing into his hands.

"Dixon, Kowalski." Murphy's voice cut in. "Go help them out. Stark and Usher, hold your positions."

Kowalski's face appeared at the edge of the hayloft. They exchanged a glance and Kowalski smiled, clearly relishing the chance to even the score with Blake. He swung his legs over the edge and slid down the edges of the ladder, the old wood creaking in protest under the big man's weight. A couple of seconds later, he had opened the doors and was gone into the night.

Stark tried to remember how long it had taken them to cover the ground between the cars and the house. Five minutes, perhaps? Moving relatively quickly but not hurrying. The ground was treacherous in the snow, so chances were they wouldn't make much better time on the way back.

More bursts of fire sounded, from at least two different weapons. Stark had an urge to forget the order and follow Kowalski, but he knew Murphy was right to hold them back here. It would play into Blake's hands if they all charged off into the woods. And so he kept his powder dry, gazing out through the hole in the wall, listening to the voices relaying the situation out at the car.

Murphy spoke again, his voice calm despite it all. "Abrams, come in. Jennings, come in."

Another distant burst of gunfire and Markham's voice came in again. "Abrams is down. Jennings, too, I think. I've got him pinned down in…" The rest was drowned in another burst of fire, and then Markham repeated the last few words. "One of the cars."

"Help is on the way," Murphy responded. "Keep him pinned."

Stark got to his feet and moved across the floor of the barn to the north side, looking for another gap in the wall so he could at least look out in the right direction. Nothing on this side. He moved back to the doors, one side still open from Kowalski's departure, and cautiously peered out. If he stood on the right-hand side, he could see in the direction of the cars. He listened to the sporadic gunfire and the occasional yells. He looked for muzzle flashes, or anything in the darkness. He could barely make out the line of trees through the snow: It registered as a solid black wall that kept all of its secrets.

Stark felt a familiar and unwelcome visitor return: that feeling in the pit of his belly when things are going bad and about to go worse. All of a sudden, nine against one didn't seem like the insurmountable odds it should have. Not when they were entirely cut off from the rest of the world, in a place where their prey had home-court advantage.

SEVENTY-ONE

I GRIPPED THE AR-15 and planted my foot in the small of Abram's back, kicking him forward as I yanked the door of the SUV open. The two men coming out of the woods dropped the plastic sacks and raised their guns. I got behind the door as they opened fire. Abrams wasn't so lucky. His body slumped hard against the door, his blood spattering the bulletproof glass.

I clicked the selector to disengage the safety on Abrams's AR-15 as bullets ricocheted off the armor plating on the door. I waited my turn and strafed the trees, hearing a cry as I felled one of the two men. From a position a little away from the cry, I heard rapid talking as the other one yelled into his communicator. I fired in the direction of the voice and ducked back into cover as an answering burst returned.

Bad timing. Perhaps if I hadn't hesitated about cutting Abrams's throat, I wouldn't have been pinned down. There had been no further shots from the position of the man I had hit, but the second was clearly alive, well, and summoning backup. The house was a short distance away through the forest, and I didn't have long before reinforcements showed up. I straightened out of my crouch to bring my eyes above the level of the window well enough. As I watched, I saw two muzzle flashes and flinched back as both shots impacted the glass beside my head. Bulletproof, but not invincible. I just hoped the guy out there wasn't carrying anything more powerful. I fired another burst to keep him occupied.

More powerful... That gave me an idea. I risked a glance around the edge of the door at Abrams's body. He had fallen back against the vehicle, his open eyes staring up at the sky. I fired another burst and grabbed him by the collar. I dragged him under the door, rolling him over. He had a small satchel slung around his shoulder by a strap. I unzipped it and started rummaging. Another burst of fire hit the side of the SUV. I wondered how close the others were.

SEVENTY-TWO

STARK HELD HIS position and watched the line of trees to the north. He kept thinking about a town called Bartella, in Northern Iraq. A town he had seen a long time ago, years before he ever heard the name Winterlong. The insurgents had gotten hold of heavy cannon and Al-Samoud missile launchers, and light infantry was no match for the heavy artillery. Stark and three others had been holed up in an abandoned building while shells rained down not more than five hundred yards away. It had taken three days before air support was able to neutralize the guns. On the face of it, the situations then and now could not be more different, and yet he felt the same powerlessness as he listened to the sporadic updates in between bursts of gunfire.

Although he, Murphy, and Usher had remained at the house and the barn, they could follow the progress through their linked headsets. Dixon and Kowalski were two minutes from the scene, approaching on separate vectors. Markham was still responding to Murphy's requests for updates. He had Blake pinned down in one of the cars, although the pinning down was mutual, since Blake was returning fire. Worryingly, neither Abrams nor Jennings had spoken since the shooting started, suggesting they were most likely not just down, but KIA. Grimly ironic, Stark thought, if the twins had actually been killed at the same time. The last burst of gunfire had been around a minute ago, and this had been the longest break in fire since the shooting had started. A lull. Stark could hear nothing but the soft whisper of snow falling through the trees.

A second later, Dixon called in to say he had reached Markham's position.

"Where's Blake?" Murphy asked.

"Still over there, I think," Markham replied. Then he remembered the communication medium and clarified. "At the cars."

"Quiet for a minute or so," Dixon added.

"You think you got him?" Murphy asked.

Markham responded after a second. "I don't know."

Silence for thirty seconds, and then Kowalski called in to say he had sight of the cars, positioned west of Dixon and Markham.

"Can you see him?" Murphy asked.

There was a pause, and Kowalski's voice came in. "I'm not sure. No movement."

Stark could picture the scene without difficulty. The three of them surrounding a hostile vehicle, wondering when and whether to break cover to check it out. Blake could be dead, he could be wounded, or he could be playing possum.

"Dixon, what's happening?" That was Murphy's voice on the line, betraying a hint of impatience.

"Unknown. No movement."

"Is he hit?"

"Unknown."

Another long pause, and then Dixon spoke. "I'm going to check it out."

"Be careful," Murphy replied quickly. "Kowalski, get in closer and cover him."

Stark held his breath and waited. Ten seconds. Twenty. Dixon had left his channel open as he approached the car. The sound quality of the headsets was so good, he could hear his breathing.

"Blake?" Markham called out. "You're surrounded. Lay down the weapon and walk out here. We won't shoot if you cooperate."

Nothing. Another twenty seconds.

"I'm going to put a couple in the car," Dixon said.

The cracks of three single shots echoes through the woods, paired up with the tinny sounds of the bullets smacking into the armor plating on the SUVs.

"No movement. Going in."

It seemed to take forever for Dixon to reach the SUV, but there were no further shots, which had to be a good thing.

"Abrams is dead," he said, which meant he was close enough to confirm. "I'm going to open the door."

"Wait," Murphy said. "Kowalski?"

Stark heard the sound of the door handle click, and a second later he heard a cry of alarm. He would never know which of the three men it came from.

"Oh fu—"

The communication disappeared, and a second later, there was an explosion from the north. This time, the fireball was big and bright enough to be seen through the woods.

SEVENTY-THREE

AS SOON AS the grenades in the SUV went up, I broke my cover behind a thick-trunked tree twenty yards away and ran flat-out for the trail. My hesitation with Abrams had been stupid, and it had nearly gotten me killed. But it had been simple enough to rig the trap with Abrams's grenades and exit the opposite side of the car. The challenging part had been putting enough distance between me and the vehicle without being seen before the reinforcements showed up. It looked like there had been two of them, in addition to the one I had been exchanging fire with.

It was as though the lessons of the last couple of days had passed straight over my head. I wasn't going to get out of this alive by acting like anything other than what I'd been five years ago: a soldier.

I had Abrams's headset now. It was top-of-the-line equipment, of course, just like Kowalski's on the train. I had been listening to the chatter between the men for the last few minutes. So far I had identified four distinct voices, including Jack Murphy's. I wondered if I should be honored that he had returned to field work just for me. I was pretty sure Dixon, the one who had tripped my little surprise, was the same one I had worked with. If so, I wouldn't be shedding any tears for him.

I knew there would be more of them. It sounded like at least two of them were in the house. Better—I caught two mentions of Bryant's name, which meant he was still alive for now and that my ruse about the bookcase in the basement had worked. Walker, who had been the man watching the road, was en route to the SUVs. No one had heard anything from out that way since the explosion, which I figured was definitely a good sign for me. I caught a break when Walker, on his way to the scene, referenced the radio silence from out at the cars.

"I thought nine against one was *good* odds."

Because of Walker's nervous chatter, I now had an answer to the question I'd asked Abrams. Nine men, maybe down to four or five now.

There was one more name I had caught that seemed somehow familiar. Usher, the one who Murphy had instructed to remain on the upper level of the house. I'd never worked with an Usher, and he hadn't spoken yet, so I didn't know if his voice would be familiar, but the mention of his name seemed to trigger something at the back of my mind. For the time being, though, I had more pressing concerns.

I made my way back up the ridge and across to the point where the trail led back down to the stables. I couldn't see anybody there, but I already knew from Murphy's instructions that there was at least one man in the barn. That might cause me a problem. I had hoped they would stick to the house for now.

From my east-facing vantage point, the three groups of buildings were laid out in front of me. The stables were closest, at nine o'clock. The barn was diagonally to my right, about two o'clock. Farthest from me was the house at twelve o'clock.

"Murphy, this is Walker."

The voice in my earpiece sounded rattled. Good. I

tensed and listened for the update. After a pause, Murphy told him to go ahead.

"I'm at the cars. Markham is unconscious but still alive, barely. Kowalski, Dixon, Abrams, and Jennings are all dead."

"Shit, what the hell—" another voice cut in. It sounded familiar. What was the name of the man I had spoken to from Chicago? Stark, I thought.

"Quiet," Murphy ordered. "Head back to the house, Walker, and be careful."

"What about Markham?"

I heard an exasperated sigh from Murphy. "Is he going to make it?"

As the two of them debated the likelihood of Markham's survival, I took stock. Five out of action, and Walker at least seven minutes away. If that was right, it left three men out at the house. That was consistent with the communications I'd heard earlier: Usher and Murphy in the house, Stark in the barn. I had cut the odds against me by two-thirds, but I was still outnumbered.

Murphy, in an uncharacteristic show of compassion, had changed his mind. He told Walker to patch Markham up as best he could and leave him in the remaining car before heading back. Which was great news for Markham, but good news for me, too.

I looked ahead at the barn, judging where best to attack. Stark would have made sure he was in a position with a view of the entrance, and probably the approach to the house as well. The barn was a ramshackle structure that had seen better days, and I hadn't done much for the upkeep since I had been the owner. All except for one thing. Something that wouldn't stand up to a thorough search in daylight.

I approached the back of the barn quickly, moving through the blind spot where the barn itself obscured the line of sight from the house and where I could not be seen from the small window in the side.

And that was when I heard Stark's voice in my ear-piece again and knew there had to be a change of plan.

SEVENTY-FOUR

STARK NESTLED INTO the northeast corner of the barn, beside a wide gap in the aluminum siding that gave him a commanding view of the front of the house. If Walker was right, Blake had taken out half of their number in one stroke. There was only one place he could be headed now. Stark kept his eyes on the line of trees, watching the open ground between the house and the barn. After a few minutes of nothing much happening, he relaxed a little, shifting his weight on the dirt floor.

Something creaked.

Keeping his eyes on the gap in the siding, he shifted his position again and heard another creak. Finally, he looked down and looked at the area of ground he was crouched on. There was a slight dip. He glanced up again at the open ground, eyes darting from the house to the tree line, before satisfying himself all was clear. He examined the dip in the floor, running the tips of his fingers over the place where it started to dip. He found a straight edge, carefully concealed under an inch of dirt.

He tapped the button on his headset and spoke quietly. "Murphy, you there?"

The response in his ear was almost immediately. "Go ahead, Stark."

He ran his fingers along the edge and found a corner. It was square. A hatch in the floor.

"I think I found something."

SEVENTY-FIVE

By the time Murphy got there, Stark had fully uncovered the edges of the concealed hatch. There was a lock on the bottom edge, the keyhole covered by a flat strip of plastic to protect it from the dirt. Stark unclipped a pocket-sized snapper bar from his belt and wedged it between the edge of the hatch and the frame at the lock. He put pressure on it and the lock broke easily. It opened on a narrow pit, about three and a half feet square and seven deep. Just enough space for a man. A bolt-hole: somewhere a person could conceal himself if the house was being searched. Stark had seen photographs of Saddam's hiding place near Tikrit, and this reminded him of it. He directed the beam of his flashlight into the hole. It was neatly dug into the earth, with the edges squared off.

"What have we here?"

As the two of them peered into the hole, Stark saw that there was a shadow at the far edge, as though a small cutting had been made in the dirt wall at the bottom. He played the beam around to confirm there was a hollow there and looked up at Murphy.

"Check it out."

Stark handed Murphy his AR-15 and dropped into the hole. It was just big enough to accommodate him. With difficulty, he crouched down to get a better look at the hollow. It was about a foot high, impossible to tell how far back it went. He crouched down on one knee and reached his hand in carefully. Immediately he felt something plastic. He took hold and pulled out a case of six bottles of water. He threw them topside and reached around in the hollow again. There were two more objects in there, both felt like boxes. One large, one small. The larger of the two contained dry rations and a Glock 19 wrapped in clear waterproof plastic. The smaller was a fireproof lockbox. Stark tossed it up to Murphy, who caught it and examined it. Without saying anything, he removed his own snapper bar from his belt and put the box on the ground. He inserted the thin, bladed end in the join between the lid and the base and twisted. The lockbox sprang open. Stark hauled himself out of the pit and looked down at their bounty. The lockbox contained two wads of banknotes: dollars and euros, a stack of ID documents held together by a rubber band...and one black flash drive.

Murphy smiled. "Looks like 'alive' just became less of a priority."

No sooner had he finished speaking than the sound of gunfire rang out from the direction of the house.

SEVENTY-SIX

I'VE HEARD PEOPLE say that Chinese have one word that means both "crisis" and "opportunity." I have no idea if that's true, but it sounds good enough to have gained currency.

When I heard Stark's communication to Murphy, I knew he had found the hatch, which was a crisis of sorts. But it also meant Murphy had immediately taken the bait, leaving the remaining man, Usher, alone in the house. Which was an opportunity. As I watched the house, I saw movement on the front porch, and then Murphy sprinted for the barn. I thought about taking the shot, decided against it. I wanted to get into the house, and I knew there was enough to keep Stark and Murphy occupied in the barn for a few minutes. Murphy was taking quite a risk breaking cover like that, which meant he wanted what was in there badly. He wouldn't be disappointed, either.

Then, secure in the knowledge that Stark would be busy examining the trap door in the floor, I sprinted toward the back door of the house. There were no windows in the upper floor facing that way, and I hoped that Usher was still on that level.

I reached the back porch and flattened my back against the wall next to the door. In the silence, I could hear movement from the barn. I reached for the back door handle and turned it. It was unlocked. I opened the back door with care and deliberation and cursed under my breath as I heard the kitchen door slam shut as the wind gusted through the house and out past me. A window open somewhere. Because of that, I had lost the element of surprise.

I stood still for a second in the hallway, listening for sounds. My instinct was that Usher would still be upstairs, perhaps in the main bedroom with its view from the front of the house. Bryant's location was easy. Whether he was alive or dead, he would be locked in the basement. But before I could check that, I'd have to flush out the sentry.

I had waited long enough to know one thing with reasonable certainty: Wherever Usher was, he was within earshot. I knew this because I hadn't heard a peep on the headset. There was no way he could have missed the sound of the door slamming. If I had been Murphy or one of the others, I would have identified myself already, or given him a heads-up I was coming. If he was far enough from me to speak without being heard, I would have heard him speaking over the communicator to confirm Murphy was still in the barn. That meant he had a compelling reason to keep quiet, which suggested that he was close by.

My unwelcome guests had had a few hours to get the lay of the land, but they would never know the house as well as me. I thought again about Walker's mention of nine against one odds. Assuming that he could count, and had no reason to lie, that left just one remaining hostile in the house.

I advanced down the hallway slowly. I held my breath as I approached the spot in the hall that would bring me within line of sight of the landing at the top of the stairs. The basement door was ten feet ahead of me: not far, but far enough to ensure I'd never make it alive.

I tightened my grip on the AR-15 I'd taken from Abrams and moved my eyes from the basement door to the full-length mirror on the wall. I hadn't spent a lot of time thinking about interior decor: Everything in the house had a function, and this was no exception. It was positioned so that you could stand in the hall-way and see the top of the stairs. If you chose a certain position, you could do so without being seen from the landing. It had taken me a while to get the angle right, but I was glad of it now. In the dull light from the window at the top of the stairs, I could see an unfamiliar shadow. Something was behind the wall at the top of the stairs. Something, or someone.

All of a sudden I remembered why the name Usher was familiar. It had been five years since I had looked at the contents of the Black Book, but that was where I had seen the name. Usher had been the one tasked with killing Senator Carlson. And now he was lying in wait again, cloaked in the shadows, ready to kill once more. I wondered how many people he had killed in the in-terim and how many of those had been innocent people in the wrong place at the wrong time. Partly by elimi-nation, partly through gut instinct, I knew the man at the top of the stairs was the man with glasses, the man who had remained nameless up until now.

Stalemate. I knew where Usher was, but he certainly knew where I was, too.

Time was not on my side either. I made up my mind and took the last step out from under the landing, turn-ing and firing a short burst at the corner of the wall at the top of the stairs. As I heard the bullets' impact into the thick wooden support pillar behind the drywall, I knew I hadn't hit the man on the landing. The sound of him moving on the floorboards just confirmed it. I ducked back underneath the cover of the landing as he responded with an answering burst, the bullets tearing into the floorboards and passing through to the basement below. I hoped that Bryant hadn't happened to be in their path. From above, I heard footsteps on the surface. Hollow and then flat as he moved across the top of the stairs and to the opposite end of the landing.

I knew the support pillar would shield him effectively, but I had accomplished my real purpose: flushing him out and rattling him into moving his position. And now the sound of his footsteps was going to help me put him down.

I had bought the house following a minor fire that had left the structure intact, but necessitated a full rebuild of the staircase and upper landing. The project hadn't taken long to complete, but I had had the opportunity to view the work in progress. That was how I knew that the opposing ends of the landing were supported by a pair of six-inch-thick concrete ledges, leaving a stretch of two-inch-thick floorboards in between. My adversary had just moved from a position shielded by the vertical pillar to one sheltered by the concrete underneath him. I hoped his adrenaline would be pumping too hard to notice the slight difference in the surface beneath his feet.

There was a pause of a few seconds while each of us waited for the other to make a move.

"Drop your weapon and I'll let you walk out of here," I called out. When there was no response, I continued. "I know you're smart, Usher. You backed off in LA."

There was a pause and then a barely perceptible noise as Usher moved. I ducked and rolled as he angled the barrel over the edge of the drop, aiming for the sound of my voice.

I waited and took another step forward.

"There's no way out," I said, ducking back into cover as he fired again. The bullets smashed into the floor a couple feet away, but the angle was no good. Sooner or later he was going to have to move from his position. I was hoping for sooner, because the shots would have alerted Stark and Murphy in the barn by now.

So far my attempts to rile him had failed. He hadn't even bothered to answer me, never mind move position. I weighed the odds and decided to force the issue. I stepped out of cover and fired blind up at the landing. The angle was just as ineffective for me, and I knew all I was doing was putting a few more holes in the ceiling.

I ducked back underneath the landing, making sure to position myself beneath the concrete. I took careful aim at the stretch of wood between the two concrete support platforms. I started to wonder if there was anything I could do to make Usher lose his cool. But then I heard footsteps again—two flat slaps and then two hollow *thunks* as he headed for the top of the stairs. I knew he was planning to rush me, spray the hallway with bullets as he ran down the stairs, hoping to take me out before I could return fire. Before he got within line of sight, I squeezed the trigger and sent a long burst straight through the floorboards at the top of the stairs just as he crossed the unprotected area. I saw the holes explode in the surface of the wood, heard a scream, and watched as the body tumbled down the fifteen stairs, landing in a crumpled heap at the bottom.

The AR-15 clattered on the floor beside him. I took no chances, lining my sights on the back of his head. When I got close enough, I kicked the weapon away and used my foot to roll the body over, keeping my rifle trained on the motionless body.

The head rolled back and the dim light from the upstairs window glinted off a single glass lens. I recognized the face from LA. The man in glasses had taken multiple hits. I switched in a fresh magazine and then crouched down beside him to take a closer look. Some of the bullets had punctured his legs, some had impacted off his body armor, and one had smashed through the right lens of his glasses.

As I straightened up, I noticed a small light in the corner of my vision, through the open kitchen door. I turned and looked inside, a feeling of foreboding growing. The kitchen was located in the center of the ground floor. I felt a cold chill as I saw a pile of shapes in the dark: stacked objects connected by wires and a winking red light. Enough C-4 to turn this place into matchsticks. Every instinct in my body screamed at me to run, to head for the door.

But Bryant was still in the basement.

SEVENTY-SEVEN

STARK TURNED HIS head toward the source of the gunfire.

"That's in the house." He looked back at Murphy, who hadn't shifted from his position and had a thoughtful look on his face. "He's in the damn house!"

Stark picked up his AR-15 and started to move toward the barn door when Murphy reached forward and grabbed his upper arm.

"Wait."

"What are you doing?"

Murphy kept a tight grip on Stark's upper arm, looking him square in the eye. "Could be an easier way to deal with that. Bryant, too. All of them."

Stark didn't get it for a second, and then he remembered the explosives in the house. Murphy's backup plan.

Another exchange of fire rang out.

"Usher's in there," he said, as though Murphy didn't know that.

Murphy held out his hand, and Stark knew what he wanted: the remote detonator that was currently nestled in the padded pocket of his combat vest. "Usher can take his chances. We've got what we need."

Stark looked back at him for a minute, trying to work out if this were some kind of black humor. Murphy stared back at him, unblinking. No joke.

Before Stark could say anything else, Murphy reached forward, grabbing at the pocket of the vest.

Instinctively, Stark ducked back. Murphy lunged at him, and Stark sidestepped again before slamming his fist into the left side of Murphy's jaw, knocking him down on the barn floor. For a moment they just looked at each other. Stark still standing, Murphy on the ground with blood flowing from his upper lip.

"I'm going in there. You can follow me, or you can sit here and wait."

Stark began to turn toward the door and heard a familiar click before he was turned all the way around.

"You forgot option three."

He turned back to Murphy. The gun was pointed directly at his head.

"Are you fucking kidding me?"

Murphy said nothing but shook his head from side to side.

"What Blake said—he didn't kill the senator, did he? We did."

"Give me the remote, Stark."

Being careful not to make a sudden movement anywhere near his own gun, Stark's hand went up to his earpiece. He tapped the team channel button.

"Usher, do you read? Get the fuck out of there. Murphy's going to blow—"

The barrel of Murphy's AR-15 erupted in white light. Stark realized he had stopped in the middle of a sentence and couldn't remember why. He started trying to speak again, but the words wouldn't come. Then his vision went red, and then black.

SEVENTY-EIGHT

I WAS HEADED for the back door when I heard the voice in my ear. "Usher, do you read? Get the fuck out of there. Murphy's going to blow—" followed by a burst of fire that I heard in stereo: a series of rapid clicks in my left ear and the unfiltered noise from farther off to my right.

And then I stopped thinking. The back door was too far away, too close to the thin drywall separating the hallway from the kitchen. There was a quicker way out. I charged through into the living room, raising my Glock and firing at the plate-glass window. It shattered around the trail of bullet holes and the glass dropped away. I caught my foot on a jutting shard of the window as I jumped through the hole. I tumbled out into the night and hit the snow, landing hard on my shoulder. I rolled to my feet and started to run just as the wave of light and heat hit me and carried me off my feet.

I landed facedown, the snow breaking my fall a little. I stayed down, hands over my head as I heard and felt large fragments of my house crash to the ground behind and ahead of me. When the larger impacts subsided, I rolled over. My ears were ringing from the blast. Black smoke was billowing skyward. As I watched, the blackness began to be penetrated by the light of dirty orange flames. After a minute I could just make out a burning husk where my house had once stood. I put a hand above my head to protect me from the small debris that was still raining down in place of the snowflakes. Murphy had missed me again. I started to struggle onto one knee, and then I saw a figure silhouetted against the flames.

Murphy's voice sounded amused. "Last men standing, huh, Blake?"

I started to get up from my kneeling position, and he shook his head. "Uh-uh. Stay right there, hoss. Toss the gun. Hands behind your head."

Slowly, I did as he asked, throwing the Glock a couple of feet in front of me. I stayed where I was, kneeling in the snow. I wondered if Martinez had been kneeling when they'd caught up with him. I wondered if he had managed to take any of them with him.

"Looks like your luck ran out tonight."

"Looks like lots of people's did," I replied, gazing past him at the burning house.

Murphy nodded. "Not exactly a perfect mission, I'll grant you. But you're not exactly an easy target."

"We can still make a deal," I said.

Murphy didn't say anything for a moment, and then he took a step closer. I could see him grinning in the flickering light from the house.

"I'm afraid you're too late. Stark found your little bolt-hole in the barn. I got the Black Book right here." He laughed at the pained expression on my face. "*Oh shit.* Damn right. Tell you the truth, you've done me a favor. With Usher dead, there's nobody left to know what really went down on the Carlson job."

"You always were a pragmatist, Murphy," I said.

He nodded. "Goddamn straight. But even so, I'm sorry it had to come to this. These last couple of days made me realize I actually missed you."

"I'm touched."

"I mean, sure, don't get me wrong—you've made things more difficult than they needed to be. But it's been so long. Made me realize they don't make them like us anymore."

"There is no us. You're nothing like me," I said quietly.

He nodded agreement, like he could afford to be magnanimous. "All right, you have a point. You know what your problem is?"

I said nothing, waited for him to continue.

"Sentimentality," he said finally. "You worry about other people. You have friends. Men like us can't afford friends."

"I bet Usher would agree with that," I said. I closed my eyes and tried to think of a way out of this. I didn't think there was one.

"He wouldn't be the only one," Murphy said in a reflective tone. He paused and seemed to make up his mind. "You tried to get Bryant out of the house, didn't you? Maybe things would have gone differently if you'd have cut your losses."

I opened my eyes again and looked at Murphy, then beyond him at the burning heap.

"Maybe."

"Anyway, enough talk."

Murphy raised his rifle, training it on my upper body.

"Aren't you going to tell me this is nothing personal?" I said quickly.

A smile of recognition at the inside joke crossed his face. "Oh, it's personal this time."

"You know what *your* problem is, Murphy?"

He stopped and smiled. I had listened to his analysis of me, so fair was fair. "Enlighten me."

"You don't have any friends left." I raised my voice.
"Shoot him."

Murphy had a split second to register a look of confusion before the spray of 5.56 NATO bullets ripped
into him. His body jerked and danced against the hell-
ish backdrop of the blaze as Bryant unloaded the full
magazine into him from behind. I flattened myself on
the ground until the burst finished and then looked up.
Murphy was down, face-first in the snow. Bryant was
still behind him, holding the rifle out in front of him
with a dazed expression on his face. I got to my feet
and covered the ground between me and Murphy in a
second, ready to wrestle the rifle from him.

When I got close enough, I realized there was no
need. The armor on his upper body had absorbed some
of the fire, but he had taken at least two in the head.
Dark red blood pumped out into the white snow as his
heart gave its last beats. I took another step toward Bryant, keeping out of the way of the barrel of the assault
rifle. When I got close enough, I gently put a hand on
the barrel and pushed it down. Bryant didn't look at me,
his eyes fixed on the man he'd just killed.

"You did good, Bryant," I said.

I had been right—difficult to miss with that many
bullets. I was glad I had made the decision to hand Bryant the AR-15 rather than the Glock after I got him out
of the basement.

*"Click the safety off here. Point at the bad guy.
Squeeze the trigger. Nothing to it."*

"Blake, I don't know how to..."

*"Safety off, point, squeeze. We don't have time for a
more detailed firearms course, okay? They're wearing
body armor, so make sure you hit the limbs or the head."*

Not bad for a first timer.

Murphy had been in the barn when he blew the house, so I knew he couldn't have seen Bryant as he left via the front door. Of course, I didn't know for sure he had gotten clear of the blast until I had seen a dark shape against the conflagration behind Murphy. I had kept him talking for another few seconds: just long enough for Bryant to get close.

Bryant let go of the rifle and it dropped to his feet. He didn't say anything for a minute. Eventually, he turned his eyes to meet mine. He shook his head as though trying to wake from a dream. "You okay, Blake?"

I nodded. "I'm okay. You saved my life. Thank you."

The words seemed to have little impact on him. He nodded absently, as though I'd told him it looked like rain.

"So what do we do now?"

I didn't answer. I crouched down and patted down each of Murphy's pockets, hoping it was still there. I found it in the left breast pocket of his shirt, my fingers closing around the tiny flat nub of plastic. The Black Book.

"First thing, we get the hell out of here. After that I'm going to need some of your technical expertise."

TUESDAY, JANUARY 12TH

SEVENTY-NINE

New York City

FARADAY HIT SEND on one last e-mail, closed the case of her tablet, and leaned back in the seat, watching the expensive storefronts of Madison Avenue as they passed by outside the car. The city had quickly returned to normal following the storm. There were still piles of snow neatly plowed to the sides of the streets, but the city had shrugged the storm off like it did everything else, and life was back to business as usual.

"Long day, Ms. Faraday?" Hank called back, his eyes darting up to the rearview mirror.

"You could say that," she replied.

It had been a very long day indeed. A day she looked forward to putting behind her. But there was one more thing to do first.

The morning had started with a post-mortem of the events at Hamilton Falls Farm two nights earlier. Only Walker had escaped unscathed. Faraday put this down to the fact that he, as lookout, had been some distance away for the duration of the action. Unfortunately, that also meant he was of limited use in piecing together the sequence of events. He had made it out in the remaining SUV with two injured comrades: Markham had been caught up in some kind of explosion, Stark he had found in the barn with a gunshot wound to the head.

Assuming at first that he was dead, Walker was amazed to find a weak pulse. Against the odds, that pulse was still going, though Stark had yet to regain consciousness. Markham had not been so lucky, succumbing to his injuries before Walker was able to get him to safety.

Seven men dead, the house wiped off the face of the earth, and no Carter Blake to show for it. If there was one positive, it was the fact that the storm and the remoteness of the battle had kept it out of the public eye. As operations went, it was an unmitigated disaster. As PR problems went, it still ranked far below the shooting of the cabbie at the airport.

Hank pulled to a stop at the corner of East Forty-Third Street, then turned in his seat and looked at her expectantly, waiting for instructions.

"Wait here," she said, and got out onto the sidewalk. She shivered as the icy wind channeled through the city's canyons bit into the exposed flesh on her face. She pulled her hat down farther. It had been a long winter already, and it would be a long time yet until spring. She turned the corner and headed toward the west-facing entrance to Grand Central.

She crossed Vanderbilt and passed under the red awnings beneath the Park Avenue Viaduct, entering the station. She moved into the cavernous space, lingering at the top of the stairs to watch as the crowds below traversed the marble concourse. It was late in the day, and the bustle down there wasn't close to how busy it got during rush hour, but it was busy enough. Hundreds of people, lots of wide-open space. Lots of exits. Trains leaving every minute for all points on the compass. It made sense for Blake to have picked this location, back when he was offering a deal.

It was five minutes to nine.

"You don't think he'll show, do you?"

Williamson had appeared beside Faraday, keeping a few steps away, not looking directly at her. An observer would have no reason to think they were speaking to each other. Just two people watching the crowds, perhaps waiting to welcome loved ones back to the city.

She had never seen Williamson outside of the operations center before. It was disconcerting to see her in outdoor clothes, away from the glow of a computer screen. Faraday shook her head. "Not really. But I wanted to be sure."

"You're flying to Washington tonight?" Faraday detected a minor undercurrent of sympathy in Williamson's question, and ignored it.

"The jet leaves at eleven thirty."

Williamson said nothing more on the subject, and they watched the crowds for another minute in silence. Faraday thought about that eight a.m. meeting tomorrow morning.

"What do you think he meant?" Williamson asked, referring to the recording of Blake's phone call to Stark and Murphy. "About how we didn't know anything?"

"Who knows, Williamson? Who knows."

She nodded and moved away from the top of the stairs. Faraday stayed put, watching for a few minutes. The big clock over the information booth on the concourse read four minutes past nine now. They had people on all the entrances, just in case.

Faraday didn't really believe Blake would show up. There was no percentage in it for him. Scott Bryant was missing—either safe or dead, and she was sure Blake knew which. Murphy's play at the house had shown that they were only too willing to come for him in the night, so why would he trust them to make another deal? And he in turn had shown them that they couldn't come after him without expecting to pay a high price.

No, she decided. She wasn't here because she expected Blake to show up. She was here because this felt like the time and place to draw a line under the operation. Blake's trail ended at the smoking ruins of a farmhouse in Upstate New York. He was gone. In the wind, as someone had said the other day. Faraday was here because this was the last vestige of a lead they had on him. She was here just in case, and now that she was satisfied he wasn't showing up, she could fly to Washington and face the music. Then, whether or not she managed to keep her job, she could go home and begin the long, fruitless task of trying to pretend this whole sorry episode had never happened.

She watched the crowds, wondering how much thought, if any, these people gave to the kind of work people like her did to keep places like this safe. The things that had to be done under the radar.

The clock read nine ten the next time she looked at it, but she stayed and watched the crowds below, searching in vain for a familiar face.

At nine fifteen Williamson appeared at her side again. "What do you think?"

Faraday closed her eyes and took a deep breath through her nose. She listened to the murmurs and happy squeals from below. "I think we're waiting for a ghost."

She told Williamson she was leaving and asked her to tell Hank to bring the car around. Walking back down Forty-Third, she turned her thoughts to the meeting with the National Security Council subgroup tomorrow morning. Questions would have to be answered. Questions about why the decision had been made to terminate a former operative on United States soil. Questions about how they had managed to let Blake slip through their fingers and what their likely exposure would be. She didn't have any good answers for that, and she suspected the one man who could have given them to her was lying in a body bag right now. *Goddamn you, Murphy*, she thought.

She stopped in the middle of the block where there was a clear parking spot and glanced back down just as her car rounded the corner. It pulled smoothly to a stop beside her. She opened the door and slipped into the backseat.

"JFK, Hank. You can take your time."

The car pulled out into traffic, turning right onto Madison. As the car picked up speed, she heard a weird tapping sound, like something was loose on the car.

"What's that?" she said, but Hank didn't seem to be listening as he passed through the intersection, switched lanes, and turned right on Forty-Sixth.

She listened more intently and decided it wasn't something loose on the car: That would have produced a more regular sound, in time with the movement of the vehicle. This was more like the noise of somebody knocking on the door. Except that it was coming from behind her.

Somebody was in the trunk.

Her head snapped back around and she looked properly at her driver for the first time since she'd gotten back in. Underneath the back of the hat, she saw dark hair instead of Hank's smooth bald skin.

"What the hell—"

The driver put his foot down as they sped east on

Forty-Sixth, covering half a block in seconds, before slowing abruptly and making a sharp turn into an underground parking lot beneath one of the buildings. They rolled down a ramp and into the lot, which was dimly lit by spaced-out strip lights. Faraday felt her heartbeat pounding in her chest.

The car stopped far away from any of the other cars, and the driver turned around, removing the hat. This man wasn't Hank. Hank, she presumed, was in the trunk. The man looking back at her from the driver's seat was a man in his midthirties with dark hair shaved close to his scalp. He had green eyes and a cold smile that didn't reach them. She had seen the face before, had spent a lot of time over the last few days and weeks looking at it on screens, but this was the first time she'd seen it in the flesh.

"Carter Blake."

"Pleased to meet you," he said. "I believe you've been looking for me."

Faraday started to reach into her coat for her cell phone, and Blake shook his head. "I wouldn't."

She released the phone and slowly withdrew her hand from the coat. "Are you going to kill me?"

"I ought to. I had a deal with your predecessor."

"A deal he should never have made."

Blake just looked back at her with the unmistakable expression of someone who could see all the cards in the deck.

"Why did you come after me?" He asked the question like he had only a passing curiosity in the answer.

"You know why. After the Crozier mess, we got a lead on you for the first time. As director, it has been incumbent on me to clean up the historical mistakes of this organization. That includes rogue former operatives like Crozier. And you."

Blake listened, a thoughtful look on his face, and then reached into his jacket with his right hand. He produced a small black flash drive, holding it between his thumb and index finger. The Book, she assumed. The leverage Blake had used on Drakakis. It hadn't been destroyed at the house. Unless he was bluffing, of course.

"You took quite a risk," he said. "Gambling you could retrieve this as well as taking me out of action. Gambling I wouldn't get upset enough about you trying to kill me to go ahead and leak the contents."

Faraday smiled for the first time. It had been Murphy's gamble, of course. She hadn't known about the Black Book until later. But there was no reason to let Blake know that. "Things have changed, Blake. Maybe what's on that drive doesn't concern me as much as it did Drakakis."

"You don't know what's on the drive," Blake said. The way he said it, it was as though it was a mild surprise to him. Maybe he really did know something she didn't.

"I'm aware that some of the activities of this organization include things that we'd rather keep quiet. But guess what, Blake? We can live with it. What's the worst that would happen? A front page in the *Times*, some manufactured outrage for a week? Maybe two weeks. However long it takes some celebrity to do something newsworthy and stupid and wipe us right off the agenda. The president will order an inquiry and maybe we get a slap on the wrist. A month later, everybody leaves us to get on with it again."

"You don't know what's on the drive," Blake said again.

Faraday felt a flush of anger. "Oh, what—you think

people really care, Blake? Nobody will care. I know what's on that drive. I know what we've done to people nobody cares about in places nobody can find on the map. I didn't walk into this job with my eyes closed— I know what went on. I know that some things happened that shouldn't have, and I know that some people worked for us who shouldn't have, present company very much included." She paused and gathered herself, lowering her voice. She was too angry to feel scared now. If Blake was going to kill her, he was going to kill her. She would go out defiantly. "Nobody will care, Blake," she said again firmly. "We do what needs to be done, and if things went a little too far in the past, then too bad. Shit happens. Nobody will care."

Blake waited until he was sure she was finished before speaking. "They'll care that Drakakis ordered the assassination of a United States senator and his wife."

The words hit Faraday like a bucket of ice water. Drakakis had ordered the Carlson hit? That couldn't be true...could it? All of a sudden it made a terrible kind of sense. Why else would he have made this deal with Blake? Why would he have purged the fingerprints hit in Fort Dodge? Why else but because he was implicated. And maybe Blake had the proof.

"You're saying Drakakis ordered you to kill John Carlson?" She tried to infuse her tone with a mocking, disbelieving edge, but she knew she wasn't pulling it off.

"No. I'm saying Murphy tried to kill me, and Drakakis ordered Usher to kill Carlson. He was going to shut Winterlong down, and Drakakis didn't want that to happen. And with all due respect, Ms. Faraday, you don't know the half of what went down."

He glanced back at the flash drive, as though surprised to find himself still holding it, and then started to put it back in his pocket. Faraday took a sharp breath, wanting to tell him to wait a second. She tried to hide the instinctive reaction, but Blake noticed. He smiled.

"All right, you can get to the point," she said. "I take it you want to blackmail me the way you did Drakakis? You want me to call off the dogs?"

"Exactly how many dogs do you have left?" Blake snapped back, all humor suddenly absent from his tone.

Faraday said nothing, suddenly feeling the urge to avoid his stare. Blake gazed at her until she looked away and then continued talking.

"I'm not here to make a deal," he said. "I tried that before, and look how it turned out. We're way past deals. I came here to give you a warning: Don't come after me again."

"And what about the Black Book?"

"That's the other reason I came here. As of five minutes ago, that drive is worthless to either of us."

"What the hell do you mean?"

Blake's eyes left hers for the first time and glanced at the tablet beside her on the seat.

"Front page in the *Times*. That was what you said, wasn't it?"

Faraday felt a sinking sensation in her stomach. She kept her eyes on Blake, resisting the urge to pick up the tablet. He had to be bluffing. *Had to be.* Except that Blake had followed through on every one of his promises up until now.

"I hope you don't mind, but I gave it to a few others as well. *Washington Post, USA Today, Wall Street Journal...The Guardian, Le Monde, Die Zeit.* CNN. The BBC. I forget the complete list."

Faraday couldn't take it any longer. She grabbed the tablet and flipped the case open, switching it on.

It was all over the Internet. It was the big story. The only story. *Government Death Squad. Carlson Assassinated by US Intelligence Agents. Conspiracy.* Faraday swiped from site to site, scanning a few lines of each devastating article, every headline drilling into her soul a little more.

"Maybe you can get ahead of this, if you're smart," Blake said. She looked up, realizing she had almost forgotten he was there. "You weren't there for most of that, after all. Maybe you woke up at night sometimes, wondering if you were doing what you should be."

She opened her mouth to say something. She didn't know if it was going to be a threat or a plea or something in between, but suddenly she couldn't remember. Whatever she had been about to say wasn't important. It could do nothing to this man who had just destroyed them. Destroyed her. And all because Murphy had persuaded her to go after him.

"I don't want to see you, or anyone who works for you again, Faraday. If you try to come after me…I'll find a way to *really* hurt you. Is that clear?"

Faraday dropped the tablet on the seat. She closed her eyes and nodded. Message received.

And then, as quickly as he had appeared, Carter Blake was gone. Faraday barely registered the noise of the door slamming shut. She barely heard the sound of his footsteps echoing off the concrete walls of the underground parking lot. She kept staring ahead at the place where he had last been.

In her coat pocket, her cell phone began to ring.

TWO MONTHS LATER

EPILOGUE

Colorado

THE EARLY-EVENING drive from the county airport had been slow going at first, but as we headed north, the roads seemed to clear up. I settled into an unhurried cruising speed of fifty and thought about the events of the last few weeks as I snatched glances at the beautiful scenery of the Animas River Valley during the occasional straight sections of the winding road. The days were getting longer, and the sun was still way above the level of the San Juan Mountains.

The revelations about Winterlong's operations, and particularly the assassination of Senator Carlson, had provoked a shitstorm in Washington. Faraday had been right about the initial reaction: widespread shock and disbelief, an announcement by the president, a full investigation. Charges. Jail time. She had been wrong about the other thing: It had taken weeks to drop off the front pages, and the aftershocks were making themselves felt all these weeks later.

The special operations organization unofficially known as Winterlong had been disbanded, of course. That was an understatement. All personnel were called into Washington pending an exhaustive investigation of their actions going back for the previous decade. A couple of men were already up on murder charges. The information on the Black Book showed that Usher had carried out the Carlson hit, which meant that my killing of him had robbed the nation of a trial. Everyone from senior personnel to the lowest levels had been hauled over the coals and charged on any hint of involvement with the crimes of the organization.

At all times, spokespeople for the Department of Defense were at pains to point out that Winterlong was a bad apple, an outlier. A concealed tumor. By virtue of its classified and top-secret status, it had been allowed to operate way beyond its original remit and authority without the knowledge of anyone outside of its immediate command structure. Catastrophic mission creep, they called it. It was a convenient line. It also happened to be mostly true. But not entirely. It would have been impossible for them to operate and continue to be funded without someone higher up knowing a little about what they did, even if all that person knew was not to ask more questions.

Faraday had taken my advice. She had managed to get in front of the investigation before it could really pick up momentum. She had cooperated fully, explaining how Drakakis had covered up the worst activities of the group, aided and abetted by Murphy and some of the other men. The black hats. She agreed to testify in the hearings, cooperating fully. She explained how she had been focusing on cleaning house, thwarted again by Murphy, who had manipulated her into authorizing seek-and-destroy missions against former operatives. Her career had taken a hell of a hit, but she might just stay out of jail.

After the events at the house, when the worst of the blizzard had abated, Bryant and I had made our way

back to the nearest town. I had called John Stafford at
Moonola from a phone booth, reversing the charges.
After letting him vent his anger at me for a couple of
minutes, I told him I had good news and I had bad news.
Being a pragmatist, he asked for the bad news first, and
I gave it to him: Bryant had gotten away from me, and
I had no leads on his whereabouts. The good news was
I had both copies of MeTime, and he would quickly be
able to verify that no other copies had been made. I was
sending those to him by secure courier.

Stafford still wasn't happy about letting Bryant go,
and now he was even less happy about doing so without having a chance to berate him in person. I told him
I hadn't finished, that I was returning the software together with a full refund of his fee. It's not often that I
fail to deliver, I said, and for the sake of my reputation,
I couldn't take his money.

Stafford had mulled it over and decided the deal was
acceptable, assuming he could authenticate the MeTime
copies and that no other copy ever turned up anywhere
else. Damn right it was acceptable. A priceless asset returned to him for the price of a phone call. Bryant had
helped me out by cracking the sunset code on the Black
Book and setting up secure coordinating distribution
to the media. Considering that, plus the small matter of
him saving my life, I felt that I owed him one.

"Are we nearly there yet?"

The sweet voice from the booster seat in the back
pulled me out of my reflections and ruminations. I
glanced in the rearview mirror to see Alyssa Bryant's
face creased into a ball of impatience.

I glanced to my right and exchanged a smile with
her mom. Jasmine Bryant was wearing a red summer

dress and a black cardigan in deference to the lingering chill in the air.

"She beat me to it," she said.

I calculated how far we had to go. "Fifteen, twenty minutes."

There was a grunt from the back. "That's for-*ever*."

Eighteen minutes later, we crossed over the Animas River itself, the tires thumping on the expansion joints of the bridge, and entered the town of Durango, Colorado. A couple of minutes later we took a left off the main road onto a short cul-de-sac of four modest-sized houses. I pulled the Ford into the gravel drive of the house at the far end, applied the hand brake, and turned off the engine.

Jasmine got out, opened Alyssa's door, and started to unbuckle her. I got out of my side as the front door of the house opened. Scott Bryant appeared in the doorway and bounced eagerly down the steps, before slowing down and walking out toward us. He looked as though he wanted to run but was holding it in check. He was wearing jeans and a white button-down shirt, and he looked more relaxed than I'd ever seen him. Jasmine and Alyssa were still getting out of the car and hadn't seen him yet. He held his hand out and we shook.

"So you found them." He smiled.

I affected a look of being insulted. "Of course I found them."

Jasmine straightened up at the sound of his voice, and they exchanged a look. Neither of them said anything, but a second later were pre-empted by a four-year-old comet on a straight trajectory for her daddy.

Bryant caught her in his arms and lifted her up, grinning from ear to ear. "My girl. How did you get so big?"

"Spaghetti, mostly," Jasmine answered.

Bryant kept Alyssa aloft and turned to look at Jasmine. "I thought she hated pasta."

"We'll bring you up to date." Jasmine smiled.

With a little complaint from Alyssa, Bryant put her down and drew Jasmine in for a kiss. "It's gonna be okay now," he whispered.

Jasmine said nothing, but she nodded as though she knew it was the truth.

They had all entirely forgotten I existed, which was fine by me. I gave them another few moments to enjoy their reunion and then cleared my throat.

"So I have to get going."

"You don't want to stay for dinner?" Bryant asked.

"Is it spaghetti?" Alyssa cut in.

"Pizza," Bryant answered.

"Yuck."

"Thank you," I began, "but…"

"Please, Carter?"

I looked down at Alyssa's big brown eyes, my mouth opening to make an excuse, and then surrendered, powerless.

Jasmine and Alyssa went ahead of us. Bryant and I tagged along behind, taking our time walking up to the big old house. There was a red mailbox with the name *Milo* hand-painted on it. I repeated it out loud.

"Previous owner, I guess," Bryant said. "I've adopted it for now. Scott Milo. What do you think?"

"You don't really look like a Scott Milo."

"Who does?"

"Good point."

We got to the door, and Bryant looked like he'd remembered something. "So what about you, Mr. Man-With-No-Name? What's the identity of the week now?"

I smiled. With Winterlong out of action, there didn't seem much point in starting out on a whole new name. Not yet, anyway.

"I'm still Carter Blake."

"Still?"

I thought about it, really for the first time, and nodded. "It just seems to be my name now."

Bryant grinned. "Come on in."

The smell of something good emanated from inside the house. We went inside for dinner. Over conversation and jokes and stories, I began to remember that there were good things in the world, too. I thought about Carol for the first time in a while and wondered where she was now. Wherever she was, I hoped she was with friends, thinking about the good things.

An hour later, full of pizza and soda and ice cream, I was back in the driver's seat, cruising along the highway as the sun dipped below the hills and plunged the world into twilight. For the first time in a long time, I wasn't thinking about the past anymore. I was thinking about the road ahead. I was thinking about all the other roads this one connected to and the ones those connected to. I was wondering where they would take me.

* * * * *

Get 4 FREE REWARDS!

We'll send you 2 FREE Books plus 2 FREE Mystery Gifts.

Harlequin® Romantic Suspense books feature heart-racing sensuality and the promise of a sweeping romance set against the backdrop of suspense.

FREE
Value Over
$20

Get 4 FREE REWARDS!

We'll send you 2 FREE Books plus 2 FREE Mystery Gifts.

FREE
Value Over
$20

Both the **Romance** and **Suspense** collections feature compelling novels
written by many of today's best-selling authors.